D1568636

Lillian Russell

37

LILLIAN RUSSELL

A Biography of "America's Beauty"

Armond Fields

McFarland & Company, Inc., Publishers
Jefferson, North Carolina, and London

By Armond Fields and L. Marc Fields
From the Bowery to Broadway:
Lew Fields and the Roots of American Popular Theater (1993)

PN 2287 .R83 F54 1999

Cover photograph: In 1906, Lillian and Joseph Brooks, her manager, used this portrait to publicize her venture into dramatic comedy. The image was designed to make her appear eternally youthful, reminding admirers of her splendid days in comic opera. (National Portrait Gallery, Smithsonian Institution. Benjamin J. Falk, 1853–1925. Chromolithographic poster, 78.5 × 58.7 cm [30⅞ × 23⅛ in.], 1906. NPG.87.228.)

Frontispiece: Lillian Russell as Fiorella in *The Brigands*, 1889, at the height of her comic opera career. (National Portrait Gallery, Smithsonian Institution. Benjamin J. Falk, 1853–1925. Photograph, albumen silver print, 14.4 × 9.8 cm [5¹¹⁄₁₆ × 3⅞ in.], 1889. NPG.80.79.)

British Library Cataloguing-in-Publication data are available

Library of Congress Cataloguing-in-Publication Data

Fields, Armond, 1930–
    Lillian Russell : a biography of "America's beauty" / Armond
Fields.
      p.   cm.
    Includes bibliographical references and index.
    ISBN 0-7864-0509-0 (case binding : 50# alkaline paper) ∞
    1. Russell, Lillian, 1861–1922.   2. Actors — United States —
Biography.   3. Singers — United States — Biography.   I. Title.
PN2287.R83F54   1999
792'.028'092 — dc21
   [b]   98-38736
                                             CIP

Manufactured in the United States of America

McFarland & Company, Inc., Publishers
  Box 611, Jefferson, North Carolina 28640

Acknowledgments

In creating this biographical and theatrical history, I relied upon the interest and expertise of many people. I am grateful for their cooperation and assistance: John Ahouse, University of Southern California, Special Collections Library; Miles Kreuger, Institute of the American Musical; Maryanne Chach, Shubert Archive; Melissa Miller-Quinlan and Maria Beach, University of Texas, Harry Ransom Humanities Research Center; and Beverly J. Cox, National Portrait Gallery, Smithsonian Institution. I also relied on the resources of the following institutions: University of California, Los Angeles, Microfilm Library; Chicago Historical Society; Clinton, Iowa, Historical Society; Mormon Library, Salt Lake City; New York Public Library at Lincoln Center, Billy Rose Theater Collection; The Museum of the City of New York; The Theater Museum, Research Division, London, England; The Library of Congress; The Carnegie-Mellon Library; The Historical Society of Iowa; and the New York City Vital Statistics Bureau.

John Farrell, a dedicated researcher, editor and friend, gave valuable assistance toward the completion of this book. I thank him profoundly for his contributions.

I offer loving gratitude to my wife, Sara, who for years has patiently and considerately lived with my passion for theater history, who listened to my discoveries and ideas, and who supported my efforts in making this book a reality.

Contents

Introduction

$\mathcal{C}$olorful and boisterous first nights were the rule in New York theaters of the 1880s. Everyone attended, from the elegantly attired Four Hundred vying to see and be seen, to young people dreaming of stardom.

Broadway ended at 42nd Street. The streets and theater exteriors were lit by gas lamps, the great electrical displays still years away. A reservoir was located where the New York Public Library now stands. The Academy of Music, Wallack's and Daly's were famous theaters. Just around the corner from them stood Tony Pastor's Fourteenth Street Theater, the popular variety house. The Cafe Martin was a rendezvous for gourmets; and the Hoffman House, with its murals of corpulent nudes over the bar, was one of the most famous drinking places in town.

People went to serious plays to see such great actresses as Maude Adams, Julia Marlowe, Minnie Madden Fiske and Ethel Barrymore. But they went with equal frequency to the frolic and fun of comic operas, variety shows and burlesque. Popular theater in those days made the harsh and indifferent city seem intimate and romantic.

In this branch of theater — gay, bold, colorful and effervescent — Lillian Russell became the outstanding symbol of the times. She was a star who blazed across America's entertainment horizons for more than 30 years, from the aftermath of the Civil War through the first political intrigues leading to World War I. A woman who went from church singer to America's highest-paid popular entertainer, from Midwestern innocent to sex goddess, from fashion trendsetter to feminist, she was proclaimed "The American Beauty" as audiences everywhere were dazzled by her larger-than-life personal appeal.

Russell lived and performed during a period of social tumult, particularly for women, who in those years were seeking unprecedented rights to self-identity and independence. Russell was a significant player — indeed, a leader — among those of her era who rejected Victorian proscriptions to seek recognition based on one's public "cash value." This was a period of robber barons and millionaires making their fortunes in the westward extension of empire. It was an era of invention: electricity and the telephone, automobiles and railroads. This period saw the rise of factories

1

and mass production; an increase in political corruption; and the creation of an urban middle class with newly discovered time for leisure pursuits. The emergence of industrial and cultural expression coincided with, and contributed to, the development of American popular theater and the star power of its performers.

One of this era's "New Women," Lillian Russell quickly learned the rules by which the fittest survive in theater. She used her stardom as a means to attain material wealth, mobility, social status and power. At once egocentric and generous, she championed women's equality while immersing herself in the elegance of *la Belle Epoque*. She was strong-willed and determined. Both men and women were awed by her phenomenal successes. Her beauty and youth, the freshness of her sympathetic voice, and the natural grace of her acting combined to fascinate theater audiences on two continents.

Russell made more money for the theaters where she performed than any other woman of her generation. As a public figure, she set new rules of social behavior, new goals for women to achieve, new standards of fashion and beauty. She stretched the boundaries of turn-of-the-century sexual relationships and moral codes.

Lillian Russell. She was once a household name, followed avidly by a society in which celebrity was the end, and the means for the most part were irrelevant. Even in retirement, during the last decade of her life, her every public act, every public appearance was a performance.

Russell's death was every bit as theatrical as her life. There were three funerals. The one in Pittsburgh included a military escort and was attended by members of Congress. In New York, there were two memorial services at Broadway theaters, with cheers and cries from theater folk and devotees ringing down her final curtain. President Harding declared three days of national mourning.

Today, three-quarters of a century later, Russell is virtually unknown. Like most larger-than-life performers of her time — including politicians, social reformers and sports heroes — she has all but vanished from the public mind. Her last national exposure came 18 years after death, in the Darryl Zanuck–produced movie *Lillian Russell*, starring demure Alice Faye. The film was a pastiche of mythology and love interests that Russell herself would have rejected as preposterous.

Yet a remarkable truth remains: Each generation since Lillian has produced a similar celebrity whose goals and successes have mirrored hers. Mae West, Marilyn Monroe, Madonna — each has carved out a unique niche in our pantheon of heroines, continuing the legacy that Russell initiated. And what Russell achieved during her reign is all the more astonishing considering that she did not enjoy the benefit of mass media, which can develop national celebrities overnight. Maybe that's why Russell remains obscure, while Mae, Marilyn and Madonna are remembered. All four, however, became famous through a combination of talent, luck, cunning and self-promotion.

Russell starred in more than 70 theatrical productions during her 40-year career. She shared the stage with such luminaries as Lionel Barrymore, Blanche Bates, Digby Bell, Jefferson de Angelis, William Collier, Weber and Fields, De Wolf Hopper, William Farnum, Della Fox, Marie Dressler and Raymond Hitchcock. Her business managers, for better or worse, included Henry Abbey, Rudolph Aronson, George Lederer, T. Henry French, Sam Shubert and Col. John A. McCaull, the theater impresarios of the gilded age. She appeared in numerous variety and vaudeville companies throughout the United States, spending 40 or more weeks a year on tour. She also performed in England, France, Germany and Belgium. She even managed her own troupe, the Lillian Russell Light Opera Company, for a number of years.

Russell began performing at a time when female artists were singing popular songs simply as one act of a variety show. They were called soubrettes ("ladies' maids" in French). In stage jargon, a soubrette was a pretty, flirtatious singer, a marginal entertainer at best.

A female might receive tribute for her acting in serious theater, but those on variety stages were considered merely pleasant musical diversions. Russell was not satisfied to play this limited role on stage. She wanted recognition for herself and for women performers in general, to legitimize their position in theater. The fact that Russell achieved this goal within only a few years of her stage debut points to her amazing skill at self-promotion, as well as her hard-nosed business acumen in negotiating contracts with some of the legendary producers of the day.

Russell was also a major force in the growth and acceptance of comic opera, or *opéra bouffe*. Her performances, both on and off the stage, popularized musical theater on the Great White Way and throughout America's hinterlands. Audiences were attracted to her portrayal and personification of women as both beautiful and independent. Unlike the militant suffragists who marched in the streets, Russell spoke to a more genteel, middle-class, urban woman — one who had more time for leisure, beauty aids, fashion and club activity, and who sought greater self-identity in a male-dominated society. She was successful in that world because she played the game harder and with more gusto than her opponents.

There is no question that she was commercially driven, seeking wealth and fame. An astute businessperson, she ran a cosmetics company, pioneered new fashions, wrote newspaper articles on staying young, sold Liberty Bonds, spoke for the women's vote and participated in politics, clearly demonstrating her diverse abilities and talents. Obviously, there was more at stake for Russell than simple box office success.

The crucial ingredient in Russell's triumphs was performance, whether captivating an audience with her voice and resplendent, jewel-studded gowns, or competing in vigorous corn-on-the-cob eating contests at Delmonico's with Diamond Jim Brady. These kinds of performances are perishable commodities, and Russell knew it. Because they predated recordings and film, her stage performances are lost to us today. But her performances in terms of human behavior have been repeated through the years by Russell's successors, and in that way we continue to see her influence.

Today, comic opera, from *Der Rosencavalier* to *Showboat*, continues to entertain audiences. The musical has become so much a staple of American theater that it is easy to believe it has always existed, and thus forget its origins and the stars who created the genre. Through the life of Lillian Russell, we can relive a portion of American theater history and understand its contributions to our culture. When we read about the issues for which Russell fought, the social standards she challenged, and the happiness she provided, it seems her era is kindred to ours. She arouses our interest and persuades us to embrace a bit of nostalgia. At the same time, we become aware that some things never change.

Chapter One

From Prairies to Pastor's

*V*ariety halls in the 1870s and 1880s were considered unpleasant places, saloons with live entertainment. As described by journalist John McCabe in his 1882 guidebook of New York, most of them were "dumps and honky-tonks." But many of the sinister descriptions of theaters featuring "smutty roughhouse turns and afterpieces" were based on the perceptions and prejudices of proper New Yorkers, who looked condescendingly on the immigrant audiences that attended them. Not all these venues, however, were dens of distaste.

Tony Pastor was a devout Catholic and family man who believed that the variety hall could be a place for respectable spectacle and admiring audiences. Pastor was born in New York City in 1837, in a hotel room on Greenwich Street near Battery Park. His father was a violinist who played in local orchestras; his mother operated a perfumery out of their home. As a child, Tony displayed an interest in mimicry and acting. At the age of eight, Pastor made his formal debut as an entertainer. His performance of song and recitation attracted a temperance group, and they persuaded his parents to allow Tony to perform at their weekly meetings.

At 14, Pastor sang at Barnum's Museum. After some years of touring with minstrel shows and circuses, he opened his first music hall, at 444 Broadway. Later, he obtained the ownership of Volk's Garden, a German concert saloon, and renamed it "Tony Pastor's Opera House," featuring the best of variety artists. Pastor also appeared on stage singing original songs, becoming a feature on his own bill. His introduction of "The Star Spangled Banner" at the beginning of each show is widely considered the first time the anthem was sung on a variety stage. According to a local newspaper, when he asked the audience to join in the chorus, "the roof of the building flew off."

Pastor emphasized comedy, dancing and singing — no fighting, freak shows or "blue" sketches. He outlawed rowdy behavior and bad language in his theater. By the time he opened his Fourteenth Street Theater (between Third Avenue and Irving Place), he was already a highly popular showman. At his new theater, Pastor also banned drinking and smoking. At the same time, he advertised to both men and women, a calculated bid to increase his ticket sales and emphasize the wholesomeness of his entertainment. Audiences at Pastor's represented the widest cross-section of New Yorkers seen at any theatrical event of the day.

November 22, 1880, was a blustery night highlighted by the city's first snow of the season. Theater goers rushed to the ticket office to be in their seats before the curtain went up at eight o'clock sharp, an on-time opening that had become a tradition at Pastor's.

The theater was relatively small but lent itself well to the intimate performer/audience relationship that characterized variety houses. It contained a family circle (a Pastor innovation designed to seat both women and children), a parquet, several rows of orchestra seats and a few private boxes. Total seating capacity reached about a thousand. A proscenium arch covered the stage, supported on each side by two large floor-to-ceiling columns decorated in bas-relief. Its heavy velvet, deep-red curtains, draped and tasseled in gold braid, were by far the richest of any variety theater in town.

Precisely at eight o'clock, the curtain rose. But to the surprise of the audience, impresario Tony Pastor himself walked onto the stage. Depending on where members of the audience were seated, they either clapped politely (from the orchestra seats), cheered loudly (from the balcony) or pounded their feet on the floor and whistled (from the gallery). As Pastor stepped forward to the gas footlights, he waved his hand for silence.

"Ladies and gentlemen, friends and customers." He paused for effect. "Tonight, I have a most unusual treat in store for you. At great personal trouble and expense, I have brought here for your admiration and entertainment the beautiful English ballad singer...." He paused again. "Ladies and gentlemen, I give you a vision of loveliness and a voice of gold — Miss Lillian Russell."

Pastor was demonstrably a master of show biz hype. The beautiful young performer he had just introduced had been given her name only a few days earlier. She was hardly from England; in fact, she had never been out of the United States. Nor had engaging her caused Pastor any trouble or expense.

Nonetheless, the moment would prove historic: the official inauguration of Lillian Russell's musical theater career. Not yet 21, only a few years removed from Midwestern prairies, her only stage experience in the chorus of an obscure company, Russell that night launched a phenomenal career that would see her become one of America's greatest stage entertainers and a quintessential symbol of the country's Belle Epoque.

Helen Louise "Nellie" Leonard was born on December 4, 1861, in Clinton, Iowa, the fourth daughter of Charles Egbert Leonard and Cynthia Van Name Leonard. They had seven children: five girls, Ida Kate, Leona, Harriet, Helen Louise and Susan (in that order), as well as two other children who died shortly after birth.

Charles was an aspiring newspaperman and printer, founder and owner of Clinton's first newspaper, the *Weekly Herald*, with two competitors in neighboring towns. Cynthia organized schools during the week and preached against slavery on Sundays at the local Episcopal Church. The couple were natural community leaders. The Leonard family heritage in America dated back to the Pilgrims' landing at Plymouth, Massachusetts.

Ancestor John Howland had been 33 when he and his fellow passengers disembarked from the *Mayflower* in December 1620. He was single and a skilled carpenter, a valuable member of this party. Like the others, he had left England because of religious oppression. Shortly after the Pilgrims settled in, John married Elizabeth Tilley, daughter of one of the group's nominal leaders. In a generation when only girls were born to the family, the Howland name was lost, but a family descendant married John Harvis Leonard in the early 1800s. Of this stock, Charles was born in October 1829 in Jamestown, New York.[1]

When Charles was ten, his parents moved to Mt. Clemens, Michigan, his father having been appointed Judge of the Circuit Court. At age 15, he was apprenticed to learn the cabinet-making trade. He didn't like it and took up printing instead, obtaining a position as a "printer's devil" in the office of John N. Ingersoll, who owned the only newspaper printed in the county. Charles advanced to pressman and compositor and, at 19, moved to Detroit to work for the city's daily newspaper, the *Advertiser and Tribune.* Two years later, he was hired by the Buffalo, New York, daily newspaper as superintendent of printing.

Though her own American roots were more recent, Helen Louise Leonard's mother was also of pioneer stock. In the early 1800s, the Van Name family had emigrated from Holland to Staten Island, New York, after purchasing some farm land there. Some members of the family moved to Buffalo, where Cynthia's mother married Daniel Hicks, at the time an interpreter and lawyer for Chief Red Jacket, one of the last of the Seneca Indians. Cynthia Van Name Hicks was born in February 1829. Along with receiving a good education (rare for girls at the time), she learned to ride, shoot and swim as well as her older brothers.

As a teenager, Cynthia declared her independence from the conventions of the day. In Buffalo, she became the first woman to work behind a counter as a salesperson. She also became a member of Buffalo's first Woman's Social and Literary Club.

In 1852, Charles and Cynthia met at a community gathering dealing with the disposition of the local Indian reservation. They found themselves in agreement regarding the protection of the Indian lands, at that time a minority viewpoint. Apparently advanced by Cynthia, their marriage took place within months of their meeting. Charles had expressed some hesitancy, because he was unsure about remaining with the Buffalo newspaper and, without a job, would have no way to support them. In spite of his concerns, Cynthia convinced him that, wherever they lived, their talents and abilities would be recognized.

A year after they married, the couple moved to Detroit, where Charles held various printing jobs. Homesteaders like Charles and Cynthia led the first large-scale migration from the East to the new frontiers of Midwestern cities. Their two-day trip from Buffalo to Detroit was endured in "Zulu" railroad cars. These were built in two sections, containing double berths made of wooden slats, separated by a narrow aisle. Passengers padded the slats with their own blankets and clothing. The railroad cars also contained a cooking stove so passengers could prepare food en route. At the end of the journey, the cars would be disinfected prior to their return East.

Unfortunately, their three years in Detroit were a time of infrequent employment. Carpenters were needed more than newspapermen. But where to go from here?

Initially, the Leonards thought that Chicago, already a rapidly growing industrial center, would offer them an opportunity for employment. But upon arriving there, they found themselves uncomfortable with the frenetic activity of the city, its crowded conditions and its smoky air. Purchasing a wagon with their last funds, they headed west again. Charles had heard from friends that Clinton, Iowa, a small town on the Mississippi River, had no newspaper.

A wagon trip from Chicago to Clinton, over pitted and unmarked roads, took at least two weeks (longer, if it happened to rain). Mostly, the Leonards camped by the roadside at night. Their possessions consisted of clothing, books and a few pieces of furniture. Aurora, Illinois, population a little over 1,000, was the largest town they would pass though. There were days when they rarely saw anyone, whether farmer or traveler.

Clinton lay on the west side of the Mississippi River. The narrowness of the river just upstream from the town allowed ferries to take wagons across, at one of the few places along the river that offered accessibility to either side. Clinton was built on bluffs overlooking the Mississippi, providing distant views in all directions. This served as protection against possible Indian attacks.

The town now had a population of more than 2,800 people, mostly English and German immigrants. During the early 1850s, Clinton residents established a school system, local post offices, a courthouse and a jail. Prior to the Civil War, thousands of miles of railroad track had been laid in the area, telegraph wires strung and new farm equipment brought in. Since there were no other towns as large for 30 miles around, Clinton had a thriving business community. It even boasted a hotel, where the Leonards stayed when they arrived. The proprietor of the hotel waived payment, because the Leonards intended to remain in Clinton.

Within a few months, Charles had set up his newspaper, a small home was fashioned in the back of the newspaper office, and Cynthia gave birth to the first of their daughters. The economic panic of 1857 almost forced the closing of the paper, but Charles survived the financial storm by forming a partnership with H. B. Horton to operate a printing firm along with publication of the newspaper.[2]

By the spring of 1861, the Leonards had become a respected family in Clinton. And the town was growing rapidly. The railway had reached the city from Chicago. A military barracks had been built, and a training center started as the Civil War threatened. The arrival of soldiers and their families swelled the population of the area, as well as the coffers of local businesses.

With Cynthia on the executive committee, Clinton ladies formed a Soldiers' Relief Association in cooperation with the Iowa Sanitary Commission. The association dedicated its efforts to supply "extra comforts for the 18th Regimental Hospital." A short time after, Cynthia and Mrs. C.W. Simmons opened a soldier's home, the first in Iowa, to take care of discharged and ill soldiers.

On the day Helen Louise was born, Cynthia was reported to have been singing in the church choir. Already in labor, she sang to the end of the services, accompanied the family back home, retired to the bedroom and promptly gave birth.

Little "Nellie" Leonard received her first press notice the day after she was born. In the Clinton *Weekly Herald* appeared an announcement:

> Born to Mr. and Mrs. Charles Leonard, at their home on Fourth Avenue,
> December 4, 1861, a bright baby girl, weighing nine and one-half pounds.

The home referred to in the notice was situated in the center of the Clinton business district, directly behind the *Herald's* office, across the street from the Iowa Central Hotel, then the largest in the state and one of the finest west of Chicago.

Though the office stood on Fourth Avenue, the Leonard home actually faced onto an alley. Shortly after Nellie's birth, the family moved to one of the nicest residences in town, with four bedrooms, a view of the river and a live-in domestic servant.

Nellie was a bright, aware and pretty blond child, cared for by the maid and her older sisters (Cynthia was continually involved with her hospital responsibilities). It was reported that Nellie inherited her good looks from her father, also blond and considered a man of "fine appearance." While the family was comfortable, the cost and scarcity of goods due to the war meant modest living.

During the first years of her life, Nellie was indistinguishable from any other Clinton toddler. She played in the crab apple orchards, went wading in the Mississippi and sat for long hours on a log with her sisters, watching the river traffic. The family was musically inclined, due primarily to Cynthia's influence. In addition to having sung in a church choir for many years, she could play the violin and guitar. The Leonard home was frequented by local singing and musical societies, the five girls being willing participants during these get-togethers.

In 1863, prompted by the move of the local railroad offices to Chicago, Charles decided to move his printing plant to Chicago, where he hoped to take advantage of the expanding railroad business. Cynthia favored the move because it offered her greater opportunity for involvement in the women's rights movement, an exciting extension of her anti-slavery and hospital work. Her recent public pronouncements on these subjects had been making Clinton friends and neighbors somewhat uncomfortable, to the point of calling Cynthia "a social reformer," a distinction she thoroughly enjoyed. Charles did not encourage her activities, but he did not discourage them either. The girls were excited about the move to a big city.

Charles sold the newspaper and printing plant. With the proceeds, he transferred his firm and moved the family to a rented home on the west side of Chicago, near his new downtown offices. Nellie was two years old.

Chicago in the 1850s boomed because it had become the transportation center of the nation. Railroads were now the city's major industry. By 1856, only a few years after Charles and Cynthia had first wagoned their way through, Chicago had become the hub of ten major railroad lines, with some 3,000 miles of track. Nearly 100 trains arrived and departed every day. It was now the largest city in Illinois, with a population of 100,000.

Chicago grew even more rapidly during the Civil War. Cattle from the West were streaming into stockyards. The grain trade thrived, making the city the nation's chief grain market. The city's manufacturing industry also grew, utilizing European immigrants as factory laborers. With all this growth, support businesses like printing and publishing plants would surely be needed.

When Charles and Cynthia traveled by wagon from Chicago to Clinton, it had taken them two weeks. Seven years later, when they returned to Chicago by train, it took them one day.

Charles quickly became occupied with administering his growing printing business. Nellie's older sisters were enrolled in school, and Nellie was jealous of the fun they seemed to be having. To placate the child, Cynthia taught her to play the piano. But Cynthia had other, more important interests at the moment.

She first organized a fair for the benefit of the Freedman's Aid Society. She then helped found the Chicago branch of Sorosis and edited its publication for some time.

A few years later, Cynthia led the spiritual faction of the women's suffrage movement, at one of the first suffrage meetings held in Chicago.[3] But this social militancy had profound effects on the family.

Steadily withdrawing from Cynthia, Charles showed displeasure with his wife's behavior but never confronted her about it. Actually, he gave it tacit approval by publishing two pamphlets she wrote dealing with women's rights. His only direct defiance of Cynthia's activities was to join the local Masonic organization. With Cynthia away from home so frequently, Charles took over raising the children. Though removed from actually rearing her children, Cynthia continued to make the critical decisions regarding their lives, particularly that of Nellie.

When the time came for Nellie to enter school, Cynthia decided, possibly as a challenge to Charles, to enroll Nellie at a Catholic elementary school for girls, even though the Leonards were Episcopalians. The school was run by the Society of the Sacred Heart, a religious order with roots in the French aristocracy, which provided a strong intellectual and moral foundation for its exclusively female students. The Society had moved to Chicago in 1858; eight years later, it was housed in a large brick building, attended by almost 1,000 students. It actually operated two schools for girls: a free school for children whose parents were unable to afford tuition, and a boarding school for more affluent families. The learning climate at the school was disciplined; each student was given much personal attention, and Nellie's talents were carefully nurtured.[4]

Nellie thrived in this environment, taking music courses and violin lessons given by Prof. Nathan Dyer. But her singing voice created more excitement, and she began taking private lessons from a Prof. Gill. Each year, Gill's students would perform in a recital at Chickering Hall, the main concert hall in Chicago. At age 11, Nellie sang her first songs before an audience, "Let Me Dream Again" by Sir Arthur Sullivan and "Connais-tu le Pays?" from *Mignon*. The newspapers gave her performance complimentary notices, one of them declaring that she sang "like an old professional." Such notices soon convinced Cynthia her daughter had the talent to become an opera star.

Voice lessons now became mandatory. Nellie studied with Madame Jennivaly, who, not surprisingly, encouraged her to become a "great opera singer," much to Cynthia's satisfaction. Along with these lessons, Nellie sang in the choir at the St. John's Episcopal Church, which the family attended. By the time she was 14, Nellie sang with her brother-in-law, Edward Schultze, a tenor of some note in the city, and her sister, a good piano accompanist. Public appearances at Kimball Hall followed, and she was favorably reviewed by the public and the press.

Over the years, the nuns of the Sacred Heart had become quite attached to their bright and talented student and spoke often of her virtues. Now, with Nellie about to graduate from their care, they also noticed she had blossomed into a very attractive young woman, warning Cynthia that Nellie would "turn men's heads."

Encouraged by her daughter's comprehensive talents, Cynthia decided to send Nellie to the Park Institute, a finishing school for girls, and to hire Madame Scherhenberg, a former opera singer, as Nellie's voice teacher. Over the next two years, Nellie became proficient in singing leading opera scores from *Martha*, *Faust* and *Don Giovanni*. In December 1877, at 16, Nellie sang the lead in *Time Tries All*, her first full-length performance, given at Chickering Hall. Along with her "sweet" voice, a mature stage presence was favorably noted.

The situation at home, however, had been deteriorating for some time. Charles' business had gone into decline. To obtain clients, gain some reputation and support a fellow Mason, Charles agreed to publish the works of Col. Robert Ingersoll, a well-known but controversial lawyer, politician and writer. Ingersoll's books and speeches attacked orthodox Christian beliefs, proposing agnosticism. This gained Charles momentary notoriety but did not create any new business. Nor did the devastating Chicago fire help Charles' financial and family affairs.

As the world's lumber capital, commercial outlet for the vast forests of the North, Chicago was built almost entirely of wood — houses, churches, stores, grain elevators, factories, streets and sidewalks. The year 1871 was unusually dry in Chicago. Very little rain fell during the summer months. By autumn, the city was kindling waiting for a spark to ignite it.

On the evening of October 8, a fire started in a barn on the southwest side of Chicago. Within a few hours, fanned by strong winds, the flames raced north and east through the city. Fire brigades were quickly overwhelmed. All they could do was warn people living ahead of the fire to evacuate as fast as possible. Traffic jammed on many streets as families in wagons filled with household goods desperately sought to flee the rising tide of flame. Many people never escaped their own neighborhoods. Hopes that a body of water would stop the fire were shattered when it leapt across the Chicago River and drove panic-stricken families toward Lincoln Park on the north side of the city. Hundreds of other families found refuge by jumping into Lake Michigan. The conflagration raged for more than 24 hours. It devoured almost all downtown and North Side homes and businesses, killing more than 300 people, leaving 90,000 homeless and destroying some $200 million worth of property.

Of the people remaining in the city, most were unwillingly idle, dependent upon the first of months of provisions yet to arrive. Troops attempted to restore gas and water. Nearly all business and government records were burned. News was impossible to obtain because newspaper offices were burned out. However, a few days after the fire, in a bold public statement, the leaders of Chicago proclaimed they would "speedily rebuild the city" and that the "secession of industry would be short." They kept their word.

Cynthia was able to use her nursing experience to help care for the injured and homeless. The older girls helped out as well. Luckily, the fire had spared the Leonard home, if not Charles' printing plant. He relocated the business temporarily near his home to keep the firm in operation. In addition, he obtained another partner, Charles Knight, and together they rebuilt the firm on its original site. But it would be a number of years before Knight and Leonard became profitable.

Cynthia, on the other hand, was now in her ascendancy as a crusader for women's rights. She had organized the Good Samaritan Society, a shelter for homeless prostitutes. After the Chicago fire, on behalf of the destitute women of the city, she carried her crusade to City Hall, lobbying politicians about their sinful behavior toward women. One result of her efforts was the decision to place matrons in Chicago prisons.[5]

Cynthia began a correspondence with Susan B. Anthony, the suffrage leader in New York. The three older Leonard girls had by now grown beyond the family, leaving only Nellie and Susan at home, with Charles as parent-designate. Cynthia grew increasingly angry at Charles, not only for his financial difficulties and his activities as a Mason, but also his decision to continue his business relationship with Inger-soll, an act she considered irreligious and impious. At the same time, she had pro-voked the ire of many politicians in Chicago, who raised barriers designed to restrict her suffrage activities.

Cynthia decided New York would be her next stop, not only to fulfill her own destiny but also, like a true "stage mother," to promote her daughter's professional career. For his part, Charles was very sad to lose his "favorite," Nellie, but evidently glad to be rid of Cynthia. The fact that he did nothing to argue against or prevent Cynthia's taking the girls to New York suggests that he had already accepted his wife's decision.

Nevertheless, the parting at the train station proved melodramatic. Cynthia avoided the painful emotions by busying herself with the luggage and locating seats. Nellie and Susan cried, as did Charles; but he tried to raise their spirits by telling them about the marvelous sights they would see in New York. Prophetically, he assured Nel-lie that she would soon become famous. "Don't forget to study and work hard for your employers," he told her. "And please write to me often."

The train trip from Chicago to New York took almost two days, passing through Cleveland, Buffalo and Albany, then paralleling the Hudson River into Grand Cen-tral Station. Coach seats were uncomfortable and food had to be carried or quickly purchased at train stops. Windows were kept tightly closed because the soot and smoke from the locomotive blackened clothing and faces. But for two young women like Nellie and Susie, the excitement of embarking on a new adventure compensated for any inconveniences.

For the last two hours of the trip, eyes wide and all but mesmerized, they eagerly took in the bucolic river valley, with its whitewashed villages and their characteristic church steeples. Then the exotic city itself—tall buildings, lined up in military file, street traffic thick with omnibuses, wagons, carts and people of all sorts and man-ners of dress, colorful signs naming businesses and proclaiming the virtues of their pro-ducts, all in a wide variety of languages. When the train finally entered the cavernous station and passengers gathered their belongings to disembark onto the platform, the girls encountered wildly waving parties (shouting to get the attention of the new arrivals) and black porters in uniforms with shiny brass buttons, hauling big-wheeled baggage wagons. Everywhere was the clamor of people and machinery, all seemingly running in random directions.

For the girls, making their way through the crowded station and finding a stage to take them to their new home was a thrilling adventure. And the ride to the board-ing house was equally exciting, crossing a wide river on a ferry to Brooklyn.

The move to New York took place in October 1878. Cynthia, Nellie and Susan took only their clothes and personal belongings with them. Once settled in the Brook-lyn boarding house, Cynthia quickly joined Susan B. Anthony and left Nellie (16) and Susan (14) under the care of the boarding house manager. Susan was enrolled in pub-lic school, leaving Nellie ample time to get acquainted with the city. As part of her desire to further Nellie's opera career, Cynthia persuaded Dr. Leopold Damrosch, a celebrated and revered voice teacher, to accept her daughter as a pupil.

Born in Posen, Prussia, Dr. Damrosch had received his degree in medicine. But he chose instead to join the Weimar orchestra as violinist under conductor Franz Liszt. Damrosch came to the U.S. in 1871 to conduct the German Choral Society. When he first met Cynthia Leonard, he was giving singing lessons to selected students and had just founded the New York Symphony Society. Damrosch found that he could not turn down the determined Mrs. Leonard.

His studio was close to the heart of the theater district in the Bowery, and Nellie soon became aware of the vitality of this unique section of the city. When she first arrived in New York in 1878, Broadway — as we know it today — did not yet exist. The street had become famous for its exclusive hotels, restaurants and shops. It was sometimes called the Ladies Mile, because of its retail shopping district. But years would pass before Broadway became synonymous with theater entertainment.

North of 23rd Street, there were no theaters. Most of them were clustered around Union Square (14th Street) — at least the more reputable ones like Wallack's, Daly's and Booth's. There, serious plays were performed. Musical comedy then

Lillian was 17 and taking vocal lessons from Dr. Leopold Damrosch. Weekly trips to Dr. Damrosch gave her the opportunity to visit the Bowery's variety houses. (Harry Ransom Humanities Center, the University of Texas at Austin.)

existed only in its most skeletal forms. Harrigan and Hart farces caught the attention of theatergoers, and Tony Pastor's variety house featured the top performers of the day. The last of the minstrel shows were being performed before audiences who had no familiarity with black face or the minstrel traditions.

Down a few blocks was the colorful and notorious Bowery. It was in the Bowery that the art and business of popular theater was born — in its dime museums, beer gardens and variety houses. It would not take long for an intelligent and cultivated young woman to see that the area was "shady," a place to observe humanity at its best and worst. The Bowery was crowded with immigrants — German, Italian, Irish predominantly — all seeking their own versions of the American Dream. Bowery streets teemed with extremes of the human condition. But its cultural milieu of tenements, stores and street vendors, foreign languages and similarly various entertainments awed both visitors and locals alike.

To headstrong and self-confident Nellie, the Bowery's allure proved irresistible. She began extending her visits to Dr. Damrosch to include visits to the surrounding theaters, taking in both serious plays and popular variety, particularly at Tony Pastor's Theater, which had a rare policy of welcoming women to its shows.

Life in New York for Cynthia and her daughters was undoubtedly difficult. Since most of her time was devoted to the suffrage movement, Cynthia held no job. Along with her work for Anthony, for which she did receive a small stipend, Cynthia organized the Science of Life Club and managed a benefit for starving women and children in Ireland. She also received monthly checks from Charles to "pay the rent." Both Nellie and Susan had part-time jobs (Nellie worked in a candy store) which generated their own spending money. But where the money to pay Dr. Damrosch came from remains a mystery.

During the summer of 1879, when theaters and variety houses were habitually closed, Nellie tried hard to get auditions to perform for the coming season, which started in September. She first chose the variety houses, because they hired more singers and changed their shows weekly. Yet all her efforts ended in rejection. The managers kept telling her she had "a nice face, a nice voice, but no personality."

Nellie did not tell her mother of these forays into the land of "sin and depravity," as popular theaters were perceived by Cynthia. Indeed, actors and actresses in popular theater were generally thought of as consorting with the Devil. Had she known of Nellie's job-hunting, Cynthia's fury would have been overwhelming. Often Cynthia would come home to find Nellie gone, and she demanded to know where Nellie was. But Susan always came up with plausible excuses to protect her sister.

Just as Nellie had all but given up her quest for employment, she met Walter Sinn, son of Col. William Sinn, who happened to be the owner of the Park Theater in Brooklyn. Mrs. Sinn, Walter's mother, liked Nellie, not only for her beauty and pleasant company, but also as a prospective wife for her son. She suggested that Nellie see E.E. Rice, the producer of *Evangeline*, who was at the time auditioning singers to fill his chorus. Mrs. Sinn facilitated the audition with Rice, apparently as a motherly gesture to Nellie. When Cynthia was told of this "act of kindness," she was against Nellie's auditioning but pleased that her daughter had been recognized for her talent. This one time, Cynthia relented, giving Nellie the opportunity to perform.

Chorus girls with angelic voices were hard to find. The want ads in the *New York Clipper*, a weekly theatrical newspaper, listed many job opportunities, some paying as much as five dollars a week. Rice noted that Nellie had a fine voice and was also quite pretty. She was immediately hired and told to report to Rice early in September. *Evangeline* was scheduled to open at the end of September, at Boston's Globe Theater.

It was an exciting event for Nellie — her first theater job, singing in the chorus for a famous producer, and starting her first tour out of town. Cynthia, however, was ambivalent. While gratified that a well-respected person like E.E. Rice acknowledged Nellie's talent, she was unhappy that her daughter would be singing something other than opera. She was even more disturbed that Nellie would be alone in another city, away from her mother's watchfulness. Yet she realized that little could be gained by attempting to prevent Nellie from fulfilling her ambition.

At the beginning of rehearsals, the chorus was taught all of its songs, apart from the rest of the play. Every day a choirmaster worked very hard with the women (there were no men in choruses). The entire production had to be ready to perform in three weeks. After learning its songs, the chorus was integrated into the production and sang with musical accompaniment from the orchestra. In these productions, the conductor and orchestra, anywhere from 15 to 25 musicians, were permanent members of the cast.

The conductor for *Evangeline* was a 22-year-old British musician, Harry Braham, who had arrived a year earlier from London to further his musical career. He came from a Jewish family of musicians and conductors, two of whom later achieved recognition in musical theater. Harry was a tall, lean, handsome young man, with cheerful eyes and an engaging manner. He directed the orchestra with a low-key, easy going demeanor that encouraged his group to play their best. He had an equally attractive effect on the young women in the chorus. Many desired his attention. Only one, however, was of interest to Harry.

Pictures of Nellie at the time reveal her allure. As stage photos, they suggest a winsome, shy girl from the

Harry Braham, Lillian's first husband. He was musical director when Lillian joined the chorus of *Evangeline*, her first professional performance. Two months later, they were married. (Harry Ransom Humanities Research Center, the University of Texas at Austin.)

country. They mask the highly motivated, determined young woman who was quickly learning about life in the urban environment. Nellie was confident, assured and intelligent, and already had focused aspirations to perform beyond the limitations of the chorus.

The two became friends quickly. They would go off together after rehearsals, Harry taking Nellie back to her boarding house at night. The seriousness and rapidity with which the relationship developed bothered Cynthia. An immigrant, an itinerant musician and a Jew was not her choice as Nellie's companion. And Cynthia had reason for concern. Within a few weeks of their meeting, Harry was taking Nellie to his Washington Square rooms. At some point during this period, prior to their opening in Boston, Nellie realized that she was pregnant.

Her liaisons with Harry continued during the tour in Boston. By the time the

company returned to New York in November, Nellie was fully aware of her predicament. Declaring their love for each other, the couple decided to marry and then
announce their elopement to all interested parties. Nellie seemed happy about the situation, even though it meant temporarily diverting her ambitions. Both, however,
feared most Cynthia's reactions to the news. It would not be a pleasant meeting.

Their marriage took place on November 4, 1879, in the City Hall offices of a justice of the peace. In attendance were some friends from *Evangeline*. Immediately after
the ceremony, the newlyweds went off to rehearsal. They planned to tell Cynthia that
evening, after the performance, when Harry took Nellie back to the boarding house.

The family confrontation turned out to be more animated than the evening's performance. After Cynthia recovered from the initial shock, her usually controlled
temper flared. With frequent pauses for appeals to Divine intervention, she lurched
back and forth across the room, screaming and pointing accusatory fingers. Cynthia
refused to acknowledge the marriage. She accused Harry of seducing her daughter
and threatened police action. She threatened to lock Nellie in her room to prevent
her from singing. At the same time, she sank to the floor and begged forgiveness for
having ignored her daughter while pursuing her own activities. In a final act of fury,
Cynthia swore she would no longer speak to them.

Ultimately, practicality prevailed. The Leonards moved to another, larger boarding house in Manhattan, on West 34th Street. Obviously, the newlyweds needed a
room of their own; and it would be helpful if they were closer to the theater district.
Cynthia also found it more convenient, since it meant she was within blocks of Susan
B. Anthony's office. The new boarding house catered to entertainers. After breakfast
was served, the dining room was converted into a practice area for singing and dancing. Exchanging news and rumors was natural among the performers. Nellie spent
an hour each morning singing songs from the show, as well as other currently popular pieces to broaden her repertoire. After lunch, she and Harry would rest before
heading to the theater for the night's performance.

Evangeline played until early February 1880, at a succession of theaters — the
Standard in New York, the Park and Haverly in Brooklyn. Nellie and Harry followed
their usual routines each performance day. Cynthia continued her non-communica-
tion policy, although frequent messages were passed along through sister Susan. The
couple grew increasingly concerned as the show neared its close. Harry had not yet
secured his next position. And it was obvious to Nellie she could not take on another
singing assignment because her figure was changing. With that acknowledgment,
Cynthia would have to be included in any future plans. Yet the long-feared confrontation turned out more pleasantly than the couple had anticipated.

Apparently, Cynthia was already aware of Nellie's condition and was waiting for
the moment when Nellie would suggest they talk about it. Cynthia not only acknowledged the situation but appeared quite solicitous, acting like a grandmother-in-wait-
ing. However, she still would have few words with Harry, only reminding him of his
responsibility to find and hold a job. Overall, the family situation settled down, with
Cynthia now openly planning for the baby's arrival and care.

It was some months before Harry secured another job, conducting an orchestra
at a variety house in the Bowery, but at least his contract would continue through
June. Nellie decided to use her time at home to renew singing and acting lessons.
There was no question in her mind that she was planning to return to the stage after

her child's birth. Cynthia, not surprisingly, was firmly against the idea.

On June 7, 1880, a boy was born to the Brahams, named after his father, Harry. A day later, a census taker visited the boarding house to collect the required vital statistics. Little Harry was listed as one day old. Cynthia gave her age as 50 (correct); Nellie said she was 19 (but not until December) and an actress; and Harry said he was 25 (actually 23). Cynthia indicated she had no occupation, making no mention of her suffrage activities.

A large room had been prepared for the parents and their new child. They had a New York City summer to care for little Harry, with frequent assistance from Cynthia and Susan. Cynthia spent her time playing with the baby while communicating little with the parents. Harry hunted for work. Nellie continued her voice lessons. As the family waited each month for Charles' checks to arrive, funds were scarce. Sympathetic to Nellie's situation, the

Tony Pastor, the acknowledged father of "variety." He transformed variety into high-quality entertainment for the whole family and gave many new performers (including Lillian) their first chances to perform. (Harry Ransom Humanities Research Center, the University of Texas at Austin.)

boarding house manager made additional food available for the baby.

In September, Harry was interviewed by Tony Pastor and won the job as orchestra conductor for the season. While he and Nellie were elated with his new job (the salary was good and Pastor was a respectable owner and manager), Cynthia bemoaned the "low class" environment around Pastor's theater. In reality, Pastor operated one of the cleanest variety houses in town.

At the time, Tony Pastor was known as the "Bowery Autocrat" and "The 14th Street Impresario." In later years, he would be labeled the "Father of Vaudeville." His pioneering efforts in the 1860s and '70s popularized and refined this type of entertainment, which he named "variety."[6]

A Pastor show consisted of nine acts, plus an afterpiece. Each act was a specific, highly skilled performance — juggling, trapeze or tight rope work, acrobatics, comic skits, buck-and-wing dancing, comic and sentimental songs and instrumental solos.

The first act was designed to get the attention of the audience. The fourth act was the headliner, just before the intermission. The second part of the show built to the after-piece, usually a skit composed of the various performers in a comic or dramatic presentation. And the impresario performed as well. A short, rotund, mustachioed man, always dressed in a tuxedo, sporting diamond studs and a collapsible opera hat, he would entertain the crowds with song and dance, often making up new lyrics to satirize the affairs of the day. Pastor hoped the audience would leave the theater eager to return next week when a new bill would be playing. His theaters were usually filled with satisfied customers. Pastor not only made his variety shows enjoyable, he also featured most of the top variety stars of the season, supporting them with strong publicity and promotion.

A spot on a Pastor program was prestigious. To perform at Pastor's meant exposure and an opportunity to build a career. Many top performers, like Edward Harrigan, Pat Rooney, George M. Cohan, Weber and Fields, the Irwin Sisters and Gus Williams credited Pastor with their show business beginnings. Aware of Pastor's reputation, Nellie and Harry were rightly excited about Harry's new appointment.

The theater season of 1880 opened at Wallack's famous house with a burlesque from London, *Grim Goblin*. Harrigan and Hart reopened their Theatre Comique with *The Mulligan Guard's Picnic*, the music written and conducted by Harry's cousin, David Braham. Willie Edouin put on a comedy called *Dreams, or Fun in a Photographic Gallery*. Other foreign successes with first New York showings included *La Fille du Tambour-Major*, an *opéra bouffe* at the Standard; *The Pirates of Penzance* at the Booth; and *The Sultan of Mocha* at the Union Square. Tony Pastor's innovation for the season was the inclusion of a series of extended skits, in addition to the usual variety acts.

Harry's work for Pastor was commended, and the young conductor was encouraged by the audience reactions to the shows. As was common at Pastor's, the theater was filled every night with so many standing room patrons that simply walking the aisles became a vigorously contested elbow-jabbing competition. One early autumn evening, the young couple determined the time was ripe. Having Pastor's ear, why couldn't Harry suggest that Nellie be given an audition? The notion presented some exciting possibilities.

The next day, Harry spoke to Pastor on behalf of his wife. Their timing could not have been better. Since Pastor was just planning his upcoming schedule to include more extended skits, among them some satires of Gilbert and Sullivan, he would need singers. Pastor readily agreed to hear Nellie the next day.

On the way to the theater, Nellie seemed calm. But alone in a dressing room, preparing to sing, the moment nearly overwhelmed her. Long-held hopes were finally being realized; a failure would be devastating. Of course, Mother must not be told until Nellie knew her venture was successful. And how would Pastor himself react? As she strode purposefully on stage, Nellie could only rely on her previous experience of performance to allay her self-consciousness.

With an accompanist playing the piano and Harry looking on, Nellie sang an operatic piece and one of the popular songs she had been practicing during the past few months. When finished, she stood perfectly still, holding her breath. For a few moments, she heard only absolute silence.

"Can you start next week?" asked Pastor.

Nellie was stunned. But she quickly recovered and readily accepted.

A story goes that Nellie answered, "Oh, I can't! I haven't anything to wear on the stage." Pastor was reported to have put a $50 bill in her hand, saying "Buy a dress with this. Pay me back at the rate of $10 a week, out of your salary." Her pay was purported to be $75 a week. In fact, it was $25 a week, and she wore the dresses that she had from *Evangeline*. But Nellie Leonard Braham was hired! Singing on the stage! In Tony Pastor's theater!

Besides discussing the pieces she should prepare to sing, Pastor suggested that Nellie change her name. He had his business manager Harry Sanderson draw up a list of first and last names and pin them to a board for her to look at. Together, Pastor and Nellie examined them and toyed with various combinations. It was Nellie who chose "Lillian Russell," because the "ll's" in the name made it sound "musical." Pastor agreed and asked Sanderson to prepare programs to include that name. Nellie Leonard had become Lillian Russell.

Nellie/Lillian and Harry now had to tell Cynthia about the latest episode in her daughter's career. Surprisingly, Cynthia responded calmly, asking only, "Is the salary satisfactory?" No question she was pleased with her daughter's stage success. But "Lillian Russell"? It would take more than a few performances for Cynthia to accept her daughter's new identity.

On the evening of November 22, 1880, when Tony Pastor addressed his audience, proclaiming Nellie's loveliness and golden voice, he launched Lillian Russell on her illustrious career. Now the real work began.

Chapter Two

She Couldn't Say No

*I*n her autobiography, written in 1922 for *Cosmopolitan* magazine, Lillian stated, "I grew up in an atmosphere of freedom. My mother never lost her temper."[1] She went on to relate a specific episode between her and Cynthia that occured when Lillian was seventeen:

> One day I appeared in my mother's sitting room to tell her that I was going out to tea. She did not approve of the person who was to take me, but all she said was, "I wouldn't go out with that man, Nellie."
> "I don't care, I'm going," I said calmly.
> "You're not going," she said, still gently.
> I considered a moment. I might be self-supporting but I had never before disobeyed her. However, "You can't whip me, can you?" I asked her coolly. "No," she said more coolly than I, "I can't whip you, Nellie, but I can prevent you from going out with that man."
> I didn't answer. Confidently, I trotted back to my own room and went on with my dressing. I shall never forget the dress I wore when I returned to her a few minutes later. It was a pale, pink organdie, frilled and crisp, and with it I wore a big print hat which was trimmed with pale pink apple blossoms, and which I thought was quite irresistible.
> "Well," I said bravely, "I'm going, mother."
> My gentle mother did not answer. She very calmly picked up a pitcher of water and turned it over on me, drenching me to the skin, ruining my hat and frock and soaking my hair. She did not lose her sweetness for an instant nor her gracious dignity.
> "I told you I would prevent you from going," she said quietly, "and I have."

While Lillian Russell was a highly successful performer for many years, adored by her audiences and sought-after by theater managers, she was, personally, a troubled woman. Clearly, many of Lillian's conflicts and decisions in life seem attributable to the strained relationship between her and Cynthia.

In an apparent attempt to reconcile her feelings about Cynthia, Lillian wrote a glowingly respectful portrait in *Cosmopolitan,* extolling her mother's virtues and strong influences on her life. In reality, however, the two had waged psychological warfare from the time they arrived in New York.

Until that time, throughout Lillian's childhood and early adolescence, Cynthia had maintained tight control over every significant aspect of her daughter's life (school, music lessons, recreation, manner of dress), always amply justified by moralistic declarations. Cynthia's demands and requirements were strict; as Lillian recalled, "she never permitted disobedience":

> All that we five girls ever became, we owed to her. The way we spoke, the way we stood, the way we behaved, were all due to her teaching. She never permitted us to speak ungrammatically or to stand ungracefully, and every little talent we possessed was trained and trimmed and polished until it stood out bravely."[2]

Along with this discipline, Cynthia impressed upon Lillian and her sisters her strong religious beliefs, dissent from established authority and her feelings about men. Yet, among the five sisters, it was only Lillian who rebelled and fought back, her conflicts with Cynthia assuming all the characteristics of what psychologists would call a love-hate relationship. Throughout her life, Lillian was conflicted about the relationship with her mother, alternately displaying hostile feelings and behavior to punish Cynthia and then, feeling guilty and contrite, making protestations of love and respect to honor her.

Cynthia's influence had been considerable. She was a religious zealot, an ardent churchgoer who preached about the perils of earthly sin and frequently invoked God to support her views. Her frontier evangelism found new focus in the women's suffrage movement after the move to Chicago. It allowed her to combine two personal crusades into a single noble struggle, at once fighting both sin and male domination.

All evidence suggests that Cynthia did not like men. She believed them to be unworthy rulers over women; they were usurping tyrants who had to be put in their place. Her domination of Charles extended over all family affairs, his business, and their moving to venues more suitable to her career. She fought the politicians in Chicago, more because of their treatment of women than any civic transgressions they may have committed. Her militancy then stretched to the streets of New York, where she became an aggressive and outspoken supporter of Susan B. Anthony and the suffrage movement.

Just after arriving in Chicago, Cynthia began a correspondence with Anthony. When Anthony visited the city, she stopped to visit Cynthia. Indeed, it seems likely that Anthony persuaded Cynthia to move to New York to assist in the suffrage crusades. Through Anthony, Cynthia met Elizabeth Cady Stanton. What better role models for Cynthia? Anthony never married. Stanton married and had seven children, but she was in continual conflict with her husband and left him to join the suffrage cause.

When Chicago politicians questioned Cynthia's qualifications, she supported her positions by claiming to have been a *Mayflower* descendant. In reality, it was Charles who could rightly claim such ancestry. But, typical of his passive manner, he allowed her to assume the patrician identity. In New York, Cynthia constantly used this claim on behalf of her suffrage efforts, particularly when she ran for mayor. Indeed, Cynthia's presumption to American "aristocracy" was so often repeated that it seems doubtful Lillian ever knew the tortured truth of her mother's claim.

With equal determination, Cynthia attempted to intercede in the romantic lives of her daughters. Supposedly caring only to assist them in finding the "right" husbands, she in fact rejected almost every suitor when marriage seemed imminent. The three oldest daughters ultimately married men approved by Cynthia. Lillian and her younger sister Susan chose their own husbands in spite of Cynthia's vociferous objections. Being close to Lillian in New York afforded Cynthia constant opportunity to remind her daughter of her poor taste in male companionship. Whenever Lillian took up with a man, she seemed to ignore her mother's protestations; yet, when the relationship broke down, Lillian would always turn to Cynthia for sympathy.

Cynthia's antipathy to authority (closely related to the issue of male dominance) was equally strong. Men, particularly those who happened to be one's employers, were not to be trusted. They would never pay a woman what she deserved. They would simply promote her for their own benefits, which were primarily money-related. Not surprisingly, Cynthia frequently insinuated herself into Lillian's contract and salary disputes, denigrating theater managers (read: males) for their ill-treatment of her daughter. Among theater managers, a vituperative letter from Cynthia, always published in a local newspaper, came to be considered a badge of professional honor.

No doubt this conduct deeply affected Lillian and influenced her professional behavior. She craved adoration from her audiences, particularly from men; and her professionally self-destructive actions probably stemmed from her guilt about "breaking the rules." Cynthia's psychic demons surely took their toll on Lillian's emotional life.

Lillian was an intelligent woman, cognizant of and sensitive to the social environment around her. Her maturity as an actress and her self-assurance in performance made her keenly aware of her beauty and the public's response to it. She fully exploited these attributes in all aspects of her life. Unlike other performers of the time, Lillian worked hard to maintain her voice and constantly improve her acting, knowing that these commodities were essential to sustain her audiences. As a result, she repeatedly proved she could make money for her employers; that knowledge gave her the ammunition to demand and obtain appropriate payment for her services.

Still, Lillian remained ambivalent about men. She liked being with them. She delighted in competing with them. She enjoyed their adoration, including the many gifts they bestowed upon her. She was married four times and had many suitors, many of whom came from elite circles of society. But all of her marriages were inconveniences in their own way, used more as platforms for her career aspirations than to manifest love. Except for her last marriage, at age 51, to a newspaperman, she chose men whose self-identities were relatively weak and who could be relied upon to acquiesce under the pressure of a strong-willed woman.

During most of her career, Lillian repeatedly displayed dysfunctional behavior, perceived by theater managers as the egocentric manipulations of a prima donna yet by her audiences as a justifiable response to economic forces that blocked women from personal achievement. At moments when she was about to capture stardom, she would peremptorily leave a show, either feigning illness or finding reason to dispute a contract. Her marriages were glorified by the press to royal proportions; her divorces became the soap opera serializations of the day. Contradictions abounded. She spoke for health and fitness, only to engage in eating contests at famous New York restaurants. She demonstrated great generosity to her fellow performers off-stage, then would get one fired because he was "acting carelessly."

These personality and behavioral traits cannot be examined out of context, however, because the social and cultural mores of her time played a prominent role in Lillian's trials and triumphs. Her appeal to a new middle class of women — who had more leisure time to read magazines, attend the theater and cater to the latest fashions — made her a role model for both their fantasies and aspirations. During this period, more women were advocating and attempting to put into practice the combination of marriage and career. The percentage of women in professions grew rapidly during the latter part of the nineteenth century. Public views of the temperment of women (presumed to be emotional, subjective and irrational) were changing in response to an accelerated emphasis on rationalism, scientific standards and objectivity. Yet despite these relatively enlightened advances, some theater managers perceived Lillian as possessing the traditional temperment of women precisely because she argued for and insisted upon equal pay.

The latter part of the nineteenth century also saw the beginning of the women's suffrage movement and its development from a "crackpot scheme" devised by a few radicals to a broad-based coalition of both elite and working-class women. The movement's most dramatic growth came through militant tactics on the street rather than tea parlor oratory. But it quickly co-opted the mainstream forces of the day, using parades, the press and the podium to spread its belief in women's equality.

One of the pivotal venues where the movement was able to gain a foothold and expand its message was the theater, particularly popular theater. Here, women were able to perform — on a stage, in public, in all manner of costume, displaying many talents beyond physical beauty, in equal roles with men, often with much publicity. These women were mobile, self-sufficient, independent contractors of their talents, earning a respectable income. From the shy *soubrettes* of the 1870s, they attained star power within a decade, at the same time spreading popular theater to the heartland of the country and soon seeing their achievements proclaimed in Edison's electric lights on Broadway.

Lillian was not only the beneficiary of this new awareness and appreciation of female performance; she was also a leader in making it a legitimate influence. Her timing could not have been better. While feminism and the suffrage movement were rarely mentioned in the entertainment business, they nevertheless were significant contributors to its advancement. When the vote for women became a controversial social and political issue, many women performers, including Lillian, supported it vigorously. Yet her involvement illustrated Lillian's ambivalence about her mother: She disliked Cynthia's militancy on behalf of the suffrage movement, only to become a spokesperson for it herself after Cynthia died.

These social forces also changed the public perception of women, from their playing a willing, secondary role as homemaker for husband and caretaker of children to their being oppressed and "wronged" by men. This became particularly true when women had the opportunity to publicly present their side of the story. Lillian was able to employ this argument a number of times. In each episode, she appeared to win the support of her audience. It not only enhanced her reputation, it also filled the seats. Theater managers complained about her behavior, until they counted the take at the end of the week.

The media revolution, abetted by the mass circulation of newspapers and women's magazines, turned an anecdote into mythology and a stage costume into a fashion craze. Other related forms of communication contributed to the gigantic increase in visual stimuli and merchandising message. Music sheets made popular songs available to all. Outdoor advertising, whether in streetcars, on billboards, barns, telephone poles, taxis, or even rock outcroppings, found marketing display space. The promotion of old holidays and the formation of new ones, like Mother's Day, offered ever more reasons for purchase and consumption. Even hot air balloons promoted the goods and services increasingly available, along with popular theater performers. The theater publicist became a very important contributor to a performer's success.

It was in this milieu that Lillian gained her fame and was able to maintain celebrity for so many years. That she was aware of, able and willing to manipulate mass media attests to her business acumen. She made herself and was, in turn, made by others — audiences who worshipped her performance, both on and off the stage; the press that followed and repeated her every word and action; and the "new" women who perceived her as a catalyst for their personal desires and goals in life.

When Lillian began her career at Tony Pastor's Theater, she was a month shy of celebrating her nineteenth birthday. Married for a year, she had a five-month-old child. She and Harry were living in the same boarding house as her mother and sister, depending on them for child-care assistance. Lillian's total professional stage experience was three months. Though both she and Harry earned salaries, some of it had to be used to support Cynthia and Susan.

Initial response to her performances prompted Pastor to teach Lillian more about effective stage behavior. He showed her how to enter the stage, how to face the audience, how to take bows and how to handle encores.

In variety, if audiences liked a song, they wanted it repeated. If the performer asked the audience to join in, the audience was captured. Repeated encores were usually mentioned in the newspapers as a sign of success and so increased the appeal of the performer. In fact, Pastor would sometimes employ "plants" in the audience to generate encores for his singers.

Pastor also suggested to Lillian that she learn new songs each week so they could be regularly introduced, thereby changing her act frequently. This was important, because many customers might then be induced to return to a particular theater each week.

In her second week at Pastor's, Lillian introduced a new song, "Moonlight at Killarney." Irish love songs were popular at the time, and the *New York Clipper* noted that many encores were requested. By her third week, Lillian was not only singing, but also acting in a short skit, a burlesque called "Needles and Pins."

A month into her career, Lillian faced her first competition on Pastor's bill. Florence Merton was thought to be as pretty and talented as Lillian, and audiences responded accordingly. The two contested one another in songs that demanded the singer reach high C a number of times. While no winner seems to have been selected by the audience, the *New York Clipper* singled out Lillian as "Pastor's new beautiful balladist."

But Lillian's initial successes soon began to affect her marriage. She was spending an increasing amount of time at the theater rehearsing. Harry was becoming jealous of her success, particularly the flowers and candy she was receiving from a growing number of admirers. At the same time, Cynthia complained that both of them were paying little attention to the baby. Still, she enjoyed seeing her daughter perform and was proud of how the audiences responded to Lillian's singing.

In early January 1881, a young woman was hired to care for the baby. One afternoon, Harry came back to the boarding house after rehearsals to find the baby crying and the woman in tears because she had accidentally stabbed the baby in the stomach with a diaper pin while she was changing him. The baby was bleeding, and Harry was unable to stop the flow. A doctor was called, but by the time he arrived, the baby had gone into convulsions. Harry panicked. Neither Lillian nor Cynthia could be reached. The Braham baby died shortly thereafter.

Soon after the initial shock and sadness, recriminations followed. While the young woman was blamed for the blunder, both Lillian and Cynthia accused Harry of complicity in the child's death. He was so upset by the episode that he was unable to work for weeks. Lillian, however, missed only two days of

To help her build public identity, Tony Pastor had Lillian pose for publicity pictures to be distributed to audiences. One of the first theater managers to use this marketing technique, Pastor heavily promoted his performers. (Harry Ransom Humanities Research Center, University of Texas at Austin.)

performance. Pastor was aware of the situation and suggested to Lillian that she take some time off to recover. She refused. Not only did she feel that her career was in jeopardy, but domestic life with Cynthia had grown increasingly uncomfortable.

Cynthia now took the opportunity to express to Harry all that she disliked about him. She blamed him for the seduction of her daughter and their marriage, and for incompetence with the child. Her reproaches became so intense that Harry moved out of the boarding house. Yet Cynthia continued her constant censure of Harry, upbraiding Lillian, "I told you what would happen." Cynthia insisted that divorce was now the only remedy.

Lillian's primary concern, however, was her career. She was not about to give it up. Indeed, she wished to devote even more effort to professional development. At the time, Pastor was preparing the first in a series of travesties on Gilbert and Sullivan operas. He chose Lillian to be a featured player in these skits. Sensitive to her needs, however, Pastor allowed her to practice the new role for three weeks, without having to perform each night at the theater, yet still receiving a salary. The confidence that Pastor showed in her increased her professional aspirations.

The *Pie Rats of Penn Yan* opened in February, one of many travesties of Gilbert and Sullivan being performed on variety stages throughout the U.S. (much to the chagrin of the original authors). Copyright law in the U.S. stated that publication of a foreign manuscript, even in the author's own country, automatically made it public property in this country. Gilbert and Sullivan's *The Pirates of Penzance* had opened at New York's Fifth Avenue Theater on September 30, 1879. American managers were free to reproduce it any way they wished; many variations were prepared, all of them intended to capitalize on the success of the original opera.

Pastor's rendition was well-received. Lillian played the role of Maria (Mabel, in the original) and was reviewed positively by the *Clipper*:

> Lillian Russell, vocally, is an exception to the other members of the cast, and her singing in the principal role is worthy of much commendation. She has not only a sweet soprano voice, but one which she uses in a skillful manner, making even the more intimate numbers of her score, which keeps much of the *Penzance* music charmingly effective.[3]

Pastor ran the show four weeks and followed it with a travesty of *Olivette*, a hit opera playing at Daly's Theater. Lillian played the title role with such success that the newspapers were calling her "most deservedly a favorite." Even the proper *New York Dramatic Mirror*, which usually condescended to the antics of burlesque and variety, was impressed by Lillian's performance:

> Miss Lillian Russell as Olivette gave additional proof of her adaptation to the requirements of *opéra bouffe*. She acted and sang most charmingly, and was faultlessly costumed. If the young lady does not allow adulation to conquer her ambition and elevate her too high in her own esteem, she will become a bright and shining light on the lyric stage.[4]

Lillian's "faultless costume" was a boy's sailor suit, cut to feature her voluptuous form. She sang "In the North Sea Lived a Whale" to the delight of the audience. Many encores followed. And the (largely male) audiences seemed to find both voice and figure equally attractive.

The observation by the *Dramatic Mirror* reporter had been astute. Pastor too noticed the rapidly developing impact of Lillian's success. The repeated encores, the long and frequent applause and the increasing attention from "stage door Johnnies" seemed to be affecting her self-perceptions. When Pastor sought to review Lillian's weekly performances, it was becoming increasingly difficult for him to consult with her.

At the end of March, Pastor began preparations for his company's spring and summer tour. Theaters in New York usually closed during the summer because of the heat and the attendant decline in the size of audiences. Touring netted comfortable profits for both managers and performers during an otherwise slow period. It also brought New York companies to audiences in many cities anxious to see them. A Pastor tour usually took what managers called "the existing circuit": Philadelphia, Baltimore, Washington, D.C., Pittsburgh, Cincinnati, Chicago, Cleveland, Buffalo,

Boston, Providence, and Brooklyn. Sufficiently large theaters and railroad accessibility were the primary reasons these cities were included.

Instead of selecting Lillian for the company, Pastor chose the Irwin Sisters. He felt that Lillian needed more acting experience, and he wished to get her away from Cynthia. So Pastor loaned her to Willie Edouin's Company, which was touring the western part of the U.S. Edouin was an old friend of Pastor and an excellent stage manager. While disappointed about not accompanying the Pastor troupe, Lillian did see the opportunities afforded her as the female star of Edouin's group. To encourage her in the decision, Pastor raised her salary to $50 per week, a welcome increase, since performers had to pay for their own room and board while on tour.

Touring companies of the early 1880s had developed a set of rules that governed the type of acts and their placement in the show. A typical Edouin bill had 9 to 12 acts, depending on the number of performers available on any given day. Each slot carried its own status, according to where it fell in relation to the intermission and the end of the program. The act appearing just before the intermission afforded Lillian high status, though not the highest. The top headliner (traditionally male) appeared second from last; this was the act everyone had been waiting for. The final act, the afterpiece, was usually a comedy skit in which all the individual performers appeared together.

Edouin's tour was Lillian's first experience working in a road show, and she learned quickly about the business of touring. Travel arrangements and housing were usually handled by the manager. Bookings were arranged so that the longest train ride lasted less than a day, usually on Mondays, when the theaters were dark. The Edouin Company, however, began their tour faced with a transcontinental train ride, from New York to St. Louis, then directly to San Francisco. They left New York on March 30, performed two days in St. Louis, and pulled into San Francisco April 16 to prepare their opening. Upon arriving at San Francisco's Standard Theater, they found it had been closed for a month.

When touring performers reached their destination, they usually stayed at a boarding house that catered to theater people. In many cities, actors were considered undesirables, and it was not surprising to see signs in boarding house windows that read, "No dogs or actors allowed."

Performers slept two-to-a-room. The boarding house provided meals. Actors would often be given advance checks to purchase drinks, charged against their salary. Some would use the checks for poker chips; others would redeem them at week's end for extra cash.

Lillian adjusted quickly to the daily routine. She slept late and ate a large breakfast to prepare for a long morning of rehearsals. If the theater was nearby, rehearsals would be held there. If not, they would be held in the dining room of the boarding house. After a light lunch, Lillian had the afternoon off to take care of personal business — letters to Cynthia or her sisters, doing laundry, or just strolling and seeing the sights. Lillian found these walks fascinating, as — with the exception of Chicago — she had never before seen any of these cities.

For most performers, boredom was a problem; and for veterans of touring companies, drinking and gambling became outlets to pass the time. Dinner was usually served around six o'clock P.M. An hour later, the performers were at the theater preparing for their acts. Theaters had few dressing rooms, usually cramped and cold, often in the basement. Few had wash basins; actors washed at long troughs, one for men, another for women. Basement dressing rooms were often shared with rats which, on occasion, would be found with greasepaint on their faces.

San Francisco was a revelation to Lillian. The gigantic bay teemed with boats of all shapes and sizes, seemingly bent on mutual destruction, only to veer away from one another at the last moment. A whole section of the city was filled with Chinese immigrants, their stores bedecked with indecipherable symbols and colorful banners. People shouted their wares, and animals ran through the streets and alleys. On top of the city's hills gleamed proud homes and hotels for the rich. At the bottom of the hills, humble shanties for the poor were patched together from whatever materials could be found. The city was a gambler's paradise. It offered all manner of potentially lucrative risks, from faro tables to mining stocks, all available to anyone determined to beat the odds. Though long a thriving seaport, San Francisco had been an incorporated city for only 30 years.

Entertainment was a profitable business in San Francisco. Eleven theaters were already in operation, with still more being built. Performances started after dinner and continued to the early morning. For the more legitimate variety houses, shows started after ten P.M. and concluded after midnight. Legitimate theater was just beginning to find an audience in the city; most shows were designed for easy laughter, gravity-defying acts and pretty dancers — the kind of entertainment less refined audiences could understand and enjoy. The Willie Edouin players offered two shows sure to "wow" these customers.

Fun in a Photography Gallery was a typical slapstick, rough-house comedy made up of turns by each of the performers, built around the title's theme. "Babes in the Woods," an opera travesty filled with song and dance, starred Lillian as the Fairy Queen. In one scene, she wore tights and sang a song that encored every night. While women in tights were not new to the stage, the sight of Lillian striding provocatively across the boards had the audience falling off their chairs. Men vying to see her after the show were equally ebullient. She accommodated this herd of suitors by frequently appearing at local restaurants after the show.

The program continued for five weeks, to enthusiastic and demonstrative audiences; unfortunately, they were neither large enough nor sufficiently remunerative. And all was not well behind the scenes. Manager Locke, who had booked the company into the Standard, had grandly paid their railroad fare and promised a large percentage of the gross receipts. But after securing the lease on the theater, he came up short on money to pay the performers. At the end of the run, the Edouin Company received much less than they were promised and discovered they had no return tickets home.

A report in the San Francisco paper downplayed their plight:

> Willie Edouin's business at the Standard was fair during the entire engagement although the excellence of the entire company deserved better recognition.[5]

Entertainment reporters rarely mentioned bad news, unless they were treated poorly by the theater.

Next stop for the company was the 16th Street Theater in Denver, Colorado. It took them nine days to get there. Just prior to opening, a number of the performers fell sick, including the Edouin children. Performances in Leadville had to be canceled. The company was rapidly running out of funds to support their housing needs. Lillian had never experienced a situation like this and could only hope she had enough money to get home.

When the show closed in Denver, the company disbanded. As usual when a touring company ran out of bookings or money, members of the company were expected to fend for themselves. Since Edouin had promised Pastor to look after Lillian, however, he invited her join his family on their return to New York.

In the end, the young performer arrived safely home. But the tour had been a financial disaster. Not yet 20, on her own, Lillian had experienced both the adulation of the audience and the trauma of an empty purse. She swore to herself that the latter would never happen again.

When the New York theater press reported the company's demise — it was news because an Edouin enterprise was usually successful — Lillian was featured — not only her engaging performance, but also her off-stage activities. What began as rumor and innuendo soon came to be accepted as fact, in part because she never denied the charges. Lillian's stage appearance in tights was singled out as an "exploitation of beauty." Reports also noted her smoking in public and having slept in the same railroad car as the men of the company. Neither of these "revelations" was ever verified. But they had a considerable effect on Cynthia, who was very upset that her daughter, upon touring for the first time, had yielded to the evils of man. The reports also had an effect on a number of New York theater managers, who saw an opportunity to capitalize on Lillian's sudden notoriety.

When Lillian at last reached New York, she attempted to explain to her mother what had actually occurred on the tour. Mr. and Mrs. Edouin supported Lillian's version of events, verifying her good behavior during a difficult time. Their report comforted Cynthia and relieved Lillian of her mother's pressure to abandon performing. For his part, Pastor lost no time in persuading Lillian to join a small road company touring New England for a month, before the fall theater season began. As it would give her additional acting experience, as well as some money, Lillian quickly accepted.

The Variety Troupe, as they were called, consisted of newcomers to the variety halls who, in a few years, would themselves become stars. Among the group were W.F. Carroll, Bryant and Richmond, the American Four and the Four Cohans, including a brash youngster, Georgie. The *New York Clipper* reported the group played to "crowded houses" in towns throughout Massachusetts and New Hampshire, on tour to the end of September. Lillian was feeling more relaxed and confident about her performances; Pastor believed she had matured professionally and was now ready to scale new heights in her career.

Only a few blocks from Pastor's 14th Street Theater, yet miles away in quality of production and class of audience, was the Bijou Theater, under the direction of Col. John A. McCaull, one of New York's most successful impresarios. McCaull was preparing a new show called *The Grand Mogul*, a comic opera, to open at the end of October. Pastor suggested that Lillian would be an excellent choice to play the role of the snake charmer, D'jemma. Col. McCaull agreed, and Pastor transferred his contract with Lillian to the colonel. Lillian was promised an increase in salary, to $75 a week, if she agreed to perform. Seeing the opportunity to play a leading role in a new comic opera production, staged in a prestigious theater, she immediately accepted.

After serving the Confederacy during the Civil War, John A. McCaull had become a lawyer in Baltimore. One of his clients was John T. Ford, a long-respected manager who owned theaters in Washington, D.C., Baltimore and Philadelphia. (It was in Ford's Washington theater that Abraham Lincoln was shot in 1865.) Ford was interested in managing D'Oyly Carte in the U.S., to perform Gilbert and Sullivan operas. He sent McCaull to New York to negotiate the contract. When Ford was found to be in financial trouble, McCaull eagerly took over his interests.

McCaull's plan was to import foreign comic operas; as a producer, he was the first to stage them successfully. He also promoted the development of American comic opera. With Rudolph Aronson, he built the Casino Theater, the first in New York designed especially for musicals.

The Casino opened its doors in 1881, after months of delays attributed to both financial and construction problems. It was of elegant if florid Moorish design. But the fad for such architectural display had already passed; by the time it was completed, it looked dated. Another innovation that didn't work was the decision to place the auditorium on the second floor, requiring patrons to climb stairs to get to their seats.

The first show performed there was a failure, not because the show was a bad production, but because the interior had not yet been finished. Patrons complained about the lack of heat, poor lighting and temporary seating. The theater was closed, then reopened two months later, with all construction completed. A year later, it would be closed again, the interior gutted to relocate the auditorium on the ground floor.

Meanwhile, *The Grand Mogul* opened at McCaull's Bijou Theater on October 29, 1881, to mixed reviews. Lillian, however, was praised by the *Clipper* as the show's "most attractive performer":

> Miss Russell, whose voice is familiar to the frequenters of Tony Pastor's Theater, where she has been a bright particular star for some little while past, was the most attractive performer in the cast, and this is not only by a handsome face and graceful figure, but by a pure, fresh voice in admirable tune, and used with a good method; she is not so good an actress as singer, but with experience should remedy this, as she is both intelligent and young, and an artist for light opera of more than usual merit.[6]

The *New York Dramatic Mirror* alluded to the "fascinating and exuberant Lil."

But in a secondary role, her efforts were not enough to keep the show entertaining. A month after opening, the show was revised, with a new libretto, cast changes and a new name: *The Snake Charmer*. Lillian was now the star performer. Her role as D'jemma was enhanced and her costumes altered to emphasize her figure. In spite of these changes, however, the show still did not appeal to large audiences, and it closed three weeks later. Her contract reverting to Pastor, Lillian had little choice but to return to him. Yet her Bijou experience revealed the career directions she was determined to pursue.

Cynthia beamed with pride that her daughter, only 20 years old, had been elevated to star status. Lillian was welcomed back to the boarding house. But Cynthia had recently received another shock when daughter Susan appeared in a short skit at Pastor's. She too, it seemed, now wanted to become a performer. Diverting maternal anger to the political situation in New York, Cynthia decided to run for mayor on the suffrage ticket.

That same autumn, Tony Pastor made plans to produce a travesty on Gilbert and

Sullivan's most recent opera *Patience.* The new opera had premiered in New York at the Standard Theater in September 1881, and was still there by year's end, playing to full houses. Pastor chose to delay his opening of the travesty until Lillian became available.

Tony Pastor's *Patience* or *The Stage Struck Maidens* opened January 23, 1882, with Lillian in the title role. She was ably supported by the Irwin Sisters; Jacque Kruger; a talented comedian, Dan Collyer; and Frank Girard. The *Dramatic Mirror* reported Lillian to be "the best representative of Patience on the American stage," astonishing praise from a newspaper that rarely complimented variety. The *Clipper* favorably observed her effect on the audience:

> Lillian Russell, who was specially engaged, produced a very favorable impression as Patience, her pleasing voice and artistic vocalization being rewarded with the warmest marks of approbation. She was the recipient of several floral offerings when she first appeared.[7]

Pastor localized the show's plot: 20 love sick maidens became 20 stage-struck girls; the soldiers became the Coney Island militia; and the male

Lillian as D'jemma in *The Snake Charmer,* formerly *The Grand Mogul.* The original show flopped, and its replacement fared little better. Lillian played the lead in the revised version and made her first personal hit at the Bijou Theater, New York's premier showplace for comic opera. (Harry Ransom Humanities Research Center, the University of Texas at Austin.)

lead was changed from a poet to a despondent stage manager. Sullivan's original music was retained.

The production was a hit, and Lillian became the most discussed young performer in the city. A story was told that Gilbert and Sullivan themselves saw Lillian perform and offered her a large salary to join them. In reality, neither of the gentlemen was in the country at the time the Pastor show was playing. But Lillian was

Lillian in Pastor's version of Gilbert and Sullivan's *Patience*. Her voice and beauty quickly gained attention from audiences, the press and "stage-door Johnnies." (Harry Ransom Humanities Research Center, the University of Texas at Austin.)

indeed affected by the attention of the press and the flattering rumors, not to mention Pastor's box office receipts.

In a bold move, Lillian proposed to Pastor that a separate opera company be built around her, managed by him, to launch shows at his theater, then tour. Pastor apparently liked the idea. He announced at the end of February that "the Lillian Russell Opera Co. would commence its season at Tony Pastor's Theater April 10." A large ad was produced, featuring the new company and boasting the show would be "handsomely mounted, elegantly costumed, with superb properties and appointments." But Pastor was not pleased with Lillian's desire to renegotiate her contract, which still had some months remaining.

With Lillian continuing to receive rave reviews from the press, Cynthia believed that her daughter was not fully appreciated by Pastor and was wasting her talent by appearing in his variety shows. She suggested Lillian confront Pastor with an ultimatum. Lillian vacillated.

After 11 banner weeks of *Patience*, Pastor decided to produce a new show, again starring Lillian. It was to be a travesty, called *Billee Taylor*, written by an English composer, Edward Solomon. The original version had been produced in February 1881, and tallied over 100 London performances, an excellent run for any foreign work not by Gilbert and Sullivan.

Lillian agreed to the role but remained unhappy with her salary. Just prior to the opening of the new show, the *New York Clipper* featured Lillian on its front page (a portrait engraving), with an accompanying personal and professional profile highlighting her success at Pastor's. The story had been carefully edited by Lillian to keep certain facts from the public — her marriage and baby among them — while other items were falsified (the Western road trip was termed a success). At the same time, her demeanor toward Pastor changed from hesitant to temperamental.

Billee Taylor opened April 10. In anticipation of another Pastor hit, the *Clipper* spoke of Lillian's "fresh and tuneful voice" and predicted the show would be "well received." It was. The staid *Dramatic Mirror* was again uncommonly stirred by her performance:

> Lillian Russell as Phoebe is charming; she sings the music like a transmigrated nightingale, acts like a materialized Grace, and looks like Venus after her bath.[8]

Soon, the festering disagreement between Lillian and Pastor erupted into open warfare. She demanded a new contract. He refused to meet her demands. After two weeks as Phoebe, Lillian left the show, and it closed. The press reported that Lillian had become ill and could not continue. Cynthia, of course, produced, directed and stage-managed this episode, suggesting to Lillian that she "bring Pastor to his knees." While Lillian did argue with Pastor about her contract, she also felt guilty about embarrassing him, because of all that he had done on her behalf. To remove herself from this unpleasant situation, Lillian retreated to Chicago to recover from her "illness" and visit her father. She never again played for Tony Pastor.

The *Clipper* reported on her exit from the show and the city:

> Lillian Russell left the city for Chicago, Illinois, where she will remain until August for rest and recuperation, of which, her physician says, she is sadly in need. Her quiet departure gave rise to a rumor that she had eloped with the son of a wealthy Wall Street operator, but it was speedily dispelled by a public explanation made by the young lady's mother.[9]

Lillian remained in Chicago with her father for two months, away from the scrutiny of the New York press. Nevertheless, rumor and speculation surrounded her. She was said to be ready to return to Pastor's; she was to appear at Wallack's Theater in a new show; she was reported too ill to get out of bed. All the while, she was actually in contact with various theater managers who regarded her a viable commodity. A letter to the manager at Niblo's Garden got an immediate response when she suggested reviving her role in *Patience*, this time in its original Gilbert and Sullivan version. The manager saw and seized an opportunity to fill seats at his theater during the summer, when most other theaters were closed. He signed Lillian, and *Patience* opened at Niblo's on June 15. Immediately, both Pastor and McCaull claimed Lillian was still under contract to them; the argument soon spread to the local newspapers. The press, however, came out on Lillian's side and warned her about the warring ways of theater managers.

> Lillian Russell is old enough in the profession to walk alone, and to defend herself against the assaults of competing managers; but the young lyric-artist would fare better to keep out of wrangles and managerial disputes, and "let those who make the quarrels be the only ones to fight, etc." Just as soon as a young actress or vocalist gets her head above ground and begins to make herself heard, just so soon will managers growl and fight about her possession, especially if she should happen to be favored with a pretty face and a nicely molded figure.[10]

This would not be the only time the press would rise to Lillian's defense as "the wronged woman." The *Clipper* also recommended that Lillian hire a manager to negotiate contracts for her, indicating it was not a job for women.

In "Billee Taylor," Lillian appeared in her first "trouser" role on the New York stage. Successfully obscuring her voluptuous young body, it was a daring bit of costuming, one that probably contributed to the show's short run. (Harry Ransom Humanities Research Center, the University of Texas at Austin.)

Despite favorable reviews, Niblo's Garden closed *Patience* after two weeks. Whether the closure was due to hot weather and low attendance or publicity about the dispute among the managers, no one would admit. Lillian returned to the boarding house and mother to await her next show.

Of little notice to Lillian and Cynthia at the time was the announcement in the *Clipper* that Edward Solomon, the English composer of *Billee Taylor*, had just arrived in New York to lead a production of *The Vicar of Bray*, a comic opera to play at the Fifth Avenue Theater. It was reported that Solomon was accompanied by his wife, Edith Blande. More accurately, she was his companion, who also happened to be the play's leading lady. The opera opened the first week of October 1882; one week later, it closed, "a designated failure," according to the press.

Meanwhile, with apologies from both sides, Lillian and Col. McCaull had agreed to forget their differences and resume working together. Essentially, Lillian elected to fulfill her contract stipulations. The result was the revival of *The Sorcerer*, chosen because it would capitalize on the current popularity of Gilbert and Sullivan operas. Typical of a McCaull show, the production was well-mounted, and Lillian was in fine voice and splendid costume as Aline, the leading role.

While the show was well-received and seemed destined for a long run, Lillian remained dissatisfied about having to work under the old contract. Negotiations between her and McCaull reached an impasse in November, and Lillian became "ill" for two days. Because she had no understudy, McCaull was forced to close the show. For the next month, Lillian's availability to perform changed day-to-day, decreasing ticket sales and angering McCaull. Finally, in December, the *Clipper* reported:

Lillian Russell is again out of the cast of "The Sorcerer" at the Bijou, owing to a relapse of the illness from which she has recently been suffering.[11]

The contract conflict between Lillian and McCaull escalated. Cynthia contrived to complicate the issue by regularly notifying the press of her daughter's health problems. Regarding one such communication, the press observed:

It is becoming clearer every week why Miss Lillian Russell has given her manager so much trouble from time to time. She is a puzzle even to her physician. She is represented now as more seriously ill than ever. The modern prima donna has become a fragile, perishable little thing. It is too bad.[12]

A reporter wanted to know if Cynthia was protecting her daughter or admonishing her.

Through the early months of 1883, Lillian remained at home, still recovering from the previously reported illness. Her legal troubles with Col. McCaull continued when he was granted an injunction against Lillian, preventing her from performing for any other manager. To maintain public exposure during this time, Lillian sang free Sunday concerts at the Cosmopolitan Theater. In March, Lillian appealed McCaull's injunction; the legal battle went to court.

Lillian played in *The Sorcerer* at the Casino Theater. The designer of the program attempted to draw a likeness of Lillian, framed by the first letter in the theater's name, a novel notion at the time. Two months later, she and Edward Solomon were on their way to London. (Harry Ransom Humanities Research Center, the University of Texas at Austin.)

Representing Col. McCaull was the law firm of Howe and Hummel, the most successful (and notorious) in New York. Attorneys Howe and Hummel had defended hundreds of accused murderers, as well as countless other clients seeking a divorce or negotiating a theatrical contract. It was said the firm could find "loopholes large enough for those convicted to walk through standing up." They had already represented such celebrated entertainment giants as P.T. Barnum, Edwin Booth and Lillie Langtry. Lillian never stood a chance.

McCaull's injunction was continued, and the judge specified conditions under which the contract would be enforced. If Lillian did not pay back advances on her salary, she had to perform for McCaull until the contract ran out, at the rate of $150 a week. If she refused to perform, she had to repay all loans and still could not perform elsewhere until the contract ran its course. As a gesture to Lillian, Col. McCaull stipulated that she would not be required to go on tour with the company at the end of its New York run.

Upset about losing her appeal, Lillian initiated conversations with a number of rival managers to appear in their upcoming shows. But this belligerent response would further complicate her situation.

The appearance of a new suitor may also have had something to do with Lillian's assertive state of mind. Edward Solomon had been introduced to Lillian at the Bijou Theater the previous month. Raised in a Jewish family of musicians and actors, Solomon had become a successful composer and conductor of comic opera in England. McCaull had signed him to come to the U.S. to produce his show *Billee Taylor*, as well as write other shows. A tall, dark man with highly polished manners, Solomon's charm was considerably greater than his ability to keep promises. He asked Lillian whether it was agreeable to her that he visit while she recuperated. She expressed her willingness, and he was seen calling on her every day. At each encounter, he shared the latest theater gossip, discussed his current projects, and played the piano for her. "Naturally," wrote Lillian in her memoirs, "I fell in love with him.... While I was convalescing, he would sit at the piano and play for me. He had the peculiar gift of expressing in a melody the serious and the romantic."[13]

Edward Solomon showed his interest and concern for Lillian at a time when others were expressing displeasure with her behavior. And, unlike Harry Braham, he was a man already well-known and successful.

Cynthia, however, was not at all pleased with the blossoming love. It seemed to her a reprise of the Harry Braham affair—a musician, a conductor, an Englishman and a Jew—romantically sweeping her daughter away. Lillian later acknowledged her mother's dislike for Solomon and suggested that this reaction may have been a factor in her love for him:

> My mother objected to him strenuously and for once she forgot her sense of humor and was rude to him — so much so that she brought upon herself the responsibility for my marriage to Mr. Solomon, for her unkindness and rudeness to him only called for my deep sympathy, a feeling which always accentuates love in a young girl's heart.[14]

While courted by Solomon, Lillian was forced to continue her contract with Col. McCaull by appearing in an Offenbach operetta. *The Princess of Trebizonde* premiered at the Casino Theater on May 5, 1883. McCaull again had his mind on the summer box office potential afforded by Lillian's appearance. Leading the Casino orchestra was Edward Solomon. On Lillian's desk at home rested a number of contracts from various managers, all for appearances the coming season. One day, in apparent pique against McCaull's constraints, Lillian signed them all. One was with Brooks and Dixon, who had no play available. Another was McCaull's renewal. Augustin Daly offered a play in his theater. The Boston Museum Theater encouraged her to star in her own review. And impresario John Hollingshead urged Lillian to appear at the famous Gaiety Theater in London.

Her decision to sign all the contracts no doubt created considerable anxiety for Lillian. And she had reason for concern: the effect on her reputation, reaction from the press, her love affair with Solomon, and Cynthia's involvement in her professional and personal affairs. It was a heavy burden for a 21-year-old, especially one with but three years' experience in the entertainment business.

The couple's situation was further complicated when Solomon wrote to one of the theatrical papers complaining about the acting in one of his plays. He later denied having written the letter, but tensions between the cast members and their musical conductor ran high.

Lillian and Edward agreed there was only one way to deal with these problems — sail for England. The *Clipper* reported:

> The pair, that is to say, Edward Solomon, the composer, and Miss Lillian Russell, for whom he composes, left suddenly for England last week. The departure was sudden, but the program was old. Months ago, a grieved lady called upon us and foreshadowed it, but requested that nothing be published in regard to it.[15]

The "grieved lady" had been Edith Blande, Solomon's previous companion and leading lady.

Making matters worse, a reporter from the *Dramatic Mirror* had begun following Lillian since hearing a rumor of her possible departure. Finding that she had purchased tickets on the *Lydian Monarch*, the reporter rushed to Cynthia to verify the story. She remarked that a daughter would surely tell her mother of any such trip. But she was deeply shaken by the implications of the news.

The ship carrying the two lovers sailed from Jersey City on June 9. Left in their wake were numerous conflicting contracts, irate managers, debts, a puzzled audience and a very angry mother. Cynthia blamed Col. McCaull for forcing Lillian to leave the country. McCaull, in turn, accused Cynthia of interfering in Lillian's affairs and giving her bad advice. The press noted that both were correct.

Yet the press also condemned Lillian's behavior as officious and egocentric, suggesting that she never return to New York again. The *Clipper* published a poem, wryly dedicated to their "dear" Lillian:

> As we write, Lillian Russell is on the high seas, and we hasten to get off this before she gets off the steamer:
>
> > "Heed not the idle gossip that attends her as she sails,
> > The wild and loony rumors or the interviewer tales.
> > The *Clipper* in its enterprise the real reason nails:
> > She is hurried to 'the other side' to mash the Prince of Wales!
> > And she'll do it, or break her voice."[16]

Chapter Three

Return of the Prodigal Daughter

The inspired collaboration of John Hollingshead, William Schwenck Gilbert, Arthur Seymour Sullivan and Richard D'Oyly Carte dominated London musical theater in the 1880s with their innovative productions of opera comique.

In late 1868, John Hollingshead opened the Gaiety Theater, which quickly became noted for its operetta and burlesque attractions. Burlesque shows in England were actually travesties or satires on popular or famous productions, often with songs interpolated from other sources. Hollingshead helped to break the barriers of morality in Victorian London by making his shows acceptable to the middle class. Prior to his innovations, well-bred and proper people were reluctant to attend the theater because plays and actors were considered immoral. If, however, a play was perceived as educational — not entertainment — it would be accepted as a worthwhile enterprise. Composers of the time wrote oratorios and cantatas based on religious themes to satisfy the public. Some travesties at Hollingshead's theater were written by William Gilbert. A number of oratorios performed at the Gaiety were composed by Arthur Sullivan.

While the English music hall was a popular pastime during the period, it was patronized solely by the lower classes. Comic opera would not become acceptable to the English middle classes until the 1890s, almost a decade after it had been embraced by that group in the U.S.

Hollingshead persuaded Gilbert and Sullivan to collaborate on an operetta that would be original, moral, melodic and humorous, designed to win over a skeptical audience and morality-driven critics. The result was an operetta called *Thepis* or *The Gods Grown Old*, which opened at the Gaiety in December 1871. Critics labeled it "grotesque" opera and predicted its failure. Surprisingly, even though it didn't follow the usual formula of burlesque or operetta of the day, the show ran into spring of the following year. Even with this moderate success, however, Gilbert and Sullivan were reluctant to continue their collaboration.

At the time, Richard D'Oyly Carte, a young concert agent managing London's Royalty Theater, was looking for operas to fill his bills. Through Hollingshead, D'Oyly Carte had met Gilbert and asked the librettist to write a production for him. Gilbert, in turn, went to Sullivan and persuaded him to participate in the D'Oyly Carte commission. The result was *Trial by Jury*. From its opening in March 1875, the production was well received and sustained a run of more than 100 performances, exceptional for an operetta. In spite of this success, Gilbert and Sullivan did not renew their collaboration until late in 1877, due primarily to other theatrical commitments, as well as the difficulties that developed when they did work together. Their new operetta, *The Sorcerer*, proved a great success. And with it, the golden years of English comic opera began.

When receipts for *The Sorcerer* began to decline, managers wanted a new opera to attract audiences. In May 1878, less than six months after their initial ground-breaking success, Gilbert and Sullivan produced *H.M.S. Pinafore*, which leapt forward so dramatically in its artistic development that critics did not know what to make of it. In the opera, the British establishment was satirized, its mores turned into comedic episodes, and its upper class trivialized. Initially, audiences loved it. But the critics struck back with a vengeance, ticket sales declined, and the show seemed near to closing. D'Oyly Carte was purported to be racing to influential newspapers to prevent them from predicting the show's demise. It seemed that English comic opera was going to die as quickly as it had been born.

But Arthur Sullivan, conducting a concert at Covent Garden, decided at the last moment to include some songs from *Pinafore* in the performance. Much to his surprise, the audience approved the songs and rushed to purchase *Pinafore* tickets. Not only were weeks of advance tickets sold, but sheet music by the thousands was also being purchased. Sensing a business opportunity, D'Oyly Carte put together traveling groups to perform the show throughout England. He also decided to take a great risk by sending a company to America, where the comic operas performed were traditionally of French and German origin.

In November 1878, *H.M.S. Pinafore* opened at the Boston Museum Theater. Within three months, there were eight companies performing the show in New York theaters. Unfortunately for Gilbert, Sullivan and D'Oyly Carte, American copyright law was such that the authors received no royalties on the use of their opera. Theater managers could interpret it or interpolate its material in any manner they wished. Among those who rushed to produce a travesty on the original was Tony Pastor. By the spring of 1879, *Pinafore* was the most popular attraction in the U.S.

In 1883, the Gaiety Theater, still managed by John Hollingshead, was one of many London theaters featuring comic opera. Constantly seeking to outdo one another, all of them vied for productions featuring lavish spectacle and well-known performers. Hollingshead had been following Lillian's progress in New York and decided to offer her a contract to sing in London. An added incentive was the popularity of Edward Solomon in England. In the U.S., he was considered a mediocre composer who simply happened to be Lillian's companion in her escape to London. In England, however, Solomon had an enviable reputation as an accomplished pianist, orchestrator and composer, one particularly respected by Sullivan. Ironically, it had been D'Oyly Carte who persuaded Solomon to travel to the U.S. to produce his hit *Billee Taylor*, one of Lillian's first stage successes. With both Solomon and Lillian at

Lillian and second-husband-to-be Edward Solomon preparing for their opening of Solomon's *Virginia and Paul* at London's Gaiety Theater. The critics didn't care for her flouting of English stage decorum; nor did they like Solomon's comic opera. (Harry Ransom Humanities Research Center, the University of Texas at Austin.)

the Gaiety, Hollingshead envisioned a profit-making coup. He cared not at all that his performers were slipping out of contracts and debts in the U.S. In fact, the trans–Atlantic controversy would no doubt increase ticket sales.

Lillian opened at the Gaiety Theater July 16, 1883, in *Virginia and Paul*, with words and music by Solomon. Early reaction to Lillian was positive and polite.

The heroine was sustained by a lady new to London. This was Miss Lillian Russell, who has many personal attractions to recommend her. Miss Russell has a sweet and pure voice, and sings with much fluency. One of her songs, 'The Silver Line,' a waltz-melody, was encored. Miss Russell sang it charmingly, as she did all the music of the opera, and her vocal skill, combined with her attractive appearance and graceful acting, made a distinctly favorable impression, and justifies us in speaking of her as the most fascinating comic-opera artist we have had from America for years.[1]

Reaction to Solomon's opera itself was lukewarm and his lyrical abilities were questioned. Still, London audiences enjoyed and supported the show.

Lillian's success was soon blunted, however, by the filing of a lawsuit, tendered by William Henderson, on behalf of his new partners, the American impresarios Brooks and Dickson, to enjoin her from appearing at the Gaiety or any other English theater. The suit was precipitated when Brooks met with Lillian and confronted her about the broken U.S. contract. When she refused to acknowledge it, Brooks contacted Henderson to take out the injunction. Henderson's lawsuit exposed Lillian's deal with Brooks and Dickson: she was to appear in ten cities for a nine-month season, at a weekly salary of $250, plus traveling expenses. Lillian would be required to furnish her own costumes and sing in shows cooperatively selected with Henderson, Brooks and Dickson. The contract had been signed in March 1883.

The salary was considerably greater than what she was currently earning, and she would have had more flexibility in performing (advantages not normally afforded an actress at the time). The British press was perplexed as to why she had run out on the contract. At the same time, managers in London began to question Lillian's commitment to perform in England.

The New York papers used this suit as an example of Lillian's capricious behavior and summarily exiled her from the stage.

> Miss Lillian Russell, when she left this country on her wild goose chase with Edward Solomon, was under engagement to William Henderson. Lillian had made a good reputation in this country, principally on account of her pretty face. Her little escapade when she was engaged at Tony Pastor's theater was forgiven because the public was pleased with a new face and wanted to give Lillian a chance. In the midst of a popular engagement at the Casino, Miss Russell suddenly went away, and at the same time Mr. Solomon disappeared. Miss Russell has killed herself in this country by her escapade with Mr. Solomon. She is of no earthly use to us in the future.[2]

The British judge, however, threw out the case, agreeing with Lillian's counterclaims. When Brooks and Dickson sold their contract to Henderson, she argued, it voided her agreement with them. Moreover, Brooks and Dickson had neither a good reputation nor sufficient money to mount a comic opera and pay reasonable wages. She pleaded that any performances with them would have jeopardized her theatrical reputation.

The New York papers suggested that Lillian had "hoodwinked" the judge. American justice would not have been so lenient.

Though Lillian prevailed in court, London audiences were affected by the coverage of the lawsuit; attendance at the Gaiety declined. Worse yet, Lillian proceeded to make another major *faux pas* on the stage, offending audience sensitivities even more. On her costume she wore a "flaming" broach emblazoned with the word "Ned" (Solomon's nickname). Members of the audience hissed when they saw it. The press wondered where Lillian had learned her stage behavior.

> The male habitués of the Gaiety Theater thought that the letters meant that Solomon had taken a lien upon Miss Russell. So they have resolved to vote Miss Russell as of no account. The moral of this is that broaches having a history should not be worn in public.[3]

Virginia and Paul ran a total of only four weeks. Disgusted, Hollingshead gave up his contract, admitting his inability to understand Lillian's etiquette. But other managers were not dissuaded. Two weeks later, it was announced that Lillian would appear at the Gaiety in *Pocahontas*, a new operetta written by Solomon. The show was presented in early September, but played only one week.

At about the same time, D'Oyly Carte approached Lillian with a proposition for her to appear in Gilbert and Sullivan's new opera, *Princess Ida*, which would open at the Savoy Theater, then London's premier showplace for comic opera. It was rumored that William Gilbert was attracted to Lillian and, after she agreed to do the role, had asked her to rehearse in his private quarters. When she refused to comply, he fired her. Lillian promptly sued him for breach of contract.

The reality was much less colorful. While Lillian had indeed been asked to play the lead role in the Gilbert and Sullivan opera, the potential liabilities of the Henderson injunction persuaded D'Oyly Carte not to pursue the arrangement. That, however, did not prevent Lillian from suing Gilbert for canceling her engagement, at the rate of $250 a week. Like many theatrical lawsuits of the day, the claim was withdrawn after a few weeks.

In early 1884, Lillian was signed to appear at London's Alhambra Theater in *The Beggar Student*, another Solomon production. This opera never opened, as managerial displeasure with both Lillian and Solomon had mounted to almost boycott proportions. The couple's London sojourn now took on an additional complication: Lillian was pregnant, the baby due sometime in May.

Since no London venues were available to them, Lillian and Solomon were quick to realize the potential benefits of a continental tour. Solomon sponsored a company to perform his hit opera *Billee Taylor*, with Lillian in the leading role. He himself would conduct, while D'Oyly Carte handled the bookings. Starting early in March, the tour took them to Belgium, Germany and France. Because of the weight gain attendant to her pregnancy (she was now topping 160 pounds), Lillian changed her costume to flowing gowns and reblocked her stage activity to reduce movement. Apparently, no one noticed any differences because no one in Europe had ever before seen her perform. Reports from various cities indicated the show enjoyed a good deal of success and even some profit. But the stress and constant touring wore Lillian down and, at the same time, eroded her relationship with Solomon.

Predictably, a rumor surfaced that Lillian was getting homesick and would return to New York "as soon as she could." It was reported she had accepted an offer from a Mr. Wetherall, the husband of actress Emma Abbott, for a season in the U.S., for the regal sum of $4,000 monthly. While the offer of employment may have been true, the reported salary was proven to be greatly exaggerated. It was significant, however, that the New York press continued to follow — and feature — Lillian, in spite of their supposed dislike of her behavior.

In early April, almost eight months pregnant, Lillian was still performing. Each performance was an ordeal, but Lillian felt she had to continue because of their need for money. Brussells shows were well-received, and the company was booked into the Renaissance Theater in Paris. Two days later, the papers announced:

> It is reported that the highly successful *Billee Taylor* tour of Lillian Russell
> in the French provinces has been brought to an abrupt termination by the
> illness of the prima donna.[4]

Lillian gave birth to a girl, Lillian Dorothy, on May 10, 1884, in London. The baby's last name was listed as Braham, since Lillian was still legally married to Harry.

Within a month, Lillian was up and about, soliciting work among London theater managers. She vigorously asserted the success of her tour on the continent and her increasing popularity as evidence of reason for employment. The manager of the Alhambra Theater attempted to engage Lillian to appear in a burlesque, *Black-eyed Susan*, but was reminded by Col. McCaull that she was still under his contract until May 1885. The Alhambra deal fell through.

To the press, both the manager and Lillian agreed to say that the show did not suit her and that she had withdrawn from the part. But McCaull's reminder provided Lillian the opportunity to contact him, and they discussed a return to the U.S. and the Casino for a show to open in December. McCaull took these discussions to mean he could promote her return in the newspapers, and he stated that she was engaged to appear in *Nell Gwynne*, a new comic opera.

Brooks and Dickson, however, refused to be ignored. They countered that Lillian was still under contract to them and would tour with the *Bluebeard* company upon her return. The dispute carried through the summer, each manager claiming to own her performance. Now more than a year old, the conflicting contracts remained unsettled. All the while, they prevented Lillian from obtaining work in London.

August brought more press coverage in both New York and London. The *New York Clipper* reported:

> Sunday newspapers are busy with the name and fame of Lillian Russell. One says she is under cover in this city. It is untrue! Another says that she is rearing a 4-month-old baby in London.[5]

The *London Era* published three articles about Lillian:

> When Lillian Russell opens here, in January next, it will probably be in *Pocahontas*, which Edward Solomon arranged for Londoners.

> Lillian Russell protests against the manner in which she has been treated by certain newspapers in England, and adds that 'the facts of the case will soon be heard, as an action for libel is pending'.

> In connection with the action of libel brought by Lillian Russell and Solomon against *The Topical Times*, that paper says that it intends to give Miss Russell every opportunity to establish her fair fame in the witness box.[6]

The libel suit never reached the court. An agreement was apparently negotiated between the parties. Nothing more of the issue was reported in the press. The suit did, however, assist Lillian in obtaining employment. *Polly*, Solomon and Mortimer's comic opera, was engaged for the Novelty Theater and opened November 8. It was well-received by both audience and critics and ran for seven weeks, to the satisfaction of performers and manager alike. A rejuvenation of *Pocahontas*, this time with libretto by Sidney Grundy and music by Solomon, was being prepared to open at the Empire Theater the end of December. But no sooner had Lillian apparently mended her stage life than she was faced with a new domestic crisis.

The London papers reported on an article published in New York regarding a suit for divorce that Harry Braham had filed against Lillian. Adultery was the claim:

> Harry Braham has commenced a suit for absolute divorce against his wife, Helen Louise Braham, professionally known as Lillian Russell. Edward Solomon is named as the co-respondent, and it is charged that the defendant deserted her husband, and on June 8, 1883, left this city for England with Edward Solomon, with whom she has since continued to live as his wife, and to whom she has borne a son. The suit has been entered in the Brooklyn, New York, Supreme Court, and no answer has as yet been put in. Mr. Braham married Miss Russell about five years ago.[7]

Pocahontas opened December 26. Unable to generate a reasonable audience, it lasted only two weeks. The reports on Lillian's love life had had their effect. To Lillian, it seemed clear her London adventure was at an end. The *Clipper* reported on her impending return the day she, baby Lillian and Solomon left England: "It is stated that Lillian Russell and Edward Solomon are about to return to this country." They arrived from England nine days later, on February 8, 1885, to be greeted at the dock by Cynthia and Susan, as well as a biting *Clipper* article:

> Lillian Russell now regards herself as an ample authority on 'The Baby's Mouth, and What to Do With It.' She has had only eight months experience, it is true; but during all that time she has been blessed with the wisdom of Solomon. And she has brought her little Experience and its music and her little Edward Solomon and his music with her from England.[8]

Not surprisingly, there was no work awaiting Lillian or Solomon. The next few months proved difficult; theater managers refused to deal with her. While no specific boycott was ever acknowledged, it seemed more than coincidence that no New York manager had available a comic opera that could have been strengthened by her presence. (In the six months following her return to New York, eight new comic operas had their debuts.) Evidently as her only alternative, Lillian agreed to perform for "25 of the gross" at a number of Sunday evening concerts to be presented at the Bijou Theater. Edward Solomon would lead the orchestra. The *Clipper*'s first report on her "American reappearance" frankly indulged in damnation by faint praise:

> Lillian Russell, in a concert at the Bijou Opera House Sunday evening, February 15, brought out a large audience. Miss Russell sang her familiar 'Silver Line' and several other selections, and was conventionally encored. Her voice exhibits a marked loss of power, and she is not so personally attractive as she was before she left this country rather suddenly with Edward Solomon two years ago. The latter gentleman led the orchestra.[9]

Lillian sang three Sunday concerts to houses that were "fairly filled." It gave her an opportunity to regain some exposure — at least to theater managers — and earn some wages. Indirectly, her efforts proved fruitful.

In an agreement with Col. McCaull, E.E. Rice obtained control of Lillian's contract. Rice planned for her to appear in the first American performance of *Polly*, the show she had last played in London. As Lillian's first employer in 1879, when he had hired her for the chorus of *Evangeline*, Rice had ever since taken due credit for her discovery. He was now ready to take credit for reintroducing her to American audiences. Rice knew it was something of a risk, but believed Lillian would still attract large audiences. The plan was to play *Polly* in New York through June, then (when summer audiences dwindled in the city) take the show on tour.

In the meantime, Harry Braham's proceedings for divorce against Lillian were closely followed by the press. In March, the suit was sent to a referee. In April, Braham was to testify but didn't appear; the hearing was postponed. When he did appear, the hearing was postponed again. Lillian's new lawyers, the notorious Howe and Hummel, succeeded in preventing any adverse publicity from getting into the papers to hinder her comeback. In her previous New York legal battle, Lillian had lost the case largely because the Howe and Hummel firm opposed her. This time, she hired them to represent her, the first of many skirmishes in which they pleaded her case. Howe and Hummel managed to delay the final disposition of Braham's case until May 6, when Judge Donahue granted the divorce. Notice was not posted in the *Clipper* until the 16th.

On May 11, before the posting, Lillian and Solomon took the ferry to Hoboken and were married by Reverend Dr. Ellerich at the Reformed Church. The only other people at the ceremony were two members of the *Polly* company. Cynthia refused to attend.

The marriage was kept so secret that Lillian was listed as "ill" and unable to appear on May 12 and 13, while she and Solomon were in fact celebrating their honeymoon. On the 14th, however, "she was sufficiently better to sing at the matinee of *Polly* when the house was packed."

Through the middle of June, *Polly* played to good houses, and Lillian gained confidence about reviving her reputation with the public. Theater managers closely monitored the audience and box office receipts to determine if Lillian still had a future. The press, particularly the *Dramatic Mirror*, remained negative. But the sudden appearance of a new legal revelation would soon alter everyone's opinion of Lillian

An advertising poster of Lillian as Polly Pluckrose in *Polly* at the Casino Theater. It was her first show after returning from London in 1885. In spite of negative comments regarding Lillian's broken contracts and London escapades, she played to full houses for the eight-week run of the show. (National Portrait Gallery, Smithsonian Institution.)

and give her a unique opportunity for a swift return to prominence.

The *New York Clipper* received a copy of a letter sent to a London newspaper by Lily Grey, an English actress. Grey stated that she had been married to Edward Solomon in 1873 by a local registrar and later married to him by a rabbi. She also claimed to be the mother of his daughter. The *Clipper* noted that "she cannot comprehend how he could marry Lillian Russell in this country." The shock waves of this exposé spread throughout theatrical circles and into the newspaper's gossip columns.

Solomon denied the accusation but quickly retained a lawyer to defend him. Lillian refused to believe that Solomon had committed such an error of judgment, and she publicly supported his innocence. Cynthia, on the other hand, took the news as justification for her suspicions of him. She reminded Lillian of the contempt she had expressed for Solomon when he and Lillian had left for England.

For the next several months, Cynthia publicly campaigned against him, damning Solomon for stealing her daughter's affections and misguiding her theatrical career. Lillian carefully avoided saying anything to the press and stayed away from her mother, if for no other reason than to prevent the press from equating a visit with support for her mother's pronouncements. Her strategic assumption of a "low profile" in the matter was made easier when the *Polly* company traveled to Boston for an extended run in June.

Cynthia soon received another surprise. Much to her chagrin, her youngest daughter Susan had joined a variety company some months before. Now an announcement in the *Clipper* delivered a message that Susan had neglected to communicate to her mother.

> Susie Russell, a sister of Lillian Russell, will be married next week to Owen Westford. Both are of the *Wages of Sin* company.[10]

Susan had taken Lillian's last name for her own stage career. She was marrying a man almost as quickly as Lillian had married Harry Braham. A newspaper even noted that the name of the company seemed appropriate for the actions of a Russell. For once, Cynthia was speechless. It would be more than a year before she spoke to Susan again.

Polly ran at the Boston Museum Theater for five weeks. In a bold publicity move, E.E. Rice renamed the company Rice's Lillian Russell Opera Company, an excellent maneuver to build the ego of his star while advancing business. The *Boston Globe* reported that the show played to "excellent business" the entire five weeks, "the fair Lillian being the magnet of the company." There was no question that the headlines generated by the Solomon/Russell/Grey marriage triangle boosted box office receipts.

But instead of continuing their road tour, the company returned to New York and retired for the summer. Lillian's confidence in Solomon seemed to be eroding, due both to newspaper reports and to Cynthia's campaign against her daughter's "deceiver." And these increasing doubts became public when it was reported that Solomon had left their 77th Street home for an indefinite time. Still, Lillian and "Ned" rehearsed together every day, working on a new opera that Solomon was writing for her. All the while, their every activity was closely watched by the press, and rumors multiplied.

Lillian delayed the road tour of *Polly* until the middle of September. She and Solomon were still living apart but working together. While Cynthia was happy to have contributed to their domestic separation, she continued her efforts to professionally discredit Solomon in numerous letters sent to newspapers and questioning his honesty. Rather than convincing Lillian that Solomon was wrong, however, Cynthia's publicity assault resulted in Lillian's professing support for him even more. A "strange melange," the papers called it.

The renewed tour of *Polly* began officially in Peoria, Illinois, on September 17, 1885. From Peoria to Detroit, Cleveland, Buffalo, Syracuse, Ithaca, Elmira and Albany, they played in every city that had a good-sized theater. Then, as typified an E.E. Rice tour, the company visited more traditional venues, large cities in the Midwest and East. Everywhere they played, the crowds were enormous. Ecstatic audiences thronged to see Lillian perform.

As newspapers, including those in New York, reported her triumphant successes, a new tone of admiration and respect seemed to permeate their reportage. Sly digs and biting comments disappeared. The Solomon adventure was rarely mentioned, and when it was, Lillian was portrayed as the poor-woman-deceived. The New York papers had once again taken her side, declaring, "This is no way to treat a lady!"

To the surprise of Rice, the tour proved a great success. The bigamy trial of Grey vs. Solomon was delayed a number of times, which helped to keep it out of the papers and potentially affect ticket sales. Lillian and Solomon continued to work together, although even this limited contact was creating tension between them. Lillian, Jr., now almost 18 months old, had been taken along on the tour but now was being cared for by a maid, because of the child's increasing mobility and the added attention she required.

Lillian found herself invited to elegant parties put on by the social elite of the city. In her memoirs, Lillian recalled her visits to the homes of Stanford White and the Vanderbilts, relating how much she had enjoyed them. How often these visits took place (or whether they actually occurred at this time) is somewhat questionable; but they surely did occur a few years later.

Lillian was now introduced to the thrills and exhilarations of the racetrack, as well as the gambling that accompanied it. At the races, she was immediately recognized, her every trip dutifully reported by the press. And when she lost some money on the horses, it seemed to make no matter, as she was believed to be the highest-paid actress on the stage. That distinction was not yet fact, though it shortly would be. Less than a year since her inglorious return from England, Lillian had become an esteemed and admired "household word." In turn, she extended equal affection to her audience.

The ever-industrious Solomon devised Lillian's next stage triumph, a departure from his usual work. *Pepita* or *The Girl with the Glass Eye* opened at the Union Square Theater on March 16, 1886. Pepita's father builds human-like robots. A female robot, designed to sing and dance, breaks down, and Pepita (Lillian) takes its place. Conveniently, a male tenor robot also breaks down, and Pepita replaces the broken robot with her lover. Ultimately, all parties realize the love of the leading singers to be genuine. The mix-up is clarified, and a wedding/ballet finale ends the play.

Pepita was an immediate success. Surprised when Lillian played a violin to accompany one of her songs, the audience proved all the more delighted. Solomon was gratified to see his songs encored so many times at each performance. But there the collaboration broke down.

Less than a month after Pepita's opening, the *Clipper* disclosed:

> Lillian Russell, the star of the company, is "out" with Ed Solomon. The rupture has been growing for some weeks and nobody is surprised at the outcome. The break is purely domestic, and Miss Russell's mother figures in it, as a thorn in Solomon's flesh. There is talk of divorce on both sides. Meanwhile, husband and wife continue to work, and the houses have naturally increased with the publicity of the quarrel.[11]

Arguments and accusations were exchanged in the press. When reporters interviewed one party and obtained quotes, they immediately scurried to the other to repeat what had been said, always requesting a rebuttal. The reportage read like a script from one of Lillian's comic operas. Lillian said that her reason for the separation was the pending charge of bigamy, suggesting that if Solomon were declared innocent, they would reunite. Having already publicly denounced Solomon as untrustworthy, Cynthia was in her glory. Here was actual proof; she had always known he was a liar. Solomon blamed Cynthia for the trouble, accusing her of filling his wife's head with distorted stories. In a brief moment of paternal lucidity, he wondered aloud what would become of Lillian, Jr., now under the exclusive influence of her mother and grandmother.

Things got worse for Solomon. A month later, he was brought to court on two additional claims: a theater manager in Cleveland sued him for a $675 debt for stage dresses; a lender demanded payment of $3,500 borrowed for living expenses. Solomon claimed that his wife was no longer contributing to the family finances, although "she occasionally gave him some money." Solomon's financial records were demanded, but he admitted their examination would be a futile task because he had no money. He also indicated he was returning soon to England. Actually, he had been enjoined to return to face the bigamy charges in court. After he left the U.S., he and Lillian never saw one another again.

Through all of this turbulence, *Pepita* ran to excellent box office returns for 67 performances, closing the season of the Union Square Theater and then traveling to Boston for another three weeks. Boston audiences, however, were not as taken with the plot. Or was it the adverse publicity? It was decided to close the show for the summer, rework it and hope to reopen in September. Ironically, a new member of the cast in Boston was comedian Fred Solomon, Edward's brother, who had just arrived in the U.S.

Admitting exhaustion from the events of the spring, and glad to get away from the scrutiny of the press, Lillian retired to a hotel in Bath Beach, Long Island. There she rested with Lillian, Jr., and Cynthia. Having lost her campaign for mayor of New York (Cynthia had been the first woman to run for public office in the city), she was devoting her energies now to assisting poor immigrant Irish children.

Lillian was now 25 years old. She had experienced two marriages, two births, hundreds of performances in scores of cities, numerous tussles with theater managers over wages and contracts, and the rigors of touring. She had become a public figure with adoring audiences, on the undeniable ascent toward a glorious career in comic opera.

In a moment of contemplation, however, she wondered whether this was the life she really desired. Performance success, yes; domestic trauma, no. How could a woman, one who passionately desired to be a professional, manage both lives adequately? Whenever about to achieve her dream, misfortunes occurred to prevent her from winning the prominence she sought.

Retire? Return home? Cynthia would be satisfied with that decision. But never Lillian.

To her, the decision was clear. She was young and talented. She had already proven her worth. Large audiences paid top dollar to see her perform. There were new goals to achieve, new heights to scale. Besides, what other woman at the time actively strove to overcome the barriers raised against her sex? As she wrote later, reflecting on her decision, Lillian admitted, "I look back now with wonder at my fearlessness. I can now only attribute that fearlessness to my youthful ambition."[12]

In August, Lillian gave Solomon another chance — in the form of one of his recently written operas. *The Maid and the Moonshiner* opened at the Standard Theater on the 16th. Critics wrote that her singing was creditable but labeled the opera "a failure." It closed after 12 performances. Lillian had planned to go on tour in the fall, but the *Pepita* company had disbanded and no financial backers stepped forward to revive the show. Lillian also found that New York theater managers remained hesitant to hire her. The recent Solomon episode hadn't helped.

Fortunately, John Duff, owner and operator of the Duff Opera Company, was about to start a tour but had just lost his female lead. Would Lillian be interested? The company would be on the road for seven months, and the performers would sing three different operas: *Iolanthe*, *The Mikado* and *A Trip to Africa*. But the salary was good, $300 a week. Since New York managers had proven unresponsive and the salary Duff offered was more than she had been receiving, she signed to perform with Duff's opera for three seasons. The tour would open in San Francisco; Lillian clearly recalled the financial disaster that had overwhelmed the Edouin Company the last time she had performed in that city, six years ago.

The Duff Company performed all three operas in San Francisco, two weeks for each, to full houses, and for a much more sophisticated audience than Lillian had experienced before. The local critics reported, "Lillian Russell has secured for herself a large share of public attention."[13] Again, articles referred to her performances both on and off the stage.

A special train took them east, to Salt Lake City, Denver, Kansas City and Minneapolis. They performed before "legitimate" theater audiences, many of whom were seeing comic opera and Lillian Russell for the first time. Newspapers from each city reported that the Duff Company was playing to profitable houses, and singled out Lillian as "a great hit."

The only event to remind Lillian of her recent tribulations was an article in the *Clipper* about Solomon:

> Edward Solomon was arrested in London on a charge of bigamy preferred by Lily Grey, who avers he was legally married to her in 1873, and that, though he deserted her in 1875, he has never been divorced from her, and he has since wrongfully wedded Lillian Russell. Miss Grey was born Fanny Isaacs. Solomon was remanded for trial and, after a short stay in jail, furnished bail of $500. Solomon claims he is innocent.[14]

In a related news release, the *Clipper* reported, "Cynthia says she is glad of it. She 'told Lillian so.'"[15]

Luckily, this news was overlooked or ignored by the press in the cities where the Duff Opera Company was performing.

As the company moved east, their program changed. The Gilbert and Sullivan operas were dropped from the repertory, replaced by *Gasparone* and *Don Caesar*, which in turn were replaced by *A Trip to Africa*, an attraction now performed almost daily. The inclusion of eight "Black Amazons" seemed to give the opera a lift, and the scene where Lillian performed in their presence received many encore requests. After touring through New England, the company stopped in Brooklyn early in January 1887. It was now almost four months since Lillian had been home to see her daughter.

Returning to its tour, the Duff Opera Company (now advertised as the most successful touring company of the year) traveled through Eastern cities and returned to some of the Midwestern cities to "crowded houses" and "SRO with encores freely demanded." If Lillian needed affirmation of her talents, she was now getting it — in spades. Audiences received her "with every demonstration of delight." However, an episode in Philadelphia caught the attention of the ever-vigilant *Clipper* when Lillian convinced Duff to discharge the leading tenor because he was upstaging her. The *Clipper* questioned why Duff had agreed to her demands.

In April 1887, the Duff Company returned to the Standard Theater in New York. These would be Lillian's first real performances in the city since her return from England two years before. It appeared that New York theater managers had finally forgiven her, that she had "paid her dues" after her misbehavior toward them. Conveniently for all concerned, her increased popularity and drawing power provided persuasive evidence on her behalf.

The company opened April 11 with *A Trip to Africa*, their new drawing card; "the houses were big, the company scoring a hit." The same opera had failed to make an impression on critics and audiences at the same theater three years before, but neither Lillian nor the eight Black Amazons had then been in the cast.

The continuing saga of Lillian and money made headlines yet again. Solomon claimed bankruptcy, owing $7,000. Creditors agreed to accept 5 percent on the dollar. Lillian herself was sued for $800, for costumes that she had been furnished in 1882. She refused to pay at first, alleging she had been underage at the time. But her counselors, Howe and Hummel, suggested that she pay the debt and end the case, and she accepted their advice. Two other costumers took the opportunity to tender lawsuits against Lillian for stage dresses, allegedly unpaid. They too were quickly paid off.

The Duff Company closed its season in June. It had been a profitable year, and plans were made to begin rehearsals again at the Standard in November. In the meantime, Lillian took the chance to rest and be with her daughter for the longest period since Lillian, Jr.'s, birth. But to Lillian, "rest" meant an almost equally arduous mix of work and play. She instituted daily singing lessons from "a proper singing teacher." When asked about this regimen, her view was:

> I only want to play the roles allotted to me in comic opera better than anyone else who ever sang them, or better than anyone who was in the line with me.[16]

This burning desire to be the best in comic opera continued throughout Lillian's career, and she worked hard to maintain the edge. As she became more prosperous, she hired preeminent operatic singing instructors to keep her voice at its best. Few singers of the time were as motivated to "have been a pupil of some of the great singing masters."

Playtime was divided between attending horse races and appearing at fine restaurants. *The* places to be seen in New York then were Saratoga (racetrack) and Delmonico's (restaurant). Lillian frequented both.

Saratoga had been known as a watering place and spa dating back to pre-Revolutionary days. During the 1800s, it was transformed from a meeting place for health-seeking hypochondriacs, Bible-thumping evangelists and the Temperance Society, to a magnet for the fun-seeking social elite. Along its main street, ornate hotels were built with vast porches from which to "keep an eye" on the strolling crowds. Stately carriage drives into the countryside were everyday excursions. Champagne balls alleviated the tedium of imbibing the waters and bathing at mineral spas. A gambling casino was constructed to adjoin the lake regattas and race track. On any given day, a visitor might rub shoulders with Cornelius Vanderbilt, Jay Gould or J.P. Morgan or trade quips with Henry James, U.S. Grant or Mark Twain. Once Broadway became an accepted milieu, one could see and be seen with Victor Herbert, Flo Ziegfeld, Anna Held, Diamond Jim Brady and Lillian Russell.

Delmonico's was the restaurant patronized by theatrical stars of the New York stage, both serious and variety performers. Agents and managers were always in attendance, listening avidly for gossip that might lead to signing top stars and productions. Newspaper reporters, who seemed to know everyone, were considered the "messengers" of the day; their task was to keep all parties informed of current events. The food and drink were excellent, and portions plentiful. Dinners might continue for three hours, with courses and discourses taking place at any table. Impromptu bets were often placed — not on horses or cards, but on who could drink the most and still walk out the door, or who could consume the most corn-on-the-cob at one sitting. A visit to Delmonico's was considered an adventure.

In this environment, Lil-

One of the few pictures of Lillian and Dorothy, circa 1888. By this time, Lillian was performing on the road for more than half the year, Dorothy being cared for by Cynthia. Lillian, Dorothy and Cynthia spent summers together at Saratoga. (Harry Ransom Humanities Research Center, the University of Texas at Austin.)

lian spent many evenings when she was not performing. During the time a show was running, she permitted herself no after-performance dinners. Only on Saturday and Sunday nights did she patronize a place like Delmonico's.

A summer of racetrack and restaurant visits, absent from the rigors of performance, amply contributed to Lillian's naturally statuesque physique. She gained considerable weight, and was now more than 160 pounds. References to her "pudginess" began appearing in the papers. Lillian attacked this problem in the same way she maintained her voice. She embarked on a rigorous fitness program to retain what her audience called her "hourglass figure." With a few months of vigorous exercise and fewer trips to the restaurant, she returned to her proper weight, around 140 pounds. She stood five feet, five inches tall, with a bust size of 38 inches, a waist size of 24 (in a corset) and a hip size of 40. Styles of the time emphasized these dimensions and

Lillian was seen as possessing the optimal female proportions. At age 26, it was fairly easy to control her weight; future bouts would prove far more difficult.

A trim, healthy and well-rehearsed Lillian was ready and eager to open in *Dorothy*, November 7 at the Standard Theater. She remained under contract to the Duff Company, but was loaned to a group of London producers to perform in the attraction. This would be its first U.S. production, the show having already had a long run in London, outdrawing even Gilbert and Sullivan's *Mikado*. The music for *Dorothy* had been composed by Gilbert and Sullivan's conductor Alfred Cellier, who sometimes worked with Gilbert when he and Sullivan were feuding.

The plot involved two young, cultivated English women who volunteer as barmaids during a festival. Two young men fall in love with them. The action revolves around mistaken identity, social class distinctions and disguises, in one of which Lillian played the role of a man and engaged in a duel. Playing a man required that she appear in tights, which at the time seemed to bother her not at all. The show ran for less than 50 performances and closed the middle of December. London-based shows didn't seem to fare any better in the U.S. than American performers did in London. American audiences found *Dorothy* pleasant but inferior to other current shows.

Duff next launched *The Queen's Mate*, convincing Lillian and the company to practice their parts on a transcontinental train on their way to a mid-January opening in San Francisco. The company had only one dress rehearsal on stage before opening night, and the production was ragged for the first week. Still, audiences hailed the show as outstanding and gave Lillian many encores. In one scene, Lillian, dressed as a page, again was required to wear tights. The audience loved her all the more. *The Queen's Mate* played to packed houses throughout its tour, traveling west to east from January to April. The press, even New York papers, reported on Lillian's continued success and noted the maturity of her performance.

Returning to New York, *The Queen's Mate* opened at the Broadway Theater on May 2 for what the papers said was "a summer run." Duff was taking a risk playing his attraction during the summer, something that was rarely done. The few times it had been attempted, most shows soon closed due to the heat and consequent poor attendance. While the show did well in May, it began to falter in June. And Lillian grew dispirited. Performing in heavy clothing, in 90-degree temperatures, was indeed hard labor. Particularly in the stuffy New York theaters, summer performances were extremely uncomfortable for audiences and performers alike.

In mid–June, Lillian announced her retirement from the cast. Duff replaced her with another singer, but the show lasted only one more week. He acknowledged his mistake but advertised that *The Queen's Mate* would reopen in August. Lillian expressed unhappiness with Duff's plans, because August was at least as uncomfortable as June. She could not break her contract with Duff over his decision, but she would not forget the inconvenience. At least the hiatus gave her time to spend with her daughter, who was now three years old.

As Duff promised, *The Queens Mate* did reopen at the Broadway on August 13, to "fair business." It remained there through the end of September, when Duff decided to put it on the road. That usually signified that an attraction was losing its New York appeal and needed a new milieu. Touring was generally a last-ditch tactic to make a show profitable. But in productions where Lillian was starring, it was a strategic move.

Her reputation had become so great that long ticket lines became the norm. Outside New York, no one cared about her personal life. If her marital problems were discussed, Lillian — poor Lillian — was seen as "a betrayed woman." To the public beyond the Hudson River, she was a free woman, her life a glamorous panoply of stage and restaurant entrances. She had become a symbol for "modern" women (who admired her emancipated life) and a lust object for men (who dreamed of pleasure-filled nights with her). All eyes now focused on Lillian the "American Beauty," as she was now proclaimed.

For the month of October, *The Queen's Mate* played in Chicago, where business was excellent. While in the city, Lillian spent some time with her father. His business had improved when he took in a partner, and he was now living comfortably enough to see his daughter perform often, even if it meant taking a train to another city to do so. Charles Leonard continued to print books for Ingersoll, the outspoken agnostic who was becoming famous for his speeches nationwide. Indeed, having been booked for a series of Sunday lectures at some Broadway theaters, Ingersoll was now headed for New York.

For Lillian, Philadelphia, New Haven, Boston and Brooklyn were the next stops, then back to New York for the opening of an opera new to Duff, *Nadjy*. The year had developed very satisfactorily for Lillian. She surely felt vindicated, having proven to theater managers that she possessed star power, no matter what they might think of her personally. She had created a large, nationwide following comprised of both sexes, one of very few performers to have achieved this at the time. The year was capped by the announcement that Lillian had signed with Rudolph Aronson, colorful manager of the Casino Theater, to appear there in April in an all-new comic opera. Only one hurdle still remained: Her contract with Duff had not yet expired.

Conflicting reports were published about her performances. In Philadelphia, she was ill. She had left the company, which was denied. She was relieved of her role in *The Queen's Mate*, to rehearse her new opera. She was arguing with Duff about her contract. She was in love and planning to marry. In what was becoming a characteristic occurrence, rumor and speculation surrounded her whenever the press sensed a story. But the intrepid *Clipper*, having obtained a letter from Duff to Aronson, was able to clear up the confusion:

> Mr. Duff, knowing that he had engaged Lillian Russell for the revival of *Nadjy*, which occurs January 21, will apply for an injunction restraining her from playing. Mr. Duff says that Miss Russell is under contract to play under his management until next May. Miss Russell had a misunderstanding with him in Philadelphia a few weeks ago, and has since declined to play with the Duff Co. on the score of ill health. All of which is permissible, according to her contract with Mr. Duff.[17]

The dispute went quickly to court. Lillian again retained the services of Howe and Hummel to represent her. The issue, as presented by her attorneys, did not merely concern a contract. At stake was a fundamental disagreement between Duff and Lillian about her wearing tights.

The judge initially granted the injunction to prevent Lillian from performing at the Casino.

> Judge Dugro of the Supreme Court upon the application of Henry Thompson, council for Mgr. J.C. Duff, on January 9, granted an injunction restraining

Lillian Russell from appearing at the Casino under the management of
Rudolph Aronson. Miss Russell contracted with Mgr. Duff in October 1887,
to appear in operas during the seasons 1887-8-9 at a salary of $300 a week.
Her fickleness displayed itself, and she left Mr. Duff. He is willing to over-
look the desertion and abandonment on her part, and take her back, if she
will only keep away from the Casino.[18]

It soon became obvious, however, that Lillian wanted to break the contract with
Duff to sign with Aronson. The argument about wearing tights was presented as her
rationale for separation from Duff.

The first intimation that Mr. Duff had that she would leave was when she
told him that she could not consent to appear in tights any longer, and
would join the Casino Company.[19]

Duff fought back: "He [Duff] said that she never objected to tights before. He
characterized her objection as a subterfuge."[20]

Howe and Hummel were able to get the injunction vacated by posting a bond
of $2,000 to cover damages, in case any should be awarded to Duff. This allowed Lil-
lian, at least for the time being, to perform in any show she desired. The argument
about wearing tights, however, became front page fodder for the press. The story
unfolded like the plot of a comic opera—indeed, better than most.

While Lillian was performing in Chicago, she had written Duff that she could
not join the company on its way to Philadelphia on Saturday, their travel day. Instead,
she would travel on Monday at 10:00 P.M. if Duff would send tickets for her and her
maid. If Duff did not send tickets, she would travel as she pleased, and Duff could
put on an understudy, if necessary. Duff responded the next day and enclosed the tickets, but pointed out to her that he had chartered a special train to take the company
to Philadelphia. The company was playing *The Queen's Mate* at the time, and Lillian
was wearing tights in her role.

When the company was in Philadelphia, Lillian again wrote Duff. This time she
complained that wearing tights was injuring her voice and causing her to catch cold.
She also stated in the letter that she would "never again appear in tights." Her voice,
she said, was her prime consideration, as "I depend upon it entirely for my support
and will not jeopardize it by wearing tights." Lillian suggested a change in the opera
so that she might wear boots and coat instead. She ended by saying she had been
singing so much that her voice was strained and she had decided to rest for two
weeks.

Duff indicated his surprise that Lillian objected to wearing tights. He referred
to a meeting between them when the opera was first being discussed. Lillian had been
told that it would be necessary for her to wear tights in the part, and she had replied
that she did not mind "a little thing like that." In fact, Duff said, she had shown
eagerness to wear them. He asked her what she was going to do about the apparent
impasse.

Lillian replied by sending Duff a certificate from a doctor, in which the physician said he had forbidden her from appearing in tights if she wished to preserve her
voice. Along with the certificate came a note from Lillian suggesting that, even though
wearing tights would compromise her health, she might go to Boston and wear tights
for two weeks "for a monetary consideration—$450 a week. She would then return

to New York and perform without tights, at her current $300-a-week salary. Duff refused her terms. As it clearly undermined her case, Howe and Hummel were furious with their client for making such a demand. It took some quick talking to prevent the judge from siding with Duff.

Duff submitted Lillian's letters as evidence of her perfidy. Lillian's lawyers called T. Henry French and Rudolph Aronson to the witness stand to testify that, in their opinion, Lillian "stood at the head of her profession as a comic opera singer." Anything that might prevent her from fulfilling her talent would be unfortunate both for the singer and her vast audience. Next, on her own behalf, came Lillian, elegantly dressed and tightly grasping a lace handkerchief poised to dab the tears that would inevitably flow. This was one witness the lawyers did not have to rehearse to elicit a judge's sympathy.

Lillian admitted the authenticity of the letters. Her only defense was that it would surely ruin her voice if she

Lillian as Etelha in *Nadjy*, at the Casino Theater. Though she had obtained release from contractual obligation to the Duff Company because she was forced to wear tights on stage, her role in *Nadjy* seemed to present no such problem. (Harry Ransom Humanities Research Center, the University of Texas at Austin.)

continued to wear tights. She stated that she had been on the stage for twelve years and had not worn tights for eight years before joining Duff's company. (She mentioned nothing about having worn tights for months in the touring company, with apparently no ill effects.)

Her counsel questioned her about suggestions made by Duff to Lillian regarding her manner of dress, that she might wear woolen garments underneath her silk tights. Clearly insulted by such a suggestion, she noted that nature had been "exceedingly generous" to her. She then favored the court with a monologue upon the precise aesthetics requisite to wearing tights on stage. Tights, she explained, must be absolutely symmetrical in form; and, if woolen undergarments were worn, it would ruin the symmetry of the effect. Tights were much like thin silk stockings, and to wear a woolen garment between silk and flesh would obviously spoil her otherwise pleasing proportions. Having emphasized the splendidly obvious, Lillian rested her case.

A week later, the judge ruled in favor of Lillian, not only absolving her of breaking the contract with Duff, but also siding with her on the issue of tights. The press, which had been reporting the details of the court proceedings, hailed the judge's edict that "Lillian's figure was a national asset and had to be protected from all hazards." The leading theatrical newspapers, the *Clipper* and *Dramatic Mirror*, took opposite sides of the argument. The *Clipper* supported Lillian; the *Mirror*, conspicuously moralistic and chauvinistic, believed that Lillian had stepped beyond the bounds of propriety. Such actions as she engaged in, the *Mirror* opined, threatened the social mores of the time.

Visualizing both the seats at his theater and his cash box filled, Aronson was elated with the result of the case and the accompanying publicity. Lillian was free to rehearse her part in *Nadjy* (now Aronson's property) for its opening in Chicago at the beginning of 1889. For the season, she was to receive a salary of $20,000, more than any other performer had ever earned on a New York stage.

Chapter Four

The Queen of Comic Opera

As the 1890s commenced, the pace of change accelerated throughout American musical theater. The number of new productions declined, yet their quality improved. Comic opera still dominated, strongly influenced by imported attractions from London. But the first offerings of native productions found their way to the stage as precursors of the home-grown creativity that would dominate theater within a few more years.

During this period, an explosion of theater-building took place, not just in New York, with many venues moving to uptown Manhattan, but in every city across the country. More theaters meant more touring companies, and more touring companies meant more performers. In the early 1890s, the demand for entertainers was so great that circus acts, minstrel singers and dime museum freaks were incorporated into touring theatrical companies to fill bills. "Stealing" performers was at once a manager's greatest fear and perceived as a unique opportunity. At the same time, increasingly sophisticated audiences demanded better productions. Companies had to carry more scenery and more costumes, even additional orchestra members, to meet the expectations of theater manager and audiences alike. If these rising standards were met, companies could reap the harvest of their efforts and return sizable profits to their sponsors.

Two other important factors contributed to this phenomenal growth — the improvement of railroad travel and the development of a publicity and promotion system to advertise attractions. Railroads had now laid track through towns of all sizes, and passenger business was on the verge of making more money than freight. Passenger comfort had greatly improved, with plush seating (in first class) and toilets in each car. Private cars were available for the society's elite. And the increasing speed of trains allowed passage from one city to another within hours. The era of touring company one-night stands was but a few years away.

Publicity and promotion for the masses went far beyond the daily newspaper. Visual images in color, made possible by a dramatic new lithographic innovation, were mounted everywhere — streetcars, wagons, taxis, delivery vans and signs atop buildings. Wherever space for an advertising sheet existed, one was being posted, legally or not. One of the primary uses for this new medium was promotion of theatrical productions and performers. And the targeted recipients of this advertising onslaught were the emerging social group of middle-class women.

This popular movement was epitomized by the magazine *Ladies' Home Journal.* It was founded in 1883 as a feminine — not feminist — periodical catering to middle-class identity and consumerism. It featured articles and editorials on family diet, domestic comfort, personal hygiene and the use of leisure time. It presented all of these issues in an up-to-date and sophisticated manner. The ideals of feminine beauty were defined, and the image of the contemporary woman was described and elevated. She was voluptuous, with a full, round face and long hair, usually blond, either pulled back or braided. Not surprisingly, Lillian Russell was featured as the personification of this ideal. So much so that one writer pondered which had come first, the definition or Lillian.

The *Journal* featured stage stars and their recommendations for beauty and health because, simultaneous with this media emphasis, came a rapid growth in the cosmetics industry and the beginning of the beauty parlor. By 1890, the *Ladies' Home Journal* could boast a following of millions of women; it was not alone. Other magazines like *Mumsey's, McClure's* and *Everybody's* were also directing their attention to middle-class women.

Daily newspapers reacted accordingly. They now included sections on fashion news (where theatrical stars would promote new fashions), women's topics (ranging from child-rearing to serialized novels) and a woman's page that included household hints and club and society news, along with biographies of well-known women. Theater sections of newspapers seemed to blend with women's "doings," as more women became recognized stage stars. New features also included an advice column, local-color reporting and the human-interest story, which helped to assuage the increasing anonymity of urban living. All of these topics featured high-profile people, particularly females, because they represented the "new" women of the age. Among these female symbols, arguably chief among them, was Lillian Russell, who not only allowed herself to be made a symbol, but also ably assisted in the effort.

The arrival of publicity and promotion also meant the introduction of the modern theater program and the emergence of the theater publicist. A small, bushy-haired and fiercely mustachioed German printer, Leo Von Rosen, was the inventor of the modern theater program in its booklet form. Old programs were a kind of broadside, dating back to Revolutionary times, whose principal artistic feature was usually a portrait of toothsome young women advertising Sozodent. By condensing the format to a more compact, easy-to-handle form, Von Rosen enlarged the possibilities for advertising and performance-related material. His basic form can still be seen in theaters today.

All major theaters and companies added publicists to their retinue, as they would an orchestra conductor. And none was more talented and creative than J.W. Morrisey, hired by Rudolph Aronson to promote the Casino and his new star, Lillian Russell. Like most publicists of his time, Morrisey had moved up through the ranks of theater publicity, from advance man (plastering signs on poles a week before a company arrived in town) to full-fledged publicist (preparing press releases for the newspapers and "planting" rumors in restaurants and saloons for eager reporters to include in their columns). Morrisey quickly obtained a reputation as the "king" of publicity men, partly because he was unafraid of taking risks. That he happened to have top performers to promote seemed to be overlooked.

There is no question that Lillian was already an excellent attraction by the time she signed with Aronson. But the job Morrisey did in promoting her performances at the Casino went a long way toward building her stardom. Among his contributions was the innovation of presenting souvenirs to the audience each time a production reached its fiftieth or one-hundredth performance. The promotion was unfailingly mentioned in the newspapers and became a sign of the attraction's success.

Morrisey refined this gimmick with Lillian's shows,

To promote her image as a stylish matron as well as a comic opera star, Lillian posed for a number of photographs distributed to women's magazines, to be included in articles featuring her as a fashion leader. (Harry Ransom Humanities Research Center, the University of Texas at Austin.)

offering a velvet-lined box of candy to all women in the audience at each performance milestone. His judicious handling of the many floral displays accorded Lillian made each event a performance in its own right. He made use of the new "commercial art" form by printing chromolithograph images of Lillian, in full costume for her Casino shows, and selling them throughout the city. (On tour, these would be sold only at the theater featuring Lillian, so Aronson would get a share of the profits.) When Morrisey found that the Kodak process could be used to reproduce pictures cheaply, he offered audiences signed photographs of Lillian.

Unfortunately, there is no measure of how many ticket sales Morrisey's activities contributed to the box office, but there is no question that his use of these techniques, at a time when they all but guaranteed display and exposure for a stage performer, assisted Lillian's ascent to stardom. That Lillian had now become the highest-paid performer on the New York stage contributed strongly to this equation for success.

Lillian's first show for Aronson was *Nadjy*, which opened at the Casino January 21, 1889. It was a French import with the familiar comic opera plot. A count's nephew loves Nadjy, but he is commanded by his king to marry a girl the emperor had kidnapped for him. Naturally, his love of Nadjy triumphs in the end. As Nadjy, Lillian was an immediate success, the papers reporting "the *Nadjy* revival brought forth splendid houses at the Casino."

Two events made this run of 118 performances noteworthy. The first occurred soon after the show opened. In an apparent dispute between Lillian and Francis Wilson, the lead tenor, he was fired by Aronson for "acting carelessly." The specific reason for the firing is unknown, but it had been requested by Lillian. Wilson sued; but like most such suits of the time, it died in a few months. The second event occurred in mid-March. Aronson announced that the Casino was to be fully electrified, one of the first theaters anywhere to institute this improvement. A new outdoor electric sign created crowds in front of the theater for months. Lillian's name became one of the first ever to appear "in lights" on Broadway.

Nadjy continued to May 4, well beyond what Aronson had planned, since he wanted to introduce his next production, *The Brigands*, before the summer season. The new show was delayed to a May 9 opening because Lillian became ill and could not sing for almost a week. When *The Brigands* did open, she was still suffering the effects of her illness and had to retire from the cast for another week. Still, the *Clipper* reported, "Lillian Russell, though suffering from a cold, was beautiful to look upon and interesting in her acting, costumed with bewildering richness."[1]

It relieved Aronson to see that the show would have a long life once Lillian returned to the cast. In addition to the lavish production values he had created for the attraction, Aronson had also hired a new musical director, Gustave Kerker. Born in Germany, Kerker had moved with his family to Louisville, Kentucky, where he began his musical education. He played in the city's theater orchestra and soon became its conductor. While E.E. Rice was on tour, he enjoyed an operetta Kerker had composed and offered him a job. His competence as a conductor got him the job at the Casino. His willingness to include interpolations in the staging of operas was welcomed by performers, including Lillian. In a few years, Kerker would become one of America's leading comic opera composers.

From the time of her return to *The Brigands*, Lillian filled the seats. At its fiftieth performance, women were given satin sachet bags; at its one-hundreth performance, everyone in the audience received a signed photograph of Lillian. Each week, at the Saturday matinee, Lillian was "florally remembered." Matinees had become an important social and cultural occasion for young women, who attended afternoon performances unescorted. They dominated the audience and had the opportunity to display the latest styles and fashions. That Lillian should be their idol was not surprising.

The Brigands was originally written by Offenbach, with an English translation by William Gilbert. It was updated, with its lines more Americanized, by Edgar Smith. At the time, Smith was assisting in the preparation of comic opera dialogue. In a few years, he would become Weber and Fields' chief writer of satire and musical comedy.

The show ran for 145 performances, throughout the entire summer, finally closing in the middle of September. It became the top-selling attraction in New York and helped to prove that shows could draw large audiences during the "hot" months. It also signaled a change in the behavior of summer audiences. Two other events helped: the opening of the Casino's roof garden and the fact that variety houses, such as Tony Pastor's, remained open in spite of the heat. Both the proliferation of fresh and pleasant "roof gardens," providing relief from the oppressive heat of New York summers, and the presence of "variety" entertainment offered at once new leisure-time options to people and additional employment for performers.

Actor/comedian Fred Solomon joined *The Brigands* midway through its run in New York and was signed to continue on its tour. Fred was the brother of Edward Solomon, Lillian's estranged husband. Like his older brother, Fred had a reputation for being attractive to women. Rumor soon had it that Fred and Lillian were sharing more than the stage; considering the intriguing complications this possibility could present, the rumor seems not entirely out of the question. In a move quite uncharacteristic for the day, it was announced that Fred Solomon's wife would join him on the company's tour.

Boston was their first stop. At the Hollis Street Theater, the show's run was extended from two to four weeks. *The Brigands* attracted "extremely large audiences" and Lillian "scored well." The tour took the company to Pittsburgh, Chicago, Philadelphia, Baltimore and Washington, D.C. Every city reported "a solid success," "crowded houses" and "profitable business." In Baltimore, the show received special recognition:

> There was an uninterrupted flow of large receipts; the success of the engagement is noteworthy from the fact that a four week's operatic run without change of bill is something of a rarity in this city.[2]

Everywhere that Lillian performed, she was acclaimed "a hit." When *The Brigands* returned to the Casino in January 1890, the audiences were "large and demonstrative" and Lillian "was greeted with especial cordiality." The show ran until the third week of February, more than 300 performances overall, including the Casino and on tour. No other comic opera had achieved such a continuous run before. Yet Aronson was planning an even more lavish production for Lillian to follow *The Brigands*, one that would serve to elevate her to regal status: Queen of Comic Opera. What better title for such a production than *The Grand Duchess*?

Press coverage of *The Grand Duchess* rehearsals was interrupted by a debate, apparently incited by a comment Lillian made regarding a change in career to grand opera. Cynthia openly supported such a move. The theatrical newspapers, however, suggested that Lillian stay in comic opera, where she was "tops," rather than go to grand opera where she would be on a "lower rung" than Patti or Calvé. Aronson stopped all debate on the issue, very possibly intentionally staged by Morrisey, by announcing that Lillian had signed a new contract for two years, at an increased salary, and "she will therefore not appear in grand opera, as has been intimated."[3]

The Grand Duchess opened February 25, 1890, the most extravagant comic opera spectacle staged to date. It was immediately embraced by critics and audiences alike. One reviewer wrote:

Lillian in the title role of *The Grand Duchess* at the Casino Theater. For this, her most famous part in comic opera, the press labeled her "Queen," an honorific she carried until her death. (Harry Ransom Humanities Research Center, the University of Texas at Austin.)

The Grand Duchess is a feast for the eye and a delight to the ear. Not in many a season has there been put forth a more commendable presentation of Offenbach's still charming work. It has filled the Casino to capacity and the prospect that it will run into summer is almost certain. The real triumph of the opera is achieved by Lillian Russell, who has never sung to better advantage or acted with greater intelligence and spirit. She has surprised even her warmest admirers.[4]

Lillian's entrance was electrifying and dignified. It was snowing. Dressed in an ermine ensemble, Lillian sat in a sleigh at the top of a hill (at a back corner of the stage). The sleigh slowly descended toward the footlights, while she waved in noble greeting to the audience. If their requests could have been granted, the opening would have been encored repeatedly.

The original production had first been presented in Paris in 1867, the story of a great lady's love for a common soldier who, unfortunately for her, is in love with another woman. Even though she promotes her beloved to general, he remains loyal to his sweetheart. Aronson's production took the opera into what Gerald Bordman, the theater historian, defined as a "musical circus." The show ran for 108 performances, ending May 31. Lillian and the company were exhausted, having been performing constantly, practically every day, for close to 17 months.

During the show's run, a notable event demonstrated Lillian's national popularity. She — or rather her voice — had been chosen for the first public display of Bell's new long-distance telephone line between New York and Washington, D.C. President Cleveland would be on the receiving end, and Lillian was to sing the "Sabre Song" to him. A line was laid from the phone exchange into Lillian's dressing room. She sang into a large metal funnel; another funnel was in President Cleveland's office. With Cleveland were actors De Wolfe Hopper and Francis Wilson, Lillian's not-so-friendly former colleague. After her song, the president congratulated her performance. Hopper enthused, "Queen, you never sang better. Your voice was delightful and clear. We all enjoyed it immensely." A few days later, it was announced that Edison was to have Lillian sing into his new phonograph. Though the heralded event never occurred, it did help to sell more tickets.

Lillian, with her daughter and mother, was loaned ex-Senator George B. Dean's cottage at Cornwall-on-the-Hudson for the summer. Being hours by train from the restaurants of Manhattan and a day's travel from Saratoga, the chosen venue served as a self-imposed rest. Disciplined as she always was about her singing, Lillian continued daily practice sessions with a singing teacher who stayed with the family.

Despite the success of the two latest shows, Aronson was having trouble keeping his lease on the Casino. He had been the original owner of the theater (along with Col. McCaull) but had been forced to sell it off to a group of bond-holders. As long as he paid the interest on the bonds and delivered a dividend to the bond-holders, he could retain the lease. While Aronson regularly paid the interest, he was accused of providing no dividends, even though he had made a good deal of money during the last year and a half. The bond-holders, led by William Steinway (of piano fame), were attempting to take both the lease and Lillian's contract from Aronson, to operate the theater themselves. The court temporarily agreed with Aronson, but he maintained only a tenuous hold. Lillian's future actions would determine his management of the theater.

Poor Jonathan was Lillian's next production at the Casino, opening October 14. It proved to be an even greater success than *The Grand Duchess*, running 202 New York performances before going on tour. Besides Lillian, *Poor Jonathan* also starred Jefferson De Angelis, a revered actor, and Fanny Rice, a younger version of Lillian, still more comedienne than singer. The plot told of an American millionaire (all comic opera the plots seemed to employ either millionaires or European royalty) who, deserted by his protégé, is talked out of committing suicide by his cook. It was a German opera with an American setting, itself a novel notion. One of the scenes, however, showed Negroes incongruously picking cotton in New York City. The scene was changed to take place at West Point, with cadets instead of Negroes, marching rather than picking cotton. The sensibilities of the American audience had to be considered.

Like Lillian's previous openings at the Casino, this one too quickly gained enthusiastic plaudits. The *Clipper* declared:

> *Poor Jonathan* has justified its choice. The comedy opera has attracted very large and highly delighted audiences, produced under the direction of Heinrich Conreid. Lillian Russell, making her first appearance this season, met with a royal greeting — a flattering denotement of the esteem in which she is held by New York lovers of light opera. Miss Russell, indeed, is now, beyond doubt, the most popular American prima donna, and her value as an artist seems to be constantly growing. She was in admirable voice after her summer's rest, and she sang her music with thorough intelligence and accuracy.[5]

The *New York World* likened Lillian's performance to grand opera:

> She was superb in appearance and in voice, and went through her role with the ease and grace of a Patti.[6]

Opening night festivities were enhanced even more by one of Lillian's admirers. First nights at the Casino were inundated with bouquets for the performers sent by friends and admirers (not to mention the theater publicist). Usually, these floral tributes were exhibited during the first two acts in the lobby of the theater, where the audience could see them and examine the cards of the senders. (A joke among theatrical reporters was to rearrange the cards on floral pieces before they were sent up to the stage.) At the end of the show, the flowers were carried down the aisles to the orchestra pit, where the musicians then handed them up to the performers.

At the conclusion of opening night, when all the performers were receiving their flowers and taking their bows, a woman ran down the center aisle, pushing ushers aside and shouting, "Brava, Russell, Brava!" Upon reaching the orchestra rail, she threw a large bouquet at Lillian, squarely hitting her. The audience was stunned, momentarily

Lillian as Harriet in *Poor Jonathan* at the Casino Theater. The show played for an unprecedented 29 weeks in New York, more than any other comic opera to that point in time. Only because Lillian tired of performing it did the show finally close. (Harry Ransom Humanities Research Center, the University of Texas at Austin.)

speechless, then demanded that the woman be thrown out. But the orchestra leader recognized the woman and assured the audience it was all right: The enthusiastic woman was Lillian's singing teacher. A teacher's best advertisements were her pupils, and this teacher was not about to miss such a promotional opportunity. Lillian graciously acknowledged her gift and applauded her teacher with delight.

Poor Jonathan was midway through its run when it was revealed that Aronson and T. Henry French were discussing Lillian's contract. French, the son of play broker Samuel French, was manager of the Broadway Theater and the Garden Theater in Madison Square. He favored comic opera productions and, like Aronson, strove to make them visual spectacles. Obtaining Lillian's services was all he needed to become the city's leading impresario.

French caught Aronson at a delicate time. Litigation regarding the Casino lease was continued, and Aronson faced sizable outlays of money to retain possession of the theater. Unfortunately, he didn't have enough to stay in business for another year. His contract with Lillian ran only to October; without her, he would lose all drawing power. (The claim that Aronson had made a few months previously, purporting to have re-signed Lillian, had been for publicity purposes only.)

At the same time, French offered Lillian a contract that Aronson could not match, let alone improve upon. Lillian had been making $400 a week with Aronson; she was offered $500 a week by French. Even more important were French's additional guarantees: Lillian would receive 15 percent of the gross (which included ticket sales, concessions and programs), and she would have no understudy.

The implications of this arrangement were unheard of in the business. No other performer had ever enjoyed such a contract. Considering Lillian's history of abruptly terminating contracts, French was taking a high risk, but he believed her tremendous public appeal would generate great profit. For their part, his fellow theater managers were outraged by French's acquiescence to Lillian with regard to her receiving a percentage of gross sales. It would force them to set up new negotiating standards with other top performers. They cared less about her demand to eliminate understudies. A performance without Lillian on stage would generate a small audience, and they would leave the theater disappointed anyway.

Not surprisingly, French outbid Aronson for Lillian's services. It was estimated that Lillian might earn more than $50,000 a year under French's management. The *Clipper* announced:

> Lillian Russell will not remain at the Casino after this season. She has signed a contract with T. Henry French to become prima donna of his new opera company, which will occupy the Garden Theater next season. *La Cigale* has been secured by Mr. French, and in this he will introduce Miss Russell on the stage at the Garden.[7]

The news created even greater interest in *Poor Jonathan*, and the show was "turning away people at every performance." Aronson had to delay his next production in order to deal with the audiences' overwhelming desire to see Lillian in her last appearances at the Casino. At the attraction's one-hundredth performance, women were given silk sachets; at the one-hundred-fiftieth performance, everyone in the audience received bonbons. Tributes to Lillian continued throughout the run.

One Sunday evening, she was presented with a Chinese golden pheasant dinner, offered by delegates from the Poultry and Pigeon Association. Another convention group gave her a Chinese pug dog. At one show, Aronson sold the entire house to the National Association of Builders, an unprecedented event for New York theater:

> For the first time in the history of the theater, a performance was given at which the daily sale of admission tickets was entirely suspended. The auditorium was decorated with silk flags and souvenirs of the play were given to each delegate. Lillian Russell was called before the curtain after the second act to receive a basket of flowers from the Chicago delegates.[8]

Thanks to Morrisey's efforts, the two-hundredth performance of *Poor Jonathan* was publicized throughout the city. In what promised to be his final promotion for Lillian, Morrisey's biggest problem proved to be replacing posters that were stolen by admirers. Crowds outside the theater delayed each performance; floral displays were stacked into the streets. The house itself was draped with flowers, picked clean by the audience as it left the theater. Morrisey also provided souvenir programs, marked with "200" on the cover, for the entire audience.

Two days after this gala evening, *Poor Jonathan* closed at Aronson's Casino. Two more days later (May 7, 1891), *Apollo or the Oracle of Delphi*, starring Lillian, opened at French's Garden Theater. Besides the regular evening performances of *Poor Jonathan*, she and the cast had been rehearsing the new attraction for a month. French was known to dislike delays when introducing new productions. Yet even with these extraordinary demands on her time, Lillian volunteered to participate in benefits for fellow performers who had been ill or were unable to continue their careers. As much as Lillian was considered "tough" with theater managers, she was known to be generous with her time and money for needy colleagues, a trait that endeared her to peers.

Apollo lacked both the vigor and the catchy music of *Poor Jonathan*, but it had Lillian. The *Clipper* reported:

> The music was neither a revelation nor a delight, and the libretto was not more than so-so. But Lillian pleased the Garden's big audience, and probably it will be retained all summer.[9]

The *Dramatic Mirror* was more emphatic:

> Lillian Russell did much to save the operetta from musical collapse. In addition, it may be said that her beauty and the magnetic charm of her fascinating personality lent romantic realism to her embodiment of Apollo's oracle. It is safe to predict that the operetta will draw at the Garden so long as Miss Russell remains in the cast.[10]

Despite its poor reviews, Lillian kept *Apollo* alive for 65 performances, until July 11. The press echoed what had become a phenomenon of audiences hypnotized by Lillian's aura:

> Theatergoers flock to the Garden box office to worship at the comic opera shrine of *Apollo* and Lillian Russell.[11]

Not to miss an opportunity, Aronson exercised the option he held on Lillian's services through October and reopened *The Grand Duchess* to run for one month, billing it as Lillian's farewell appearance at the Casino. The press reported she was "unsurpassed in this role:"

> In point of beauty, she reigns a queen on the comic opera stage. And with regard to her vocal preeminence — well, go and hear her. There never was a Gallic songstress who could sing as charmingly as our own Lillian.[12]

Morrisey had one last fling. The final performance of *The Grand Duchess*, Lillian's last at the Casino, was a floral extravaganza. The *New York World* featured the event on its front page:

> Lillian Russell's Good By [*sic*] to the Casino. Grand Duchess Lillian Russell Bids It Adieu in Flowers.

> Everybody was at the Casino last night. Everybody wanted to have the last peep at the Queen of Comic Opera ere she made her farewell bow before the Casino footlights. Enthusiasm, affection and regret were equally mingled, for all who were there admired Miss Russell, who is popularity personified

with the whole company, from the property boys behind the scenes to the leading soubrette. The ushers were kept busy, carrying up floral tributes which were without number.[13]

Lillian was reported to have received these honors with "elegant modesty."

The newspapers noted the next day that Lillian, her daughter and mother were to leave for Europe. Actually, they traveled to the Thousand Islands in upper New York State where Lillian went fishing. At the same time, however, she began rehearsing on the songs for her official introductory production with French, *La Cigale*. With her on this trip were her singing teacher and Mrs. Scott Siddons, a well-known actress with a reputation for being one of the most expressive performers on the stage. Mrs. Siddons had agreed to tutor Lillian to improve her acting.

A new lawsuit involved Lillian indirectly, but mostly exposed the lack of proper

Program for the *Grand Duchess*, the second time it was introduced at the Casino Theater. Attendance of *Apollo* had declined, and Casino manager Rudolph Aronson wanted the return of full houses. Theater programs represented an excellent advertising vehicle, particularly for pianos, because such programs could target a select group of consumers who were musically oriented. (Harry Ransom Humanities Research Center, the University of Texas at Austin.)

copyright laws protecting theater performers. Benjamin Falk, a photographer who worked for many performers, including Lillian, sued another photographer for publishing photos of her, alleging that it infringed on his copyright. He also asked for a preliminary injunction to prevent sale of these photos, which were being sold to manufacturers of smoking tobacco. Lillian wrote a letter to the court, objecting to her photo being given away to "induce customers to purchase boxes of cigars and packages of chewing and smoking tobacco." The offending photographer was also accused of altering the design of Lillian's photos to evade the law. However, the judge refused to grant the injunction, on the grounds that it had not been shown that Falk was suffering irreparable injury. The ruling came as no surprise, since other people in theater — authors, song writers, even stage designers — were frequently unable to maintain legal ownership of their material. It would be another decade before copyright laws were established and enforced to protect the authors of intellectual property in entertainment.

La Cigale was taken from the La Fontaine fable, "The Grasshopper and the Ant." The dramatic version focused on two nieces, one who longed to go on stage, the other domestically inclined and recently married. Lillian played the role of Marton, who reaches stage stardom but spends lavishly while her thrifty cousin saves for the future. In a faint, Marton dreams of returning home penniless, only to find herself repulsed by her cousin. Upon awakening, she discovers her true love and mends her spending ways, and all ends happily.

The music was written by Edmond Audran, composer of *Olivette* and an admirer of Lillian who once promised to write her an operetta. The production included a number of interpolations by the young Ivan Caryll, who would soon become one of America's foremost composers of operettas. Carl Streitman played the male lead, his first appearance in the U.S.; Louis Harrison played the comic, and Susan Leonard played a duchess. It was Susan's third appearance with her older sister, with more shows to come. Playing the second lead was Attalie Claire, a young singer who was quickly singled out for her "sweet voice" and received "long continued applause" for her efforts.

Critics praised the show and the performers:

> *La Cigale*, with Lillian Russell, at the Garden Theater October 26, is one of the most successful that has taken place since Jenny Lind sang at the old Castle Garden.
>   Miss Russell has made the best hit of her remarkable career, as Marton. She displayed a genuinely remarkable intensity and fire, and worked the house up to a pitch of enthusiasm.[14]

The *Dramatic Mirror*, usually reserved when complimenting stars, stated:

> A new horizon has opened before Lillian Russell. She is no longer the mere toy of comic opera; she is a star of opéra comique, and she shines peerlessly in its firmament.[15]

In their constant effort to make comic opera a native art form, the *Dramatic Mirror* further declared:

> Miss Russell is a purely American product. We have, therefore, the more reason to be proud of her ascent.[16]

The press, however, held off any indication that the show would be a money maker because of the performers' high salaries and the exceptional production values. French anticipated this and raised the cost of seats to $2.

The desire to see that theater in America became more Americanized was a particular editorial policy of the *Dramatic Mirror,* and it became even more fervent as American productions and performers began to dominate the stage. This view appeared at a time when comic opera was beginning to lose its appeal. Nearly all comic opera had been imported to America. Each year, productions increased in lavish spectacle. But only those operas in which Lillian performed seemed to be hits. She herself was not affected by the general decline of the genre, because of her star power and nationwide appeal. (Those grueling "provincial" tours paid off.) Support she gained from female audiences also tended to separate Lillian from other performers and distinguished her work from other comic opera productions.

Audiences were only now beginning to discern a distinction between different forms of stage presentation. Variations on the typical and familiar operettas were being modified to feature more speech than singing, more portrayal of everyday people than royalty, more ensemble performance than individual stars — all factors presaging the components of twentieth century American musical comedy. And there was an upstart rapidly capturing the attention (and the dollars) of middle-class audiences — vaudeville. Even though the *Mirror* had strongly supported serious theater over variety, it too was now beginning to acknowledge vaudeville as an all-American product.

Along with its idealization of American-made products, the *Dramatic Mirror* also viewed performers as symbols for society to emulate or vanquish, depending on the editor's judgment of their moral stature. Lillian had already scaled the perceived pinnacle of artistic virtue. She would soon experience their moral wrath.

The start of 1892 promised continuous success for the Garden Theater's prosperous triad of *La Cigale*, Lillian and T. Henry French. Enter the Gerry Society (a.k.a. the Society for the Prevention of Cruelty to Children). Organized and led by Elbridge T. Gerry, a New York socialite and moral crusader, this private group was publicly entrusted with enforcing the laws concerning the on-stage appearance of children under the age of 16. These laws, however, seemed to be enforced in a selective manner, depending on favoritism, payoffs and moral judgments by Gerry, usually designed to obtain the widest publicity for his group.

When Gerry initiated his campaign, his attention had been directed to the "lower" forms of entertainment, variety shows and dime museums. As his impact on theater managers increased, however, he expanded his investigations into "legitimate" productions as well. At the time of his evaluation of *La Cigale*, Gerry's power to decry "immoral lawlessness" on the part of theater managers was a potent and intimidating force with which to reckon. By turns anxious and outraged, managers were already employing lawyers and politicians in an attempt to curb his zeal.

In one scene of *La Cigale*, as reported by *The New York Times*: "Particularly good were the movements of a group of dainty children and their grasshopper dance."[17]

Gerry directed French to remove the children from the show. French had no choice but to follow Gerry's demands. Lillian attempted to persuade Gerry to allow the children to perform, but Gerry refused. When the children's parents reported their disappointment, they remarked about the children's love for Lillian and the kindnesses she had shown them.

Changing the scene did little to detract from the success of the operetta, but Gerry's indiscriminate actions against *La Cigale* became a catalyst among managers to inhibit, if not altogether end, Gerry's interference. Over the next six months, managers and the theatrical newspapers campaigned to rein in Gerry's power. Litigation was initiated against him; bills were introduced in the city council and state legislature to restrain his activities and disband his organization. None entirely succeeded, but in a year's time his activities had been lessened. Gerry's crusade was compared to Anthony Comstock's concurrent, self-styled battle against alleged obscenity.

At the same time, sadness descended on the industry when it was learned that Col. John McCaull was ailing:

> ...the man who did more than any other single individual to establish and sustain comic opera in America is now broken down in health, beyond all hope of recovery and reduced in fortune. Col. McCaull is living a reclused life in Baltimore and suffering from paralysis."[18]

Lillian as Marton in *La Cigale* at the Garden Theater. The show was a comic opera version of "The Grasshopper and the Ant" and became another signature production for Lillian. Over a period of three seasons, she performed it more than 300 times to audiences across the country, notably at the Chicago World's Fair. (Harry Ransom Humanities Research Center, the University of Texas at Austin.)

Sponsored by McCaull's old partner Rudolph Aronson, a benefit was planned at the Casino to honor McCaull and collect money on his behalf. Lillian was the first to volunteer her services and money. The affair was suffused with nostalgia for all the theater people who attended, and it netted over $3,500. McCaull died a year later, having spent this time bedridden, completely paralyzed.

French made a mistake in scheduling *La Cigale* at the Garden Theater for the middle of February. He had underestimated its profitability, not taking into consideration the potential return from increasing ticket prices. Now he had no choice but to put the show on tour, in order to fulfill all the commitments previously made in cities where *La Cigale* was scheduled to appear. Managers would not tolerate having to change a bill that featured Lillian Russell.

La Cigale's closing night at the Garden proved a tour-de-force for Lillian. French had arranged to present Lillian's autograph (on a card commemorating the last show) to all the women in the audience. She herself had planned to give a short speech at the end of the performance. Yet all this was superseded by the devoted attentions of her audience.

At the end of the second act, just as the curtain was about to drop, three ushers rushed to the stage carrying a red satin cushion, upon which rested a large star, set with 89 small diamonds. The gift had been subscribed by a number of admirers as a testimonial to their "Queen." The attendant ovation brought Lillian to the footlights to accept the gift. Bowing graciously, she took the cushion from the musical director, spoke a few words of thanks, threw kisses to the audience, bowed again and retired from the stage. When she appeared in the third act, Lillian wore the dazzling star in her hair. Cheering loudly, the audience erupted in appreciation of her gesture, momentarily stopping the show.

Boston was *La Cigale*'s first tour stop, at the Globe Theater. Just before the first show, the Press Club put on their annual entertainment for the city's theater people. Lillian was invited and attended, as did other members of the company. Appearing for the press was always considered important, particularly when a company was about to open a run.

La Cigale quickly received acclaim and SRO signs appeared at every performance. But the success of the operetta itself ran second to press coverage of a stage confrontation between Lillian and Attalie Claire, the contralto and second lead. The disagreement between them had begun months earlier. When Claire arrived in the U.S. from London, having been hired by T. Henry French to appear in his opera company, she found that it was now the Lillian Russell Opera Company to which she had been signed and that she was to "assist" Lillian on stage. Claire did not care for this arrangement and stated her opinion clearly, both to French and Lillian. In reaction, Lillian snubbed Claire. The tension continued during their run in New York and broke into open hostility in Boston, aided by the activities of a number of Claire's admirers.

A group of young men from Columbia College began almost nightly demonstrations for Claire while the show was still in New York. Unknown to most people, one member of the Columbia group, Alfred Kayne, was in love with Claire (they were later married) and enlisted his colleagues to celebrate her performances. Kayne and his friends continued this activity in Boston, attending every show and presenting Claire with flowers, rings and dinners. As prima donna, leading lady of the company, Lillian objected. Claire's response was that she was "no one's pendant, that she is independent and she, too, has her friends."

Lillian reacted by refusing to allow the collegians' flowers to be passed over the footlights. Claire publicly expressed displeasure with the edict. Lillian then declared that Claire could not wear on stage the rings that had been presented to her by the Columbia men. The press gleefully suggested that the rings were larger than those worn by Lillian. In spite of Lillian's demands, Claire wore them anyway. The *Boston Globe* noted:

> Miss Claire wore the rings just the same, and Miss Russell's eyes flashed with indignation even more brilliantly than did the diamonds.[19]

Kayne and his Columbia colleagues continued to send Claire flowers. Each night the floral bouquets grew more magnificent, to the point where they were unable to fit through the front entrance of the theater. To deal with this obstacle, the Columbians rented a store window next to the theater and had the floral displays put on public exhibition.

Lillian's own admirers rushed to her defense.

> The friends of Miss Russell assert that Miss Claire avails herself of every chance to attract attention. They say that the part of Charlotte, played by Miss Claire, is that of a quiet, demure country girl, whereas the contralto makes Charlotte a forward coquette. They also assert that Claire should not wear $1,000 rings and wash dishes with white kid gloves on.[20]

During an interview with reporters, Claire responded by pointing out she was 12 years younger than Lillian and not as "full blown." Prior to the next show, her

Columbia admirers chose to make a garden of roses along Claire's pathway to the theater. At another performance, when Claire sang her initial solo, the Columbians threw her large bouquets from their box seats. The *Globe* observed:

> Miss Russell and Miss Claire still embrace each other, as the action of *La Cigale* demands, but it is noticed that these scenes are cut as short as possible.[21]

Taking advantage of the controversy, the *Boston News* decided to conduct a contest among readers to determine who was the more popular actress. As the votes poured in, the *News* printed the results each day, hawking papers each evening in front of the theater. Voting continued throughout the entire run of the show. During the tumultuous affair, there was SRO at every performance, seats being sold days in advance. Martin Drake, the theater manager, said happily that the show "will go out in a blaze of theatrical glory."

But not for Attalie Claire. Just after the show closed, the *Boston News* reported she had won the popularity contest. At the same time, Lillian forced her removal from the cast. The *Dramatic Mirror* reported:

> Attalie Claire, having been forced out of the cast of *La Cigale* by Lillian Russell, has returned to her apartments at the Bartholdi in this city. She is still a member of the cast and appeared at T. Henry French's office to draw her salary.
>
> Miss Claire has a magnificent diamond star that cost $1,000. It was presented to her last week by the *Boston News*, in token of having received more votes than Miss Russell in the contest.[22]

The episode disturbed Lillian greatly, not only suggesting her vulnerability as the leading comic opera star, but also reminding her of the increasing competition from younger performers. Such challenges, coupled with her own observation that comic opera was beginning to lose its appeal, could have an influence on her future marketability. The situation would have to be carefully monitored.

Her concerns were heightened when the *Dramatic Mirror* berated Lillian for her behavior on stage and her attacks on Claire. A star should not behave in this manner; a star should assist the newcomer to attain success. Was Lillian becoming too conceited, carried away with the adulation of her audience? She could fall as fast as she had risen, the *Mirror* suggested. Such comments trailed Lillian and the company into Chicago, where the local press reported, "The opera was a great disappointment" and commented further, "The opera and the fair but jealous Lillian are attracting but fair houses."[23] The *Mirror*, continuing its editorial chastisement, declared, "Lillian Russell should wave the palm of peace at Attalie Claire. And Attalie should admit that Lillian is not so dreadful old, after all."[24]

The box office in Chicago was not good, but when the company played in other cities on the tour — St. Louis, Pittsburgh, Washington, D.C., and Philadelphia — it was as if no one had heard or cared about the controversy. Lillian was still "The Queen," and theaters were jammed with appreciative audiences. Newspapers in these cities mentioned nothing of the dispute. Instead, considered newsworthy was the fact that Lillian was traveling from Chicago in a private Pullman car named the "Lillian Russell." Also not mentioned, except in the society columns, was the composition of the audiences now attending Lillian's performances — fashionable crowds, women dressed in sumptuous style, the social elite. Most of the rest of the theatergoing public, a far broader segment, was instead paying increasing attention to the new, middle-class entertainment called vaudeville.

Unlike comic opera, vaudeville was perceived to be home-grown entertainment, a uniquely American invention. To confuse the issue, some of the better vaudeville companies were now adding to their programs skits that resembled, or parodied, comic opera productions. Audiences increasingly focused on the "comedy" in comic opera, as these works were satirized by the vaudevillians.

La Cigale closed its tour in Brooklyn at the end of May to "large and appreciative houses," people having forgotten about the winter's debate regarding Lillian's professional behavior. Lillian was preparing to travel to Europe to spend the summer. Lillian, Jr., would accompany her mother. Cynthia planned to stay home and attend to her suffrage activities. On the boat with Lillian was manager T. Henry French, to discuss their plans for next season.

French had astutely observed the changes in audience preferences, quite noticeable in New York and other large Eastern cities. Operettas were losing their appeal, particularly those that were imported. Foreign performers were not receiving the adulation afforded them in previous years. Even the great Richard Mansfield was close to bankruptcy. New comic operas would have to be refined and prove themselves on the road before playing New York theaters. The cost of mounting comic opera productions had increased substantially, due to both elaborate staging and the extensive travel required to make a profit. New theaters were being built in towns never before considered "on the circuit," and quality productions were demanded. French had to persuade Lillian that touring the country was now as important as playing in New York and that more cities, even smaller ones, would have to be included in her tours.

They also discussed the need for companies that could perform repertory, since audiences in a given town were quickly saturated if only one production was presented. Lillian would now have to be prepared to sing three different operas on the same tour; company members would have to be versatile (able to sing and act various roles); property people would be required to carry more scenery and develop systems for faster build-up and tear-down. To economize further, the number of musicians would be decreased by enlisting local people to play in the orchestra. While Lillian was earning a sizable salary, it was obvious to her that she would now be working harder for her income. The coming season promised to be difficult for any comic opera company seeking reasonable profit.

A summer in England served as respite from the season past and preparation for encroaching challenges. Lillian chose to tour the country in a coach, lounging for a few days at various spas, being entertained by theater colleagues and minor royalty. Traveling with her was Geraldine Ulmar, a fellow performer of comic opera in London. Following Lillian's strict routine, they practiced singing daily. A July issue of the *Clipper* announced Lillian's forthcoming schedule:

> Miss Russell will sail for home July 20 and begin her season at the Baldwin, in San Francisco, late in August. On Sept. 5, at the Baldwin, *The Mountebanks* will have its first performance in this country, Miss Russell singing the part of Teresa. It will be given in New York at the Garden Theater December 26.[25]

When Lillian landed in New York, reporters were waiting at the dock to question her "about everything from politics to matrimony." She accommodated them all:

> Miss Russell is in good spirits over her new part in *The Mountebanks*, has several new songs written by Ivan Caryll, is in raptures over Mmes. Melba and Calvé, and thinks European theaters, climates, vegetables and women are all inferior to the American institution and product.[26]

Early in September, Lillian, the entire company and T. Henry French left Grand Central Station on a special train bound for San Francisco. Lillian had a private car, called the "Grassmere" (but quickly renamed the "Lillian Russell"); among its furnishings was a piano for her to rehearse with. The company's departure from the station could have been a scene from one of Lillian's shows:

> Miss Russell appeared just a few moments before departure. She entered the throng with perfect composure, displaying all the elegance of an unruffled temper, and did some charming acting before she waved adieu to friends from the rear platform as the train moved out.[27]

The train consisted of seven cars, including three cars of scenery. Performers rehearsed on board each day of the week-long trip. San Francisco reporters were sent to Sacramento to intercept the train and interview Lillian, but the train arrived at midnight, and Lillian was sleeping. No one dared awaken her, and the interviews were delayed until the train's arrival in San Francisco. A Press Club dinner preceded the opening, to introduce Lillian personally to local journalists. It was reported to be a great success.

The Mountebanks opened September 22, to enthusiastic audiences and approving critics:

> Lillian Russell opened her annual season at the Baldwin Theater. The prizefighters, the presidential candidacy, the cholera, the strike and all else were not able to affect the fair Lillian's popularity, and from the moment she first set foot on stage, the city has been a whirlpool of excitement. SRO every evening. Ninety-five in the cast, eighty-five brought from the east. Miss Russell's success was apparent from the start. Her voice is pure and sweet, and she sang with the greatest ease. Her acting was natural.[28]

While Lillian was deemed a hit, *The Mountebanks* itself was considered only an average play. And within a short while, the press was chiding Lillian and French for their comments about being slighted by the social elite of the city. The show played to full houses, but French was glad to leave town.

Now the grueling tour began in earnest, to cities never before visited, to audiences whose only experience of Lillian derived from newspapers and magazines. The towns of Los Angeles, Stockton, Portland, Ogden, Salt Lake City and Denver were played in rapid succession, usually for one-night stands. Finally, the company stopped in a familiar city, St. Louis.

As initial reactions to *The Mountebanks* had predicted, the show soon faltered, replaced by *La Cigale* as the featured presentation. Apparently, American audiences were unable to appreciate the *Mountebanks* plot, which portrayed complications arising from taking a magic potion that made all men who drink it "exactly what they pretend to be." All the action took place in a picturesque Sicilian mountain pass, early in the current century. It was not one of Gilbert and Cellier's better shows, especially in the U.S. The audience asked: Where is Sicily? The press questioned: Who needs a potion to behave the way people normally do?

In contrast, audiences in all cities thoroughly enjoyed *La Cigale*. Each performance was a social event, a place where it was of benefit to "be seen," even though (or possibly because) ticket prices had been raised. By the time the Lillian Russell Opera Company reached Chicago on Thanksgiving Day, their performance at the Columbia Theater was sold out. A Chicago paper declared, "Miss Russell was as charming as ever and her company is stronger than she has ever had."[29]

In hopes of achieving a booking coup, Chicago promoters asked Lillian to consider performing at the Columbian Exposition (1893 World's Fair) during the coming summer. Both Lillian and French thought it a good suggestion. To aid in their decision, the manager of the Columbia Theater offered them an increased percentage of the ticket sales. A deal was agreed upon; a contract signed. Lillian and her company would appear in May, at the beginning of the Exposition, and play an unprecedented 16 weeks, throughout the summer. The engagement had the potential of providing a very prosperous summer. It also offered the company the luxury of summer employment and no travel.

Yet, just as things seemed promising, problems with Lillian, Jr., caused Lillian anxiety. The tensions had been precipitated by Lillian herself a few months previously, but there had been little she could do about it while on tour. At the beginning of autumn, just before Lillian and company left for San Francisco, Lillian, Jr., had been placed in a convent for schooling and care. Apparently, Lillian felt it would be better for the child than being at home with Cynthia. But the manner in which the young girl was left at the convent remains questionable.

Lillian, Jr., was taken to the New Jersey convent. While walking the grounds, she was asked by attending nuns to go to the flower shop to buy "some pretty posies." When the girl returned, she found her mother gone and only the nuns to offer solace. In her autobiography, Lillian, Jr. (later called Dorothy), wrote about her feelings at the time:

> I didn't want to be separated from my mother. I appreciated all the kindness shown me, but I was homesick, and this homesickness brought on an illness that lasted two years.[30]

While unhappy, she nonetheless attempted to apologize for her mother's behavior:

> I was reaching an age where it wasn't good for me to remain in the backstage environment. Mother, busy always, sometimes on tour, couldn't attend me. She visited me as often as she could, but when she was on the road she couldn't see me naturally.[31]

In a few months, Lillian, Jr., was returned home, under Cynthia's care. At the same time, Lillian arrived in Chicago where she celebrated her thirty-first birthday, receiving many salutations, floral bouquets and letters from friends and admirers. A quiet evening with her father was subdued and reflective.

Considering the emotionally charged circumstances, it seems odd that an announcement appeared a few days later in a New York paper noting that Lillian, Jr., had performed "as a pianist in a concert by pupils of a local school in Steinway Hall." How had she been able to accomplish this in light of the recent traumatic events?

On the company's return to New York, *The Mountebanks* was still undergoing changes; French refused to stage the show until he believed it was properly prepared. Instead, the ever-popular *La Cigale* opened at the Garden Theater on December 26, with many cast changes, and proved "an emphatic success."

Up to this time, for all her public appearances and constant press coverage, Lillian's private life had been modest and relatively simple. A small home on West 43rd Street served her, Lillian, Jr., Cynthia and a maid. Its prime feature was the multitude of photographs of theatrical people covering the walls. Lillian never gave interviews at home, nor did she often invite people for dinners or parties; it was more professionally advantageous to be seen in a public place with a colleague or admirer. Only a few years before, Lillian had described her life at home (that is, when she *was* at home):

> Do you know that I have few intimate friends, that the visitors to this little home of mine do not number a dozen all told and that I am glad of it. They are not of those who love the loud things that blazon light. There is a charm and a peace in my simple home existence.[32]

That all changed at the beginning of 1893, when she moved to a large brownstone home on West 77th Street, near West End Avenue and Riverside Drive, the most fashionable section of Manhattan. The home, its furnishings and its ambiance now had to be in keeping with her professional persona as stage star and public icon. Lillian's move "uptown" was a newsworthy event. The press reported each day's activities; all awaited the first reports concerning the inside of her new home, ultimately described in detail by all of the New York papers.

The brownstone had four floors. The top floor was reserved for servants, now including a maid, two housekeepers and a coachman. The third floor was for Lillian, Jr., and also contained a few guest rooms.

Lillian's sitting room, bedroom and bathroom comprised the second floor. The sitting room held a piano, and it was here that she practiced and rehearsed. Lillian's bedroom was decorated in traditional Victorian style, massive ornate furniture and brass accessories. The bed frame was made of brass, draped with silk ribbons and surrounded by mirrors. In a large display case were collections of souvenir spoons and snuffboxes. A divan covered with pillows, encircled by Turkish memorabilia and an incense burner (almost a duplicate of a stage setting in one of her operas), graced an alcove off the bedroom.

The first floor had four rooms — a parlor, drawing room, dining room and kitchen. The three public rooms were decorated in the same Victorian style, with large pieces of furniture, elegantly carved, and yards of hanging velvet drapery, interspersed with Japanese cabinets and tables. Large China vases containing palm leaves, wall ornaments and yet more mirrors adorned the rooms. Pink and blue dominated, in various hues. Oriental throw rugs abounded.

Lillian's home had become a magnet for celebrities, with Lillian as hostess. Parties and dinners were held each week, shared with currently popular theatrical people, politicians, the social elite and individual admirers. What had once been defined as a simple home now became a stage assemblage designed for a non-stage performance. An observer of the scene suggested it was getting hard to distinguish Lillian's stage roles from her private life.

At last, French judged *The Mountebanks* ready to be performed, but some company resignations — stage manager and second lead contralto — again delayed the opening. It was intimated in the press that these last-minute resignations might have been "inspired" by Lillian. The new show was given its first New York performance on January 11, 1893, to be met with a mixture of compliment and criticism. The compliments were for Lillian's singing and acting:

> Miss Russell must have been proud of the tumultuous applause that greeted her upon her first entrance and that was duplicated frequently during the course of the performance. Miss Russell dominated the work, singing with her customary brilliancy and acting with unexpected piquancy and vigor.[33]

Even the support staff was considered excellent, though the audience proved resistant to characters named Giorgio Raviolo, Luigi Spaghetti, Risotto and Elvino di Pasta. Nonetheless, the score and plot were severely criticized, the score considered "rather disappointing," the plot "doubtful."

In less than two weeks, it was announced that the company was rehearsing *Girofle-Girofla*, to be presented as a replacement.

Women's suffrage had been dormant in New York for almost a decade, having reached its greatest activity with street demonstrations and parades in the middle 1880s, highlighted by Cynthia's candidacy for mayor. A suffrage revival occurred in 1893 on two fronts: actions by the more radical Susan B. Anthony wing (which used the issue of political corruption to promote its cause) and the emergence of elite groups of women who viewed suffrage as a way to improve women's social status, particularly that of their own class (and at the same time further their political equality). This latter movement prominently influenced premier female theatrical performers.

Asked to join this new group, Lillian agreed without hesitation. Thus, the Professional Women's League of Theatrical Performers met on January 23, 1893, to identify its purposes and goals. First, and most important, the women chose to work toward better professional treatment and compensation; second, to assist destitute and sick female performers. They would accomplish this by sponsoring socials and giving benefit performances. The group members recognized that they had a unique opportunity to achieve their goals because of their celebrity and ability to influence public sentiment. Lillian was considered an excellent model to emulate, because of her success in obtaining higher wages, better contracts and a voice in her theatrical career.

Though it dealt solely with theater matters, this was Lillian's first involvement on behalf of the suffrage movement. Nevertheless, Cynthia was ecstatic about her daughter's decision since it supported her own lifelong crusade. But she questioned Lillian: "Could rich women really support a grass-roots movement?"

Lillian participated with the group when she was in New York, made frequent monetary donations and performed in fund-raising benefits, but there are no indications that she espoused any of its rhetoric. Still, it was a significant first step, one in a long series that (especially in later years) would come to demonstrate her commitment to the issue of equality for women.

Meanwhile, to the amazement of Lillian, T. Henry French and the theatrical press, *The Mountebanks* attracted large audiences for far more than six weeks. At its one-hundredth performance, women in the audience received a silk box filled with fine candies; attached to the box, an American Beauty rose, compliments of Lillian Russell.

On March 3, *Girofle-Girofla*, already performed during two previous seasons, was revived at the Garden Theater. The review was tepid; it was "not up to date," "not funny," and contained "old music." Response to Lillian, however, was congratulatory, no doubt because she saved the production from failure.

Of even greater significance than Lillian's success or the production itself was the outcome of a debate raging in New York's City Council, a major social and cultural confrontation that involved theater managers, politicians, lawyers and religious leaders. Ultimately, it was agreed that women were now to be allowed to appear bareheaded in theaters. French's Garden Theater, with Lillian as its main attraction, was first to initiate the new law.

A combination of productions—*La Cigale, The Mountebanks* and *Girofle-Girofla*—was now presented on tour in Brooklyn, Boston and Philadelphia, to prepare the company for its extended run in Chicago during the Columbian Exposition. Audiences in all three cities responded well to the repertory idea. It demonstrated the full range of Lillian's abilities and offered more opportunities to see her perform. Among theater managers, they saw her increasing public favor as a lucrative opportunity and promptly advanced prices. As her company approached Chicago, the press took note of advertising for Lillian's entrance to the city:

> Lillian Russell is immensely popular in local circles, which conditions added to her generous and scholarly advance heralding, making clear sailing for weeks to come.[34]

Or so hoped everyone involved with the World's Fair and its attendant entertainments.

Chapter Five

The Queen's Consorts

$\mathcal{D}$owntown Chicago in May 1893 was a tourist's delight. Sunday dinner could be had for one dollar. Lakefront hotels like the Victoria and the Leland offered rooms for only three dollars a day. The atrium of the Great Northern Hotel boasted a large tropical garden, complete with palm trees. The New Sherman House featured a mandolin orchestra. Florists sold American Beauty roses for five and ten cents each.

Just down the street from these grand hotels, the ornate Columbia Theater had for many years presented high-class shows. In 1881, it had been built by the Haverly brothers as Chicago's premier theater, aptly named the Haverly. Four years later, hard times forced the brothers to sell it to Charles McConnell, who renamed it the Columbia in honor of Christopher Columbus. The Columbia was the largest theater in the city, with the largest stage area; managers bragged about its elaborate and modern dressing rooms. Tours of the theater were given to show visitors its "behind-the-scenes" activities. The management of the Columbia may have been the first in the U.S. to offer such theater tours.

The Lillian Russell Opera Company began its summer run at the Columbia one week after the gala opening of the Columbian Exposition, popularly known as the Chicago World's Fair. Both Lillian and T. Henry French counted on the attraction of the Fair to bring in a large audience and sizable profits to their presentations at the theater. Promoters of the Fair counted on the exhibition to make Chicago seem "the wonder city of the U.S." and an example of the "wonderful accomplishments of a young nation." Their hope was to attract people from all over the world to demonstrate "the stupendous results of America's enterprise."

Only three years before had Chicago won (beating out New York City) the right to represent the U.S. in its four-hundredth anniversary celebration of the discovery of America. In a last-minute move to outbid New York, a group of Chicago businessmen came up with the offer of an additional $5 million—which they in fact did not possess—to win approval. Confident New York financiers were shocked by Chicago's victory and claimed fraud. How could a new, industrial city beat out the cultural capital of the U.S.?

Appeals to politicians and the federal government failed to change the result. The

New York press then spent the next two years belittling Chicago planners as "immature purveyors of the country's culture" and "unfit to represent the U.S. to the world community." Referring to Chicago's brash boasting of having outbid New York for the World's Fair site, Charles Dana, a reporter for the *New York Sun*, suggested readers should pay no attention "to the nonsensical claims of that windy city." The phrase caught on and became a figurative symbol of Chicago as the "windy city," a reference made even today, though its meaning now applies more to the city's weather than its bragging rights.

Chicago in the early 1890s was a perplexing urban paradox. It had demonstrated rapid reconstruction after the great fire of 1871. The city had doubled in size in 15 years and now had a population of close to a million and a quarter. At the same time, its phenomenal growth had been accomplished without systematic planning or control. The city was a prime example of America's industrial development and all the difficulties such unrestrained growth created (problems in housing, waste, water pollution, traffic and crime). The city offered stark contrasts between wealth and poverty. Yet despite all this, Chicago was designated to demonstrate America's cultural achievements.

One important component of the potential success for the Fair was popular entertainment and its ability to attract and amuse large numbers of visitors. Performance was viewed as a significant complement to scientific, educational and technological exhibits. Fair promoters worked hard to generate enthusiasm and support for entertainment because of the financial rewards it could potentially bring. Within a short time, they received hundreds of requests from theater managers, musical groups, amusement vendors, restaurants and circuses, all of which looked upon the Fair as a way to make a fortune in a few months. Such crass commercial concupiscence was not exactly what the Fair officials had in mind.

An argument ensued about the role and placement of Fair amusements. Some planners, led by religious groups, wanted to keep entertainment out of the Fair altogether. But the realization that considerable revenue would be lost by eliminating amusements and concessions convinced the planners to allow select groups to operate within the Fair grounds, restricted to an area called the Midway Plaisance. The "Midway" soon became the common reference to a circus aisle lined with concessions. Planners did not, however, consider what might take place outside the fairgrounds, beyond their jurisdiction.

The entertainment agreed upon by the planners was exemplary, eclectic and popular. Paderewski, the great Polish pianist, would offer recitals; Walter Damrosch (son of Leopold Damrosch) would conduct the New York Symphony Orchestra; "Gentleman" Jim Corbett would give boxing demonstrations; an Algerian group would present exotic dances, featuring an enchanting young acrobat named Little Egypt; and Sandow the Strongman (managed by Flo Ziegfeld) would ripple his muscles for squealing young women.

Outside the fairgrounds, however, visitors had a wide variety of other entertainments from which to choose. Circuses were set up in vacant lots. Large tents were erected to house a temporary stage and rows of folding chairs in order to offer vaudeville shows. Store fronts were converted into miniature stages upon which jugglers, fire eaters and freaks performed. For those seeking even more compelling thrills, some shows offered "blue" material and scantily clad performers. Most of these attractions operated irregularly, depending on the Fair's daily attendance.

Less than a week after the Fair opened, the international financial world was thrown into turmoil. The Wall Street stock market crashed, a victim of a combination of overproduction, overspeculation, wildcat enterprises and the effects of the McKinley Tariff. Passed by Congress the previous year and sponsored by owners of large corporations, the law shut out competition by the creation of trusts and monopolies. The Panic of 1893 hit the Fair hard. Early attendance had fallen below expectations because of poor weather. It immediately decreased to the point where planners were concerned about their ability to continue operations.

Chemical National Bank in Chicago closed its doors, putting great financial pressure on the many exhibitors and theater managers who had taken out loans from the bank. A number of downtown theaters went "dark," and others struggled to survive with reduced audiences. The temporary amusements outside the fairgrounds suffered equally; some just "folded their tents" and left town.

The attractions within the Fair itself, however, kept it solvent through the early turbulence. When the weather improved and the immediate effects of the Panic subsided, attendance slowly began to increase. Two decisions by the planners appealed to visitors: the Fair would remain open three nights a week until 11 P.M.; and, in a bitter debate with local religious authorities that also involved the federal government, the Fair was given approval to open on Sundays. By July, attendance had reached more than 100,000 a day and seemed to be increasing. Only after the Fair closed in October did the full effects of the Panic hit Chicago, creating large unemployment and poverty. It took the combined financial power of Philip Armour and Marshall Field, who assumed control of the Illinois Trust and Savings Bank, to assure depositors their personal holdings were guaranteed.

The downtown theaters struggled through May and June with small audiences. Even Lillian could not combat the situation. The *Chicago Tribune* seemed generous in its review of her show:

> Lillian Russell had established herself beyond question in favor with our showgoers. Business has been evenly good, but not up to the standards her presentation would warrant.[1]

In fact, everyone was losing money and wondering whether there would be any kind of turnaround. The *Clipper* reported, more realistically, "Business is not good. The number of shows doing good count on one hand. Five more shows closed."[2]

When Fair attendance began to rise, attendance at the downtown theaters followed. Both were boosted by a timely and welcome side effect of the Fair — a significant increase in the number of conventions meeting in Chicago during the late summer and fall. It was estimated that more than one-third of Fair visitors in September were affiliated with some convention. Indeed, the Fair was purported to have launched Chicago as a "convention" city. Because of their proximity to hotels, the surge in convention business could not have been more advantageous for downtown theaters.

By late June, the papers were reporting:

> Lillian Russell and her admirable singing cohorts gave *Girofle-Girofla* with great artistic and financial success, each performance bringing out the SRO placard.[3]

Theaters reopened. Outside the fairgrounds, other attractions raised their tents again to entertain visitors. Prosperity returned, both to the entertainers and to the Fair itself.

Central to the attractions on the Midway Plaisance was Chicago's answer to the Paris International Exposition of 1889 and its introduction of the Eiffel Tower. Designed by American engineer George W. G. Ferris, the Fair's giant steel wheel was considered a technological innovation unsurpassed in physical mechanics. The first Ferris Wheel was 264 feet high (some 20 stories) and, when fully loaded, could carry 2,160 people. Not surprisingly, it was the most popular attraction of the entire exposition.

Adjacent to the Midway was another major breakthrough, this one cultural. The French ambassador cited the Woman's Building as an "outstanding effort of the World's Columbian Exposition in the realm of ideals." Yet it had not even been considered in the original planning for the Fair. Only the redoubtable Susan B. Anthony and her suffragist cohorts had made this remarkable exhibit a reality.

Although the overall image of women it portrayed was inconsistent, the Woman's Building sponsored an unprecedented official recognition of women. On one hand, it extolled the virtues of the self-sacrificing Victorian woman; on the other, it insisted that women were able to compete fully with men. The building was designed by a woman architect; all of its fine art was made by women, including the internationally famous, Paris-based, American Impressionist painter, Mary Cassatt. Exhibits and demonstrations presented the arts of cooking and child-rearing. A model kindergarten (an innovation in education) operated each day, providing care for the children of Fair participants and visitors alike. Weekly discussions on politics, social values and the roles of women in society were led by Anthony, Jane Addams and Mrs. Potter Palmer, chair of the Women's Department of the Fair and "queen" of Chicago society.

To an observer, the Fair presented this conflicting picture of the American woman, just as the larger society was struggling with the role of the "new" woman and her middle-class aspirations. Just down the promenade from the Woman's Building stood a 60-foot statue of the Republic — secular, chaste, indeed virginal — representing the ideal American woman. A few feet away, young Arabian girls performed sexually provocative dances. A nearly naked Sandow entertained women with his magnificently muscular physique. Outside the fairgrounds, prostitution was big business. And a few miles to the north, Lillian Russell manifested the new womanly virtues of independence and equality, to audiences both on and off the stage.

Girofle-Girofla gave way to *La Cigale* in July, with continued success.

> Lillian Russell is in the third month of her generally successful engagement. Miss Russell's business will maintain a profitable basis; her performances bring delight to the hearts of all comers.[4]

Lillian's off-stage performances likewise impressed all who saw or read about her exploits in the daily newspapers. Because of her familiarity with and availability to reporters, she received more press coverage than all of Chicago's social elite.

In order to visit the race track, Lillian changed her matinees from Saturday to Thursday. Later, she dropped Saturday evening shows altogether, to embark on weekend trips to other cities, booking private train cars to accommodate all her guests.

She sponsored frequent picnics, often for charity. She was party to afternoon carriage rides to the Fair, outings that sometimes included visiting royalty. Her frequent visits to the race track, usually with Harvard-educated heavyweight boxing champion turned actor "Gentleman Jim" Corbett or rough frontiersman-turned-smooth Wild West Show impresario "Buffalo Bill" Cody, were reportable social events in themselves. One of her initial excursions received front page notice.

With her usual entourage, Lillian attended Derby Day at Washington Park. The social elite of Chicago, proudly puritanical, did not admire actresses in general and were very uncomfortable with Lillian in particular. Her appearance in the exclusive clubhouse caused no little apprehension among the women, and the doyennes of Chicago society requested that Lillian be asked to leave. According to the *Chicago Tribune*, she did so willingly, being given, out of consideration by the management, "one of the best [boxes] in the grandstand." To the consternation of these "proper" women, Lillian received admirers between each race and "all sorts greeted her." As Emmett Dedmon wrote in his book, *Fabulous Chicago*:

> If society did snub her, its satisfaction must have been spoiled the next day when the reporters put her name at the top of their lists of women at the races.[5]

The race track was Lillian's primary amusement. Her visits to the best local restaurants were a close second. Breaking one of her old rules, she frequently went out to eat after an evening performance, followed from the stage door by reporters and accompanied by a high-profile, elegantly dressed, bejeweled admirer named, appropriately, "Diamond Jim" Brady.

James Buchanan Brady's life could not have been more different than Lillian's. Born in 1856, of Irish immigrant parents, he grew up in one of the toughest waterfront sections of lower Manhattan. His father owned a saloon, and Brady's youthful experiences at the establishment would later lead him never to drink. His mother was a warm and tender person who always had a helping hand for the needy. Though he strongly disliked violence, Jimmy Brady was a fat young boy who learned to rely on his fists to open a narrow path inside a constrained world.

At age 11, a loner, unhappy with his new stepfather, he quietly left home to work as a messenger in a hotel. Four years at the hotel taught him much about the social behavior of the time. He learned manners and how to speak correctly. He also learned how to be a "sport," an important aspect of socialization that would help him throughout his career. A "sport," he noted, usually wore a heavy, gold watch chain, flashed diamonds, spoke in a booming, confident voice and, at appropriate times, ordered drinks for the house. Young Brady's hotel experience also developed his appreciation for food, both in quality and quantity.

At 15, he was hired to work in the baggage room at the Grand Central railroad terminal. Meanwhile, he put himself through night school to learn reading and penmanship. Within two years, his good work got him appointed station agent; a year later, he was elevated to office clerk; and, at 21, he was appointed chief clerk, at a salary of $50 a week. Earning a respectable income gave Brady the opportunity to purchase good clothes, eat at the best restaurants and attend the theater. He soon became infatuated with the actress Lotta Crabtree and closely followed her career as an anonymous, adoring fan.

Brady left the railroad to work as a salesman for a railway supply firm. While his demeanor as a salesman was somewhat crude, he was friendly, genial and honest; he knew the railroad business thoroughly. The result was almost instant success. Within three years, he became the company's top salesman. His timing could not have been better; he was selling railroad equipment at the height of railroad expansion during the 1880s. Using his knowledge of the industry to instill confidence, he became a shrewd judge of his customers. His philosophy of "if you are going to make money, you have to look like money" translated into a public persona that wore more diamonds than others, spent more money than others, and had more women at his side than anyone else. Not surprisingly, when asked to describe the man, a fellow salesman called him "Diamond Jim."

Collecting diamonds became a passion for Brady. On his travels, he would haunt pawnbrokers in every city, buying the gems after hard-nosed negotiating. At the same time, having become a well-known salesman and larger-than-life social hound, his ongoing interest in entertainment made him a theater buff and frequent first-nighter, while his free-spending habits gave him entrée to the theater's inner circle.

The Panic of 1893 hit the railroad business particularly hard. Within a few years, most railroads were in receivership. Luckily, Brady had no money invested in railroads or stocks. Instead, his entire estate was in cash and diamonds, so he was generally unaffected by the Panic. Since he had little to do during the summer of 1893, he decided to vacation in Chicago, taking in the Fair and visiting all the good restaurants he could find.

When Lillian came to Chicago, she rented a fashionable home on the South Side, in the same neighborhood as the Armours, Pullmans and Fields. Lillian, Jr., came with her, along with Cynthia, maids, carriages and a coachman. While Lillian performed and partied, Lillian, Jr., was taken to the Fair or beach each day and accompanied her mother on weekend excursions. Cynthia spent all of her time with Susan B. Anthony or occupied by events at the Woman's Building. Not once did she venture to visit Charles. He had been badly hurt by the Panic and, in the late summer, had to declare the bankruptcy of his printing firm. Ever loyal to her father, Lillian helped him out financially until he could reopen, a year later.

Yet for all her publicity and brilliant reputation — possibly *because* of it — Lillian was not accepted by the Chicago social elite, as she was by their peers in New York. Consequently, she had little choice but to associate with fellow entertainers. Meanwhile, Brady regularly attended her shows and frequently invited her to dinner. Lillian soon replaced Lotta Crabtree as his theatrical idol. Their dinners together became the catalyst that created a life long friendship between two apparently dissimilar people.

While their early years and upbringing had been very different, Lillian's and Brady's needs and motivations proved to be quite similar. Both performed in an unconventional but effective manner, often going beyond the acceptable boundaries of propriety to achieve success. Both knew the value of an adoring and loyal audience. Both sought love, affection, confirmation of their behavior and uncompromising trust to fill the void of loneliness that pervaded their private lives. Even their physical differences — they were often labeled Beauty and the Beast — made them all the more compatible, as the relationship never threatened to "deteriorate" into romance.

Brady was attentive, devoted and loyal to Lillian. He was kind, gentle and delighted in her career as much as she did. He felt honored to enjoy her company and to be accepted by her. A lonely man who was well aware that his spending habits attracted friends, Brady knew that the many diamonds he gave Lillian would not alter their feelings for one another. In fact, he was proud that she used them in the same way he would; after all, it made headlines for them both.

Likewise, Lillian was able to confide all of her problems and conflicts to Brady because he could be trusted. His native insight into human behavior, honed by many years as a salesman and negotiator, helped her both professionally and personally. She depended on his advice. And when her public performance was under the microscopic scrutiny of strait-laced society, she could turn to him for companionship and understanding. Diamond Jim Brady was Lillian's only non-romantic male friend, and their friendship lasted until his death in 1917.

Together, they achieved great gourmand triumphs in Chicago restaurants, highlighted by contests to determine who, at one sitting, could eat the most corn-on-the-cob, Brady's favorite food. Reporters covering these contests would bet among themselves about how many ears of corn might be consumed by the contestants. Brady would always win (legend had it that he possessed an enlarged stomach), but Lillian proved fiercely competitive.

At the start of one contest, Lillian excused herself prior to the food's being brought to the table. Returning, she gave a package to the restaurant owner for safekeeping, sat down with Brady and began the gustatory orgy. Afterwards, as she and Brady were leaving, Lillian retrieved the package. Asked by reporters what was inside, she revealed her secret strategy. The package contained her corset!

In spite of continual sellouts through August, rumors spread that Lillian and T. Henry French were about to terminate their business relationship. Along with the announcement that the Lillian Russell Opera Company would close at the Columbia September 2 came the declaration that Canary and Lederer had obtained a lease for the Casino Theater and:

> …they claim they have contracted for the service of Lillian Russell, who will head her own opera company bearing her name, which will be the permanent attraction of the house.[6]

It was reported that Lillian would receive $700 a week and half the profits.

French was in financial trouble. The cost of running the company, not to mention that of Lillian's salary, was more than he was able to generate, even from a good run at the Columbia Theater. French had been unable to lease a theater in New York for the coming season and had no new show in which he could feature Lillian. He had no choice but to give her up.

Canary and Lederer, on the other hand, had joined forces to obtain the Casino and take advantage of Lillian's popularity, only enhanced by the fact that her Chicago exploits had been duly covered in the New York papers. Canary had the money; Lederer was the theater business professional.

George Lederer was the same age as Lillian and had begun his professional career at age 12, acting in a comic opera production. Over the next decade, he wrote vaudeville sketches and worked at the drama desk of the *New York Journal*. His first producing venture came in 1878, and he soon became a prosperous manager through his profitable touring companies and hard-nosed, financial approach to management.

George W. Lederer, who, with Thomas Canary, took over management of the Casino Theater in 1893. Lederer had spent the previous fifteen years turning out mediocre shows. As boss of the Casino for almost a decade, however, he became famous for producing many successful comic operas and musicals.

Obtaining the lease on the Casino, which he held for almost a decade, made him one of the most successful producers of the time.

Canary and Lederer took official possession of the Casino at the end of October. A few weeks before, they initiated rehearsals for their first comic opera production, *Princess Nicotine*, starring Lillian, to open November 20. Their plan was to play the opera on the road for a few weeks before opening in New York, but the plan was never implemented because preparing for the show's elaborate production values took longer than expected.

During rehearsals, in a little-noticed press announcement four days before the opening of *Princess Nicotine*, the New York Supreme Court gave consent for the annulment of Lillian's marriage to Edward Solomon. She was granted permission to resume use of her maiden name and given sole custody of Lillian, Jr. A free woman again, Lillian was quoted as saying:

> You think I am going to be married at once. But I am not. I am done with married life. Watch me for five years.[7]

Princess Nicotine opened November 20, to a full house, loud cheers for Lillian and good reviews from the critics. Given the overall response to the new show, lamentations about the decline of comic opera seemed premature. Like most of Lillian's shows, the supporting cast was excellent. It featured Digby Bell, who had been stolen from Klaw and Erlanger for a price; Charles Bigelow, an accomplished comedian; and a newcomer to the comic opera stage, Marie Dressler, a young (24), self-effacing actress with a pleasant voice, who could elicit riotous laughter with her stage pratfalls. Gustave Kerker, now the dean of musical conductors in New York, led the orchestra.

The story told of the marriage between a pretty cigarette maker, Rosa, and a rich tobacco planter. The local governor wanted Rosa for himself. After the usual series of complications, misinterpreted intents, escapes, returns, and explanations came the inevitable happy ending. The *Dramatic Mirror* reported:

> *Princess Nicotine* appeared to have caught the fancy of the first night audience at the Casino. This was due primarily to the singing and magnetism of Lillian Russell in the title role, and secondarily to the melodiousness of the score and the romantic nature of the story. Miss Russell received a double encore for her rendering of the cigarette song at the end of the first act, and was frequently applauded throughout the performance.[8]

Dressler played the role of the Duchess. For Lillian, she was the perfect comic foil. Not a pretty woman, large by even the standards of the time, Dressler bumped and stumbled her way across the stage, tripping or falling over every conceivable obstacle, real or imagined, to the delight of the audience. It was a

Program for *The Princess Nicotine*, with Lillian as Rosa. It was during this run that Signor Giovanni Perugini was hired to sing the leading tenor role. Within a few weeks, audiences noticed that there was more than simply acting going on between Lillian and Perugini. (Harry Ransom Humanities Research Center, the University of Texas at Austin.)

role she had already perfected in previous variety shows and was to make hugely successful in the future.

Dressler had been born in Canada in 1869, into a family comprised of an unstable father and a warm, gentle, and loving mother. Her father, authoritarian and prejudiced, had a severe temper. But he loved music and performed it often, both at home and as a livelihood. Because of his erratic income, however, the family moved often. Marie was an ugly child, both fat and awkward. But her sister Bonita was considered beautiful. Where Bonita got attention because of her beauty, Marie found she could get attention and elicit laughter by being clumsy.

Dressler found the stage a way to earn a living simply by acting out the way she naturally behaved. Coupled with a good voice, a talent for improvisation and the ability to remember her lines, she quickly obtained work in touring companies. An early, abrupt marriage to a fellow actor lasted only a short time and convinced Marie that

MARIE DRESSLER

Though Marie Dresseler had a long and successful career in musical comedy and vaudeville, it was her later appearances in both silent and talking pictures that provided national recognition and plaudits for her acting skills.

her career had to come before any romantic attachments.

When Dressler tried out for the role in *Princess Nicotine*, Lillian took an immediate liking to her. She, in turn, respected Lillian, who also became her mentor. The friendship was a mutually beneficial attraction of opposites that seemed to satisfy their symbiotic needs.

Dressler was not physically attractive and seemed to wear clothes in a haphazard fashion. She was a natural comedienne, a "joker," instinctively adept at slapstick. Lillian's elegant, poised, confident, graceful demeanor made a dramatic contrast. Moreover, Dressler was in no way a threat to Lillian, no female competition.

Dressler looked upon Lillian as the embodiment of all that she wished for herself yet knew she could never attain. In fact, she obtained considerable vicarious satisfaction simply by being close to Lillian. For her part, Lillian seemed to view Marie as a younger sister who sought guidance and training in both the theatrical and social arts. Like an older sister, she could protect Marie and assist in her career. When Marie mentioned the salary Lederer paid her, Lillian got her friend a raise. When one of the companies Marie was employed by failed, Lillian took her in until a new job was found. And Marie often stayed at Lillian's 77th Street home when playing in New York.

In many ways, their personal experiences were parallel. Each had one parent who was irrational and one who was loving. Their homes had been ruled by authoritarian people. They both sought affection, love and recognition, but found it only in the world of theater. Neither woman seemed able to find the "right" man. No doubt they spent long hours discussing their respective lives, both personal and professional. It was not surprising, then, that Marie Dressler became one of the few genuine female friends Lillian ever had.

While the Casino was constantly filled for *Princess Nicotine*, Lederer continued to tinker with the production itself. Dialogue was added; Lillian was given some new songs to sing; performers were replaced. Lederer reported that, because of the show's improvement, *Princess Nicotine* would remain at the Casino until March before going on tour. He also announced that, on December 22, Signor Giovanni Perugini would replace Perry Averill as lead tenor.

"Signor Perugini" had been born Jack Chatterton in upstate Michigan in 1855. Until he appeared in small roles in operatic companies in the 1880s, very little is known of his early years. By that time, he had changed his name, grown a mustache and adopted the somewhat affected if stylish persona of a dashing, aristocratic Italian tenor with an excellent voice. Henry Abbey hired him to sing opposite the celebrated Adelina Patti at the Metropolitan Opera, and Perugini's career singing premier operatic roles was assured. He seemed to be more favorably received in Europe than in the U.S. and spent most of his professional time there. For the three years previous to appearing in *Princess Nicotine*, he had been performing in London.

Perugini had sailed to New York in the fall for a vacation, accompanied by Madame Nordica, the Metropolitan Opera's prima donna. On the ship, for amusement, they hired a famous palm reader to tell their fortunes. The reader examined Perugini's hand and, after a moment's consideration, stated, "You are going to be married shortly."

"Nonsense," exclaimed the tenor, believing the suggestion preposterous.

"You will be married within the year, to one of your own profession," the reader went on. Both Perugini and Nordica laughed at the suggestion and dismissed the man. "You may laugh," he insisted, "but before next summer arrives, you will be the husband of a great singer and beautiful woman."

No further thought was given to the prediction.

While Perugini was resting in New York, the Clipper announced that Perry Averill was to be replaced in *Princess Nicotine*. Perugini acted on the news immediately, believing he could fill the role more artistically. He wrote to Lillian, asking for an interview regarding the tenor part. She replied amiably and set up an appointment at her home. Lillian had never heard Perugini sing, but she had met him several times in the past at social gatherings. And, after one of Averill's "off-nights," Digby Bell had remarked, "Queen, why should Chicos be performed in this ridiculous way, when so fine an artist as Perugini is going to Italy because no one in America has sense enough to engage him?"

Arriving for the appointment with Lillian, Perugini found that she was not at home. Indignant, he returned to his quarters and wrote her another letter indicating his displeasure about the snub he had received. Lillian wrote back immediately and apologized. Their next interview ended in the employment of Perugini for *Princess Nicotine*. It was the beginning of a whirlwind romance reminiscent of a comic opera plot.

In the first act of the opera, Chicos (Perugini) climbs a tree to wait for his lover (Lillian). When he sees her enter, he gives a great sigh of love. Separating the branches, he descends from the tree to embrace her and express his ardor. Within two weeks of Perugini's taking over the tenor role, both audiences and people backstage noticed that more than mere acting was taking place.

A week later, January 11, 1894, the *New York Herald* scooped everyone else with the headlines:

Signor Giovanni Perugini (a.k.a. Jack Chatterton), Lillian's third husband. Lillian was initially attracted to his elegant dress, polished European manners and professional demeanor. His egocentric behavior, abusiveness and desire to co-star with his new wife soon persaded Lillian of their incompatibility. (Harry Ransom Humanities Research Center, the University of Texas at Austin.)

Lillian Russell To Wed Again

The Comic Opera Diva Will Marry Tenor Perugini in This City After Easter

She Is Tired of Single Life

Then, Too, She Hopes Her Marriage Will Put an End to the Gossip About Her[9]

The announcement surprised everyone. The newspapers made a point of reminding Lillian that, only a month earlier, she had stated she was no longer interested in marriage.

Yes, I did say only a few months ago that I was done with married life, but I've changed my mind. Why? Well, I'll tell you. Signor Perugini is a gentleman; he is a dear, good fellow and he has asked me to marry him.... But in addition to that, I am tired of reading these reports of my approaching marriage in the papers. I am only a woman, after all, and these rumors — all of which have been false, of course — have both annoyed and hurt me. I hope my marriage will put an end to that sort of thing.[10]

Lillian's audiences wanted to know why she should get married in any case. They seemed to enjoy her more when she was single. Manager Lederer pointed out that a clause in his contract with Lillian stipulated she agreed not to marry while working with him. "I jokingly reminded her of that," he said, "but, of course, we shall impose no objection to her marriage." He knew it would help the box office considerably. A *New York World* reporter confirmed the story with a visit to the show's evening performance and an interview afterward.

> The way she made love to Chicos last night was simply outrageous, and he — well, his voice fairly trembled with emotion; and Lillian — that is Rosa, the Princess Nicotine — dressed in her white bridal attire, and looking more lovely than ever, sang her "Good Night" song.[11]

When the reporter saw her backstage, "her cheeks were flushed with excitement" and "her eyes beamed with tenderness."

"Yes, it is true," she said. "I am to be married. There ought to be some happiness in store for me; my road, heretofore, has been rocky enough." The reporter surely agreed with that assessment.

The marriage date was set for March 18. The fact that Perugini was Catholic and Lillian Episcopalian seemed to be of little import. But a few days later, a judge of the State Supreme Court raised questions about Lillian's remarriage. State law required that, before a divorced person could remarry in New York, the person to whom the decree had been granted had to have lived a good, moral life for the past five years. Lillian and Perugini decided to marry at her home January 20, but her attorney, Mr. Hummel, informed her that she could not marry in the state, at least for the present.

Lillian flew into uncharacteristic rage. She proclaimed she didn't care what the law might be. Then she swore she would be married anyway. Upon receiving another note from Hummel, she quieted down but was still defiant when she reached the theater. She refused to see reporters but sent out a message that "there will be no postponement. The program will be carried out!"

Perugini seemed very disturbed, but he revealed his immediate plans, which suggested the wedding was forthcoming.

> I have won a dear, dear woman and I am very happy. Where and when the wedding will take place does not concern the public. I will give a little farewell dinner in my bachelor apartments, and that shows our marriage is imminent. There will be about 20 of my friends there and it means goodbye to the old bachelor days.[12]

They were married the next day, but not in New York. At nine in the morning, messenger boys were delivering flowers and packages at the front steps of 318 W. 77th Street. At ten o'clock, a carriage stopped before the front door. Three elegantly dressed women stepped out the door and into a carriage. They were Lillian's mother (who obviously sanctioned the match) and Lillian's sisters, Susan and Hattie. Then the door opened again. Dressed in an exquisite costume of pale pink silk, Lillian sailed down the stairs and into the coach. The coach door slammed shut. With a crack of the whip and a clatter of hooves on cobblestones, the passengers were off to an unknown destination.

The coachman had been given orders to drive fast and attempt to elude the reporters who had stationed themselves around Lillian's home since the previous evening. The intrepid reporters, however, not duped by the circuitous route taken by the coachman, held close on his heels. Down Columbus Avenue, through 59th Street to Fifth Avenue, then south to 42nd Street and Broadway sped the entourage. Cynthia had discovered the pursuers and was seen waving a menacing finger at them. Down 14th Street the procession rattled, heading for the Hoboken ferry.

With considerably less fanfare, Perugini had already made his way to Hoboken via the downtown ferry. With him were his valet and best man. At Justice of the Peace Moeller's house, all awaited the bride.

When Lillian arrived, she rushed up the stairs to be greeted by her husband-to-be. "Hello, Jack," she greeted him, grasping his hand. "How do you feel?"

Within minutes, in the center of the parlor, the ceremony began. Beside Perugini's attendants and Lillian's relatives stood Leander Richardson, the only press representative allowed.

The ceremony was brief. The bride and groom exchanged rings. As Perugini slipped the band on Lillian's finger, he bent and kissed her hand. Upon being pronounced man and wife, he kissed her tenderly on the lips and remarked, "Now, gentlemen, each in turn. Let there be no crowding." Justice Moeller was first and, according to Richardson, "threw his three pretty daughters watching into a panic."

The entire ceremony lasted 12 minutes. On her way out the door, Lillian handed the judge tickets for a box at the Casino for him and his family to occupy that evening. Returning to their 77th Street home, the couple spent the afternoon in seclusion. A bridal dinner was held, which included the entire party, plus Madame Nordica, Lillian's favorite opera diva. In deference to the Lenten Season, there would be no formal function until after Easter, when the many wedding gifts were displayed, along with the names of the donors.

Reactions from the interested parties were varied. The *Dramatic Mirror* commented:

> It may be supposed that Lillian Russell and Signor Perugini are singing and acting the leading roles with more spirit and intensity than ever before.[13]

A skeptical theater manager observed:

> Don't you think it is unwise for a prima donna like Russell to be married? Americans don't like married prima donnas, and I am very suprised that Lederer gave his consent.[14]

Perugini talked about going "from bachelorhood to ... paradise?"

Susan, Lillian's younger sister, remarked, "It is all very pretty. But Nell, dear, if your memory should want jogging at any time, come to see sister Susie."

Both Dressler and Brady were taken aback by Lillian's quick decision to marry Perugini. Brady responded stoically. Dressler did not like Perugini — she often chided him for his pomposity — and warned Lillian that her decision was a grave mistake.

Lederer was forced to put *Princess Nicotine* on the road at the end of January, because he had not paid the lease interest demanded by the Casino bondholders. (There was some question whether he actually had the money to pay it.) Lillian became aware of Lederer's predicament and reacted by beginning to explore other professional possibilities. One such opportunity was to sing with Henry Abbey and appear in London in the fall.

The *Princess Nicotine* tour took the company to Baltimore, Brooklyn, Washington, D.C., Philadelphia, Boston, Hartford and New Haven (where it entertained the Yale students), always playing to full houses and excellent reviews for Lillian. By contrast, Perugini was mentioned infrequently; when he was, it was as Lillian's husband. The tour was profitable, enabling Lederer to pay his debt and allow the Lillian Russell Opera Company to return to the Casino by the end of March.

But Lillian and Perugini were now having obvious marital problems. Company members noticed periods of time when the two didn't speak to one another. Midway through the tour, they secured separate dressing rooms. Lillian would attempt to extend the evening after the show, apparently delaying the time when she had to return to their rooms. Marie Dressler reported an episode in which Perugini requested of Lederer that he be co-starred with Lillian. When Lederer refused, it seemed to Dressler that Perugini became abusive toward his wife and upbraided her in public.

The company returned to the Casino and opened March 27 with a revival of *Girofle-Girofla*. Lederer believed it was too soon to play *Princess Nicotine* again, and he was aware that *Girofle-Girofla* was one of Lillian's greatest triumphs. The reviews reflected positive audience reactions both to the comic opera and to Lillian; Perugini, however, was not at all pleased.

Lillian in the dual role of Girofle-Girofla, in the comic opera of the same name at the Casino Theater. It was during this run that she and Perugini separated, generating considerable negative publicity for Lillian. (Harry Ransom Humanities Research Center, the University of Texas at Austin.)

> *Girofle-Girofla* was revived before an audience that overflowed the seating spaces. It is doubtful if Miss Russell ever sang the dual role as well as she did on Tuesday night, and she certainly never threw more spirit into her acting of it. Signor Giovanni Perugini was more interesting from mere juxtaposition, than he was effective either vocally or in acting.[15]

The increasingly strained relations between Lillian and Perugini did not prevent them from giving a reception at their home after Easter. It was billed as Lillian's first formal social affair as hostess. In reporting the party, the press described Lillian's gown, the service, the food and the guest list. None mentioned anything about Perugini.

In fact, very few of Perugini's friends had been invited. Among the theatrical managers attending were Oscar Hammerstein, Rudolph Aronson, Canary and Lederer; correspondents from London and New York papers appeared in abundance; also attending were a number of comic opera composers and librettists. Friends included Digby Bell, Madame Nordica, Marie Dressler and Jim Brady. Reporters noted that Lillian and Perugini seemed to ignore each other throughout the party. What was going on between them?

Girofle-Girofla played at the Casino until the end of April, then went on tour in

Eastern cities. Lillian's definitive break with Perugini occurred in Philadelphia. During one of the show's scenes, Perugini made derogatory asides to Lillian, unintelligible to the audience but loud enough for other performers on stage to hear. Dressler was so outraged by his comments that she threatened, "I'll throw you into the bass drum," and chased him to his dressing room.

A few evenings later, in their hotel room, Perugini became physically abusive to Lillian and attempted, according to her rescuers, to throw her from the window of their seventh floor rooms. Lillian directed him to leave and never again return to her 77th Street home. For the next two weeks, however, they continued to perform together.

At the Amphion Theater in Brooklyn, some stage behavior between them received newspaper coverage. Allusions to matrimony in the script caused audiences to hoot, laugh and nudge one another in obvious derision of the "happy couple." When Perugini tried to kiss Lillian, she stepped behind another actor to evade his embrace. A duet between them was peremptorily cut from the third act. Even the theater manager was surprised when Perugini appeared at all in the last act. The fact that the audience had made fun of Lillian annoyed her immensely.

At about the same time, and not coincidentally, Lillian announced she would not perform under Canary and Lederer's management the following season. Supposedly, they could no longer afford her; and their debt threatened the continued use of the Casino. As part of a suggested settlement, Lillian would fill the remainder of the season, and Canary and Lederer would release her at the close of the present tour. Henry Abbey was said to be ready to sign Lillian for the coming season.

This time, instead of being in sympathy with Lillian's problems, as they had so often been in the past, the theatrical press published editorials expressing disapproval of her behavior:

> There seems to be nothing left for Lillian Russell to break — not even a contract. She has signed with Abbey and left her late manager lamenting. Miss Russell and her extraordinary affairs, matrimonial and otherwise, have occupied an utterly absurd amount of space in the columns of the daily press, off and on during the past ten years. The thing has been overdone to such an extent that the public is getting nauseated. It is a matter of public note that Miss Russell's business fell off and her audiences guyed her during the final weeks of the tour.
>
> There are limits to toleration, as there are limits to patience. After a certain point of unsavory notoriety is passed, it takes more than artistic ability to restrain the public from open revolt. There are certain social laws which may be broken once too often by persons in public life.[16]

Lillian struck back. In an exclusive interview with the *New York Herald*, she stated her position concerning Perugini and their marital disagreements. She considered Perugini artistic and refined, a man with "grace of manner and spirituality." Even so, she noted, her consent to marriage had been reluctantly given and "the night before the ceremony was performed, I sat and thought gravely over the subject, fearing that I was about to make a mistake. I was grossly deceived!"

To her dismay, she had found that Perugini wanted to rule her, dictate who should be her friends, where she should go, what she should do. He had even threatened to discharge her servants.

She went on to say, "If a woman marries a man she can respect, she'll cherish him." She had accepted him as an equal, but he had not reciprocated. Perugini had even admitted during one of their arguments "that he had never loved me, but that he had married me for artistic position purely."

Lillian finished by leveling a threat:

> I do not wish to injure the unfortunate man. But if he should dare to attack me in the public prints, should presume to answer what I charitably assign as the only reason for our separation, I will come forward with details that will astonish people.[17]

Instead of defending himself, Perugini sailed for England, promising to return in the fall to press a lawsuit for divorce. The company had closed the season two weeks early, "caused by bad business, due to the airing of Miss Russell's marital troubles to the public." It was announced that Lillian would appear in London in July, under Abbey's management. Lillian's business representative Edward Peiper also mentioned that:

> ...Miss Russell will remain in Europe and appear there in public for at least a year. She will sing both in Great Britain and the continent.[18]

But no sooner had the announcement been issued than newspaper headlines disclosed that Lillian was confined at home, ill due to a "necessary surgical operation." She would be unable to leave for England as soon as promised.

According to the newspapers, it had been Lillian's intention to retire to a private hospital to undergo the surgery. Instead, she decided to have the operation at home. For security reasons?

Why?, inquired the reporters. What kind of surgery was performed?

Lillian's family physician, accompanied by Cynthia, informed the press that Lillian had suffered from "a simple ailment, incident in many cases to motherhood." The operation was successfully performed, said Cynthia, and Lillian would be able to leave her home in a week. A short rest in Saratoga would follow.

Reference was made to the fact that the current "trouble" had arisen from the birth of Lillian, Jr. Reporters pointed out that the birth had occurred ten years previously. Other observers suggested that Lillian's decision to undergo the operation at home indicated a desire for secrecy. Moreover, why was the operation taking place now, at so crucial a juncture in her career?

All available information implied that Lillian had an abortion. Had she been impregnated by Perugini? Possibly, though Lillian would later claim their marriage had never been consummated.

While Lillian recovered and prepared for her trip to London, she was handed a summons to appear in court, courtesy of Canary and Lederer. The managers had received an order in the New York Supreme Court restraining Lillian from appearing under any other management until after the expiration of her contract with them, an obligation that supposedly extended for another year. Lillian ignored the restraining order and continued her travel preparations.

To protect his own investment, Henry Abbey's lawyers gave notification they would appear on Lillian's behalf, thus freeing her to go to London and perform in Abbey's new production. Indeed, Lillian and Abbey left together for England at the end of July.

The following week, arguments in the case against Lillian were heard. Much to the consternation of Canary and Lederer, the judge delayed his decision.

In the meantime, Lillian began her rehearsals for *The Queen of Brilliants*, a new comic opera that was to open at the Lyceum Theater, London, in September. The *Dramatic Mirror* suggested that Lillian was again leaving the country with marital problems and broken contracts trailing her, just as she had done in 1883.

In the press, Abbey bragged relentlessly about the new opera. The chorus would be 100 voices strong; performers from the U.S. were being brought in to support Lillian, including Lillian's sister Susan and Susan's husband, Owen Westford. The *London Referee* confirmed Abbey's preparations:

> It will thus be gathered that everything that astuteness and money can obtain will be brought into requisition by Mr. Abbey for Miss Russell's support during her forthcoming London season.[19]

Back in the U.S., a New York Supreme Court judge declared that Lillian might sing for any manager she chose until October 1, when the vacation season ended. After that date, however, she was enjoined from singing for anyone other than Canary and Lederer. Lederer immediately cabled Lillian:

> Injunction restraining you from singing from October 1, 1894, sustained. Rehearsals begin September 10. You are requested to report Casino, New York on that day.[20]

Lederer went on to claim that "she cannot settle with us. We want her here by October 1 to go on tour under our management as her contract binds her to do."

Lillian refused Lederer's demands. Preparations for the opening of *The Queen of Brilliants* continued. The New York press calculated that Lillian would have to leave for New York one day after the opening of her London engagement in order to return in time for the requisite performance in the U.S. "In that event," they surmised, "her London engagement would be the shortest on record."

The Queen of Brilliants opened at the Lyceum Theater September 8, to a large audience. In spite of Lillian's performance, the comic opera itself proved a flop:

> Lillian Russell has never been in better voice. There is nothing more gorgeous on the light opera stage. It is a mediocre play with a weak book and the music is not catching. The excessive magnificence of the scenery actually smothered the performers. Dullness seemed to be the unpardonable sin of both composer and author.[21]

Critics pointed out that Lillian had more costume changes (nine) than songs (three). "The audience wants singing, not posturing," they proclaimed.

Soon after such critical reviews of the show, the lawsuit with Canary and Lederer was suddenly resolved. Obviously, Abbey was concerned about the financial prospects of the production and eager to keep his losses to a minimum. The theater managers agreed to share the benefits and burdens of Lillian's management. She would return to the U.S. to open at Abbey's Theater, New York, on November 5, in *The Queen of Brilliants*.

Newspapers now shifted their attention to the Jersey City court where Perugini had just filed divorce papers against Lillian. He claimed desertion and his wife's refusal to live with him. He stated that his domestic troubles were due to Lillian's infatuation with playing poker, which she indulged with other men to all hours of the night. He further stated that his wife ignored his expressed wishes regarding her choice of friends; he didn't like Dressler or Brady. "She refused to obey my instructions and asserted her right to do as she pleased," Perugini claimed.

When Lillian suggested Perugini was abusive and conceited, he responded hysterically:

> She used my rouge; she misplaced my manicure set; she used my special handkerchief perfume for her bath; she always wanted the best mirror. ... Once when I became excited because she had moved my bandolier, she threatened to spank me, and she did, with a hairbrush, too. You must publish a contradiction of what Lillian said. I want you to say she laces and wears false hair and is horribly made up, and is not the least bit pretty off the stage.[22]

HENRY E. ABBEY

Henry Abbey managed some of the country's greatest actors, among them Edwin Booth and E.A. Southern. He was instrumental in bringing acclaimed foreign performers and productions to the U.S. In 1893, he built Abbey's Theater to promote legitimate theater on Broadway.

It was in response to these accusations that Lillian intimated their marriage had never been consummated. Though her assertion deflected any connection between her surgery and her marriage to Perugini, it unavoidably raised other questions regarding the propriety of Lillian's behavior.

In spite of Perugini's remarks, Lillian's recent adventures were regarded quite negatively and her popularity suffered a precipitous decline. Pictures and quotes disappeared from women's magazines, and the daily press buried reports of her activities in a distant corner of the theater page. Just prior to her opening at Abbey's Theater, New York, the *Dramatic Mirror* published a scathing editorial, not only denouncing Lillian's behavior, but even disparaging her physical appeal:

> Lillian Russell went to London, was seen, failed to conquer, and has returned, bringing her complacency back intact. *The Queen of Brilliants*, in which Miss Russell will appear soon at Abbey's, seems to resemble an

overstuffed woman. Of ribbons and geegaws there is a superb abundance, of real qualities of excellence there are few.

It is impossible to feel serious disappointment in Miss Russell's foreign experiences. In point of popularity, it is true, she has long held first place in the field of American comic opera, but her prominence and success does not strengthen faith in the knowledge, the taste, or the judgment of the numerous class that forms the following here of a prima donna of this order.

Miss Russell possesses beauty of the doughy sort that ravishes the fancy of the half-baked worshippers of pink-and-white pudginess. But the beauty that has its roots in acute intelligence and sparkling animation, she possesses not. She sings well enough. Her acting powers resemble those that are generously displayed in the front row of the chorus.

When you compare the performance Miss Russell hasgiven in such classics as *La Grand Duchess* and *Girofle-Girofla* with those of any of the women, French, English or American, that were mistresses of this effervescent art, the wonder is that Miss Russell's ponderous exhibitions have been received with a large measure of public favor.

There is nothing champagney about her, there is only a bovine self-complacency, supported by spiritless, puttified "good looks" and a well-trained voice in which I have never been able to detect the sympathetic quality. Sympathy indicates sensibility, and sensibility is not Miss Russell's most conspicuous attribute, either as a prima donna of comic opera or otherwise.[23]

The Queen of Brilliants opened November 7 at Abbey's Theater. Reviews of the comic opera were caustic:

If the original English book was worse than the present one, it must have been a very bad work. There is a story, of course, and that which by courtesy may be called a plot, but it is extremely difficult to discover it during the progress of the performance, and it would be utterly incoherent without the aid of the auditor's imagination.[24]

The combination of negative publicity and critical reviews doomed the show. Attendance was light; financial losses were high. To Abbey's relief, *The Queen of Brilliants* closed in four weeks. The *Dramatic Mirror* offered no reference to Lillian, writing only of the show. Other newspapers discussed what the proper manners of an actress should be, and the fact that Lillian had broken all the rules. The *Clipper* reported, almost gleefully:

The engagement that Lillian Russell closed at Abbey's on Saturday night was the worst patronized of any she played in this city. Circumstances indicate that her popularity as an individual attraction is waning rapidly.[25]

When the curtain fell that night, Lillian returned home miserable, anxious and humbled. The tumultuous events of the year had taken their effect on her. Her career appeared to be in ruin. A good portion of her public had deserted her. Almost overnight, public and professional opinions about her had forever changed the understanding of what it meant to be a "prima donna." A phrase once intended to confer high praise on an actress or singer whose gifts and skills won her recognition as "first lady" of a company would now come to be used as derogatory code, indicating excessive ego, volatile temperament and a penchant for flouting social norms.

For the moment, only Jim Brady remained by her side to console her, hold her hand and remind her that Lillian Russell had redeemed herself before.

Chapter Six

Requiem for Comic Opera

"Is Miss Russell in?"

"Yes. She is expecting you."

A moment later, Lillian, splendid in an elegant gown and an abundance of diamonds, rose to receive her visitor. She gave her the hearty Lillian Russell handclasp and the dazzling Lillian Russell smile, then led the woman to a dressing room chair. The dark-eyed, dark-haired woman, dressed in mourning clothes, carried a worn traveling bag.

"Mrs. Haverly," Lillian exclaimed, "how clever of you to come among your friends and give us a chance to buy the things we need, without the bother of going to the shops."

As the woman opened her bag, Lillian continued, "I want some cold cream, some powder and some rouge. And of course, some toilet water. All named after Jack Haverly, you say? Then, of course, they are the best."

The contents of the bag were quickly placed on Lillian's dressing table and a crisp green note was transferred from Lillian's gold chatelaine to the woman's plain, black leather purse. For a brief moment, Lillian studied the woman in mourning, then again extended her hand.

"Mrs. Haverly," she observed, "you are the most cheerful 'broke woman' I ever met."

Every night, carrying her wares, this woman called at the stage doors of New York theaters; some bejeweled personality like Lillian always swung them open for her. She was the recent widow of Col. Jack Haverly, former manager of 14 theaters and 22 road companies, who had provided early employment to Frohman, Hayman and McKee, among the most prosperous managers of the day, and who had himself made and lost over $3 million in his career.

When the woman departed, leaving Lillian alone, the room seemed desolate. "That could be me," Lillian thought. "I could be forced from the stage. And then what would I do?"

Shaking her head in wonder, dusting a bit more powder on her cheeks, Lillian prepared for the evening's performance of *The Grand Duchess*. She was well aware that the show was barely surviving, and one-night stands on the road were increasingly fatiguing. There seemed no doubt that what she did best, comic opera, was losing its market appeal and that she herself had lost a good deal of drawing power. These were insecure times. And it provided little consolation that the specific aspect of performance she had known was not an isolated incident. Musical theater, in general, had entered a period of transition.

With its foreign origins and alien themes, comic opera was rapidly losing favor among American audiences. As U.S. authors, composers and librettists discovered and celebrated America in their scripts and music, American musical comedy developed along distinctly different lines. The newly discovered authenticity of American life, American characters, American manners and customs allowed authors to discard European royalty, foreign armies and exotic and legendary plot lines. As middle-class audiences increasingly embraced vaudeville, comedic farce and musical theater, so too did these theatrical forms increasingly reflect the lives and experiences of a self-consciously "American" audience.

A significant contributor to this change in approach was an old friend of Lillian, De Wolf Hopper. In the early 1890s, his comic opera *Wang*, generated a good deal of popularity and longevity. While its locale was foreign, it was written by an American composer and featured American slang. The show also featured a pert and comely singer, Della Fox, wearing tights and short skirts. Her refreshing simplicity and direct approach to acting satirized the pompous affectations of traditional comic opera.

Back in 1888, Hopper had begun reciting (at Wallack's Theater) a poem clipped from a San Francisco newspaper. His rendition of "Casey at the Bat" soon proved wildly popular. By the early 1890s, Hopper was being urged to recite the poem at his every stage performance. What could be more American than baseball? The poem did not by itself change people's minds about comic opera, but its popularity vividly symbolized the reorientation toward musical theater's new American forms.

A few years later, Hopper played in *Dr. Syntax* with his wife and leading lady, Edna Wallace Hopper. The last scene of the farce-comedy featured a boat race between Harvard and Columbia. Hopper judiciously altered the winner of the race depending upon where the show was playing. In 1896, Hopper appeared in *El Capitan*, its music written by John Philip Sousa. The transformation of American musical theater had by then become familiar to everyone, from authors to audiences.

During the middle 1890s, theater managers and the press alike were using the terms "comic opera" and "musical comedy" interchangeably, although few could give either form a specific definition. It would take the team of Weber and Fields, opening their Broadway Music Hall in the fall of 1896, to lend definition to musical comedy entertainment and chart the direction of its growth during the following decade.

Collateral to these new theatrical trends were changes occurring in New York theater audiences. The primary audiences were now solidly middle-class and included both women and children. Popular theater was the most frequently attended and most widely enjoyed leisure pastime. Audiences were markedly increased as New York became a mecca for tourists. One of the reasons that summer productions now prospered was the dramatic rise in visitors to the city. More theatergoers translated into more theatrical attractions and more theaters. During this period of expansion, there was also a significant increase in the number of new theaters built uptown in the new and more fashionable areas around Broadway and 42nd Street.

Another contributor to larger theater audiences was the accelerated production and distribution of popular songs, to the point that the late 1890s became identified as the "Golden Age of Ballad." Pioneering songwriters, among them Stephen Foster, James A. Butterfield and George Cooper, had ignited an interest in ballads that dealt with the trials and tribulations of the American lifestyle.

Within a few years, traditional songs like "Clementine," "There Is a Tavern in the Town" and "I'll Take You Home Again, Kathleen" evolved into popular, contemporary compositions by songwriters like Harry Von Tilzer, Paul Dresser, Jimmy Thornton and Charles K. Harris, not to mention the stirring marches of John Philip Sousa. The music publishing business grew rapidly, due to the entrepreneurial efforts of promoters like Joseph Stern and the Widmarks. Popular songs of the mid-1890s included "The Sidewalks of New York," "When You Were Sweet Sixteen," "After The Ball," "The Band Played On" and "Sweet Rosie O'Grady." The sale of sheet music, to be played and sung at home and in saloons and beer gardens, increased dramatically, making millions of people familiar with the latest songs and the shows for which many of them were created. Audiences now wanted to be familiar with the music before they attended a show.

Along with the expanding sheet music business came efforts by singers "selling" new songs from the stage, and hoping to become publicly identified with them. It could mean many thousands of dollars additional income for both singers and publishers if such a popular bond could be forged. Many stage performers made their reputations by interpolating new songs into the shows in which they appeared. Just as audiences continually requested Hopper to recite "Casey," they also requested soubrettes to repeat their particular signature songs, often as a "tag-on" added to whatever the current production happened to be.

As popular theater expanded and matured as an industry, a number of shrewd and enterprising entertainment promoters saw an opportunity to take control of its assets (namely, its performers and theaters) and turn them into sizable financial rewards for themselves. By virtue of their astute capacity for business and with uncompromising ruthlessness, they formed a theatrical trust, commonly referred to as the Syndicate.

During the 1895-96 season, it was revealed that a combination of theater managers was being formed to gain control of theaters throughout the country. Chief among these managers were Nixon and Zimmerman in Philadelphia and Klaw, Erlanger, Hayman and Frohman in New York. By early in the year, through agreements and leases, they had obtained control of 37 first-class houses. To each of these houses they guaranteed 30 weeks of attractions. In return, the theater managers would have to accept such performers and attractions as the Syndicate gave them, on the dates it stipulated.

The Syndicate was able to make these demands by signing touring companies and individual performers for extended periods of time. If a local theater manager wanted to have continuous entertainment for the season, he had no choice but to sign with the Syndicate. If a performer or company wanted to have continuous bookings for the season, they would have to agree to the Syndicate's mandates. Managers who opposed this system tried to organize against the Syndicate but failed. Leading performers like Richard Mansfield, Nat Goodwin, and Francis Wilson also attempted to form a coalition of actors, but it never achieved any bargaining power, due to the high costs involved (largely for lawyers and lawsuits) and the unpredictable, transitory nature of an actor's box office appeal.

Within a few years, the Syndicate became so powerful, controlling multiple theaters

in large cities and at least one high-class theater in smaller cities, that few performers could hope for a continuously booked season unless they agreed to the Syndicate's
terms. When the *Dramatic Mirror* sent out a query to 65 theater managers in major
U.S. cities asking their opinion regarding the Syndicate, they received only six replies.
When Francis Wilson drew a cartoon representing the Syndicate as an enormous
octopus, each tentacle labeled with one of the myriad restrictions the voracious beast
imposed upon actors, no newspaper would print it, for fear of losing the advertising
revenues received from Syndicate-controlled theaters.

Initially, Lillian was unaffected by the Syndicate because of her contractual relationships with such powerful impresarios as T. Henry French and the tandem of
Canary and Lederer. Theaters in the cities she played were affiliated with these
national managers, and no local manager would turn down a Russell engagement anyway. By 1897, however, Lillian's managers were being pressured by the Syndicate to
the extent that, if they wanted a show to appear in a given city's best theater, they
had to agree to play numerous smaller theaters in one-night stands. In response to
these demands, Lillian stipulated in her contract that she would play no matinees during one-night stands and would perform no more than six times a week during such
road trips. Yet by early 1899, her tour was entirely dictated by the Syndicate. She
strongly disliked their influence and, later, openly fought them. Other producers
who later opposed the Syndicate included the Shubert brothers and David Belasco.

There was more to Lillian's crisis than the decline of comic opera or the rise of
the Syndicate. For personal and professional reasons, she now had to seriously attend
to reestablishing her audience appeal and box office drawing power. While appearing on the road in *The Grand Duchess*— the replacement for *The Queen of Brilliants*
fiasco— her focus had been distracted by a number of unfortunate events. In late
January 1895, she was informed that Edward Solomon had died while held in jail for
failure to pay his debts. A few weeks later, she fell on stage and injured her leg. A
local newspaper suggested her notorious late-night activities might have contributed
to the mishap. A letter from Cynthia informed her that Lillian, Jr., had decided to
change her name to Dorothy, out of respect for a friend who was dying. Cynthia suggested that her granddaughter was probably just looking for a little self-identity.
"Dorothy" was now almost an adolescent and had openly expressed distress over her
mother's long absences.

Yet satisfied and responsive road audiences always raised Lillian's spirit and
resolve. They seemed completely unaffected by or even aware of her problems in New
York. If they were aware, it evidently made no difference. Lillian remained their
"Queen." In Chicago: "Lillian Russell crowded the theater and drew the largest receipts
in the history of the house." In Philadelphia: "Miss Russell is in excellent voice and
is repeating her past successes." In an effort to maintain the company's attractiveness,
Lillian and Abbey decided to add *La Pericole* to the touring repertoire before performing the new show in New York. The decision was rewarded with SRO performances throughout the remainder of the tour. Abbey was very pleased, not to mention
relieved, both by audience response to Lillian and press coverage of her performances.
Possibly, the return to New York in April would be better than he had anticipated.

La Pericole opened at Abbey's Theater on April 29, playing to a packed house. It
was an auspicious return to a venue where, only five months before, Lillian's performance, both on and off the stage, had been strongly criticized.

> Miss Russell was more than satisfactory in the role of the fascinating street singer of Lima, and has rarely, if ever, done better work. She gave a very spirited performance and did more and better acting than she has shown for several years.[1]

Success in New York, however, was short-lived. When her lawyers announced that she was mortgaging her 77th Street home to raise some $19,000, in order to pay off debts resulting from the Perugini affair, the press was quick to remind readers of Lillian's past transgressions. At the same time, Abbey informed the press that *La Peri-cole* would have to be withdrawn to make way for a new opera, *The Tzigane.* Apparently, he had contracted with the authors, Edgar Smith and Reginald de Koven, promising them that their show would appear at his theater by the middle of May. Lillian had not been made aware of this arrangement and was angry about having to rehearse a new show while performing another. She argued that giving up a proven success for an untried vehicle was always risky, particularly during these tenuous times for comic opera. Her assessment would soon prove correct.

The Tzigane opened at Abbey's Theater on May 17. The show had a traditional comic opera plot. Lillian played a Russian gypsy, Vera, in love with an army officer but commanded to marry a serf, one of her own class. She runs away. Years later, now a woman of standing, she returns to find that her first love has been faithful to her. In the predictable finale, they marry joyfully.

The show was panned by critics. They pointed out that it had not been adequately prepared, citing a number of instances when Lillian had to be prompted. The *Clipper* reported:

> Mr. Smith has little reason to be proud of his book. Its lyrics are quite satisfactory but its dialogue is without merit of any sort. Miss Russell is not fitted either by temperament or vocal training for the satisfactory rendering of such music as was allotted to her. The three comedians — Jefferson de Angelis, Fred Solomon and Joseph Herbert — labored hard to make dull roles effective.[2]

Amazingly, the show continued to draw good audiences into June, beyond the normal summer closing date for New York theaters. Abbey optimistically predicted the show would run until the middle of July, but Lillian became ill and remained out of the cast for a week. Theater attendance immediately declined. Even upon her return, Abbey decided to close on June 18, promising to reopen with the same production in August.

For the summer, a recovering Lillian rented a 16-room cottage in Great Neck, Long Island, on the shores of Manhasett Bay. There she rested and took up a new sport, automobile driving. During her second driving experience, traveling 18 miles an hour, she was stopped by the police for speeding. She decided that automobile driving was hazardous and accepted Brady's suggestion that bicycling was better for physical fitness.

Lillian was also very concerned about the increase in her weight during the past season. What better way to reduce and, at the same time, promote the new fad of bicycle riding currently sweeping the country? Each day, she and Marie Dressler traversed the roads of Great Neck. Within a short time, their daily route had been charted by local residents who would stand by the roadside, wave to them, or offer refreshments as they passed.

Because of the intense heat in the city that summer, Lillian proposed to Abbey that playing New York in August would be unprofitable. Since Abbey was already faced with considerable debt, he agreed. They planned to reopen the season in Boston on September 9.

Boston audiences proved more receptive to Lillian and *The Tzigane*. The Globe commented, "Lillian Russell and her company have met with very great success during the past week."[3]

The second week was equally successful, but Lillian and Abbey decided to replace *The Tzigane* with *La Pericole* anyway, to maintain the company's drawing power. The success of this decision persuaded them to alternate performances of the two shows throughout the tour, which was to take them for the first time to Washington, D.C., Montreal and Toronto, as well as Buffalo, Cleveland and Chicago, one of Lillian's favorite cities in which to perform.

Even with full houses, the cost of the productions and touring added to Abbey's steadily increasing debts. To cut costs, he released the leading tenor and a number of bit players, to which the Chicago papers quickly reacted:

> [T]he management has resolved to get along with cheaper people. Now let us see what the public will think of such a policy.[4]

But Chicago audiences didn't seem to care. To them, the production was "a great success" and Lillian was "a dream." The *Tribune* pointedly noted:

> Lillian Russell has not lost her popularity in Chicago, however faithless the public may have proved to her in New York.[5]

Receipts for three weeks in Chicago topped $26,000, the most ever achieved at the Columbia Theater to that point in its history.

The tour continued through the Midwest, and then into new territory, performing in Nashville, Memphis, New Orleans and Atlanta. Lillian played to SRO audiences in these cities, in which people had long heard of but never yet seen her perform. Two additional shows were added to the repertoire, *The Little Duke* and *The Grand Duchess*. *The Tzigane* was dropped, but Lillian and her troupe were still singing three different operas, in some cities on successive days.

An interesting and press-worthy sidelight of the tour was Lillian's use of the new gold-plated bicycle Brady had given her. No matter the city, each morning Lillian rode the streets, to the great enjoyment of the viewing public. Reporters followed her route and interviewed her at the end of each day's exercise. By this time, Lillian had become a strong, vocal spokesperson for the benefits of biking, and her comments about losing weight and improving her health were frequently mentioned. Every article also described in detail the bicycle Brady had given her. In addition, Lillian made a contribution to bike-riding fashion. For comfort and facility, she wore what was described as a "split skirt." Within a few months, her outfit had blossomed into a national fad.

At one of the company's stops, Pittsburgh, they were going to inaugurate a new first-class theater, the Carnegie Music Hall. To test the acoustics of the hall, Lillian was asked to sing "The Star Spangled Banner." When she started to sing, she realized she could not remember all the words. She had no option but to ask the stage hands if anyone could help. One of them, up in the flies, volunteered. He came down to recite the words to her. Another hand produced a brown paper bag, which had until that moment held his lunch, upon which to write Francis Scott Key's immortal verse. Lillian then proceeded to sing the song and promised never again to forget the lyrics. In her memoirs, she recalled the embarrassing incident:

> You may be sure I learned the words to that song at once — never to be forgotten again. A nice lot of patriots were we, that party of Americans. I have been obliged to sing that old patriotic song many thousand times since that day, but I have never started to sing it without seeing the words written on a crumpled brown paper bag.[6]

The last two weeks of the tour, performing one-night stands in 12 cities through Pennsylvania and New York, were very fatiguing for the company. In typical Abbey fashion, the demanding manager directed the company to rehearse a new comic opera, *The Goddess of Truth*, to open at his theater upon their return to New York City. Lillian's concern about the lack of adequate rehearsal time, which had caused her performance to meet with critical disapproval at their last opening, was disregarded by Abbey due to pressure from his creditors. Just before the new show's opening, Abbey's financial problems were made public.

A rumor in the press suggested Abbey would not be Lillian's manager next season because of the financial losses he had suffered. Another rumor indicated Lillian was about sign for the coming year with T. Henry French. When French had managed Lillian before, she appeared in *La Cigale* at his Garden Theater, and his net profits were reported to be more than $100,000. A week later, however, the *Clipper* announced:

> The arrangement between Lillian Russell and T. H. French is off. It is probable, in spite of all that has been said regarding Russell's desire to find a new manager and Abbey and Grau's wish to abandon a star on whom they have lost large sums of money, that Russell will continue under Abbey and Grau's direction next season. Mr. French yesterday received a letter which stated that certain complications had arisen, and that Russell would be under the A. and G. banner next season.[7]

The "complications" happened to be Abbey's creditors. They believed he would not be able to pay off his debts if he didn't have Lillian appearing during the year. While always risky, a show with Lillian had a better chance of success than one without her. Abbey seemed satisfied with the decision. Lillian, however, remained discontented and continued her conversations with other managers.

The Goddess of Truth opened February 26 to initially good reviews:

> The fair Lillian wore some handsome gowns, acted with unusual spirit, and even somewhat of abandon, and sang with good effect.
>   She was somewhat too pronounced in the osculatory duet with Richie Ling, the tenor, but the audience seemed to enjoy this episode more than anything else in the opera, and redemanded the duet so often that Miss Russell cut the kissing out altogether in the final encore.[8]

But in the following weeks, attendance dropped off dramatically. By the fourth week, Abbey was concerned (and his creditors dismayed) at the production's rapid decline. They had no choice but to close the show and give up Lillian's contract. As a temporary measure, they agreed to replace *Goddess* with *The Little Duke* and put it on a short tour. To compound the problem, during the last week of the show's

Diamond Jim Brady: What he lacked in physical appeal and social grace, he made up in flamboyant parties and diamond-studded first-night theater appearances. The long-term friendship between Lillian and Brady, as well as his devotion to her, became legendary.

appearance in New York, the house had to be closed because Lillian was ill (or so it was reported). Her absence from *Goddess* and the rumors about her leaving Abbey produced more negative press, as it had after the Perugini episode.

The Little Duke was introduced April 6. According to the *Clipper*, Lillian did not fit the part:

In the title role of this work, Miss Russell gives the convincing proof of the truth of her recent assertion that nature has been generous to her, though the pecuniary results of the final fortnight of her engagement here may afford substantial reason for her donning the costume required. The fair Lillian has grown somewhat matronly since the days when she looked so handsome in *The Queen's Mate* and, viewed from an artistic standpoint, her present venture is much to be regretted. She cannot look the part, nor is her style of singing such as can give proper expression to the music of the role.[9]

It was fortuitous for Lillian that the company left on tour a week later. Audiences in other cities, as before, responded more positively to the production and her role in it.

Miss Russell was very cordially received and her singing won many encores. The piece was handsomely staged and the chorus was excellent.[10]

For the remainder of the tour, audiences were large and responsive, and Lillian was recognized for her good work. Returning to New York in the middle of May, Lillian continued her efforts to find a new manager. Her prospects were aided by Abbey's admission that he could not meet his creditors' demands. Although he had made money managing the ventures of Henry Irving and Sarah Bernhardt, his losses managing Lillian Russell amounted to more than $200,000, attributed in part to her high salary and percentage of the gross receipts. No sooner had Abbey's liabilities been revealed than Canary and Lederer announced they had signed Lillian for the coming season in a new comic opera, to open mid-September.

Commenting on the changes in New York popular theater evident during the summer of 1896, the *Clipper* noted that the number of vaudeville companies had doubled in two years. The *Dramatic Mirror* indirectly acknowledged the influence of vaudeville by instructing their newsboys to hawk the paper outside vaudeville houses. Weber and Fields, fast becoming America's leading comedians, purchased a theater on Broadway to present their version of classic farce-comedy and travesty. According to theater managers, the number of successful comic operas could be "counted on one hand." Lillian, however, seemed still to be surviving.

An editorial in the *New York Standard* presented an insightful summary of her position in New York's popular theater environment:

> We can't believe that Russell is done for, as the prophets of the theater insist that she is. In all essentials she is still literally the queen of comic opera. While she played to business that would disgust a farce-comedy enterprise the last weeks of the season, once out of town the absolute sovereign of the comic opera stage found herself in very changed conditions. It is only fair to add that her managers were none too anxious to make her life pleasant for her. She is hopeful and confident that by this time next year she will have fully recovered her place in the favor of the public and in the calculations of managers.[11]

An observer of Lillian's activities might have wondered if she had any problems whatsoever. To improve her health and physique, Lillian took daily bicycle rides through Central Park, often accompanied by Jim Brady and Marie Dressler. Her new costumes prompted a run on cycling clothes. They also served as impetus for women to discard the traditional Victorian dress for more liberating styles, like Lillian's split skirt and the even more daring bloomers. Apart from the physical benefits derived, Lillian enjoyed bicycling. Moreover, she saw it as an easy and popular way to capture public attention during the theater's off-season.

When Lillian, Brady and Dressler rode Central Park's trails, other traffic halted to watch and wave. Whenever the biking trio stopped to rest or have a snack, they were soon surrounded by spectators. "Keep Off the Grass" signs didn't deter the eager fans. When Lillian rested her back against such a sign, the police formed a ring to protect her from onlookers.

Vigorous exercise was balanced by frequent visits to Manhattan's fine restaurants, to join the "lobster palace" crowd, and to Saratoga, to enjoy both the waters and the horses. The Waldorf-Astoria Hotel was the new place to see and be seen, along with her usual haunts (Delmonico's, Rector's and Shanley's). Visits to Saratoga gave Lillian the opportunity to show off her black Victoria carriage, with matching black thoroughbreds; her gold-plated bicycle; or, if she cared to stroll the streets, her Japanese Spaniel, with its diamond collar. This particular Saratoga summer, she was challenged on picking winners at the races by a young theater singer, Louise Montague. Immediately, stable owners, jockeys, trainers and bookies chose sides to supply the contestants with daily tips. It was reported that neither woman had done very well, but Lillian won "by a nose" and, to celebrate her victory, threw a party for everyone involved. After two months of these active diversions, she sailed for England to rest, before starting rehearsals for her new managers, Canary and Lederer.

The fall of 1896 was to prove an emotional challenge for Lillian, at once fortified by stage successes and depleted by death. Her return to the comic opera stage was to take place in *An American Beauty*, labeled a three-act musical comedy. The vehicle had been written by Hugh Morton, with music by Lillian's old friend Gustave Kerker. Since Lillian had already been publicly dubbed "The American Beauty," what better way to enhance her career at this time?

To insure that the production would both make money and win critical acclaim, Lederer planned to have the show open on the road and tour for three months before exposing it to New York audiences and critics. Lillian continued to demonstrate her popularity and box office strength on the road, but New York critics might still be in the mood to reject her. Lederer planned to hedge against any such eventuality. But no plan could account for the impact of personal tragedy.

In early September, Charles Leonard, seeking relaxation before starting a new position in Chicago, visited his brother in Detroit. Charles' printing business had been placed into receivership the previous year and sold at public auction. Two of his former employees had opened a printing firm and asked him to be their secretary. Charles decided to travel to Detroit before assuming his new responsibilities.

A week before Lillian was to open *An American Beauty*, she received a telegram that her father had suffered a stroke, leaving him speechless and paralyzed on his right side. The attending physicians were not sure he would ever recover.

Susan and Hattie went to see their father, but Lillian felt she was unable to leave the show at this critical time. She did, however, contact Charles' brother frequently to monitor her father's condition. She was deeply saddened and had great difficulty performing.

An American Beauty opened in Elmira, New York, on September 16, to a full house. Even though written by an American author, the play was set in Europe. Its principal characters included a rich widow, some circus people, an English earl in disguise and a German prince — a typical and predictable comic opera cast. The most notable scene in the production took place in the second act, when Lillian made her entrance on the back of a pachyderm (two men inside an elephant costume). She was displayed in a "radiant garb that would have made Sheba's queen green with envy." As had been the case in many of her previous shows, Lillian saw to it that her sister Susan and Susan's husband Owen Westford had roles in the production.

While playing in Springfield, Ohio, Lillian received news that an old beau, Walter Sinn, had suddenly died. He was the son of Col. and Mrs. Sinn, who had obtained for Lillian her first professional audition (with E.E. Rice). Walter had been escorting her at the time, and Mrs. Sinn had looked upon the match as a potential marriage for her son.

A week after learning of Walter's death, Lillian received a cable from her father's brother in Detroit. Charles had just died. His body was being shipped to Chicago for burial October 13.

Lillian's initial reaction was to tell the company she could not perform that night and that she planned to attend her father's funeral. But such a decision would have closed the show for a week. Members of the company and theater management persuaded her to continue performing, since it meant income and salaries for everyone involved. (While on tour, actors received no salary if there was no performance, even if the hiatus was brief.) In addition, the theater at which the company was then

Publicity photographs like the ensemble scene above required many hours of staging. Performers had to hold a pose for as long as fifteen minutes to ensure the photo's success. Here Lillian and company portray a typical comic opera scene from *An American Beauty*. (Harry Ransom Humanities Research Center, University of Texas at Austin.)

playing had been open for only one week. A quick closure would surely have a detrimental effect on its future success. Although her emotional pain was obvious, Lillian agreed to work.

> That is what decided me — the company and their loss. Eighty people would lose a whole week's salary. Then I thought of my father and of what he would have wished me to do, and I decided to play.[12]

Both Susie and Hattie agreed. "Play. It would have been Father's wish."

The local press recognized Lillian for her strength and bravery. In New York, however, certain members of the press admonished her for failing to attend her father's funeral, questioning her values and accusing her of heartlessness. Cynthia rushed to Lillian's defense, arguing the fundamental creed of the stage: "The show must go on." Whether Cynthia was genuinely supporting her daughter and the acting profession, or whether her personal disdain for Charles influenced these comments, can only be surmised.

A few days later, Lillian fell from her bicycle and injured her ankle. She was in physical pain but paid little attention to it. While in New Orleans, however, she came down with a sore throat and could not perform. When Lederer announced that Lillian would not appear, the audience walked out, and the show was closed. In order to recover her health, Lillian went to Chicago to rest; she was then able to visit her father's grave.

Charles Leonard received an impressive funeral. Members of printing associations, Freemason associates and former employees came to honor him. A eulogy noted his outstanding reputation, his personal integrity and the fact he was a "stead-fast friend and honored associate." Yet, of his immediate family, only Ida, Lillian's oldest sister, attended the funeral. Lillian and Susie sent a grand floral offering. Charles was buried in Graceland Cemetery. When Lillian visited Charles' grave a month later, an early snow had already blanketed his place of rest.

Yet another reminder of mortality greeted Lillian in Chicago when it was announced that Henry Abbey had died suddenly in New York. According to reports, his recent financial losses had had a profound effect on an already sick man; Abbey had become despondent. Lillian was dispirited, not only by Abbey's death, but also by the *Clipper*'s obituary, which implied she had contributed to his financial ruin:

> The tour of this star proved most disastrous, as it required the profits of his other ventures to meet the losses of the Lillian Russell Opera Co. and the firm's failure was claimed to be the direct result.[13]

When *An American Beauty* reopened in Chicago at the end of November, all eyes were on Lillian, carefully watching to see how she behaved and performed. Apparently, her performances were good enough to satisfy "fine audiences" and relieve Lederer's concern about the show's future. At her final performance, Lillian celebrated her birthday — 35, she told the audience truthfully. The orchestra played a program of songs from previous shows, which Lillian dutifully sang and encored. Presents and flowers accumulated on stage, and congratulatory telegrams and cablegrams were continually brought up and given to her to read. But it was a melancholy Lillian who left Chicago after a sentimental and emotion-filled month. In fact, concern about her health was so great that a reporter from the *Dramatic Mirror* called at her home to determine if she really would open at the Casino at the end of December. She smiled, presented him two tickets for the opening, and sang him out the door.

The new "musical comedy," as it was being billed to New York audiences, was an immediate hit, the work being "well received" and Lillian getting "more than her usual quota of praise." The splendor of her voice was noted:

> She certainly can sing, and sing well, and I doubt if, all told, she has recently appeared to greater advantage, either vocally or physically, than in this production.[14]

Yet, at the same time that Lillian was filling the house nightly, other comic operas were failing, and managers were converting their theaters to present vaudeville instead. With more pages in their editions now devoted to vaudeville than to any other form of entertainment, theatrical newspapers dramatically proclaimed the demise of comic opera. In addition, many of comic opera's most distinguished performers began signing up with vaudeville companies, at salaries greater than they had ever earned before.

The one-hundredth performance of *An American Beauty* was celebrated, and women in the audience received American Beauty roses and a card autographed by Lillian. Her signed photograph was distributed to the entire audience at the production's one-hundred-fiftieth performance. The show was to run until the beginning of March, then go on a short tour until the end of the month, when Lederer planned to feature Lillian in a new attraction.

But even though Lederer was making a good deal of money from the show, he found himself in a difficult situation. His business partner and financial backer, Canary, had been stricken by a heart attack and was now near death, requiring Lederer to oversee all of the company's financial interests and production responsibilities. Lederer also had to deal with the increasing power of the Syndicate. Many of the theaters he had formerly booked directly to present his shows were now controlled by the Syndicate, and he was forced to deal with them to acquire future tour routes. For Lillian's shows, this meant first-class theaters with ample seating, week-long bookings and a routing that required short trips and low travel expenses. While the Syndicate was willing to accommodate Lederer, they pressured him to guarantee a profitable venture. They suggested he feature two or three stars to draw large crowds, a recommendation Lederer found hard to refuse. But how would Lillian feel about sharing the stage with other prominent performers, particularly another female singer?

When Lederer put the proposal to Lillian, to his surprise, she consented, agreeing that the arrangement could improve the chances for a successful run. Who was Lederer hoping to sign to co-star with her? He suggested Jefferson de Angelis and Della Fox. De Angelis was an old friend and co-star who had worked with Lillian in *Poor Jonathan* and *Apollo*. Lillian felt comfortable with him and knew he admired her singing and acting. A man of wit, he had a self-effacing approach to theatrical performance that added a welcome sense of levity, both on the stage and in the company.

Della Fox, however, according to the press, was considered Lillian's competitor. A petite blond, Fox presented herself as a simple and energetic performer who sang every role in a sweet, charming and coquettish manner. In reality, she was a shrewd businesswoman, bold and direct, who regularly gambled on anything that might sustain a wager. Her early performances had included *The Pirates of Penzance*, *Olivette* and *Billee Taylor*. It was George Lederer who first recognized her potential and, in 1891, gave her a starring role with De Wolf Hopper in the hit show *Wang*. Fox was a good comedienne, with a melodious, though not strong, voice. Given their similarities, how would she and Lillian get along together on the stage? Lederer longed to believe it would be successful; Lillian said she would wait and see.

Rehearsals for *The Wedding Day* began in early April, with apparently amiable cooperation among the stars on stage. Offstage, Lillian enjoyed some advantageous publicity by appearing with Anna Held in the audience of a number of currently running shows (followed by the usual entourage of admirers) and by purchasing the private rail car formerly owned by Lillie Langtry.

The Wedding Day opened at the Casino April 8, to satisfactory reviews. Some parts of its humor were, however, criticized as "vulgar." It too was billed as a "musical comedy," in three acts, written by Europeans, from the risqué French work *La Petite Fronde*. The action took place in France, in the seventeenth century, during an insurrection of the Frondists. Lillian was singled out as the "unopposed star" of the production:

> *The Wedding Day* hasn't any love story, and it hasn't any comedy story, but it is sweet and clean, much of the detail is diverting and there are some lively songs. Miss Russell not only was a vision, being more beautiful than she ever was, and we failed to detect rifts in her splendid voice. Mr. de Angelis is clever, is as agile as ever in dancing and sufficiently glib and humorous in speech. Miss Fox made good comic use of her very thin situations.[15]

Even with all its comic-opera faults, the show was considered a "skillful piece of work"; thanks to "the triple alliance," as the stars were being called, it played successfully. Lederer planned to present it in New York for six weeks, and then go on tour. By the third week, however, the box office had declined and tensions had begun to surface between the two female stars. During the show's fifth week, Della Fox withdrew because of a purported illness, but the ever-vigilant *Clipper* tracked her down:

[A]lthough the house was closed because of the alleged illness, she [Fox] spent the evening with a party of friends at the new St. Nickolas Music Hall. It will probably be discovered in the near future that dissentions have arisen in the happy family combination at the Casino, and that the rival stars are not the best of friends.[16]

Lillian, with Jefferson de Angelis and Della Fox, in *The Wedding Day*. The show played for almost two seasons and was the first production in which Lillian shared the stage with other top performers. After some brief episodes of ego conflict, the chemistry of their friendship attracted SRO houses throughout the country. (Harry Ransom Humanities Research Center, University of Texas at Austin.)

An understudy took Fox's part. When Fox returned two days later, Lillian ignored her on stage. The show closed at the end of five weeks, Lederer promising that it would return, with the same stars, in the fall. At the same time, a rumor spread that Lillian had received an offer from D'Oyly Carte to appear in London.

The summer of 1897 seemed dull for most folks in New York, but not for Lillian. Very few theatrical events took place, as most of the theaters were closed. Competition for visitors came chiefly from summer resorts and beaches. Not only had transportation to these places improved, but leisure package tours were now being promoted to attract large crowds. The severe summer heat in the city proved a boon to resort owners.

At first, Lillian announced she would travel to Europe for the summer. She later said she would take some apartments at a resort on Long Island and make brief trips out of town. In fact, she passed most of the season at Brady's summer home and in Saratoga.

At one of Brady's parties, Lillian met Edna McCauley, a young woman who had introduced herself to Brady and initiated what proved to be a long and intimate relationship with him. The daughter of a Brooklyn policeman, McCauley had moved to Manhattan and worked as a salesgirl until she found Brady. For Brady, their immediate liaison turned into instant love. He wanted to marry McCauley. Being more interested in the style of life he could offer her than the heart of the man himself, she always refused. Yet when she was introduced to Lillian, McCauley was warmly accepted and soon became a "regular" member in the group. Her relationship with Brady would continue unabated for more than a decade.

At about the same time, while enjoying the Saratoga race track season, Lillian renewed her acquaintance with Jesse Lewisohn, a member of New York's business elite who had frequently played poker with her during the Perugini days. Born into a family that made millions in copper, Lewisohn increased his capital by operating as a banker and stock broker. This wealth left him with a good deal of leisure time in which to become one of the city's celebrated "swells" and a constant visitor to restaurants, theaters and gaming establishments. Jesse was tall, dark and Jewish. To no one's surprise, Cynthia was not pleased about their friendship.

Lillian and Jesse began their relationship at Saratoga. During the day, they were seen betting on the horses; at night, dining in the fashionable restaurants. The twosome of Lillian and Brady had now become a mutually advantageous, cleverly deceptive foursome, Brady escorting Lillian, Lewisohn arm-in-arm with McCauley. They delighted in confusing the spectators even more when Brady introduced McCauley as his niece, while Lillian presented Lewisohn as her fiancé. For Lillian, love and affection had unexpectedly returned. She was feeling very good, almost expansive, over her good fortune. Monitoring her health and physical condition was now imperative, but accommodating the changes in her professional world would prove easier to deal with. Or so it seemed.

In August, much to the surprise of the press, Della Fox agreed to continue in *The Wedding Day* for the coming season. Three factors helped her come to this decision: she was given an increase in salary (to $600 a week); her role in the show was enlarged; and Lillian reached out in friendship to her. Ecstatic at the turn of events, Lederer rushed to the Syndicate offices to book the show for almost the entire season, the company to stay on the road the whole time. He immediately announced that "the triple alliance" would open the season in Syracuse, at the new Wieting Opera House, on September 15.

For the next few months, reviews from each city on the tour echoed the exceptional success of the production:

> A large audience saw *The Wedding Day* when it began its brief engagement here. Miss Russell's singing was as sweet as usual. Miss Fox was given every chance to display her own peculiar graces and pleased her many friends. Mr. de Angelis was as droll and original as ever. The company which supports the stars are strong. The scenery is handsome and spectacular; the opera is very impressive.[17]

Interestingly, the show was identified as a "comic opera," not the increasingly current "musical comedy," during its entire tour.

In what was becoming an annual event for Lillian, the company played Chicago

Jesse Lewisohn, heir to the country's first copper fortune, financial speculator, gambler and Lillian's companion for a decade. In later years, Lillian referred to Lewisohn as her "one true love."

at the time of her birthday, at the familiar Columbia Theater. Again, according to the *Tribune*, it was a gala evening, with gifts, flowers and telegrams inundating the stage as Lillian performed many of her hits. Three weeks at the Columbia "filled the house to overflowing, reaping good profits."

By this time, Lillian and Della Fox had become good friends. One of the features of their friendship was the creation of a never-ending pinochle game, played on trains and in hotels throughout the tour. Lillian came to respect Fox as a talented "trooper" and thoroughly enjoyed her humor. Fox came to regard Lillian as an older sister and mentor. According to the press, the obvious melding of talent and temperament made their performances enjoyable to watch. Unfortunately, Fox became seriously ill two years later and, at the peak of her career, had to retire from the stage, except for brief appearances in vaudeville some years later.

Whenever he could, Lewisohn took the train to see Lillian, since she was performing away from New York for more than six months. Gossip columns in local newspapers mentioned seeing them together at restaurants or, when possible, at race tracks. Back in New York, Brady and McCauley continued making the rounds of theaters and restaurants, hand-in-hand.

While the show made its way through the Midwest and back to the East Coast, Lillian endeavored to make plans for the coming season. Lederer had no new shows for her because he was concentrating all his efforts on the formation of vaudeville companies. Lillian had no desire to appear in vaudeville, even less as a performer in the Syndicate empire, but she found no musical comedy/comic opera productions suitable. Rumors suggested she was going to appear in London in a comic opera attraction written by Sir Arthur Sullivan. Another said she and the *Wedding Party* company were going to Australia. Yet another said that she would appear with De Wolf Hopper in a musical comedy. Finally came a report that she and Thomas Seabrooke would join forces.

When Gustav Amberg, a European producer, approached Lillian and offered her a concert tour in Europe for the coming season, along with an attractive salary (reportedly $1,200 a week), Lillian quickly accepted. She knew well that both audiences and attractive vehicles for her kind of performance were dwindling. A profitable tour of Europe, at a time when the American popular theater scene was changing, would buy her time to plan her future career. Amberg immediately announced that Lillian, singing her most famous songs, would appear before audiences, including royalty, in Germany, Austria, Russia and Holland. It promised to be an ambitious tour, even for Lillian.

Even though Lederer had planned to keep the "triple alliance" show on the road for the entire season, continued success persuaded him to return to New York for its final weeks. On April 18, *The Wedding Day* opened at the Broadway Theater (the Syndicate had already booked the Casino) and "was greeted by a large audience, proving almost as great an attraction as when seen earlier in the season." Due to heavy advance sales, what had been scheduled as a two-week engagement turned into a five-week run. Totaling both New York and road performances, *The Wedding Day* played more than 200 times. Lillian could not help but feel somewhat vindicated about her enduring box office status.

After the end of her season, personal matters had to be dealt with immediately. Perugini had finally filed papers for divorce. Lillian decided not to contest his accusations, in order to defuse any adverse public reactions that might again arise. Through her lawyer, she responded that she only wanted to get "this unpleasant episode settled." About the same time, Lillian went to court to change her name again, this time to Lillian Leonard Russell. She explained the action to the press, saying:

> I intend to play an extended engagement in Germany and I understand that the law in that country is very strict regarding the use of legal names.[18]

Did Cynthia have anything to do with the decision?, wondered a reporter. Perhaps the change had been made to honor her recently deceased father, suggested the writer who had chastised her for not attending Charles' funeral. Even a change in name served to provoke controversy in the press.

What the press did not cover (or did not know about) were Lillian's difficulties with her teenage daughter. Dorothy was having disciplinary problems at private school and had run away a number of times. The only classes she seemed to enjoy were music and dance; her only friends, said her teacher, were boys. Lillian had already been away from her daughter for nearly six months and was now planning another extended tour, so her direct influence on Dorothy (whether positive or negative) was minimal. Actually, Susan had more contact with Dorothy than did her mother. Still, Lillian felt a few months together would improve the situation. So she took Dorothy and Cynthia with her to Saratoga and delayed her trip to Europe until August. Of course, Jesse Lewisohn was also on hand, along with Brady and McCauley.

Close by the race tracks and restaurants of Saratoga whirled the roulette wheels

at Canfield's Club House. Richard Canfield had run a high-stakes gambling house in
New York for a number of years; it was the favorite wagering venue among the city's
social and business elite. Naturally, Brady and Lewisohn were welcome guests, often
accompanied by Lillian. Canfield's opening a branch in Saratoga now provided gam-
blers a year-round chance to lose their money.

To prepare herself for the coming concert tour, Lillian brought along a singing
coach and a physical trainer. Also joining the entourage were her Japanese spaniel
and her gold-plated bicycle. Lillian's battle with her weight continued — biking, then
gourmet meals; singing, then the race track — but no one seemed to question her
glamour or her beauty.

On August 7, accompanied by her sister Hattie, who could speak German, Lillian left for Berlin, via a few resorts in England. Her first impressions of Berlin were
positive, since she was housed in an elegant suite of rooms at the city's finest hotel.
When she arrived at the theater, however, her desire to perform there plunged. The
Winter Garden was indeed more garden than theater. Its myriad groups of tables and
chairs were occupied by all classes of people, evidently more intent on consuming
great quantities of beer and wine, than in attending to Lillian's performance.

Though conditions were not ideal, it was soon reported, "Lillian Russell is said
to have achieved a prodigious success upon her appearance at the Winter Garden,
Berlin."[19]

Apparently, success had its price. A professional leader of applause, whose position was an established theatrical tradition in Germany, demanded money from Lillian, or else he would suppress positive public response to her singing. She was also
advised to tip the stage manager and the musical conductor generously. Whether this
professional behavior was normal or not, German theater people obviously perceived
Lillian as a rich American star who could easily afford even their most exorbitant
requests.

She was then presented with a bill for having performed a number of German
songs without copyright authorization, an item that Amberg seemed to have overlooked. Constant importunings by flower sellers and innumerable invitations to dinner similarly became disagreeable nuisances. According to Lillian, she was stopped
frequently to show off her wardrobe and bicycle to "motley crowds" gathered at each
train station. Such annoying misadventures cannot be verified, nor can her more
positive reports of various encounters with European royalty. Nevertheless, Lillian's
enthusiasm about performing in Berlin, as well as elsewhere in Europe, deteriorated
quickly and definitively. Her negative sentiments about Germans and most other
foreigners (except the British) were probably a result of these experiences, real or fan-
cied.

> When the end of my engagement came, I breathed a sigh of joy.... How
> happy I was to reach London again.... The people I liked were there.[20]

Lillian's engagement in Berlin lasted six weeks. By early October, she was back
in London and split her leisure time between attending the races at Newmarket and
taking in the latest theater attractions. The London papers seemed just as inventive
as those in New York in manufacturing rumors about Lillian. One or another London paper seemed constantly to claim that she would be appearing in some future
comic opera on the English stage, although they tempered their revelations by

reminding readers that "her last London appearance, in *The Queen of Brilliants* was not successful." They further reported:

> Lillian Russell is now in London, having canceled her continental music hall engagements because, it is said, she did not choose to sing in countries whose language she could not speak.[21]

In addition, a brief statement in the papers noted that the divorce between Perugini and Lillian had been granted on October 21, in Jersey City.

When Lillian returned to New York on December 1, dozens of reporters waited at the dock to interview her. In her *Reminiscences*, Lillian wrote about her activities in London and a trip to Paris and Monte Carlo that had supposedly taken place during this winter. She stated that she returned to New York, after a highly successful trip, in March 1899. Both statements were untrue. Evidently, writing some 20 years after the fact, she confused the events of this European sojourn with another.

Lederer was among the crowd waiting for Lillian to disembark. He had a new musical comedy (actually, an old comic opera) available for her. If she could start rehearsals immediately, the production could open in January.

The show was a revival of *La Belle Helene*, which had first appeared in the U.S. in 1868 and been presented numerous times since. This latest version had been updated by Louis Harrison, with some new songs by Ludwig Englander. Thomas Seabrooke was to be the lead tenor. Also signed for the production was Edna Wallace Hopper, another of Lillian's potential rivals. But an optimistic Lederer believed he could effect the same kind of cooperation as had been achieved by "the triple alliance" in *The Wedding Day*. Petite, delicate, girlish and spontaneous, Hopper was almost a double for Della Fox. In fact, she had played in a number of the same shows as Fox, even serving as her replacement in *Wang*. Unlike Fox, however, Hopper considered herself a better actress than Lillian.

La Belle Helene opened January 12, 1899, at the Casino Theater. It was not well-received. As the *Dramatic Mirror* noted:

> The production was not crowned by immediate success. The performance was somewhat tiresome and certainly by no means as attractive or amusing as the extravaganzas which had become a feature of this house. Opéra bouffe is a relic of the past. Lillian Russell looked well in her showy gowns and sang well. In her centered the greater part of the interest, but Edna Wallace Hopper absorbed a large share of what remained, although her well-wishers could not but regret that she made in the last act so immodest an exhibition of herself.
>
> We fear that the venture will not be a success, mainly for the reason that we have outgrown opéra bouffe.[22]

Only Lillian's popularity kept the show alive for 52 performances before Lederer put it on the road. Backstage, Lillian offered scathing opinions of Hopper's on-stage antics and increasingly provocative appearance. Hopper had chosen to wear ever-scantier costumes, which naturally elicited loud cheering from the younger males in the audience. The *Clipper* noted:

> The excellent cast contribute in various ways to the success of the performance, although it is probable that the means employed by little Edna to woo the public furnish the best results.[23]

Nor did it help Lillian's disposition to have her own voluptuous physique adversely compared to that of the slender Hopper by Alan Dale, the *New York Journal* critic. Still, Lillian committed to continuing with the show, probably because she had no ready alternative.

Except for weekly runs in a few large Eastern cities, the company now faced a series of one-night stands through New York State and into Virginia. Surprisingly (after the less than enthusiastic response from New York City audiences and critics), *La Belle Helene* played to SRO houses throughout the tour. Reflecting the changing tastes and definitions of popular theater, a Philadelphia critic called the show "a novelty," neither a comic opera nor a musical comedy. No matter, Lillian was still praised for her performance. The same critic reported:

> Miss Russell sings the beautiful Helene, and a more fitting representative of the role could hardly be found. She made a most pronounced hit with her audience.[24]

The showdown between Lillian and Hopper came at the Lafayette Opera House in Washington, D.C. Throughout the preceding week, Hopper had been upstaging Lillian in the final act, shamelessly striving to elicit as much audience reaction as she could create. Due to her high-kicking dancing in brief costumes, she was now getting more applause at curtain calls than Lillian. Lillian wired Lederer that she could no longer perform with Hopper, who was flouting all stage etiquette. Evidently, Lederer's response failed to satisfy Lillian. She returned to New York, shutting down the show.

The public explanation given was that Lillian did not care to play any more one-night stands. New York reporters reminded Lillian that not too many years ago, she herself had upstaged other actresses by wearing tights. Lederer, angry about the show's abrupt closing and consequent loss of revenue, threatened to sue Lillian for any losses he incurred. And he soon kept his word.

Two months after *La Belle Helene* closed — the time needed to gather the financial information to construct a lawsuit — Lederer sued Lillian for $15,000, the amount he claimed to have been damaged by her refusal to continue the tour. With the aid of her law firm, the ever-ready Howe and Hummel, Lillian contested the suit.

> In a lawsuit brought by George W. Lederer against Lillian Russell for breach of contract, the parties seem to be equally desirous to push the proceedings. Mr. Lederer says he is determined to fight the matter to the bitter end, while Miss Russell says she is only too glad to have the opportunity to present her side of the case, and will do all she can to further the matter.[25]

Fortunately for Lillian, Lederer was not the only major producer in a bind for loss of a leading lady. Nor was she alone among top performers in striving to discover a new sense of direction as American popular theater rapidly and unpredictably evolved. Only a few blocks from Lederer's Casino Theater, the exceptionally inventive, acclaimed comedic duo of Weber and Fields had also reached a watershed in their own meteoric ascent to fame.

Joe Weber and Lew Fields, the sons of Jewish immigrants from Poland, had become partners at ten years of age and began their performance career playing 20 times a day for three dollars a week at Bowery dime museums. Soon they were playing in variety houses, having perfected a routine of broad comedy and slapstick in either

Irish, Dutch or blackface costumes, depending on how long and where they were playing. As teenagers, they had toured the country with different variety companies. On tour, they learned not only what would make people laugh, but also the business of operating a theater company. In 1890, when they were 23, they formed their own company and, over six years, expanded their operations to become the most successful group in vaudeville, running three traveling companies and guaranteeing banner weeks to the theaters in which they played.

They had settled on a routine of Dutch two-act comedy and physical abuse. Fields, the taller and shrewder character, would inflict punishment on Weber, short and stout (with pillows stuffed over his midriff). Together, they mangled the English language, imitating the kinds of communication problems immigrants would often encounter upon arriving in the U.S. It was a cathartic experience for their largely immigrant audiences to be able to laugh at them-

A personal picture of Lillian, circa 1898. An astute observer of the theatrical scene, she was well aware that the appeal of comic opera was rapidly declining. She soon began exploring alternative performance opportunities, which ultimately led to her signing with Weber and Fields. (Harry Ransom Humanities Research Center, University of Texas at Austin.)

selves and others, away from the harsh realities of the city streets.

In 1896, the partners purchased a deserted and supposedly haunted theater on Broadway and 29th Street, named it the Weber and Fields Music Hall and launched vaudeville, satire and burlesque programs aimed at the better classes of theatergoers. At first, their shows consisted of two parts, the first half comprised of a number of vaudeville song-and-dance specialties featuring some of the stars of the day. The second half consisted of satires on dramatic plays currently being staged in New York. These farces were filled with nonsensical plots and topical humor. Thus, *The Geisha* became *The Geezer, Cyrano* became *Cyranose* and *Tess of the D'Urbervilles* became *Tess of the Weberfields*.

By 1898, their theater was jammed with SRO audiences for an entire season.

Along with those of other prominent American and British actresses, Lillian's likeness appeared on many tobacco products appealing to male theater patrons when she appeared in comic opera. (Harry Ransom Humanities Research Center, University of Texas at Austin.)

Opening night tickets were auctioned off to luminaries such as William Randolph Hearst, Stanford White, Diamond Jim Brady and other prominent members of New York's social elite. The success of the Weberfields company allowed the partners to pay their performers some of the highest salaries in the profession.

For the 1899 season, Weber and Fields had decided to eliminate the variety part of the show and devote all their attention to travesties of current Broadway productions. For a show to be satirized on the Music Hall stage had come to be considered a mark of distinction. Indeed, managers such as Belasco and Fitch made a point of inviting Weber and Fields to their theaters, hoping their shows would be selected for parody.

A charming story came to be told about a serendipitous meeting between Lillian and Lew Fields. In this compelling tale, Lillian is sitting in Jesse Lewisohn's race track box, picking a winner by jabbing a hat pin into the program with her eyes closed. Fields jokingly suggests that if she were to use a fork, she could no doubt pick horses to win, place and show, all at once. The joke offers an opportunity for them to converse and Fields asks the key question: Would she consider joining his company? Immediately, Lillian proclaims it a fine idea. But, Fields asks tentatively, at what price? Lillian suggests $1,200 a week, a guaranteed 35 week season and all costumes paid for by Weber and Fields. On the spot, Fields agrees to the deal and they shake hands on it, supposedly the only contractual agreement between them for five years.

In reality, Weber and Fields were desperately looking for a female lead to play in their zany satires of current shows. Having just lost Fay Templeton, Weber suggested that Fields go to the race track, seek out Lillian and persuade her to join the company. While both men had considerable doubt about her ability to carry off a purely comedic role, not to mention share the stage with other stars, they were willing to give it a try. Fields already knew Lewisohn from previous race track and gambling casino encounters. Meeting Lillian would be easy; persuading her to join their comic stock company would demand all of Fields' ingenuity and talent for selling.

When Lillian actually agreed to join the Weberfields, both men were at once surprised and pleased. A public announcement at the end of July quickly followed the signing of a contract. The *Clipper*, in bold type, reported:

> Lillian Russell has signed with Weber and Fields and will be a member of their music hall stock company next season. She will play the leading role in the new burlesque, *Whirli-gig*, with which the house will open the season September 14.[26]

For Lillian, the chance to work with Weber and Fields rekindled professional enthusiasm and desire. In fact, she was as tired of performing in comic opera as audiences were tired of seeing it. But this would be a new adventure, with new acting challenges. The opportunity could not have been offered at a better time. Here was Lillian's chance to make her career adjustment within a quality professional environment, to an accepting and enthusiastic audience. But could she play musical comedy of the kind featured at the Music Hall? That's what the press and critics wanted to know:

> Weber and Fields have many very clever people under contract, people who have proven their fitness for burlesque and who have become favorites of the clientele of the house. With them, Miss Russell will have to strive for supremacy, and should she fail to obtain it, it is possible that unpleasantness may result as the fruit of her disappointment. It is true that Miss Russell may always be depended upon to make a fine appearance upon the stage. She undoubtedly possesses rare beauty, excellent taste in dress and a fine stage presence. She is prodigal in outlay for costumes, and is, moreover, gifted with a good voice and considerable vocal ability. Time, however, will take liberties even with pretty women, and while we admit Miss Russell is still fair, we pause at the word and omit the remainder of the alliterative phrase which it suggests. It is announced that in the new burlesque, *Whirli-gig*, Miss Russell will play the part of a frisky, capering French girl of 20. We can only hope she will play it well.[27]

The press further reported that, in anticipation of a new and successful season, the Music Hall was undergoing a complete renovation and "will be practically a new house when the artists are ready to play." Everyone was also anticipating a new Lillian Russell.

Reporters were said to be placing bets on whether she would make it in musical comedy. The odds were two to one against her.

Chapter Seven

Music Hall Days

Lillian's entrance to Weber and Fields' brand of musical comedy was both auspicious and audacious.

In her opening stage appearance, a slimmed-down Lillian, accoutered in a magnificent Worth gown adorned with miniature pearls, skipped sprightly from the wings to be met by cheers and prolonged applause. After singing two songs, she was encored repeatedly for both.

In her second appearance, the introduction of a travesty called *The Girl from Martins*, Lillian was seen in bed wearing a plug hat and what appeared to be a nightgown. The audience gasped. When she threw off the bedcovers and got up, the audience saw she was wearing a low-cut, off-the-shoulder evening gown. The audience, particularly the women, gasped again. Letters sent by patrons complained that the scene was too suggestive and a less revealing gown was substituted.

Lillian played Mademoiselle Fifi Coocoo, a rich and cultured Parisienne. One of her partners in the skit was David Warfield, who played Sigmund Cohenski, a millionaire Jew vacationing in Paris with his daughter. At one point in the skit, Lillian gave her dinner order to a waiter. She ended this extensive dissertation in French with the English phrase, "You may bring me a demitasse."

Overwhelmed and confused, Cohenski turned to the waiter and ordered authoritatively: "Bring me the same, and a cup of coffee."

Even though the routine had been practiced many times, Lillian still laughed openly with the audience. The critics, more than a little surprised but apparently pleased by her performance, reported:

> [T]here is little doubt that in her new field she will regain much of the popularity which once was hers.[1]

Rehearsals for the show had begun in August for a September 21 opening. Weber and Fields always opened their shows on Thursdays for good luck. Complementing Lillian was an all-star cast that included some of the most accomplished comedians on stage at the time. Besides their experience and professionalism, they possessed two attributes rarely seen on the popular stage: an ability, indeed a willingness, to share

122

the limelight with fellow comedians and a unique facility to improvise stage business, which always seemed to improve the show and give it a sense of spontaneity that audiences came to expect.

Peter Dailey, a heavyset but very graceful man, with light dancing movements, was always smiling. Dailey seemed to have a response for whatever happened on stage and he frequently deviated from the script. While such business would have distressed actors in legitimate theater, his improvisations always seemed to provide positive stimulus for the other Weberfield performers. No one ever knew how Dailey might act on stage. With him, rehearsals were a waste of time. One performer remembered that rehearsals at the Music Hall "were a madhouse," because she was never sure what other players were going to do or say, particularly Dailey.

David Warfield, another of Lillian's co-stars, had come to New York a few years earlier to appear in comic opera productions at the Casino. In one of these, he presented some memorable imitations of various legitimate actors, including a comic rendition of Sir Henry Irving. Warfield was hired by Weber and Fields to play a variety of ethnic roles. Two years at the Music Hall gained him the attention of David Belasco, who launched Warfield on a long and successful career in legitimate theater. A scene between him and Lillian in their first show together illustrates the zaniness of the production and Lillian's characteristic reactions to it.

In the so-called "Bohemian scene," Lillian gave a speech, a humorous travesty on European comic opera performers. Behind her stood Warfield, dressed in a ridiculous bathing suit and wearing a pair of large false feet. He provided an hilarious example of the Bohemians to whom Lillian referred. His costume alone provoked laughter, so Lillian had asked him to refrain from any other activities that would distract the audience from her monologue. Warfield promised he would stand perfectly still. After a few performances, Lillian noticed the audience laughing even more heartily than her own comic speech might warrant. She turned to find Warfield, standing still, as he promised, but his face uproariously contorted, presenting a disconsolate visage, with tears rolling down his cheeks. Lillian laughed so much at his antics that she couldn't finish the scene.

Charles Ross, a comic song and dance man, partnered with his wife Mabel Fenton for many years. Because of their outstanding ability to play a variety of character roles, their talents were extensively relied upon by Weber and Fields. Ross was a pleasant-looking, dapper dresser who would usually burlesque the handsome hero. John T. Kelly, a former Irish comedian with an excellent Irish brogue, played Irish roles, both male and female. Frankie Bailey, a female dancer who possessed what were purported to be the best legs in the business, showed them to advantage. Weber and Fields inserted their own two-act routines into the context of whatever travesty the company was performing. Their roles varied from Klondike miners to confidence men, highway robbers to bratty children, Union soldiers to glamorous women, all performed in dialect, accompanied by comedic business that "filled the house with laughter the entire performance."

Their performances were strongly supported by writer Edgar Smith, stage manager Julian Mitchell and composer/conductor John Stromberg. Smith had started his career adapting foreign comic operas, often for productions mounted at the Casino Theater. Upon joining Weber and Fields, he embarked on a career of writing comedy scripts that became classic burlesques of legitimate plays appearing on Broadway.

Julian Mitchell began as a dancer and later moved to direction and staging. His innovations at the Music Hall — fast pacing, developing the chorus line — gained him an excellent reputation, which led to stage direction for Victor Herbert's *The Wizard of Oz* and the first of the Ziegfeld Follies. John Stromberg, originally hired because of his hit song "My Best Girl's a Corker," soon became the Music Hall's in-house composer and conductor, a first in the preparation of musical comedy. A number of his songs, among them "Come Down Ma Evening Star," "Ma Blushin' Rosie" and "Kiss Me, Honey Do," became hits in Music Hall shows and enjoyed continued popularity long after the shows themselves had disappeared from memory.

First nights were gala events at the Music Hall, even though audiences knew that an initial Weber and Fields show was always at its worst. The chaotic nature of rehearsals often left large gaps in the script; scripted material was habitually crossed out; and the word "business" (scribbled on the side of a page) meant the players would improvise when they reached that point. A Weber and Fields show was never smoothed-out on the road like other shows before opening in New York. A first night show might last four hours. After dropping the dull material, adding new jokes and tightening the plot, the show was a fast and funny two hours a week later.

First nights inevitably brought out the social elite of the city to enjoy the Music Hall's travesties. The year that Lillian began, an auction of first-night tickets was conducted a week before the show opened, Peter Dailey serving as auctioneer. The auction was designed to eliminate the rampant ticket speculation that had occurred outside the theater on opening nights in previous years. Jesse Lewisohn paid $1,000 for two box seats; $100 to $500 bids for box and orchestra seats came from Diamond Jim Brady, Stanford White, Boss Croker and William Randolph Hearst. Displays in front of the theater more than matched those on stage, where floral tributes to the performers were placed. The streets around the theater were jammed to gridlock with fashionable carriages.

In anticipation of the new season and Lillian's introduction at the Music Hall, the entire interior had been refurbished. Reds were changed to hues of rose; worn plush exchanged for silk. Lights were shaded by old rose globes. The walls, ceiling and proscenium arch were repainted in old rose, accented by white and gold trim. A rose velvet carpet was laid. Lobby walls were redecorated with bas-relief, and all old photographs removed. The Music Hall had been transformed into a new house, fit for the elegant elite who now frequented this house of comedy.

The show received additional publicity, thanks to Charles Frohman, one of Broadway's famous producers. He was presenting *The Girl From Maxim's* at his theater and threatened to file a lawsuit against Weber and Fields to prevent them from satirizing his show. While visiting his theater, both Lew Fields and Edgar Smith had been asked to leave. The press questioned Frohman's motives:

> We cannot see how he has reached the conclusion that he will be injured by
> the proposed burlesque. His play will receive a large amount of free adver-
> tising, and presumably an increase in patronage.[2]

After all, the press pointed out, it had become a badge of honor for a show to be burlesqued at the Music Hall. Indeed, it was common to see such stellar legitimate theater performers as Richard Mansfield and Olga Nethersole in the Music Hall audience, laughing at the Weberfields' exaggerations of their performances.

Naturally, Lillian was delighted with her success in playing travesty and with the positive audience reaction to her performances. Her primary problem proved to be the difficulty she encountered in controlling her own laughter because of all the comedic business taking place on stage. It would take her some months to learn to play the "straight man." By that time, Weber and Fields realized that Lillian was not suited to perform in all the new skits they came up with as replacements throughout the season. Still, the constantly changing dialogue, new jokes, new scenes and new songs kept Lillian busy at rehearsals and her act fresh on stage. A month after first seeing a given show, a visitor to the Music Hall would often remark how different the show itself had become, even though the name hadn't changed.

There is no question that Lillian enjoyed her new role, her colleagues and, of course, her new and enthusiastic audiences. As she wrote in her memoirs:

> My first season at the Music Hall was vastly more important to me than any other that followed, as it was the means of changing the whole method of my line of work on the stage.[3]

Her career had not only been regenerated, she had also regained her title as "Queen." Lillian Russell was still recognized as the most beautiful and highest-paid female performer on stage.

The welcome combination of Lillian's new salary and the profits from some judicious investments recommended by Jesse Lewisohn prompted a real estate spree, consummated all at once in the fall of 1899. First, Lillian sold her well-publicized home on 77th Street. Actually, there was a sizable mortgage on the home, and its sale gained her little profit. In its place came what was, for Lillian, a more intimate structure on West 57th Street. The new house was more in keeping with her current needs. Dorothy was away at school; and Cynthia was now 71 years old and somewhat frail. A home was purchased for her in Rutherford, New Jersey, where she could more comfortably spend her declining years. Lillian had only one person to entertain, her intimate friend Jesse Lewisohn. Rearranging her living conditions was somewhat like rearranging her career, mused a reporter.

The new home on 57th Street was described by Dorothy as a "miniature museum." Every article in the house was an authentic antique. Lillian had collected Chinese porcelains for years and accumulated a large assortment. J.P. Morgan was said to visit Lillian to view unique specimens in her collection. Besides Marie Dressler, whose visits had by now become infrequent due to her heavy road schedule, Blanche Bates often used the guest room after a late evening of diversion. Along with frequent guest Jesse Lewisohn, Jim Brady and Edna McCauley continued to maintain the public foursome.

Another purchase was a summer home in Far Rockaway, Long Island. The estate was strategically located, within commuting distance of New York and near enough to the race tracks to play the horses. It was reported that Lillian engaged a betting commissioner to place wagers for her; he would visit her each day to collect her bets.

This summer home contained 30 rooms. There were 16 bedrooms, besides quarters for the servants, of which there were maids, two butlers, a valet, grooms, chauffeurs and gardeners. The grounds contained a vegetable garden, garage, stables, kennel, hen house, a barn for cows, a private bathing beach, tennis court and a gymnasium, which Lillian had specially built. When visitors stayed at the house, one of Lillian's requirements was that they exercise each day, employing whatever method they preferred. Lewisohn was an avid tennis player; Brady enjoyed golf; if possible, Dressler tried to avoid any exercise at all.

Weber and Fields changed skits as often as the previous one seemed to get stale or new shows or topical events gained headlines. Their first replacement for *The Girl From Martins* was called *The Other Way* (a travesty on *The Only Way*). Lillian appeared in a French peasant costume. The *Dramatic Mirror* commented:

> She has taken a new lease on life since she joined the company, and it is interesting to watch the way in which she has fallen into the jolly humor which pervades the entire organization.[4]

For the first time in her career, Lillian sang a "coon" song. Coon songs were Tin Pan Alley's interpretation of ragtime. Ragtime was an invention of black composers, most notably Scott Joplin, characterized by an up-tempo, syncopated melody. By contrast, Tin Pan Alley lyrics were usually racially stereotypical, employing plantation dialects, and always sung by whites. Like the period's most popular dance, the cakewalk, the coon song was one of the last vestiges of the minstrel show. The popularity of coon songs prompted many musical producers to interpolate them into their shows. John Stromberg was an excellent composer of coon songs and incorporated them into the Music Hall shows to good effect. Their popularity extended well beyond the show itself, an example being "Ma Blushin' Rosie," made famous by Al Jolson.

For Lillian Russell to sing a coon song was a significant change in her style. Her anxieties, however, were relieved when the *Dramatic Mirror*, the continuing arbiter of her career, reported that she "made a decided hit with it." This confirmation of her successful switch from comic opera to musical comedy inspired both Lillian and Stromberg to collaborate on coon songs for each new show.

During one of her skits, Lillian chose to wear a diamond crown given her by Jesse Lewisohn. While she was singing, Peter Dailey stepped on stage. In the middle of her song, he interrupted, "Lillian, do you have a headache?" Taken aback, Lillian responded, "Of course not. Why do you ask?" "Well," said Dailey, "if you haven't a headache, why are you wearing all that cracked ice on your head?"

Amid convulsive laughter from the audience, he sauntered off stage, while Lillian attempted to finish her song. Audience reaction to this episode was so positive that Edgar Smith decided to incorporate it in future skits with Lillian, if she were willing to have her song interrupted. Lillian thought it an excellent idea and played her role accordingly. She had great respect for Dailey. "Peter was the rarest of all comedians," she said, "the natural one to whom all thing are funny. Life to him was a bubble, and he made it seem that way to everyone about him."[5]

The company's next replacement skit was *Barbara Fidgety* (a spoof of Clyde Fitch's Civil War drama, *Barbara Frietchie*). Dailey's song "For That They Made Me Colonel" was the hit of the piece. Lillian soon noticed that Dailey knew only the first four lines of the song. Each time he sang it, he would make up new lyrics, usually in rhyme. Once the audience became aware of it, they challenged him in encores to come up with new verses. He obliged, and they were always funny.

On May 5, after a record-breaking 264 performances on Broadway, the company went on tour. A hired train took 90 people, cast and crew, along with costumes and scenery. The four-week tour to ten cities netted Weber and Fields more money than they had made all season at the Music Hall, advanced ticket prices and large theaters contributing to their profits. Like other managers before them, Weber and Fields realized that most of their money was to be made on the road.

Near the end of the season, Lillian hinted to reporters that her time at the Music Hall had been so much fun she would love to return for the following season. Immediately, she was signed. A happy Lillian retired to her summer home at Far Rockaway to enjoy the company of friends and the excitement of the races.

Back in New York, however, an historic confrontation between vaudeville artists and theater managers was about to take place. In May, theatrical papers reported that all the principal managers of variety theaters were going to meet to form a Vaudeville Trust, its purpose being to control theaters and performers in all venues, an operation similar in structure to the Syndicate's control over first-class theaters. In addition, the Trust would move to reduce the salaries vaudeville performers were receiving, claiming they were already too high. Trust spokesmen argued that supply of actors was greater than demand and the unfit had to be weeded out. They singled out as most offensive the "gold-brickers," a term describing actors who moved from the legitimate stage to vaudeville, then stayed in it because vaudeville was more profitable. In return, the Trust would provide an actor a full 40-week season, though at a lower salary, because of the season-long guarantee. They would also eliminate the need for actors to have an agent, but the agent's 5 percent fee would revert to the Trust.

In response to this ultimatum, vaudeville actors formed a group called "The White Rats." The name was borrowed from a similar group formed in London; "rats" spelled backward was "star." At their first meeting, eight people were present. By their fourth, a few weeks later, 40 performers attended. As news of the new organization was spread by the theatrical papers, applications by the hundreds poured in, many of them coming from the top performers in vaudeville.

Initially, the objectives of the White Rats were to protect the booking rights of actors, to be paid reasonable salaries, and to retain their agents; it was more a series of protective measures than a challenge to the Trust's control over theaters. By September, the group seemed to be large enough to directly confront the demands made by the Trust, and a number of individual skirmishes took place (suggesting to all that such confrontations would escalate). At first, all of the White Rats were males; none of them considered the inclusion of women performers, even though women represented more than a third of the vaudeville players. But this exclusionary decision would soon change.

In the meantime, sheltered from the friction between management and labor, Lillian, her family and friends enjoyed their summer comforts. Lillian's girlfriends, whom she dubbed the "Farm Flirts," always seemed ready to party. Frequent visits by Lewisohn and Brady, usually bearing gifts of food and wine, livened up the atmosphere.

This was also the summer that Dorothy, now 16, was introduced to the races. She had already been placing bets secretly with her mother's agent and had even won a few races. According to Dorothy, when her mother found out, she replied, "I guess there is something in heredity after all." The following week, Dorothy accompanied Lillian to the races, an event that often repeated itself until late August, when Dorothy had to return to her convent school in New Jersey.

Rehearsals for the 1900-01 season began with a rash of "mash" notes anonymously sent to the performers. It was common for members of the company to receive such notes from admirers, ranging from shy requests for a lock of hair or a piece of clothing

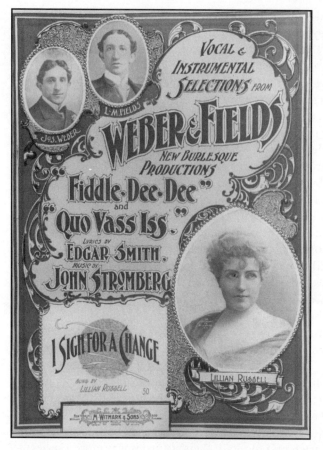

Music sheet cover. Weber, Fields, Stromberg and Witmark collaborated on publishing songs that Lillian and Fay Templeton performed in Music Hall productions.

to fervent protestations of desire. Among the notes that Lillian received was one from a goat owner who offered her a pet of his if she would use it in a skit. Another stated boldly, "I love you. Let's get married." Lillian knew it came from a cast member kidding her about past marital alliances. Another such note was received by David Warfield, who ignored it because so many absurd propositions were being passed around. When Belasco complained to Lillian that his note had been ignored, she took him backstage to talk to Warfield. Warfield was offered a sizable contract to appear in legitimate theater, a far cry from his antics as Sigmund Cohenski.

On September 6, the Weber and Fields company of comedians opened with *Fiddle-Dee-Dee*, to their usual full house of rich patrons, assorted politicos and theatrical celebrities (including Flo Ziegfeld, Abe Hummel and Julius Witmark). All had come to see what was being called "the greatest assemblage of talent ever seen on the popular stage." This season, there were two additions: Fay Templeton, who had been with the company before Lillian, and an old friend of Lillian's, De Wolf Hopper. Templeton, considered a better actress than Lillian and able to parody many of the female stars on Broadway, was just what Weber and Fields wanted for their skits. Hopper, tall and handsome in his leading man roles, added sexual glamour to the cast and proved the perfect romantic foil for Lillian.

In the first episode, Lillian played the role of Mrs. Waldorf Meadowbrook, an elegantly gowned member of the socially elite 400, who expressed her desire for travel and fun by singing "I Sigh for a Change." Later, she was joined by Hopper, who was first obliged to quiet the audience when they requested he recite "Casey at the Bat." The two sang a number, imitating the roles they had long performed on the comic opera stage. The *Mirror* commented:

> Miss Russell looked more radiantly beautiful than ever, in a bewildering costume that made the women in the audience blink their eyes. A duet brought them [Russell and Hopper] the most spontaneous and enthusiastic applause of the evening.[6]

In the second act, Lillian stood balanced on a rock, the moon conveniently shining only on her, and sang one of Stromberg's new coon songs, "Come Back, My Honey Boy, to Me." The remainder of the cast presented a burlesque of a new Broadway hit, *Quo Vadis*, translated into Music Hall parlance as *Quo Vas Iss?* The stilted classical language of the original was roughly translated into the slang of the day. Most notable in this skit was Templeton's singing of one of Stromberg's biggest hits, "Ma Blushin' Rosie." The *Mirror* summed up the evening's experience:

> [T]he new entertainment is a success from start to finish, and it looks as if Weber and Fields will enjoy another season of great prosperity.[7]

Quo Vas Iss? was followed a few weeks later by a travesty of Augustus Thomas' play *Arizona*. Lillian played the part of Sarsaparilla, the daughter of an eccentric ranch owner. The girl is hypnotized and taught to smoke. Singing a song in praise of cigarettes, Lillian smoked on stage, the first time that anyone had smoked in a comic opera or musical comedy. Shocking as her action was, no one seemed to mind. What the press did mention, ironically, was that Fay Templeton's "avoirdupois" was beginning to handicap her work.

The skit also made two other significant contributions to the musical comedy genre. First, stage effects and decor were used to enhance characterizations. Walls, dishes, saucers and cups were painted to resemble cowhide; a portrait of a cow's head sported eye-glasses and a cap to look like the rancher. Second, a chorus line of 40 pretty young women who had staggered on stage in dirty and revealingly torn uniforms, suddenly snapped to attention and performed a series of complicated dance formations. Julian Mitchell's intention was to integrate the chorus into the story and justify the girls' presence on stage.

In the middle of the season, Charles Ross got into an argument with Fields and quit, just as the company was rehearsing a new skit. Only a few hours later, Fields persuaded Charles Frohman to lend them Fritz Williams. Williams then spent the whole afternoon in a hansom cab, touring Central Park with John T. Kelly and learning his part. That evening, Williams played his role flawlessly. He was congratulated by the cast, particularly on how well he kissed Lillian with so little preparation.

After 32 weeks at the Music Hall, the Weberfields went on the road for their annual spring tour, this time for six weeks. Again, profits from the brief tour bested the long season in New York.

An episode in January forced Fields to consider leaving the show for a short time. His children had fallen very sick with scarlet fever, and his oldest brother Max had just died of tuberculosis. The press expressed sympathy for Fields and noted his devotion to his family. The fact that he remained with the company and continued to perform was lauded as evidence of his commitment and professionalism. It could not have escaped Lillian's notice that, a few years earlier, she had been maligned for doing the same thing.

Early in 1901, a strike by the White Rats against the Vaudeville Trust seemed imminent. In addition, the White Rats had formed an in-house booking agency to handle all of their members' needs, the five percent commissions from booking (previously the agents' fee) to be donated to operate the organization. They also voted to admit women to the group, acknowledging their earlier oversight. Lillian was the first woman to join, setting an example for other female performers to align themselves against the Trust.

Lillian, with (left to right) David Warfield, Lew Fields and Joe Weber, in *Fiddle-Dee-Dee*, 1900-01 season. In peasant costume, singing coon songs, Lillian persuaded critics she could perform farce comedy as convincingly as comic opera.

Aware of mounting pressure, the Trust offered to rescind the commissions at their next meeting. When no meeting took place, the White Rats called for a walkout in Eastern theaters, set for the following Thursday. The Trust then offered a temporary truce, again promising to abolish the commission. But again, nothing was done. In March, some members of the White Rats staged sick-outs, disrupting both New York and touring schedules. Finally, the Trust stopped taking commissions.

Believing they had won the battle, the White Rats were jubilant. By the summer, however, through behind-the-scenes deals and pay-offs, the Trust was able to weaken the opposition's booking arrangements and "buy" some performers with high salaries. The White Rats soon realized they had been outmaneuvered by the Trust's deception and double-dealing. Unfortunately, this initial setback rendered them a token organization for several years, given to protests and parties but no real action.

During this time, Lillian had worked hard for the organization, promoting its benefits to as many women as would listen to her about the issue. Her association with the Professional Woman's League, of which Susan was now president, helped somewhat, but most of its members were no longer active theatrical performers. When the White Rats lost a good deal of their initial vigor, Lillian felt she had wasted her energy on a cause whose leaders were evidently unprepared to effectively combat the arrogant theater managers. She knew how tough individual managers were;

a consortium of them controlling most of the vaudeville theaters would be a formidable opponent.

Despite these political disappointments, Lillian's second summer at the Far Rockaway estate seemed even more enjoyable than the first. Her stable was now filled with horses; cows roamed the surrounding fields; and the vegetable garden was large enough to supply salad greens daily. She was no longer the only stage star living in the area, as it was rapidly becoming a fashionable summer place for performers and producers. Yet Marie Dressler's situation was in stark contrast. Having just filed for bankruptcy, Dressler was staying with Lillian until she was able to sign a new contract for the coming season.

Lillian's third year with the Weberfields began on September 5 in *Hoity-Toity*. The *Clipper* reviewed the show as if opening nights at the Music Hall had become a Broadway tradition.

> Each succeeding show seems to be better than its predecessor, and the present one is just as certain of success as were any of those that have preceded it.... The house was literally packed and each member was enthusiastically received. At the close of the performance, which lasted till midnight, the stage was transformed into a bower of flowers. The leading members were called upon for speeches and made them.[8]

In the first part of the show, Lillian played Lady Grafter, a wily social matron, serving as a "straight" foil for Weber, Fields and Sam Bernard as "The Sauerkraut Kings." The second part took place on a set resembling the Yale University campus, where a rowing crew took Lady Grafter on a lake ride. As the audience watched, the scene changed to a river. Lady Grafter soon became the coxswain; as crew and leader moved down the river, slides were projected on a rear screen depicting the changing riverbank. Lillian's performance as coxswain, so incongruous with her costume and demeanor, was singled out as being "clever business."

In a later scene, Lillian was cast as the fourth in a poker game with the three "sauerkraut kings." Fields and Bernard had just taken all of Weber's money and were boasting of their card-playing powers. Even as they passed cards under the table to one another, Lillian calmly won every hand and all of their money. With each hand lost, the boys became more upset. By the end of the game, they were fighting among themselves, while Lillian happily walked off the stage counting her winnings.

Hoity-Toity ran for 33 weeks. The usual spring tour lasted only three weeks, because the Syndicate had effectively blocked the Weberfields out of most theaters in the cities they wished to visit. As a result, profits this season were minimal, which generated strains on the long-term partnership.

For the first time since the Music Hall opened, there were few new musical scores introduced. Weber and Fields didn't want to let people know that John Stromberg was ill with rheumatoid arthritis and was having difficulty composing music. During the later part of the season, he was so incapacitated that he had to give up conducting the orchestra. Hiring another conductor did little to solve the problem. In desperation, Weber and Fields persuaded an ailing Stromberg to prepare songs for the coming 1902-03 season. He tried, but was able to compose only one song, for Lillian.

When she visited Stromberg at his home in June, he could no longer walk and was obviously in great pain. But he showed her a song he was working on. "Lillian," he promised, "I will write you the prettiest song you ever sang." He died a few days later, the diagnosis being a "paralysis of the heart." Shortly afterwards, however, it was found he had committed suicide by taking poison, Paris Green, an insecticide he used in his garden. To the cast, Stromberg's loss was disheartening; to Lillian, it was as great a loss as she had ever experienced.

When his body was discovered, the song he had written for Lillian was found in his coat pocket. As Lillian received the manuscript for "Come Down, Ma Evening Star," she noticed brown spots on it, remnants of the poison Stromberg had taken. This painful image served as a poignant reminder to her each time she sang the song.

Far Rockaway now had a garage to keep automobiles. Brady and Lewisohn already drove, and Lillian purchased her own car as well. Speeding around the countryside (at 15 miles an hour) became an enjoyable pastime for friends and visitors, replacing the carriage and horseback riding of previous summers. An expensive bit of excitement occurred when the garage caught fire, caused an explosion and destroyed the automobiles owned by Lewisohn. Lillian felt it best to spend the remainder of the summer at her cottage in Saratoga.

Just prior to beginning rehearsals for the coming season at the Music Hall, Lillian saw Dorothy and Susie off to France. Dorothy, now 18 and a graduate of her convent school, was enrolled in a finishing school in Paris. Lillian had signed for her daughter to be tutored by an opera star from the Comedie Francaise, stating she would like Dorothy to study for grand opera.

On September 11, the 1902-03 Weber and Fields Music Hall season began, Lillian's fourth year with the company. *Twirly-Whirly* was called a musical comedy, in keeping with the new definition of popular theater. Along with Lillian, this season's performers included the returning Peter Dailey, Charles Bigelow, John T. Kelly and Fay Templeton. William Collier, a more than adequate replacement for De Wolf Hopper, was also hired. The usual first-night activities filled the house.

Set in Seville, the new show concerned a wealthy American stockbroker and his widowed stepdaughter, Mrs. Stockson Bonds (Lillian). To show off her wealth, she invited the local nobility to a party, but they ignored the obviously *nouveau riche* American. Snubbed, she chose to instead invite a vaudeville impresario, a naughty monkey and its keeper, a Spanish opera singer and two German army deserters (Weber and Fields) to dispense the usual comedy mayhem. Lillian sang "The Leader of Vanity Fair," which described her efforts to be chic and "smart."

There was no doubt that Lillian knew this role well. When she is snubbed, Mrs. Stockson Bonds observes, "The life of a society star is not a path of roses. I envy the little stars up there. They can stay out every night and not lose their sparkle." It was the cue for the orchestra to begin "Come Down, Ma Evening Star."

On opening night, so the story is told, Lillian cried before she could finish the song. Actually, attempting to interpret the song had previously been even more painful. During rehearsals, Lillian was never able to sing the entire song. Even the chorus cried when she started. Mitchell would say, "All right, pass the number today." This scenario repeated itself at every rehearsal until the last, when Mitchell finally commanded, "Now then, Miss Russell, we will have that song, as you and the chorus are going to do it tomorrow night! See that you all sing it!"

Critics mentioned how Lillian rendered Stromberg's final gift:

> Miss Russell's voice shook as she sang the song and she seemed on the verge of tears.[9]

While "Evening Star" was a coon song, Lillian sang it with the feeling of an opera aria; it was a deep and personal emotion she displayed to audiences. The song became her "signature" tune, and she sang it often in future years. Each time, she said, she saw John Stromberg in his last painful hours, finishing the manuscript just for her. She recalled, "I always thought of Honey Stromberg whenever I sang that song. And, strange to say, no one ever sang it in public but me."[10]

In a final tribute to Stromberg, the Weberfields (led by Lillian) staged a benefit for Stromberg's widow. It netted more than $6,000.

In the middle of December, Julian Mitchell resigned after an argument with Joe Weber. Having now lost two of his most important collaborators, Fields was very upset. What had been a quiet if increasingly apparent rift between the longtime partners now made it to the street, with rumors claiming they were quarreling and would soon separate. The reports quickly died as they continued to perform together. But even more serious problems were yet to come.

Twirly-Whirly played to full houses for 31 weeks (247 performances). Each of the replacement skits was reported to be excellent, and customers kept returning to see the "new business" put on by the company. The year's end tour ran weeks but included many one-night stands due to continued booking problems. Advanced prices in large theaters generated considerable profit for Weber and Fields. Unfortunately, as their shows prospered, their friendship deteriorated.

Often seen at gaming establishments and the race track, Lew Fields loved to gamble. In an effort to curb gambling in the city, New York's new district attorney, William T. Jerome, staged a number of raids on some of the best-known resorts in town. He also subpoenaed prominent businessmen to be questioned publicly regarding their gambling. Fields was never called, but Jesse Lewisohn was identified as a major player. When Lewisohn refused to respond to Jerome's subpoena, he was arrested while attending the race track with Lillian. Still, Lewisohn refused to answer Jerome's questions. The court case against Lewisohn took almost a year. In the end, he admitted that he was a gambler and had played at some of the well-known gaming houses. After admitting his participation, he was released from the district attorney's investigation. Through it all, Lillian remained very concerned about Lewisohn's situation, not only because of their intimate relationship, but also because a good portion of his winnings found its way into her jewelry boxes. Lewisohn's health suffered. He contracted stomach ulcers from the ordeal, a problem that ultimately contributed to a serious illness.

Meanwhile, the summer of 1903 was a memorable one for Lillian, due to her daughter's marriage — or, rather, how Dorothy came to be married. Her return from Paris had been shrouded in romantic mystery. Dorothy claimed she had been married to an Italian count during Christmas in Monte Carlo. A few months later, her supposed husband had an operation and died under anesthesia. Data suggest that Lillian was unaware of these events, if they had in fact ever occurred.

After Dorothy returned home, she was reportedly being courted by the Einstein brothers, who had escorted her during previous summers. Tracy Einstein was often seen with Dorothy, but it was Abbott Einstein who won her hand by his insistence.

In her memoirs, Dorothy stated that she and Abbott eloped to New York in September and were married by a rabbi. In fact, they were married in a colorful ceremony on August 20, in Jersey City. Dorothy's stories often bordered on the fanciful, as though she were trying hard to outdo her mother in "outrageous" behavior. She claimed:

> Abbott Einstein's mother was an Irish Catholic and he had been brought up in that religion. I had become a Catholic too. But it didn't seem possible that any clergyman but a rabbi would join in matrimony two people with the names Einstein and Solomon.[11]

In fact, the Einstein family were practicing Jews. Even though she attended Catholic schools, Dorothy was an Episcopalian. A justice of the peace married them in New Jersey.

Strongly disapproving her daughter's choice for a husband, Lillian was very unhappy. She believed Dorothy was too young and inexperienced for marriage and had ruined a promising career. She had hoped that Dorothy would return to Paris to complete her operatic training. Still, Lillian consoled herself, her daughter hadn't married someone from the performing arts.

To resolve any doubts in her mother's mind about her career intentions, Dorothy announced she was going to audition for the chorus in Sam Bernard's new show *The Girl From Kay's*. Much to Lillian's relief, Dorothy didn't get the job. But Dorothy was not yet finished with the stage. Abbott wasn't pleased by any of these activities, but seemed unable to do anything about them.

At the beginning of the century, New York (and America) was poised on the threshold of a new era. The first New York subway began operating, offering a fast and clean way to get around town. The Pennsylvania Railroad announced its purpose of entering New York via tunnel under the Hudson River, into a new terminal at 34th Street. Not to be outdone, the New York Central began construction of a new terminal on the site of the old Grand Central Station on 42nd Street. The Flatiron Building, at the intersection of Broadway, Fifth Avenue and 23rd Street, was the city's hub and its most celebrated skyscraper. As the retail district edged uptown, stores pushed the theaters before them. A new theater section, around Times Square, received a boost from the new subway. What had been the original theater district was now rapidly disappearing. Wallack's, Daly's, the original Bijou, Hammerstein's and Madison Square theaters were all gone. The famous Garden Theater was now a Jewish playhouse. Some, like the Savoy, Academy of Music, and the Broadway, were being transformed into moving picture houses.

In the U.S., two bicycle builders flew their metal, wire and paper contraption over the sand dunes of Kitty Hawk. An enterprising young man drove a car of his own design over a frozen lake in Michigan in the fastest time achieved by man to that date. President Theodore Roosevelt declared that, thanks to such exemplars as the Wright brothers and Henry Ford, the country's economic future looked bright.

It was also the period when American musical comedy became an established commercial entity. The number of shows calling themselves musical comedies increased dramatically. Attractions like *The Wizard of Oz, The Prince of Pilsen, Babes in Toyland* and *Piff!Paff!!Pouf!!!* were well received and sustained long runs. (*Oz* and *Babes* were Julian Mitchell and Victor Herbert collaborations.) Even Weber and Fields' popular brand of comedy had lost its novelty and was now faced with formidable new competition.

While the Weberfields' new show, *Whoop-Dee-Doo*, was considered a success similar to their previous annual openings, ticket sales were not as large, nor were box office receipts sufficient to pay the weekly expenses and salaries of the company. On December 30, 1903, a cataclysmic event in Chicago doomed many theaters in the U.S., including the Music Hall.

Mr. Bluebeard, starring comic Eddie Foy, was playing to full houses at the Iroquois Theater, which offered seating for 1,700 people. The popularity of the attraction was so great that it created standing room, bringing the total audience to more than 2,000. At the beginning of the second act, a spark from one of the new electric floodlights ignited a piece of scenery. Within seconds, the fire spread from flies to draperies to the stage itself. At the sight of flames, the audience panicked. A door was opened backstage, fanning the fire even more. The asbestos curtain refused to drop. The lighting system exploded, leaving the theater in darkness. Within 15 minutes, more than 600 theatergoers were asphyxiated, burned or trampled to death. Another 400 were injured.

The nation was shocked. Across the country, mayors ordered an immediate investigation of every theater in their jurisdictions. Many were found to be out of compliance with fire protection regulations and were summarily shut down. For a time, the combination of theater closures, out-of-work performers and stage hands, and a significant decline in theater attendance nearly paralyzed the entertainment industry. The disaster also had an effect on the Syndicate. Because of its questionable reputation, the Syndicate was singled out as being more careless than other theater organizations. The result was a strong anti-Syndicate campaign that damaged the monopoly considerably. The Shuberts, a new, aggressive, anti-trust company, saw an opportunity to invade Syndicate territory, which they quickly did, with impressive success.

Fire department investigators examined the Music Hall and gave the Weberfields an ultimatum — rebuild the theater or close it. Given their divergent views on the partnership's future, what were the longtime partners to do?

Unfortunately, the opening of *Whoop-Dee-Doo* had to be delayed for two weeks because Lillian fell ill and was forced to bed. When the show did open, two Thursdays later, Peter Dailey apologized to the audience for the delay by telling them the tailor had been unable to finish Lillian's trousers in time.

The show opened on September 24. For the city's social elite, opening nights at the Music Hall had become a fashion show. "Everybody who is anybody, as well as those who would like to be somebody" attended the show, reported the *Dramatic Mirror*. Wealthy women usually dressed to compete with Lillian. They were astonished when she first came on stage in men's evening clothes, smoking a cigarette.

In her second appearance, she wore one of her elegant gowns; the audience showed their appreciation for her return to femininity. The scene took place in Paris at a German beer garden. Lillian played a countess poking fun at Americans and their desire to purchase European art. When asked whether it was true that Russell Sage wanted to purchase the Venus de Milo, she replied, "True, but he wanted it cut-rate because it was damaged."

The best skit of the evening was a Weber and Fields routine with Lillian and Louis

Mann. In the skit, Lillian wanted to buy a statue of Roman gladiators. While examining the statue, Weber and Fields tipped it over and broke it. They had no choice but to themselves pose as the statue, dressing in skirts, painting themselves white and holding swords. Lillian became aware of the switch and decided to have fun with them, pinching and tickling while inspecting the "statue." When Lillian was not looking, they relaxed and changed poses. She then decided to hold a dinner in front of the statue. Hungry, the boys would steal food from the table when no one was looking, being forced to "freeze" in various ridiculous poses whenever anyone glanced at them. Each time they played the skit, Lillian had difficulty suppressing her own laughter at the antics of the comedians. Audiences found the routine hilarious.

Still, a decision regarding the company's future had to be made quickly. Believing they had no choice but to leave the Music Hall and go on tour early, Weber and Fields signed up with a small booking organization for stops in the West and Midwest. The Syndicate, in the person of Abe Erlanger, who harbored a passionate dislike for Weber and Fields, now saw an opportunity to get back at them. When the company was playing in San Francisco (their first performance after a cross-country trip), Erlanger made a deal with the booking company to gain control over the Weber and Fields route. He canceled the tour, leaving them stranded 3,000 miles from New York, without any theaters in which to play, for eight weeks.

Scrambling frantically for independent houses, Weber and Fields found a theater in Los Angeles, another in Albuquerque, still another in Denver and, thanks to the Shuberts, even one in Chicago. Seasoned troupers that they were, the company handled the inconveniences admirably. Weber and Fields, however, had now agreed to separate; by the time they reached Pittsburgh, Broadway was aware of their impending dissolution. Both Peter Dailey and Lillian announced they were not returning to the Music Hall next season. Lillian was already at work seeking future bookings, but now found it unaccountably difficult to contact theater managers.

The last show for the Weberfields would have been in Boston, but for some friends who rented them New York's New Amsterdam Theater for a final two-week run together. The fact that the New Amsterdam was owned by Klaw and Erlanger added bitter irony to the Weberfields' final act, played in a Syndicate house.

After the company's final curtain, May 28, 1904, the entire group lined up on stage, hand-in-hand, Fields at one end, Weber at the other. Everyone was in tears, including an audience comprised of the city's social, business and political elite. All the performers made brief speeches. Some, like Lillian, expressed their hope the comedy team would reconsider. When asked to speak, Fields could only gasp his dismay. Weber said in a weak voice, "We can only say we are sorry." The orchestra played "Auld Lang Syne," the curtain came down and a saddened audience slowly left the theater.

A week later, the *Dramatic Mirror* announced that Lillian would again appear in a comic opera, entitled *Lady Teazle*, a dramatization of *A School for Scandal*. The Shuberts were to be her managers, and the attraction would appear at the Casino Theater, a recent Shubert purchase.

Lillian, however, confronted another, more personal concern. Fulfilling her promise, Dorothy had entered vaudeville early in the year, singing and dancing at various New York houses. Because of her name, she was followed closely by the press. While she was commended for her overall performance, her voice was considered weak. Dorothy's career continued, though it seemed her bookings had less to do with her own talent than the fact she was Lillian's daughter. Nor was Abbott Einstein pleased with the situation. At one point, believing that a stage manager had made unwarranted advances toward his wife, Abbott punched the man. When he couldn't persuade Dorothy to give up vaudeville, he moved out of their apartment.

Lillian's spirits had fallen. The closure of the Music Hall and the separation of Weber and Fields had ended what she later described as "the best-ever years" of her stage career. Examining her performance opportunities, she found little to excite her. Even the promise of a show like *Lady Teazle* meant a return to comic opera. At 43, her voice had lost some of its range and sweetness. Would audiences notice? Would they still come to see her perform?

Chapter Eight

End of an Era

ℳaybe it was time to retire.

> Can I succeed in straight comedy or will the public accept me only if I sing a few songs and act, too? From the day of my debut on stage to the present time I have been identified with comic opera and it is therefore a grave question in my mind if the public would accept me in any role that required not the lifting of my voice.[1]

Theater managers also wondered about that, and were reluctant to approach Lillian with any shows that would present a risk to them. By her own admission, Lillian had not "worked hard" while with the Weberfields. She had taken little opportunity to improve her talents; she had perhaps even lost some of her self-discipline.

By the middle of May 1904, when new shows and performers were already signed for the following fall season, Lillian reported she had no plans for the future. She was not sure what she would do.

Yet Lillian was an astute observer of the theatrical scene and very much aware of the rapid changes taking place. She particularly noticed the changing face of audiences attending popular theater venues — "polite" vaudeville, musical comedy and a new form tentatively called a "revue." For these attractions, audiences were distinctly middle-class; they now were clearly split between younger customers, many of whom were seeing these forms of entertainment for the first time, and older, who had previously experienced these changing forms and generally accepted them.

Older customers continued to perceive Lillian as the American Beauty, but they were no longer sure at what form of entertainment she was best. Her voice still rated tops, but she was now identified with no particular style of music. The days of manager conflicts, marital problems and seemingly self-destructive behavior were ancient history. Lillian was now seen as a mature professional.

Younger audiences, unaware of or not familiar with the comic opera genre, looked upon Lillian as an anomaly. There was no doubt that she was beautiful, exquisitely gowned, a polished entertainer. But the young were less acquainted with her particular talents and skills. She seemed to have an excellent reputation, but they weren't

138

sure of what it consisted. For her part, Lillian was confident she retained an honored place among experienced theatergoers; at the same time, she was unsure of her position among new audiences.

Lillian also recognized the continuing expansion of popular theater. In actuality, she had been a contributor to it for years. During her five years at the Music Hall, audiences for popular theater had doubled; the number of touring companies had tripled. In New York City alone, the number of theaters catering to the vaudeville craze had also tripled. In cities and towns all over the country, theaters devoted to popular entertainment were being built. Stage productions had become the premier leisure-time activity. Even the limited touring done by the Weberfields had instructed Lillian on the importance of performance "on the road." Discussions with fellow performers, including Susan and her husband Owen Westford, had convinced her of the influence and impact of popular entertainment's rapidly expanding market.

Another change in popular theater was a gradual shift in the public's perception and acceptance of feminine beauty. Young female performers now tended to be petite, thin and dark-haired, with a zest and vitality that radiated strongly from the stage. What these performers might have lacked in polish and vocal control they made up for in gregarious behavior — brasher and sexier, according to some critics — that seemed to communicate an "I don't care" attitude that young audiences found refreshing and enjoyable. Lillian, by contrast, was still identified as "The Queen," a persona that connoted a far different image from those of younger women who might be considered competition.

Lillian knew from personal experience that one ought not to compete with these performers. Not that long ago, she herself had been like them, had exploited the public's tastes to her own benefit. But there still seemed to be plenty of room for all kinds of actresses on the current stage. Lillian would just have to find her particular niche.

Nor should the Syndicate be overlooked. They were now at the height of their power, controlling most of the theaters around the country, along with a good percentage of performers. They were making alliances and breaking competition at will. Still, the first signs of an organized and vocal opposition could be seen. A foundation was being created that would grow in strength during the next few years, directly challenging the Syndicate's hegemony. This challenge would come both from performers' groups and rival entertainment companies.

Lillian's feelings about the Syndicate were profoundly negative, and they were made even more so by the Syndicate's attempts to emasculate Weber and Fields. But Lillian was also sensitive to the fact that all theater managers wanted to control and dictate to performers under their command, particularly women. Thus, whether one dealt with the Syndicate or not, every contract had to be skillfully negotiated and carefully monitored, to safeguard all agreements made.

One of the Syndicate's new rivals, 28-year-old Sam Shubert, a theatrical impresario-in-the-making, now came to Lillian's rescue. As a teenager in Syracuse, about the time he decided to enter the theater business, Sam had been dazzled by Lillian when she and her company came to perform comic opera. During his ascension to theater management in New York, Sam continued to follow Lillian's career. He hoped that, at some time in the future, she might come under his management. His enthusiasm for her, however, was not necessarily shared by his brothers Lee and J.J.

The Shubert family had settled in a poor section of Syracuse, upon their arrival from Lithuania, in 1882. To contribute to family finances, Sam and Lee obtained jobs at local theaters. Enthusiastic about opportunities in the theater business, Sam became a box office treasurer. While in his early '20s, his insightful analysis of the growing vaudeville business convinced him to purchase the touring rights to a popular play, *A Texas Steer*, and the financial reward afforded by this decision started his career in earnest. What followed were five years of theater and touring company acquisitions and an increasingly keen knowledge of theater business operations. In 1900, Sam decided to move to New York to enlarge the brothers' theater leasing and ownership business, in spite of the fact that their primary competition was the all-powerful Syndicate. Even in the infancy of their company, the Shuberts were the Syndicate's chief adversary; the battle for theater business supremacy, which was to last a decade, soon began.

Their first acquisition was the Herald Square Theater in New York. Due to some fortuitous booking commitments, they were able to sign Richard Mansfield, at the height of his career. Though the Shuberts were opposed to the Syndicate, they realized that, at this point, joining them was better than fighting them, so they signed an agreement to become a Syndicate-affiliated house. They acquired the rights to two shows, *The Belle of New York* and *Arizona*, both of which became hits and gave the Shuberts the money necessary for expansion.

They entered production by presenting a problematic play, but followed with a popular musical that opened in 1902, at their newly acquired Casino Theater. The history of the Casino, its many previous managers and owners, its age and design, all contributed to an image of opulent decadence; but the Shuberts saw in the Casino the potential drawing power of one of New York's most famous theatrical landmarks.

By 1904, the Shuberts stood on the threshold of directly confronting the Syndicate. Obtaining the services of Lillian Russell would be a major step in building their reputation. There is no question that Sam Shubert was the driving force among the three brothers. Lee tended to follow his brother's lead; J.J., impulsive and combative during these early years of the company, was assigned to handle out-of-town business affairs. Within a year, however, this arrangement would radically change.

Sam Shubert knew Lillian had made no commitments to perform during the 1904-05 season. What better way to entice her than to suggest a return to comic opera? What more inviting vehicle than a musical adaptation of Sheridan's *A School for Scandal*? Shubert personally traveled to her summer home at Far Rockaway to make his proposal. His offer could not have been better timed. With Brady and Lewisohn in agreement, Lillian accepted.

On October 24, after three days of hard negotiations, a contract was signed. Lillian had been unaware of how the Shuberts dealt with performers, and *they* were unaware of how Lillian dealt with theater managers. It was an education for all of them. Issues like the purchase of gowns, touring conditions and the performance of matinees dominated their discussions.

Interestingly, Lillian agreed to a salary of only $700 a week, well below what she had been earning for the past ten years. She believed, however, that her receiving 50 percent of the net receipts would more than offset her lower weekly salary. She also persuaded Sam Shubert to include Susan's husband, Owen Westford, in the cast, at $75 a week. In a few months, all of these agreements would become a matter of contentious debate.

Lillian spent the next six weeks rehearsing, particularly the songs. Since she had not sung a complete role for more than five years, her singing teacher was in almost constant attendance. Yet according to reporters allowed into rehearsals, her voice was as strong, clear and sweet as ever. The press seemed to be enjoying her return to comic opera. Lillian reciprocated with a comment about her comeback:

> In view of the fact that the greater portion of my life has been spent in comic opera, it is not unnatural that my wishes should be for the betterment of that class of entertainment.[2]

Headlines trumpeted: "The Queen has returned!" All awaited Lillian's appearance on stage.

Lady Teazle opened at Baltimore's Academy of Music on December 19, 1904. The press called it "a big success, in every way." Three days devoted to solidifying the production and an auction of first night seats at the Casino prepared the show's New York opening on Christmas Eve.

Two issues distracted Lillian just prior to the opening. First, she expressed irritation to Sam Shubert because he had fired a girl in the chorus for not being, in his opinion, sufficiently pretty. Secondly, a report from Denver noted that Dorothy, on the road with a vaudeville company, had become seriously ill with bronchial pneumonia and was now on her way home. Dorothy would arrive on the day *Lady Teazle* opened at the Casino. Despite these severe distractions, Lillian, ever the disciplined performer, made certain that no one in the audience noticed her distress.

Opening night proved a typical Russell extravaganza. In front of the theater, crowds blocked traffic. Ticket speculation was rampant. Flowers overfilled the lobby. In anticipation of greeting Lillian's return to comic opera, audience behavior was frenetic. When she finally appeared, in a superb gown of the period, there was a theater-wide gasp of pleasure. "Younger and prettier than ever," they exclaimed.

The production was well-received. To Lillian's benefit, critics seemed to be more taken with her acting maturity than her singing. Their comments even conveyed a touch of awe:

> Miss Russell was a delightful surprise in her sincerity of acting and the really good work she did in the quarrel and screen scenes. Here was plainly shown the sure touch of the higher comedienne, for which her work at Weber and Fields gave her little opportunity. [The audience] stood up after the last curtain and shouted their approval, as the beautiful star was nearly drowned by the inrushing tide of a floral flood.[3]

Through early February, *Lady Teazle* played to capacity houses. The immediate success of the show persuaded Sam Shubert to put it on tour, even though the size of the production made a tour very expensive, more than he had ever spent for any previous show. Plans were made to start the tour in March and, if success continued, travel *Lady Teazle* to June.

These plans were abruptly changed when, on the morning of February 11, during chorus rehearsals, the Casino caught fire. Like most theater fires of the time, extensive damage occurred before firemen arrived. Four alarms were called. Extra police patrols were needed to contain the crowds that gathered to watch the conflagration. The fire raged uncontrolled for a time because the pumps were frozen and firemen could not get the water tower to work. Thick, black smoke poured from the building until streams of water finally drowned the flames. While smoke permeated the entire building, only a few rooms were completely gutted. Unfortunately, these rooms included those containing most of the scenery and costumes for *Lady Teazle*. Luckily, the chorus had quickly evacuated the auditorium, with no personal mishaps. Lillian was not yet at the theater. When she was called and told of the fire, she rushed to the Casino to assist company members, who were shaken by the experience.

Sam Shubert now had no choice but to put the production on the road, just as soon as new scenery and costumes could be prepared. That would mean at least two weeks of hard labor to overcome the losses due to the fire. (It would be almost a year before the Casino reopened.)

In a financial discussion with Sam, Lillian agreed to reduce her weekly salary to $600, on the condition that more money be given to company members because of their increased expenses while on tour. Sam readily agreed. At the same time, however, he suggested that some members of the cast, in his estimation, were not performing well and should be dropped. One he mentioned was Owen Westford.

Lady Teazle opened its tour in Albany on February 24, just ten days after the fire, an amazingly short time in which to reconstruct both scenery and costumes. Cast members were happy because they would be receiving a salary again. The Shuberts were pleased because they had been able to obtain bookings on short notice.

Unknown to Lillian, the Shuberts had formed a new corporation, the Lillian Russell Opera Company, both to safeguard their investment and transfer some of the financial responsibility. Sam, J.J. Shubert and J.J. Jacobs (the Shuberts' lawyer) were the sole directors. Having incorporated the production, any losses incurred would not revert to the Shubert organization.

The show appeared to be generating good profits on the road, but all was not smooth between Lillian and the Shuberts. Since the company had to go on tour prematurely, many "one-night-stands" had to be booked. Lillian had stipulated in her contract that she would play only six performances a week while on the road. The Shuberts booked theaters for seven performances. Lillian refused to participate. To their chagrin, the Shuberts were forced to cancel these extra engagements. In Hartford, a Shubert manager booked a matinee because the evening performance quickly sold out. When Lillian was informed of this, she wired Lee Shubert that she would not appear.

> Sam Shubert distinctly understood I would play no matinees on one-night-stands. Will not play matinee Hartford.[4]

In a threatening manner, Lee Shubert and the Hartford theater manager attempted to force Lillian to perform at the matinee. Lillian responded emphatically:

> I will positively not play the Hartford matinee. I am no slave for Shuberts or anyone else.[5]

The matinee was not played.

A few weeks later, Lillian sent a strongly worded letter to the Shuberts complaining about lack of advertising, and the resultant low turnouts in many of the towns they played. Apparently, the Shuberts had reduced advertising expenditures to save money. Lillian was also irked by their attempt to release Owen Westford, which she successfully blocked. Because of the Shuberts' continuous efforts to reduce show expenses, the Russell/Shubert relationship was rapidly deteriorating. On May 11, 1905, the arguments became moot.

To deal with litigation concerning a leased theater, Sam Shubert was traveling to Pittsburgh on an overnight train. Near Harrisburg, Pennsylvania, the passenger train sideswiped a work train that carried blasting powder. The resultant explosions killed 22 people, among them Sam Shubert.

Lee and J.J. Shubert were devastated by their brother's death. It was immediately and prematurely reported that they would sell the company. Within a few weeks, however, the surviving brothers revealed their plans: to continue operations and, according to the press, do so even more aggressively than they had in the past. That also meant acting more aggressively toward Lillian. They closed *Lady Teazle* in Pittsburgh a week later. The tour had taken the company to 27 cities in three months.

Because of the abrupt closing, Lillian had to pay for a few of the cast members' return transportation to New York. (The bookings had originally included a return to New York City.) When Lillian got back, she immediately met with her lawyer to consider a lawsuit against the Shuberts for profits due her. Lee Shubert said the show had lost money. Her own figures suggested a profit of more than $20,000, of which she should receive half. Because of personal crises, however, it wasn't until late August that Lillian was able to file a lawsuit against the Shuberts.

About the same time *Lady Teazle* closed, two disturbing domestic problems had surfaced. Dorothy, fully recovered from illness, was playing in vaudeville at the Colonial Theater in New York. Reviewers had been unkind enough to suggest that her stage appearances were solely the result of her mother's celebrated name. Even more disturbing were reports of Dorothy's drinking.

Almost simultaneously, a call from Leona Ross, Lillian's sister in Rutherford, New Jersey, revealed that Cynthia had been diagnosed as dying of Bright's disease — a kidney problem causing uremia, anemia and poor vision. She was now confined to bed, and Leona would be administering to her mother's needs. Cynthia had given up her suffrage activities a few years previously. In their place, she had adopted Christian Science, a dramatic shift in her lifelong religious beliefs.

The episode seemed to alter Lillian's feelings about her mother. Whether out of guilt or pity, her mother's virtues were now fondly and warmly praised, their long-term conflicts completely ignored. Upon her mother were bestowed the qualities of a saint; whenever Cynthia was mentioned, she was crowned with a halo of adoration. An astute reporter pointed out that Cynthia was now conveniently removed from Lillian's life; thus, Lillian could now visualize her mother as she pleased, even fabricating Cynthia as a model mother for a model daughter.

Lillian decided to move summer operations from Far Rockaway to Bay Ridge, partly to be closer to the Long Island race tracks and partly to be in a smaller house. Since she herself was feeling less inclined to entertain, and Dorothy was away, the home need not be large. Brady, Lewisohn and McCauley still visited often, but few others were coming by these days. The summer was generally quiet and restful. A late June headline in the papers, however, caught Lillian's attention: Lilly Langtry was returning to the U.S. to receive $2,500 a week to appear in vaudeville!

Within two weeks, the newspapers announced another major theatrical milestone: Lillian Russell was going into vaudeville.

No surprise is created nowadays when announcement is made of the engagement of this or that famous star for vaudeville, and when it was rumored last week that Lillian Russell had been offered a very large salary by F.F. Proctor, scarcely an eyebrow was raised. It appears, according to the reports, that Mr. Proctor's agent offered Miss Russell $2,000 a week, and that the prima donna refused to make the "plunge" for less than $4,000. It is possible that the difference may be split, and that Miss Russell may consent to work for the same amount of money that Mrs. Langtry is to receive in vaudeville next season, which is $3,000 a week. It may become a fad for prominent stars to take a dip into the "continuous," especially as the salaries offered are so very tempting.[6]

Actually, Lillian had contacted Proctor directly. They had quickly agreed to a $3,000-a-week salary, but Lillian would have to supply her own gowns.

Their formal agreement was announced mid–September: ten weeks on tour, at $3,000 a week. Her act would consist of four songs, taken from her past hits, accompanied by an orchestra. Shows would be two a day.

Lillian opened at Proctor's 23rd Street Theater October 2, 1905. Three weeks prior to the event, publicity for the opening commenced. Proctor had erected a large electric sign over the marquee of the theater and the stage itself, with Lillian's name emblazoned. Although she was only to sing songs, elaborate scenery served as a backdrop. Lillian was quoted as saying she would display 20 new dresses during the tour, one of which supposedly had been made for Queen Wilhelmina of Holland. Just the Irish-point lace trimming of the gown was worth $1,000. She added that she would change musical selections each week and was already prepared to sing 30 of them. In order to make the performance more intimate, she would have piano accompaniment only.

Lillian's opening was a tremendous success. The *Clipper* enthused:

> The greatest event in the history of American vaudeville occurred when Lillian Russell made her reappearance in the field in which she made her first success. During the years that had intervened since the night that Miss Russell, a slip of a girl, made her first timid bow at Tony Pastor's, she has made a remarkable career, and few players have been so constantly and so conspicuously in the public eye.
>
> At her first appearance, Miss Russell was perceptibly nervous, but the warmth of her welcome soon reassured her and she sang her selections charmingly.[7]

The remainder of the vaudeville bill included Josephine Cohan (George's sister) and Fred Niblo, starring in a skit about marriage (they had just been married a few weeks before); a quintet performing various antics on xylophones; and a monkey act. A number of one-reel motion pictures closed the show.

Dressed in a Worth gown, her hat and muff made of blue ostrich plumes, Lillian sang four songs, all from comic opera. Her two encores were popular hits, the final being "Come Down, Ma Evening Star," the song called for by the audience throughout her performance. Lillian now sang it without the original coon-song plantation accent.

Reports of her performances the next four weeks were equally affirming. The press pointed out that "judging from the large audience, and the presence of speculators in front of the theater, Mr. Proctor has made no mistake in agreeing to pay the salary Miss Russell receives."

While Lillian was enjoying her return to the stage, assisted by the renewed enthusiasm of audiences, Dorothy was suffering the indignities of both a failing career and a failed marriage. What made all this so immediate to Lillian was that Dorothy had returned to live at home. Critics reported that Dorothy sang "in a more or less pleasing way," a compliment any singer could do without. Short of money, Dorothy put at auction all of her household furnishings, now owned by her after the final divorce from Abbott Einstein. The auction attracted a large crowd (many of them people from the theater), but it netted only $3,000. Dorothy, however, remained determined to continue her vaudeville career.

Lillian's successful tour completed just before Christmas, and she and Jesse Lewisohn left for Europe on a three-month vacation. The legal battle with the Shuberts would have to wait until she returned. Deciding what to do next was a decision Lillian could make while going to the track in England and buying gowns in Paris.

Besides visits to London and Paris, the lengthy trip included motoring to Nice and Monte Carlo, Lillian's first excursion in southern France. While in Paris, she was joined by Anna Held and Flo Ziegfeld. A party of 12 made

Right: Program for Proctor's 23rd Street Theater featuring Lillian in her first appearance in vaudeville. It was also her first of two-a-day performances, sandwiched between Russian dancers and minstrels, on the same bill with a magician, dancing dolls, acrobats and motion pictures. (Harry Ransom Humanities Research Center, the University of Texas at Austin.)

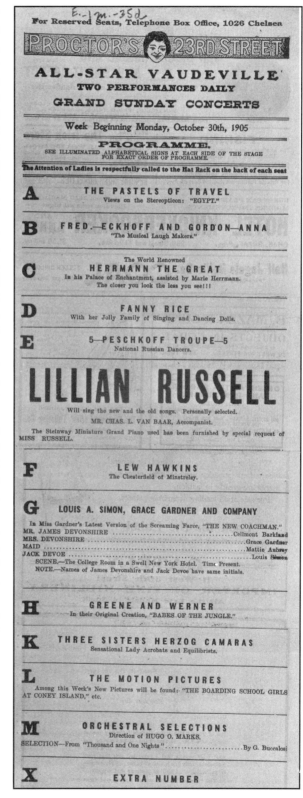

the trip in four automobiles, stopping often to sample the local food and wine. In Monte Carlo, Lillian gambled often, usually attracting a crowd which included minor royalty. In her memoirs, Lillian related a number of stories that involved various members of European royalty, though none of these reported events can be verified. Frequent trips to the Provençal mountain town of Grasse, however, were publicly remarked, as Lillian was attracted to the town's perfume factories and remarkable flower fields. In Nice, the group attended the local Mardi Gras festival. During the evening's festivities, both Lillian and Anna Held were accosted by a group of young revelers who demanded kisses from them. The stars graciously complied, much to the delight of the crowd.

Near the end of their vacation, Lillian and Anna indicated a yearning for something "American." A picnic in Anna's room offered respite from elaborate French meals. Anna made hamburgers, fried potatoes and peaches with cream — an "all-American feast," as Lillian described it.

Just prior to her return home, the *New York Herald* printed an exclusive story stating that Lillian would marry Jesse Lewisohn, if his family consented. Lillian, it was reported, did not want to be an "unwelcome guest," since Lewisohn's family were rigidly Orthodox Jews. Apparently, his family was not inclined to accept her, for reasons unmentioned. How she felt about this rejection — after all, she had already married two Jewish men — was never revealed, but it very likely contributed to a gradual cooling of the relationship. They remained close friends, and Lewisohn continued to give Lillian gifts. But the more intimate aspects of their alliance received little attention after they returned to the U.S.

Reacquainting herself with current theatrical activities, Lillian was now struck by a number of significant events that appeared to redirect the mood and energy of Broadway. Brash Georgie Cohan had opened his first major production, *Little Johnnie Jones*, in November 1904 to critical acclaim, although the show played only 52 performances in New York. Cohan wrote the book, composed the score, directed, included his parents and wife in the cast, and played the lead role. The story offered a combination of patriotism, farce and good old American corn, a formula he was to employ successfully throughout his career.

Cohan introduced two songs in the show, "Yankee Doodle Dandy" and "Give My Regards to Broadway," both of which became classic melodies representative of early American musicals. Swept up in a fervor of nationwide patriotic zeal at the time, audiences loved his performance. In quick succession, he produced *Forty-Five Minutes from Broadway* (January 1906, 90 performances in New York, with the hit song "Mary's A Grand Old Name") and, a month later, *George Washington, Jr.* (February 1906, 81 performances in New York, with the hit song, "You're A Grand Old Flag"). To the popular stage, Cohan brought a speed, exuberance, precociousness and American-style sophistication never before seen. His shows represented national confidence, a sense of superiority, and certainty of moral virtue, absent any "old-country intrigues."

Just down the street at the new Lew Fields Theater, built for him by Oscar Hammerstein, the former tall partner of Weber and Fields, united with Victor Herbert and Julian Mitchell to embark on a new career of producing and performing musical comedy, based on a coherent story, integrated songs and Fieldsian production values that easily outspent and outshone any other shows on Broadway. The show *It Happened in Nordland*, combined a European location with music hall comedy and characterization. Like Cohan's show, it too became an immediate hit, and attempts were made by other producers to take advantage of the new craze.

As if energized by new musical comedy models and new audiences looking for novelty, performers themselves reunited to confront their nemesis, the Syndicate, which up to now had dominated their careers. The White Rats, for the past few years a sleepy, ineffective organization, voted for new, more aggressive leadership. Another actors' group began negotiations with Samuel Gompers and his American Federation of Labor for possible union affiliation.

Still another group of entertainment professionals sought a way to publicly debate the Syndicate, attempting to get their side of the story to general audiences. The result was the first issue of *Variety*, published December 16, 1905. Sime Silverman, a savvy theater reporter, had the novel idea to report honestly on the entertainment business, with little regard either for advertising dollars or the intimidating power of the Syndicate. Silverman chose the name for his paper after the British word for music hall shows. He borrowed $1,500 from his father-in-law, hired a number of friends, purchased some used furniture and opened a two-room office in the Knickerbocker Building at 38th and Broadway. His first issue sold 320 copies.

Variety took a strong anti-Syndicate stance. For the first few years of its operation, much of its editorial content featured political cartoons and stories about the Syndicate's oppressive tactics and policies. Indicative of Silverman's views, his second issue contained an article about "Why the Vaudeville Artists of America Should Organize." It was a dramatic call for a more united effort against the Syndicate.

Examining the weekly theatrical papers, Lillian saw they were now filled with photographs of the latest productions and performers, many of them women. In fact, musical comedy and vaudeville were featured more often than legitimate shows. Lillian realized she must evaluate these new challenges to her career; alternatives had to be considered. Meanwhile, more immediate issues awaited her attention. What kind of job could she quickly line up? How could she force the Shuberts to pay her what she had earned from *Lady Teazle*?

Before going on vacation, Lillian had her lawyers prepare a suit against the Shuberts for her share of the profits. The Shuberts, in turn, claimed there were no profits. The court ordered a review of Shubert records to determine expenses and revenue generated by the show. Shubert records showed the production costs of *Lady Teazle* amounted to $15,880. According to them, the show had ten weeks of losses ranging from $513 to $2,700 and eight weeks of profit, ranging from $305 to $1,800. The final tally calculated a loss of $128. Lillian's own records indicated a profit of more than $7,000, of which she was to receive 50 percent. She further claimed that whatever insurance payment the Shuberts had received from the Casino fire should be shared with her. To counter her claims, the Shuberts produced a letter from Lillian admitting she had given them permission to deduct the losses of the previous week's returns from the profits of the following week and to allow production costs to exceed estimates, "to make a success."

Recent examination of weekly reports sent to the Shuberts by their local managers indicates that in fact the production had earned a small profit. But just as the Shuberts had "modified" their books, Lillian's own figures were inflated, in her favor. After some months of debate, the suit reached an impasse, with neither party able to obtain resolution. Lee Shubert was glad to terminate Lillian's contract. Lillian swore never to work for the Shuberts again.

Demand for Lillian's talents quickly came from Percy Williams, owner and manager of a circuit of first-class vaudeville houses. No sooner had she returned to her 57th Street home than he approached her with a lucrative offer for a six-week tour, at $2,500 a week. Since Lillian had not yet made up her mind what career course to take, she accepted the offer. Williams promoted the tour "as positively the last appearance in vaudeville of Lillian Russell." Opening at the Colonial Theater in New York, on April 4, 1906, Lillian sang a number of popular songs and encored them repeatedly upon request, always ending with her signature, "Come Down, Ma Evening Star." Reporting on her performance, the *New York Herald* critic wrote:

> Miss Russell made her appearance through a center door and swept down to the footlights in a creation of embroidered chiffon, [to] which the audience announced its approval and the women gasped with delight.[8]

But Williams could not persuade her to return to his theaters for the following season. Lillian now had other plans.

When she publicly announced that she was giving up singing roles for dramatic comedy, everyone was skeptical. How can she leave the kinds of performance that have made her *the* Queen?, the press asked. Does she really have the ability to play allotted roles in a dramatic comedy? Can she convince audiences that this transition will please their tastes?

Lillian herself debated these questions but was determined to take the risk. She firmly believed that her strong motivation and drive for success would make the change work. There were also practical considerations.

At least for the time being, Lillian felt she had to give up singing roles. She was not practicing voice as rigorously as before, and the strain of singing in vaudeville had become noticeable. Straight roles, where her appearance and acting would be featured, were more in keeping with audiences' changing perception of her stage career. Moreover, after her confrontation with the Shuberts, Lillian wanted to possess sole control of her earning power. It might be more risky, but a positive result would prove more lucrative. She had money to invest. Why not use it to explore new career possibilities? There was a personal reason, too: With her mother ill in New Jersey, Dorothy in vaudeville, and less reason to stay in New York to see Jesse Lewisohn, why not go on the road for a time?

To this end, Lillian contacted a friend and respected manager, Joseph Brooks, to obtain some suitable plays for her. Brooks also had a good working relationship with Klaw and Erlanger, who promised him bookings at the best first-class theaters around the country. In discussing strategy, Lillian and Brooks agreed that all her performances, at least for the immediate future, should be on the road, not in New York, because of possible criticism regarding her career change. In addition, they agreed that her roles should be an extension, a stage elaboration, of her perceived personal life (a rich woman, a member of the social elite, a horse fancier, an attractive, well-dressed matron)—in short, a personality that Lillian could satisfactorily convey to audiences with believable authenticity and sincerity. *Barbara's Millions* was announced as Lillian's first dramatic comedy vehicle, to open in Chicago in September.

Besides preparations for her new venture, Lillian spent the summer indulging in her favorite sport, the horses, and a new image-building endeavor, beauty. Visitations to Saratoga continued, but Lewisohn was seldom seen with her. She decided to establish a racing stable and purchased eight horses from Australia, to be housed at her summer home. She rode daily, until an episode in August curtailed her activity.

One morning, an automobile frightened her horse, which bolted and threw her off, one leg still attached to a stirrup. Her riding instructor quickly intervened and prevented injuries, except for a few bruises. Nonetheless, the ever-present press reported the incident, sighing with relief that "Lillian was unhurt."

The subject of beauty began to attract Lillian's attention. Much had been reported in the newspapers about her amazing ability to sustain a youthful appearance. Speculation ranged from what regimen she followed to maintain her beauty to how old she really was. She was often asked to comment on beauty-care methods, products and exercises. Frequently, she gave interviews on these subjects. In addition, Lillian was constantly besieged by advertisers, pleading with her to endorse their beauty products. She refused all offers. Given this attention to her as a perceived beauty expert, why not take the opportunity to use it promotionally? The newspapers agreed.

With Susan helping her prepare articles, Lillian began releasing stories related to health, beauty hints and personal appearance. The newspapers printed everything she submitted, and asked for more. The effort quickly resulted in her being labeled an authority on the subject; it also enhanced the public's awe regarding her appearance. However, because of the demands of a new show, Lillian was unable to pursue the project. Nevertheless, it seemed to offer interesting possibilities for the future.

Rehearsals for *Barbara's Millions* began in late August. Lillian and Brooks decided to open the play in Grand Rapids, Michigan, on September 13, to perform it a few times before presenting it in Chicago. The Grand Rapids review was almost apathetic:

> Lillian Russell appeared in the leading role, that of a California girl who has inherited a fortune from her father. The piece is a comedy without music. The star is as fetching as ever.[9]

The critical review in Chicago was devastating:

> Lillian Russell demonstrated three things at the Illinois Theater, where she made her metropolitan debut in comedy. She has shown that her beauty is as great as ever; that she has a real talent for comedy; and that the play, *Barbara's Millions*, is utterly impossible — an instantaneous and emphatic failure.[10]

The show played for two weeks in Chicago, to good audiences because of Lillian's "fame and beauty," the "curiosity to see her in comedy," and the elegance of her costuming. Otherwise, according to the *Dramatic Mirror* report, "it is flat, stale and unprofitable."

Unashamed, Lillian apologized publicly for the show's failure, assuming all the blame. But instead of closing the show, she reported that the script would be rewritten and staged again in New York, where "I would rather make a complete failure than not have its opinion at all."

While on her return to New York, a robbery returned Lillian to the front pages. At a train stop in Dayton, Ohio, she was asked for an interview by a man who appeared to be an enterprising reporter. At the end of the interview, when Lillian happened to be looking out the window, the man apparently exchanged her satchel, containing $5,000 in money and jewels, with a similar one. He quickly made his

In 1906, Lillian and Joseph Brooks, her manager, used this portrait to publicize her venture into dramatic comedy. The image was designed to make her appear eternally youthful, reminding admirers of her splendorous days in comic opera. (National Portrait Gallery, Smithsonian Institution. Benjamin J. Falk, 1853-1925. Chromolithographic poster, 78.5 × 58.7 cm [30 ⅞ × 23 ⅛ in.], 1906. NPG 87.228.)

escape from the train station. When Lillian's maid opened the bag, it was filled with paper. "They're gone! The jewels are gone!" she screamed. A Pinkerton detective was conveniently on duty and immediately launched a search.

Questioning people close to the scene led to discovery of the culprit's identity. The Pinkerton Company brought in photos from its private Rogue's Gallery and the felon was identified as John Arthur, a slick con man who happened to be a track habitué and a lover of theater. In fact, the dashing Mr. Arthur looked like an actor himself. When asked, "What do you want, your jewels back or to send the thief to prison?", Lillian replied that she preferred to have her jewels rather than prosecute the man.

The Pinkerton detective then set out to get the jewels. Once the felon was found, a deal was made to return the jewels to Lillian, with one provision: "Her silk nightgown and a pair of her stockings," said Arthur, "they were with the jewels. They stay with me." The deal was made; Lillian's jewelry was returned. A few months later, Pinkerton reported that John Arthur was seen in a box seat, apparently enjoying one of Lillian's performances.

Barbara's Millions reopened at the Savoy Theater in New York on October 8. It failed again, emphatically:

> It would be unfair to judge of Lillian Russell's abilities in the legitimate drama by her first incursion into the field. Whatever dramatic interest *Barbara's Millions* may have had in its original French form was carefully eliminated in its adaptation by Paul Potter, leaving a barren waste of dialogue and meaningless situations out of which a more capable company was utterly unable to exhort either rhyme or reason.[11]

With respect to Lillian, the critics suggested it was the vehicle that defeated her, not her acting ability.

> It may well be said to start that Lillian Russell was not suited to the part of Barbara…. It gave an intimation, however, of what she might do if she were cast in different surroundings.[12]

Four weeks later, it was announced that Lillian "will make another attempt at dramatic comedy in *The Butterfly*," to open in Philadelphia in December.

While rehearsing the new show in New York, Lillian still found time to devote to a number of charitable benefits. One of these was the annual collection for the Lamb's Club, an actors' organization that gave money to destitute or ill former performers. The event, held at the Broadway Theater, netted over $10,000. Besides Lillian, Buffalo Bill Cody, Marie Dressler, Sam Bernard and Raymond Hitchcock acted as auctioneers and performed.

The Butterfly previewed in Atlantic City, New Jersey, on December 21, before going to Philadelphia. Consensus about this show suggested it was a vast improvement. To show his continued support for Lillian, Jim Brady sent a floral tribute that filled the stage at the show's first-night performance in Atlantic City.

The show opened three days later, on Christmas Eve, at Philadelphia's Chestnut Street Theater, "delighting a packed house." Within a week, the play had achieved hit status. As reported in the *New York Clipper*:

> Lillian Russell as the Butterfly is truly a wonder, and the nightly audiences this week at the Chestnut Street Theater showed their appreciation by large attendance and pronounced applause. Her gowns are a delight to the weaker sex, and The Butterfly is an assured hit.[13]

The report was followed by an announcement that Lillian and Brooks had signed a five-year contract to develop future dramatic comedies. The company would immediately begin touring for six months, traveling to the South, Far West and Midwest before closing in Detroit. It was a very ambitious schedule. Lillian, of course, was familiar with the stresses and fatigue of touring.

Rumor suggested that Jesse Lewisohn purchased two train cars for her, and also a special train to take her to and from Bay Ridge, but there is no confirming evidence. Available information suggests that Lillian leased two Pullman cars, one for herself, the other for the company. In her car, which she renamed "The Lillian Russell," were a sitting room, kitchen, gym, bedroom and bathroom. Telephone service was hooked up to the car in each town they visited. Assisting Lillian were a private secretary, maid, chef and porter. A Pinkerton guard was hired to protect the cars. Out-of-pocket costs for company members were increased three dollars a day because of the arrangement, but Lillian gave them each an additional ten dollars a day to compensate. When they happened to play a full week in a city, Lillian rented an automobile for the company to tour the area. While on a trip of 52 towns, in 23 states, 27,000 miles in all, for 33 weeks, living in the same surroundings made travel more tolerable.

The trip through the South netted continuous "SRO business." At many Midwestern stops, when Lillian made curtain calls, audiences requested her to sing. For many of these audiences, her voice was as important as her acting:

> Again has Lillian Russell proven the existence of that good nature, which, after her beauty, is the greatest of her charms. She has determinedly gone into comedy without the musical prefix. Cries of "song, song" succeed those

of "speech, speech." Throughout the Midwest, she has amiably sung three songs instead of making one speech.[14]

Results in the Far West were equally gratifying, with "excellent houses," "large and fashionable audiences" and "SRO signs" for the attraction. Lillian's return to San Francisco was met with a fete sponsored by the local Press Club, which elected her an honorary member of the organization.

Given that she was now spending most of her time on the road, Lillian decided to sell her 57th Street home. When her decision was revealed, the papers declared, "Lillian is broke!"

"Not broke, but reallocating my life," Lillian retorted. Her books and Chinese porcelain collection would be kept at her summer home on Long Island. But she also admitted that additional money was needed to finance upcoming shows. An autumn auction of her household furnishings was planned to make that money.

The tour of *The Butterfly* ended in Detroit June 15, to a standing ovation. In her own mind, Lillian had no doubt proved she was a fine actress and, given the proper role, could more than satisfy discerning audiences. Her beauty and reputation retained their drawing power. Because she had made a great deal of money on this series of one-night-stands, she planned to do it again the following season.

That summer was a transitional period for Lillian. The long road tour and another planned for the following season meant seeing friends less often and making fewer excursions to the track. In a short two months, rehearsals for her new play would begin. What trips she did make to Long Island tracks were brief, "to reduce her turf debts," said the papers. Visits with Brady and Lewisohn were infrequent. Lewisohn was ill and somewhat incapacitated. The fact that he was unable to accompany her to the track may have contributed to her reduced attendance.

The summer of 1907 brought another of those seminal events that were giving new direction and enthusiasm to popular entertainment. On July 9, at the Jardin de Paris, a rooftop theater, Flo Ziegfeld introduced the *Follies of 1907*, a revue that combined the structure of vaudeville with musical comedy and, as promoted, the glorification of the American girl. Supposedly suggested by Ziegfeld's wife, Anna Held, the production was patterned after the French *Folies Bergère*.

What had been designed as an interim summer show proved so successful that Ziegfeld moved it to the Liberty Theater in the fall and then put it on tour. Profits from the show were so gratifying, Ziegfeld decided to mount a bigger and more elaborate production the following season. Lillian took careful notice of the way that Ziegfeld featured his female performers.

The premiere of her new show, *Wildfire*, and the auction of Lillian's household goods occurred within days of one another. *Wildfire* opened at the Grand Opera House in Cincinnati, Ohio, on September 30. The story told of a widow, Mrs. Barrington, who is left a racing stable, and nothing else, by her late husband. A nefarious trio comprised of a rival racing horse owner, a bookmaker and a naive jockey brings the action down to the final scene, in which the wave of a handkerchief determines whether the jockey should win or lose the race. Mrs. Barrington finds out about the plot, pretends to be attracted to her rival and, while in a romantic clinch, waves her handkerchief, signaling her jockey to win the race. In a final dramatic gesture, she throws the man from her arms as the jockey crosses the finish line, to the cheers of the crowd.

Lillian as Mrs. Henrietta Barrington in her dramatic comedy hit *Wildfire*. The show ran for two seasons; Lillian played the role 566 times. (Harry Ransom Humanities Research Center, the University of Texas at Austin.)

The Cincinnati critics exclaimed:

> *Wildfire* had its first presentation on any stage at the Grand last week before uniformly large audiences, and unless the local verdict should be reversed in other cities, it will be a long time before Lillian Russell is required to seek a new vehicle. It proved to be one of the most delightful comedies offered here in many months.[15]

The critics in Chicago, the show's next stop, were equally enthusiastic:

> Lillian Russell presented her new play, *Wildfire*, and the entire outfit scored an immediate laughing success. Miss Russell was very charming in the role of Mrs. Barrington. She carried her several tense scenes with credit, and ran away with the light comedy scenes. The production is a very handsome one, and Miss Russell's gowns were stunning. The performance furnishes a good, hearty laugh almost from start to finish.[16]

The auction was almost as successful financially, generating over $74,000. Attended by thousands of people, and many fellow professionals, it was conducted for three days at the renowned Fifth Avenue Galleries. In addition, many members of New York's social elite were there to look for bargains in furniture, paintings and draperies. Prices ranged from $2.50 for a piece of bric-a-brac to a painting by Vibert for $3,900. At the conclusion of the auction, all that remained were a few garden benches and a bust of Julius Caesar. When told of the result, Lillian was thoroughly satisfied.

Her satisfaction, however, was short-lived. Not ten days later, on October 21, 1907, banks in New York and the remainder of the country were struck by a "currency panic." From the moment banks opened, thousands of customers crowded tellers' windows to demand the return of their savings. In a short while, most banks had dispensed their last available cash and closed their doors.

Lillian had placed the proceeds of the auction in the Knickerbocker Trust Company, one of the banks that ran out of funds. Unfortunately, she lost all the money she had deposited. But when Susan reported the news to her, Lillian was more concerned about the Professional Women's League account than her own. It was she who had persuaded the League to invest its funds, some $3,000, in the Knickerbocker, based upon its supposed reliability. Although the bank reopened for business a few weeks later, there is no evidence that Lillian ever recovered her money from the bank. The continued box office success of *Wildfire*, however, soon replenished her purse.

Another more entertaining event occurred on the same day, a short distance away from the sealed doors of Knickerbocker Trust. An attraction imported from Vienna, *The Merry Widow*, opened at the New Amsterdam Theater. A hit operetta in Europe for two years, the production returned pageantry and foreign-inspired elegance to the New York stage, much to the dismay of American musical comedy producers. With a cohesive, understandable book, the music of Franz Lehar and new dances and fashions, *The Merry Widow* swept the country within months. Because the currency panic prevented American producers from opening new plays, *The Merry Widow* quickly became the most profitable show of the season.

Within months, many American theater managers formed companies to present their versions of it on tour. Like the Gilbert and Sullivan plays with their multitude of travesties, *The Merry Widow* had many imitators. The enterprising Joe Weber, for example, placed three *Merry Widow* companies on the road for two years and was said to have made his fortune from the effort.

This stylish Viennese opera provided an important benefit for Lillian. It rekindled public interest in comic opera and comic opera performers. Since Lillian was already identified as America's personification of comic opera, her performance visibility increased even more, especially in the country's heartland. It had been a fortuitous decision by her to continue singing old comic opera songs at the close of plays. Her singing served as a reminder to audiences, old and young, that Lillian continued as the Queen of Comic Opera.

During the fall and winter months, while the country recovered from its recent financial panic, Lillian continued to fill theaters. One-night stands through Ohio, New York and New England brought "this delightful comedy" to "fashionable and full houses." Lillian's success was so dramatic that the New York press suggested she return to the city to perform. She and Brooks considered the offer but again decided that the time was not yet ripe for her Broadway debut in dramatic comedy.

It was in Boston that Lillian celebrated her forty-sixth birthday. In honoring Lillian, the Boston chapter of the Professional Women's League made her a guest of honor at its annual reception. The occasion was attended by all the actresses who were playing in the city at the time, as well as by local members of the profession. Lillian graciously accepted their homage for having been a star more than a quarter of a century. "That long? How does she do it? How does she stay so beautiful?" wondered her adoring audience.

The year 1908 began in the same SRO fashion as 1907 had ended. Reacting to the revival of elegant costumes on stage, newspapers reported every new gown Lillian wore in *Wildfire*; she took advantage of this publicity by changing gowns every week. Miss Clipper, a column devoted to women performers in the *New York Clipper*, described Lillian's attire:

> Lillian Russell's Wildfire gowns are all extreme in mode and extremely hand-some and costly. She wears a different one in each of the three acts, and looks her own beautiful self in all of them. [Each gown was then described in detail.] Thus attired, she certainly presents one of the most beautiful of stage pic-tures, fully preserving her reputation for beauty of face and elegance in dress.[17]

It was a face and elegance that Lillian would truly need for the remainder of the year. If ever the theatrical description of "trouper" defined a performer under stress, Lillian would soon win that dubious honor. When Richard Mansfield talked about the difference between acting on stage and dealing with personal tragedy, he suggested that the tougher it was to perform, the better he did it. His insight proved equally true for Lillian.

Owen Westford was a tall, lean, somewhat frail-looking actor who specialized in portraying older, scatterbrained roles. The fatigue of constant one-night stands with the Russell company affected his acting, and he suffered from recurrent minor bouts of ill health. While the *Wildfire* company was playing in Washington, D.C., Westford became seriously ill and had to be sent back to New York. Susan was waiting to take him to a hospital for diagnosis and treatment. Deeply fond of her brother-in-law, Lillian was very concerned about him and called daily to learn of his condition. Within a week of his return, however, Westford died of a reported stom-ach malady.

Funeral services were conducted a few days later, and Lillian was the only fam-ily member unable to attend. Westford's death, however, had a profound effect on her. She blamed herself for not noticing his deterioration. It was her show, under her direction, that had evidently contributed to his illness. His lovable and gentle man-ner, which Lillian respected, made his loss even worse. As she and Susan discussed the situation, Lillian recognized the fragility of life, and her own mortality, as well as her sister's pressing needs. Susan would now be faced with decisions that affected her future. She had retired from the stage a few years before to devote her efforts to run-ning the Professional Women's League as its president, but now other decisions would have to be considered. "Go back on stage," Lillian suggested.

The *Wildfire* tour was booked to appear in a number of Iowa towns in April. One of its planned stops was Clinton, featuring Lillian's return to perform in the town of her birth. Elaborate plans were made for the event: a parade, reception, speeches, hon-ors and an extended performance that included the play and a recital afterwards. The entire county was poised to pay homage to their "Nellie."

Just a few days before, while the company was playing in Omaha, Lillian received a call from her sister, Ida Kate. Cynthia was failing. Due to the planned events in Clin-ton, however, Lillian could not shut down the tour in the event of her mother's death.

On April 10, at the age of 81, Cynthia Leonard died. Despite her numerous accomplishments, newspaper announcements identified her only as Lillian Russell's mother:

> Mrs. Charles E. Leonard, mother of Lillian Russell, died at the home of her daughter, Mrs. Edward Schulze, Rutherford, New Jersey, on April 10. Mrs. Leonard was in her eighty-first year, and death was due to general debility. She lived in Rutherford with Mrs. Schulze for a number of years. Five daughters survive her.[18]

Having been in declining health for a number of years, Cynthia died from the complications of Bright's disease. Her long career of suffrage activities ceased when she moved to Rutherford. Her influence over Lillian also seems to have ended at that time. About the same time, Lillian began talking about her mother in adoring terms, evidently attempting to build a mythology around Cynthia's philosophy of life, morality and spiritualism. Of course, Cynthia was no longer in proximity to prevail upon her daughter.

Nevertheless, Lillian was deeply saddened by Cynthia's death. Performances continued, but a pallor hung over the company as it passed through Iowa towns. Ironically, Cynthia's funeral was to be held the same day as Lillian's Clinton performance. Whether out of courtesy, business necessity or lack of knowledge, no mention of Cynthia's death was made while Lillian was in Clinton.

As she arrived in Clinton, crowds cheered and bands played for Lillian. Her carriage disembarked from the train. She entered the parade and was swept along Clinton's main street to the theater steps, where local government and business leaders presented her the city's key. A gala reception followed, continuing until evening, when it seemed the entire town pushed its way into the Clinton Theater to watch Lillian perform.

The performance itself was characteristic of old variety hall audience antics. Funny scenes from the play had to be encored, as did the final horse race scene. Many of the songs Lillian sang in recital were encored three or four times. Members of the audience sang with her; others danced in the aisles. Throughout this tulmult, flowers were continually transported to the stage.

It was past midnight before Lillian was able to return to her Pullman car. But the emotional scene of triumph and adoration was tempered by personal mourning. Within minutes, the company was on its way to Davenport, Iowa, their next stop. A plaintive Lillian gazed at Clinton's receding lights and wondered whether her mother would have approved of her performance.

A week in St. Louis gave her some time to recover, which she attempted to do by renting an automobile and speeding around the countryside. Joseph Brooks made a special trip to St. Louis to visit Lillian and assess her emotions. He was reassured to find that Lillian's efforts had "made a pronounced hit with the large audiences."

Two days later, Lillian read that her old friend and mentor, Willie Edouin, had died. While they had not seen one another for more than two decades, fond memories of her first tour and its subsequent hardships remained. It seemed to her that an era was ending. Yet even more sadness was to follow.

It was the end of the season. The company's final performance had just been concluded in Detroit, and they were preparing to return to New York for the summer. The success of *Wildfire* convinced Lillian and Brooks to offer it again, on tour, next season. While on the train, Lillian received a telegram that her friend and esteemed Weberfields colleague, Peter Dailey, had died in Chicago of pneumonia. His body was being transported to New York, where an elaborate funeral was planned. Lillian responded that she would attend.

It was raining Wednesday morning in New York, but...

> ...one of the largest outpourings of professional people ever gathered at the funeral of an actor was in attendance at the services held over the body of Peter F. Dailey. So great was the crowd that many could not gain admittance, and the personal friends of the dead comedian were there in full force. There was much genuine grief shown at the passing of one of the stage's most popular men.[19]

Among the forest of floral arrangements stood Lillian, Lew Fields, Joe Weber, Tony Pastor, Fay Templeton, Marie Dressler, Julian Mitchell and dozens of fellow performers, restaurateurs and political figures. Lillian wept openly throughout the services, giving way to tears that may have been stored up over the past few disconsolate months. There was no longer any reason to act, not in front of fellow professionals.

As a final tribute to one of the stage's most imaginative comedians, a typical Peter Dailey improvisation was recalled. Peter was on tour. While Dailey was writing his name on the register of the local hotel, a cockroach walked across the register page, stopped next to Dailey's pen and then walked away. Dailey looked at the hotel clerk and said, "I've been bled by St. Joe flies, bitten by Kansas City spiders, sawed by mosquitoes all over Jersey, but I'll be darned if I ever was in a place before where the bugs looked over the hotel register to find where your room was!"

Shubert's *Ave Maria* and Chopin's funeral march ended the services.

Once back home, Lillian and Susan discussed their summer plans, if indeed they were going to do anything at all. Both agreed that grieving at home would just prolong the unhappiness. Some decisions had already been made. Susan was going to live with Lillian temporarily. She had decided to return to the stage for the coming season and was already exploring the possibilities.

Jesse Lewisohn was again very ill. He was diagnosed with ulcers and, according to the doctors, close to death. Lillian was very concerned about Lewisohn's health, but more as a dear friend than lover. When Lewisohn's doctors recommended he spend some time in the country to recover, Brady suggested he stay at Brady's farm in New Jersey. In addition, Brady persuaded his girlfriend, Edna McCauley, to assist in Lewisohn's rehabilitation. With Lewisohn under Brady's attention, Lillian could get away for a brief vacation.

She and Susan left for Paris. It was planned as a trip to peruse the latest fashions and select new gowns for the coming *Wildfire* season. After Joseph Brooks joined Lillian in Paris to agree on her selection of gowns, he returned to the U.S. convinced she would enjoy another lucrative tour. A few days later, Klaw and Erlanger announced their plans for traveling *Wildfire*, touting its already "triumphant tour success":

> Lillian Russell, who will be seen next season in the racing comedy *Wildfire*, is at present enjoying the delights of shopping in Paris. Miss Russell will purchase several new gowns for use in the play. She will begin rehearsals the first week in August. The season of *Wildfire* will open at Asbury Park, September 5. Miss Russell will then go to the Liberty Theater, New York, for a long stay.[20]

Apparently, Lillian and Brooks believed both she and *Wildfire* were finally ready to face New York critics in her new career as dramatic comedienne.

When Lillian returned to New York, Brady informed her that Lewisohn was improving — news Lillian was relieved to hear. But Brady also told her of another development: It appeared that Edna and Jesse were in love. Brady was disturbed and angry. In contrast, Lillian seemed stoic about the news. But before she and Brady could deal with the situation, there occurred another overwhelming loss to the theatrical profession.

After more than 50 years in show business, an old and infirm Tony Pastor died in his sleep on August 26. With him were his wife, his physician and his long-time manager, Harry Sanderson. The city of New York went into mourning.

> Tony Pastor, the Dean of Vaudeville, is dead. The cause of death was weakness and a general physical breakdown. His age was against him, and worry over the fact that the famous little theater on 14th Street, which bore his name, had passed beyond his control, caused a relapse, and he sunk steadily until the end.[21]

Commemorating his passing, the *Clipper* commented:

> In the death of the grand old man of the varieties, the entire profession had lost one of its best friends and protectors. Throughout the world his loss will be felt by thousands who have loved and revered him, and with them his memory will live to the end.[22]

Pastor would have been unhappy about being called the Dean of Vaudeville. He disliked the word and the identity given him with it. Song and dance, comedy and travesty were his offerings. He had made them legitimate entertainment, acceptable to middle-class audiences — men, women and children. He had launched the careers of many now-famous performers who might not have made it without his help. He was a teacher and mentor. He never turned away a performer who was hungry or out of work. His inspiration and innovation laid the foundation for the development of popular theater. Such views were expressed by the press, performers who had benefited from Pastor's guidance, and a public that would sadly miss his stage presentations.

Along with members of the profession, Lillian attended the funeral to honor the man who had initiated her career. Laying on his casket a white carnation (the flower Pastor always wore in the lapel of his tuxedo when on stage) was all that Lillian could do in reverent memory. Indeed, she thought, as Pastor's casket was lowered into the grave, this was surely the end of an era.

A month into her fall tour of *Wildfire*, Lillian read in the *New York Herald*:

> Jesse Lewisohn, the wealthy son of a rich copper king, is to be married Sunday to beautiful New York girl, Edna McCauley. Meanwhile, Lillian Russell is wedded to her art and is making fame and money in her delightful comedy, *Wildfire*.[23]

Chapter Nine

Her Image Renewed

"I think I'd rather see Lillian Russell come into the shop on a rainy morning after a bad week's business than any one in the profession. She's a great buyer," said the manager of Worth's gown store. "She buys as sumptuously as she dresses. She likes a great deal of everything, and likes it of the best. She gives large orders. The greatest of them all is Lillian Russell."

As it happened, the man was interviewed just after Lillian ordered gowns for her season's tour of *Wildfire*.

"The women all love to wait on her. She's the only customer we have who can cure peevish Polly of her tantrums. Maxine Elliott is gracious, but remotely so. Virginia Harned reminds me of a little girl of high spirits. Maude Adams goes about her shopping hurriedly and abstractedly, and Eva Davenport jokes her way through a day's shopping.

"At any rate," the manager mused, "I'm glad to see Miss Russell, if only that she is a tonic to the saleswomen. Her entrance is a cue for everyone to smile."

For Lillian, too, this buying spree was cheering. It helped her concentrate her energy on a new season of performance. It also helped to console her after the personal losses she had suffered during the previous months.

Jesse Lewisohn's professed love for Edna McCauley did not come as a surprise to Lillian. The two had always had an admiring friendship as part of the foursome. All parties seemed to be on their best behavior to support Jim Brady, the most emotionally vulnerable of the group. When told of Edna's feelings for Jesse, Brady had become very upset. Their affair came as one of the worst shocks in his life. When questioned by the press and asked to comment on the situation, he responded diplomatically, "I am sorry but I cannot discuss the private affairs of Mr. Lewisohn and Miss McCauley." Yet his pain was apparent.

Help now came to Brady from numerous Broadway friends. Nat Goodwin and De Wolf Hopper offered stories of broken love affairs (theirs and others') as unfortunate as his own. They showed their sympathy by giving parties in his honor, luring him back to the world of first-night appearances, reminding him of his love for theater.

Lillian had known her relationship with Lewisohn was deteriorating ever since their proposed marriage had been rejected by his family. Their Old World beliefs about the acting profession were probably more decisive in the matter than the fact that Lillian was not Jewish. Lew Fields, for one, often talked about the barriers actors had to overcome to be considered legitimate and respected. Success, money and good residences alone did not seem to convince those who believed that performing was somehow sinful. So much so, said Fields, that he forbade his children to enter the profession.

When Lillian read the announcement that Lewisohn and McCauley were about to marry, she sent the couple a congratulatory note. The report of marriage, however, had been no more than rumor. The couple were indeed in love, but the actual marriage would be delayed a few months. Meanwhile, Lillian had to deal with a more profound issue. The lifelong stresses of the relationship with her mother had to be addressed.

Cynthia's death released a combination of feelings in Lillian. On one hand, she voiced respect and adoration for a woman who had spent her entire life fighting for women's freedom. On the other hand, she harbored a continuing anger toward a mother who had attempted, with some success, to impose her authority on Lillian for years. Only since Cynthia became ill had Lillian felt some easing of this constant tension. Since Cynthia's death, Lillian had experienced an admitted sense of relief.

Lillian also discovered she now had less need for male companionship. She grew closer to her extended family and spent more time with her sisters. For the most part, her fame had by now eliminated the previous struggles with managers and producers; they were just happy to obtain her signature on a contract. She perceived little competition from other female performers; they were developing their own stage personalities within an industry itself in transition. Her personal extravagances in gowns, jewelry and Chinese porcelain were now viewed as characteristic elements of her public persona and perceived as legitimate rewards for Lillian's long and successful years of labor on the stage. As 1909 approached, Lillian, perceptibly more relaxed, seemed ready to explore new horizons.

Wildfire's new season opened at the Casino Theater in Asbury Park, New Jersey on September 3. Because portions of the story had been rewritten and many of the cast were new to the production, Lillian believed it best to preview the show before opening in New York. According to some critics, who traveled from New York to view the play, the production "was as good as before"—at best, a tepid and ambiguous review.

When *Wildfire* opened at the Liberty Theater in New York on September 7, Lillian received precisely the kind of reception she and Brooks had anticipated. The reviews were not especially good, often accompanied by sarcastic references to her acting ability and the strength of the show's plot:

> Without the reputation and consequent popularity of Lillian Russell, *Wildfire* could not have lasted a whole season on the road in first-class theaters. It is doubtful whether Miss Russell and the several good actors in her support will be able to carry the play to any marked degree of success in New York. The piece is the commonest sort of melodrama. Miss Russell carries the role of Mrs. Barrington with much grace and all of her beauty. The part makes no strong demands upon her as an actress.[1]

In spite of such criticism, *Wildfire* played in New York to full houses for eight weeks, until the end of October, when its road tour was launched. Of even greater interest to newspapers than the show's popular success was an editorial debate about Lillian's age and beauty. Perhaps fomented just to sell more papers, the controversy started when one reporter noted that Lillian's daughter Dorothy was now a grown woman with graying hair. Another countered by pointing out:

> It is one of the penalties of stage service that audiences who have seen a performer for five seasons fancy it was for ten, that having been entertained by her for ten years they are certain it was for twenty-five.[2]

Estimates of Lillian's age differed by a margin of 25 years, the upper limits being the middle sixties. Through it all, Lillian just kept smiling, apparently enjoying the debate. Finally, as *Wildfire* was about to leave on tour, the *New York Clipper* referred to a copy of the respected book *Who's Who on the Stage* and pointed out that Lillian had been born in 1861, making her 46 years of age. They ended the story by exclaiming, "She is in life's midsummer. May it be endlessly prolonged."[3]

As to her enduring beauty, there was little debate. All agreed that "her beauty is a fixed and positive quality." Then, the inevitable question: "How does she do it?" In response, Lillian promised to reveal all her beauty and health secrets in the near future.

The tour started at the Hollis Street Theater in Boston. Reviews, like all those on the road, were excellent:

> Lillian Russell is having quite as marked personal success as a year ago, to excellent financial returns.[4]

The first leg of the tour lasted eight weeks, primarily one-night stands in New England. The company's return to New York in December gave Lillian an opportunity to deal with two important personal issues: the sale of her 57th Street home and Dorothy's purported second marriage.

Lillian's home had been put up for sale a year earlier. At about the same time, an auction had been held to dispose of many of her household furnishings. The auction had netted over $74,000, all of it lost a few weeks later during the bank panic of 1907. The sale of her home to Edward C. Jones had generated $60,000, some of it invested in her productions for the 1908-09 season, the remainder applied to pay off the mortgage. Lillian would now have to find another place to live, somewhere on the fashionable Upper West Side.

The situation with Dorothy was considerably more complex. She was performing periodically in vaudeville. When not working, she was living in New York with Lillian. She was often seen visiting Rector's with an assortment of male friends. In addition, stories of her gambling reached Susan, who in turn related them to Lillian. Dorothy denied the stories, blaming Aunt Susan for passing tales to her mother. Lillian, too, gave the impression these stories were untrue. When Blanche Bates related some gossip to Lillian about her daughter, Lillian responded defensively, "Are you trying to talk to me about my own child?" Nevertheless, the stories persisted.

Dorothy's brief liaison with Harry Pollak, in the process of divorcing his wife, who happened to be Lillian's friend, quickly ended when he left for England with another woman. Finally, Lillian suggested that Dorothy should leave home and, if possible, concentrate on her career in vaudeville. Dorothy responded to the recommendation by suggesting she was being sent away because her presence made Lillian appear older.

While performing in Philadelphia, Dorothy met a Japanese prince, Tetsuma Akahoshi, who was attending the University of Pennsylvania. Frequent visits, gifts and dinners evidently followed this first meeting. When their relationship became public — a New York paper claimed they were engaged — Akahoshi was ordered by his family to return to Japan. One report indicated that, prior to Akahoshi's return to Japan, the couple spent three weeks in New York on a continuous round of parties. Another report said they had left together for San Francisco, there to be married, before Akahoshi's departure. While no specific marital documentation has been found, a number of New York papers claimed they had evidence of the couple's marriage.

In December, Dorothy returned home for her mother's birthday. Lillian was quite perturbed about the press revelations regarding her daughter's behavior. When Dorothy denied the stories, Lillian professed to believe her, but apparently some doubts remained. As Dorothy wrote in her memoirs:

> I felt Mother believed me, for when she kissed me good night she said, "Promise me, you'll never do anything like that again. No matter what happens, always come and tell me about it first."[5]

Four months later, Dorothy would elope, upsetting her mother deeply.

At the beginning of 1909, *Wildfire* again went on the road, traveling to the Far West and returning through the Midwest. Most of the stops were one-night stands, made more comfortable thanks to Lillian's elegant and well-appointed railroad car. The car itself soon became something of a celebrity, pictured often in newspapers and magazines, and prompted other performers to emulate Lillian by leasing their own Pullman cars for touring. SRO and approving reviews followed Lillian throughout the tour.

While playing in Cincinnati in February, Lillian was informed that Jesse Lewisohn and Edna McCauley had been married and left for Europe on their honeymoon. Her performance that evening seemed just a bit more animated:

> Lillian Russell returned this week in *Wildfire*. The play is changed a little, but Miss Russell seems rather younger and handsomer.[6]

In San Francisco, audiences seemed to forget about Lillian's previous disparaging comments about their fair city by filling "each of the nine performances":

> Lillian Russell succeeded at the Van Ness, having opened in *Wildfire*. It is evident from her reception that the old feeling that existed in the minds of San Francisco theatergoers has disappeared and that they have forgiven the beautiful star for having once said that San Francisco was a "jay" town. She was enthusiastically applauded and was compelled to make a speech.[7]

While touring in the West, Lillian received a jolt when Brooks informed her that he had sold the rights to *Wildfire* to another manager. While she knew this was to be her last tour of the production, she had planned to retain the rights herself, so that it might be revived in the future if necessary. Examining her contract, she found that Brooks had the right to sell the play, the proceeds to be shared between himself and

Lillian. He had sold the property for $10,000, a high price, but Lillian was disappointed to see "her hit show" disposed of in so cavalier a manner. Shortly afterwards, Brooks announced Lillian's next dramatic comedy:

> Klaw and Erlanger and Joseph Brooks will give Lillian Russell a splendid production in her new comedy, *The Widow's Might*, by Edmund Day, opening September 6, at the Liberty Theater in New York.[8]

Wildfire ended its two-year journey, "one of the most profitable Miss Russell has ever had," in Milwaukee on June 12. Lillian had appeared in the production a total of 566 times, traveling to 36 states and 92 cities and towns, many of them one-night stands. Now, returning to New York, she had to find a place where she and Susan could live.

The opening of the subway in October 1904 sparked an intensive building boom on the Upper West Side. The fashion was apartment houses and elegant hotels, from 11 to 14 stories high. With elaborately ornate stone and carved-wood facades, cafés, billiard rooms, hairdressers, barbers, valets, tailors and private bus service to the theater district, the hotels were lavish enough to attract people like Lillian.

For the moment, Lillian and Susan decided to rent an apartment at the Ansonia Hotel, said to be designed by Stanford White. Actually, it had been constructed by William Earle Dodge Stokes, on the grounds of the old New York Orphan Asylum, between 73rd and 74th Streets, just off Broadway. He had retained a French architect to design the hotel. Construction had begun in 1899; the hotel, a giant Beaux Arts building resembling the great hotels of Paris, only larger, was opened about the time the subway started operation. At the time Lillian moved in, the Ansonia had already amassed an impressive list of tenants, many in the theater professions, among them Enrico Caruso, Arturo Toscanini and Flo Ziegfeld. By this time, Anna Held was no longer Ziegfeld's wife and had returned to Europe to perform. In her place was *Follies* star Lillian Lorraine, who had a separate suite on the tenth floor, within steps of Ziegfeld's own lavish apartment. On various other floors during this period lived impresario David Belasco, composer Albert von Tilzer and George M. Cohan.

Once settled in the new suite, along with Lillian's library and Chinese porcelain collection, Lillian and Susan prepared to spend six weeks in Paris, admiring French fashions and purchasing gowns, just as they had the previous summer.

Whether by design or otherwise, Lillian managed largely to elude the press on this trip. Anna Held was said to have given a large party for Lillian. She and Susan were reported to have been seen buying gowns at various Parisian shops. The only event that received widespread press attention was Lillian's return to New York, when her coat was stolen as she went through customs. It was later disclosed that the coat had been taken only as a souvenir. Nine trunks of gowns were left untouched.

Rehearsals for *The Widow's Might* began the middle of August. As was now the rule in Lillian's productions, Susan had a role in the play. Both she and Lillian felt that, at least for the time being, they should stay together.

The plot of *The Widow's Might* centered around villainous relatives, youthful admirers and money. Central to the plot was an amorous attraction between a middle-aged widow (Lillian) and her considerably younger lover. At the end of the play, the widow won her young man, an outcome that critics and audiences alike proved unable to accept with moral equanimity.

The show went through a two-day trial, September 10 and 11, at the Court Square Theater in Springfield, Massachusetts. On September 13, *The Widow's Might* opened at the Liberty Theater in New York. Lillian was praised; the play was panned:

> Mr. Day has built a piece that is only of fair caliber. It was given its most effective prop by the star, who was personally successful, and who gave the tottering comedy the needful help over the rough places. In addition to contributing a lame, halting play, with situations that were very obvious in advance, the author showed a certain disposition at times to lay on the daubs of melodrama a little too thickly. Miss Russell reads her comedy lines with infectious humor.[9]

Acton Davies, theater critic for the *Evening Sun*, pinpointed the essence of Lillian's appeal, the reason she could carry even inferior plays:

> No one could possibly have done any more with the role of the Widow Curtis than she did — in fact, we don't know any one who could have done half as much. Miss Russell never disappoints her audience. There is the open-hearted and unaffected nature of the woman herself which really wins her audience. No woman on mere voice or beauty could hold the favor of the public as Miss Russell has.

Another influential critic, Renold Wolf of the *Morning Telegraph*, summed up Lillian's performance in eight words: "A strictly Lillian Russell night — and she won."

There was no question that Lillian's appearance in the play was responsible for its survival for six weeks in New York and another seven on the road. She knew, however, that *The Widow's Might* would soon be finished and began immediately to look for a replacement.

Midway through the show's run in New York, Lillian acquired another boarder. A chastened Marie Dressler had just returned from a financially disastrous season in London. She had formed her own company to perform musical comedy, but British audiences found Dressler's brand of comedy bewildering and her "working girl" portrayals embarrassing. Having invested all her money in salaries and costumes, Dressler had no choice but to declare bankruptcy, stranding her American cast in London. By September, her liabilities amounted to more than $24,000; her only declared assets consisted of "necessary wearing apparel, worth $100."

Dressler's comedic abilities were well-known, however, and within a few weeks she was signed by Lew Fields to appear in his new musical comedy, *Tillie's Nightmare*, a show destined to become the signature performance of Dressler's career. Lillian helped her longtime friend move into new quarters at the nearby Majestic Hotel once Dressler received her first paycheck.

On the road, *The Widow's Might* did well on its abbreviated tour of Eastern cities. In Washington, D.C., it had "excellent patronage"; in Newark and Brooklyn, "good business" was reported. When the show returned to New York for its final appearance — so Lillian could celebrate her birthday at home — she played "to a capacity house."

For the first time in many years, Lillian's birthday — she was 48 — was primarily a family affair, bringing together her sisters and their families; Dorothy, who was living at home again and attempting to restart her vaudeville career; and a few friends, among them, Jim Brady, Marie Dressler and Digby Bell. Brady presented her with a

marriage proposal. But Lillian kindly refused on the grounds of their long and mutually supportive friendship. Brady then offered to build her a theater; it would be
called the Lillian Russell Theater. Again she refused, suggesting that he give the money
to charity: "There are too many poor people who need the money. It will be time
enough to name a theater for me when I am dead." (Ironically, no theater has ever
been named for Lillian.)

The Widow's Might closed quietly. In its place, Lillian and Joseph Brooks produced
The First Night by George V. Hobart, an adaptation of *Der Holbe Dicter*. The plot could
not have been better tailored to Lillian's interests and abilities. The action of the play
hinges on complications arising from a wife's (Lillian) wish to hide from her jealous
husband the fact that she has written a comic opera. She persuades a well-known play-
wright to claim authorship. The plot intensifies when the author's fiancée and the husband trail the two authors, whom they suspect of a more than platonic relationship.

The First Night opened on Christmas Eve at the Broad Street Theater, Philadelphia, also the beginning of its tour. Both Lillian and Brooks felt that avoiding New
York critics would be to their advantage. As they had anticipated, Philadelphia critics singled out Lillian's stage presence and the beauty of her gowns:

> Miss Russell fit happily into attractive stage pictures (aided materially by
> some marvelous creations of Paris modistes). In the third act, she demon-
> strates that she has skill of no mean caliber in straight comedy. At the close
> of the act, she delivers a long speech with faultless elocution, her rich speak-
> ing voice suggesting possibilities of power and feeling which might serve
> her well even in more exacting roles. Her efforts met with well-merited
> applause that was as hearty as it was sincere.[10]

Even though New York critics had been side-stepped, Alan Dale, the city's most
esteemed theater critic, made the trip to Philadelphia to see Lillian perform. In his
review, he recognized Lillian's successful professional evolution with glowing praise:

> The public's acceptance of her as a comedienne means the glorification of
> personal ambition, the fruition of three years of long, hard work and the
> consummation of the spirit of "I will" carried out in the face of obstacles
> which would have discouraged utterly a less plucky woman. Her early
> results were bad; she decided to stay on the road until she could make New
> York take notice; and then that "first night" with every critic recognizing
> her achievement and the audience giving her a royal welcome.

For Lillian, Dale's article represented "official" recognition of her current career.
His unqualified praise was a performer's "medal of honor."

The First Night's tour took the company through the Southern states (new territory for Lillian), some week-long runs in St. Louis and Chicago, and then a long
series of one-night stands in Michigan, Ohio and New York. The tour ended in
Canada at the end of May. While generating only minimal profit, it did a great deal
to enhance Lillian's public image. Other events on the tour, however, seemed to capture more headlines.

The people of Clinton wished to honor Lillian in the Iowa Hall of Fame, located
in Des Moines, in the state capitol. The suggestion immediately met with protests
from various religious groups which complained that no performer, especially one
like Lillian, should ever be honored in a state building. After rancorous debate, the

legislature barely passed a resolution to accept a painting of Lillian. It would be received by the Iowa Historical Society, then hung in the capitol building. On her way from St. Louis to Chicago, Lillian traveled to Des Moines to deliver the painting. At the presentation ceremony, members of the legislature, with some hesitation, asked her to sing, and she cheerfully complied.

At about the same time, theatrical newspapers printed comments made by a number of well-known actors in opposition to the suffrage movement. Lillian reacted strongly to these remarks, supporting the suffragists and suggesting that these actors were jealous of the opposite sex's cleverness and skill on the popular stage. While the episode was quickly forgotten, it represented Lillian's first public statement in support of the suffrage movement and signaled her entry into the national debate it had sparked. Cynthia Leonard would have been proud of her daughter. Concerning her granddaughter, however, Cynthia's sentiments would not have been as flattering.

Dorothy was in San Francisco with friends, preparing to travel to the Orient. While there, she met Robin Dunsmuir, son of a mining magnate from British Columbia. Within a few days of their meeting, he asked Dorothy to join him on a business trip to Peru to examine some mines. When she could not make up her mind, Dunsmuir left San Francisco by boat without her. On the way, he sent her a continuous string of cables expressing his love for her. Soon succumbing to his amorous persuasion, Dorothy agreed to join Dunsmuir in Mexico.

Taking the train, she met him in Mazatlan. On March 20, they were married. When informed of the impending event, Lillian was in Chicago. Her telegram to Dorothy, sent before the marriage, advised her daughter to think carefully about marital union with someone she hardly knew. Dorothy cabled back, just after the ceremony, saying only that she was very happy.

The relationship lasted only a few months. In Peru, Dorothy became ill, lonely and disillusioned with the marriage. She wired Lillian to cable her money to return home. A few days later, Dorothy boarded a steamer bound for New York. She never saw Dunsmuir again.

Lillian spent the summer of 1910 visiting her sisters in Rutherford, New Jersey, and Schenectady, New York. Automobiling now seemed to be her favorite sport. Yet, while motoring in downtown Schenectady one afternoon, Lillian hit a pedestrian who later complained of injuries, even though he had walked away from the accident scene. A few days later, the man's lawyer presented Lillian with a lawsuit demanding $5,000 for damages. The man claimed he had received unspecified internal injuries. Lillian's lawyers counterclaimed that the man had not planned to file a suit until discovering the woman who hit him was Lillian Russell. The judge deferred the case. It would take three years of court proceedings before the case was finally closed. Lillian was exonerated; the man received no money.

In August, Joseph Brooks announced that Lillian would star in a new dramatic comedy, *In Search of a Sinner*, to open on the road in September. As part of the announcement, a brief description of the plot was offered. A newspaper reporter sarcastically noted that both title and plot seemed appropriate for Lillian. No one mentioned that the play had been written by a woman, Charlotte Thompson, a professed advocate of suffrage.

Just prior to the opening, Blanche Bates organized a benefit for the Ossining Hospital, her favorite charity. To boost ticket sales, Bates asked Lillian to participate in the event. Of course, Lillian agreed. She volunteered to sing "Come Down, Ma Evening Star" and sell souvenirs. Once it was advertised that Lillian was participating, many of New York City's elite bid for tickets. First in line was John D. Rockefeller, who paid $500 to hear Lillian sing. "I've never seen her," noted the reigning capitalist, "and only heard her sing on the gramophone." His son, John D., Jr., paid $100 for a ticket, as did Gen. McAlpin, Senator Depew and other notables. To highlight the gala event, Jim Brady led a flotilla of automobiles from New York to attend the festivities.

In Search of a Sinner opened in South Bend, Indiana, September 16. It was performed three times at the South Bend Theater before moving to Chicago for its formal opening. The local press reported that Brooks "has provided his star with a splendid production."

The story tells of a widow (Lillian, as Georgiana Chadbourne) searching for a sinner who will give her a life of "blood and sinew and subduing battle," which her last husband, a relative saint, neglected to provide her. He had instead "never missed a meal" and "sat by the fireside till she wished to call him Fido." Meeting a likely prospect, Mrs. Chadbourne shamelessly throws herself at him. The pursuit begins; amorous complications ensue; but in the finale, she gets her man. To succeed in her quest, she steals flowers, converses with strangers, drops tulips onto the laps of delighted men and performs other decidedly "unladylike" acts.

It took a female theater critic, Amy Leslie, to laud the skills and talents of both Charlotte Thompson and Lillian Russell:

> Miss Russell was never so well equipped with a part, never looked handsomer, never at any time displayed so much dash, vitality, choice art and versatility and never was more enthusiastically applauded for her gracious entertaining, with thanks to Charlotte Thompson for making it happen.
> *In Search of a Sinner* shall prove one of the famous pleasures Miss Russell has given to her American public.[11]

Thompson's play was not intended as farce, nonsensical comedy or typical stage sentiment. To the contrary, in a humorous, sometimes biting way, the issue of male-female relationships was explored and debated, with the woman's side smartly and clearly stated. Lillian could not have been a better spokesperson for the play's message.

In fact, in the climactic scene, Lillian's rousing speech about the equality of women all but invariably received standing applause and cheers from women in the audience:

> What satisfaction can a true feminine find in the deep devotion of a man that no other woman can praise? What gloat is there in holding a man who couldn't love if he tried? Don't talk to me of your placid stream and placid slippers by the hearth. They're for old age, not for youth — and the man who gives you a peace like that has only that to give. Saints are all right in Heaven, with a harp and a hymn and a halo, but when I marry again you'll know the man is a sinner. I want a man, soul and body, spirit and flesh; a temper to calm, passion to curb and I to please and women to rouse. I want life — the battle of love. Women were born to fight and win and glory in the winning.

It was in Pittsburgh that this suggestive and compelling proclamation launched Lillian into two of the most engaging events of her life. Asked her feelings about the suffrage movement by a reporter from the *Pittsburgh Leader,* she startled the man with the vigor of her response:

> Woman has forced herself into a position where she has to fight for her rights, and now she is fighting in earnest. Why not take the real step of suffrage for women by abolishing the male vote.[12]

With that declaration, Lillian publicly positioned herself as an outspoken advocate for woman's suffrage, just as Sarah Bernhardt, Mary Mannering and Madame Nordica had done a few months previously. Suffrage leaders in New York joyfully awaited Lillian's return, hoping to involve her all the more in the movement's activities.

A few nights later, Alexander P. Moore, publisher of the *Pittsburgh Leader,* came to watch Lillian perform. When Lillian finished her soliloquy, he too found himself carried away, standing and applauding, as did all the women in the audience. Moore would later recall that he simply had to meet her.

Alexander P. Moore had been born in Pittsburgh, on November 10, 1867. When he was 12, he landed his first job, as a hustler in a brickyard, while continuing his studies in night school. Not liking manual labor, he obtained a job as an office boy on the *Pittsburgh Telegraph.* From that position, he rose to cub reporter, full-fledged journalist and city editor. Switching to the *Pittsburgh Press,* he rose to managing editor and part owner of the paper. A few years later, he was hired as editor of the *Pittsburgh Leader* and soon became owner and publisher.

Over the years, Moore had developed a reputation as a "fearless" spokesperson on civic and political affairs. He was a strong admirer of Theodore Roosevelt and supported him wholeheartedly during his Bull Moose campaigns. Recently divorced, after 15 years of marriage, Moore had already stated his support for women's suffrage.

Using his press title as leverage, Moore obtained a luncheon engagement with Lillian. His courtship began almost immediately. She was attracted to this strong, intelligent and independent man. A reporter for a New York tabloid gossip column coyly noted that Moore was a newspaperman, like Lillian's father, and that he was — shame on her — five years younger. Was this real life pretending to be a play — or perhaps the opposite?

The tour headed west, with extended runs in San Francisco, Los Angeles and Denver, along with many one-night stands, all to full houses. In Denver, Lillian "pleased large audiences." In San Francisco, she "opened to a big house of curious folks, who went there to see the star who has discovered the elixir of youth." The *Clipper* reported that the show had been given a new title by reviewers: *The Beauty Show.*

In almost every city Lillian played, feature articles about her youthful aspect, professional longevity and personal attractiveness were published side by side with the reviews. It was as if both audiences and critics were rediscovering her, but very differently than she had been perceived before. Now she was viewed as a mature, handsome professional, one whose presence, both on and off the stage, made people gape with reverence while captivated by her gracious, attentive and good-natured manner.

In Search of a Sinner became a national happening, and Lillian disappointed no one. Many critics questioned whether she wanted this kind of adulation. After all, it implied that she was now a veteran performer, possibly at the end of her career, a not unreasonable suggestion with regard to a female performer close to 50 years of age. Her reply: Yes, she enjoyed it. And, in one of many gracious acknowledgments to admirers, new and old, critics and audiences alike, she sincerely thanked them for their approval.

At the beginning of 1911, the tour returned to the Midwest, then headed for a long series of one-night stands in the South, a quick visit to Mid-Atlantic states, and finally back to Chicago in early April. While Lillian played cities in Ohio and Pennsylvania, a frequent caller was Alex Moore.

Although *In Search of a Sinner* was profitable, Lillian and Joseph Brooks were again having disagreements, primarily dealing with new productions they were planning to stage. Lillian had not been completely convinced that *The Widow's Might* was the correct show for her, but Brooks had prevailed. When the show was dropped, they had discussions about *In Search of a Sinner*, which Brooks liked and Lillian was unsure about. When it became a hit, Lillian acknowledged the accuracy of Brooks' prediction. Now, Brooks suggested that she give a rewritten *The First Night* another try.

Lillian demurred. When Brooks read in the *Dramatic Mirror* that she was considering a return to vaudeville, he demanded a decision about the proposed show. Apparently, the report had been based on rumor. But Lillian, attempting to maintain good relations with Brooks, soon agreed to reopen *The First Night*.

Brooks now also expressed concern about the financial results of the 1910-11 season. Lillian was playing to good and enthusiastic audiences, but few SROs; receipts had declined. In fact, the entire theatrical business had fallen off.

An editorial in the *Dramatic Mirror* stated that industry-wide receipts in large cities had declined 25 percent. Declines were even greater in smaller cities and one-night stands. Theater managers, usually reluctant to admit anything but success, conceded publicly that they were conducting business at a loss. Why the decline?

Wall Street attributed the sluggish market to the aftereffects of the panic of 1907. The prophesied recovery had never materialized; and while the country seemed prosperous, the cost of living was also increasing, inhibiting expenditures for leisure-time pursuits. (Even baseball owners were complaining about a drop in attendance.) New legislation against railway interests also had an impact on touring theatrical companies, forcing them to reduce their preferred routes or abandon them altogether. But the *Mirror* identified two other factors it believed to be the primary culprits depressing theater business: motion pictures and "the automobile craze."

There was no question that the popularity of motion pictures had been growing at a phenomenal rate among all classes of people. One immediate result was a decline in the patronage of gallery and low-priced seats in high-class theaters. Comedy and drama sufficient to meet people's needs seemed to be supplied by motion pictures. The rapid building of theaters, particularly in New York, contributed not only to the dilution of all attractions, but also to the proliferation of unworthy attractions that audiences quickly shunned. In effect, audiences were being "turned off" by stage productions because so few good ones were available to patronize.

With respect to the automobile, the *Mirror* bemoaned the fact that the new conveyance was radically changing people's habits and threatening "home life" by promoting increased mobility and a decreased sense of family responsibility, as well as ruining streets and dirtying the air. Even worse, people seemed so enamored of the automobile they were giving up the theater.

Of course, there were individual exceptions to this general decline in theater business, notably Lillian's performances, which proved fortunately lucrative to theaters that housed them. But Brooks feared that Lillian was attracted to vaudeville because, in that venue, she could command a large salary for less work and would no longer have to concern herself with the idiosyncratic demands of full-fledged stage production. He would prove correct in his assessment; however, the confrontation didn't occur until *The First Night* reopened.

Chicago audiences were presented with both of Lillian's current shows: *In Search of a Sinner* played one week at the Blackstone Theater; *The First Night* replaced it, opening there on April 10 and running for two weeks.

Reviews of the show were universally bad. Critics for the daily papers roundly booed the production. One of them published a letter from the chagrined author of *In Search of a Sinner*, Charlotte Thompson, sent to Lillian, regarding the shelving of her play: "Good luck, dear Miss Russell, and may I have the luck next time to write a play you sincerely embrace."[13]

The *Chicago Tribune*'s report on the start of the play's second week pronounced its demise: "This evening marks the beginning of the end as far as Chicago is concerned."[14]

This was all the evidence Lillian needed that changes had to be made. She severed her contract with Brooks and immediately contacted the Keith Circuit, which had already approached her, to see what she could arrange. Within two weeks, a deal was made, at $2,500 a week. Lillian Russell was back in vaudeville!

Lillian's part of the Keith circuit bill consisted of four songs and two encores, one of which was "Come Down, Ma Evening Star." Accompanying her on the piano was Dorothy, returned from her South American marital venture sufficiently contrite. On May 8, the vaudeville tour began, conveniently, in Pittsburgh, to good reviews:

> Her reception was tremendously flattering. The critics were surprised that
> her voice retains so much of its old-time charm and more astounded at the
> youthful appearance of the singer.[15]

While in Pittsburgh, Lillian spoke out again on the suffrage question. It was fully covered by the *Pittsburgh Leader,* whose owner and publisher, Alex Moore, attended every show and was seen escorting Lillian every day.

> I am not a militant suffragist, nor are most women of intelligence and
> refinement, but I believe that the time has come that some drastic action is
> necessary to persuade the men to the justice and seriousness of our
> demands.[16]

When Lillian traveled to Cincinnati, the second week of the tour, Moore was on hand to escort her again. Soon, local newspapers were reporting the impending wedding of Russell and Moore. Both parties denied the suggestion. "Both of us are single," Lillian said, "and there is no reason for people to insist we are to be married. If I get married again, I will leave the stage permanently, and I am not ready to do that at this time."

Six weeks after the disaster of *The First Night* in Chicago, Lillian reappeared in the city to sing in vaudeville. Chicago critics seemed relieved that Lillian had returned to her musical roots:

> The local press unanimously hail Lillian as having successfully "come back" into the lyric field and prophesy big success in next season's opera venture.[17]

The reference was to an announcement that Lillian planned to return to comic opera by signing with the producing team of Werba and Leuscher, at the time the largest importer of foreign productions. As Leuscher stated, "We will endeavor to secure a Viennese success for Miss Russell." What the impresarios neglected to reveal was that their deal was conditional, based on Lillian's acceptance of any opera they presented her. When Leuscher returned from Europe in July, he brought two operas for Lillian to examine. She rejected both, and the comic opera plans were terminated.

But as she had promised, Lillian as beauty expert was launched, if from an unlikely source. While in Chicago, during the *First Night* affair, Lillian had been approached by the Sunday editor of the *Chicago Tribune,* who asked her for contributions to the paper's Woman's Page. Given various themes from which to select, Lillian wrote three articles for the *Tribune.* The public response was so favorable that she was offered a one-year contract, at $12,000, to write a daily column. Her articles would also solicit questions from the public, which she would answer, one question a day. Ida McGlone Gibson, an accomplished Chicago journalist and *Tribune* employee, was assigned to assist Lillian. Susan, too, helped in the article writing. According to the editors of the *Tribune,* Lillian's pay was to be greater than that of any other woman writer.

Starting in August, the articles were an immediate hit. The *Dramatic Mirror* reported on this new episode in Lillian's career:

> In her cottage at Chelsea, near Atlantic City, Lillian Russell is writing her 'Beauty Secrets' for the Chicago Tribune. Interesting they are, too, and bearing the stamp of individuality, as they bear the signature of her whom in the Weberfields day they called "The Queen."[18]

The cottage in Chelsea was now Lillian's summer retreat. Staying with her were Susan and Dorothy. The Ansonia Hotel had not met her needs, and she had moved a few blocks away to the Majestic Hotel, an 11-story, 3-winged building on 72nd Street, a hostelry labeled "the Jewish place" by its neighbors. Though a family hotel, it boasted a roof garden and a dance hall and often sponsored concerts. Yet the Majestic, too, was only a temporary residence. Lillian was hunting for a permanent apartment, possibly suggesting to reporters that she was considering "settling down."

Both Alex Moore and Jim Brady visited Lillian frequently at her Chelsea retreat. Horses were no longer of great interest to Lillian; the seashore now seemed considerably more restful and less expensive than the race track. A singing coach again accompanied her, since it appeared she would be singing, rather than acting, in future performances.

An announcement in September revealed her plans. Werba and Leuscher, who had sought Lillian for comic opera, instead booked her to tour in vaudeville for 15 weeks, at $2,500 a week. In the company would be a young comic named Ed Wynn and the already celebrated Three Keatons. Her performance would include four songs, encores and a succession of beautiful gowns. Her companion and secretary for this tour would be Mrs. Leona Ross, Lillian's sister, who had been divorced some months before.

Lillian opened at Keith and Proctor's Fifth Avenue Theater (the Keith Circuit was booking the tour) on September 18, to an audience that had purchased all tickets a week in advance. The next two weeks included runs in Harlem and the Bronx, allowing Lillian to remain at home while performing. Meanwhile, she found a permanent place to live, a large apartment at 267 West 89th Street; Jim Brady lived only a few blocks away.

The remainder of the tour took Lillian to major Eastern and Midwestern cities. At most of these stops, crowds were at capacity; reviews were excellent. But while Lillian was concentrating on pleasing her audiences on the road, the New York funeral of a retired tailor was about to alter and refresh her stage popularity.

Lillian's old friend and theatrical colleague Lew Fields was performing *The Hen Pecks* in Chicago when he received a cable stating that his father was close to death. He immediately closed the show and caught the Twentieth Century for New York. Unfortunately, he didn't arrive soon enough to see his father alive. The funeral took place the next day. In attendance, along with the immediate family, was Joe Weber.

On the way home from the funeral, Fields suggested, "We ought to get together again, Web." Cautiously, Weber indicated his agreement. At first, the duo envisioned a high-class vaudeville company to perform in New York, then take the usual profitable road tour. A close friend, William Morris, suggested they reassemble the old Music Hall principals. But how? Many were already occupied with other shows. Moreover, their current salaries would make it impossible for such a company to turn a profit. If they could only persuade Lillian to join the company, Weber mused, the rest of the people would follow. He was correct. And the timing of Weber and Fields' request was superb.

At her new apartment, Lillian was holding an elaborate party to celebrate her fiftieth birthday. Attending the party were Dorothy, sisters Leona and Susan, Digby Bell, Jim Brady and Alex Moore. At the end of the party, Moore presented Lillian with a ring and asked her to marry him. Without delay, she accepted his proposal. They agreed to announce their forthcoming marriage at the end of the month.

On December 27, at a carefully staged press conference at her apartment, Lillian and Alex Moore revealed their plans for marriage, the ceremony to be performed in May. The ever-present *Dramatic Mirror* reflected on this new adventure:

> Lillian Russell, across the table, is as beautiful as, and more scintillant than, Lillian Russell across the footlights. Her own epigrams are cleverer than those allotted her by playwrights. Said she in the mellow comfort of the dining room of her Chinese apartment on 89th St., near Riverside Drive: "But I'm not marrying a millionaire. I leave that to chorus girls." And "I never wished I were a man. If I were, I might have been President of the U.S. and earning half my salary."[19]

The next day, Weber and Fields came to Lillian with their own proposal. "Pay me what you like," she said. "We'll make Pittsburgh the last stop on the tour and you boys can come to my wedding."

On December 30, in Lillian's apartment, she signed a contract, the first of the proposed company to do so, officially making her a member of the Weber and Fields

Jubilee Company. It was reported she seemed as elated over her signing as were Weber and Fields. Quickly following Lillian's acceptance were Fay Templeton, William Collier, John T. Kelly, Frankie Bailey and Bessie Clayton. Edgar Smith, author of nearly all the old Music Hall shows, started immediately on the libretto. They would call the show *Hokey-Pokey*.

Weber and Fields refused to state the terms of the contract with Lillian, other than to say her remuneration was very large. Later, it was revealed she was being paid $1,500 a week, well below her usual vaudeville salaries.

Following one last week in vaudeville, playing at Baltimore's Maryland Theater, Lillian joined the Weberfields in rehearsals. Like old times, jokes and routines were continually changed; no rehearsal was ever completed; activity was frenetic. As always, no Weber and Fields show would ever be perfected before the opening performance.

Hokey-Pokey opened at the Broadway Theater on February 8, 1912. A typical Weber and Fields auction of seats, an event that turned into a celebration of long-lost friends, had taken place a week earlier. The auction lasted for three and a half hours and had to be halted for the evening performance of the show currently playing at the theater. William Collier, Raymond Hitchcock and Edgar Smith acted as auctioneers. The first box seat, with the highest bid of $900, went to William Randolph Hearst. Henry Watterson, of the *Louisville Courier-Journal*, paid $500 for a box. Other high bidders were Supreme Court Justice James W. Gerard, William Morris, Felix Isman and Lillian Russell herself. Total receipts were $13,728. In 1899, when Weber and Fields conducted their first auction, total receipts had amounted to a little over $2,000.

Ticket holders started arriving at the theater two hours before show time, even though the night was very cold and windy. Outside the theater, traffic was gridlocked by a mixture of carriages, automobiles and pedestrians, all seemingly pointed toward the entrance doors. Floral bouquets filled the lobby and the stairways. Everyone was in high anticipation; the theatrical event of the year was about to begin.

As an overture, the orchestra presented a medley of Stromberg songs, eliciting applause for each. The curtain rose on a scene of the Place d'Opéra, Paris, and a drill team of chorus girls, led by Frankie Bailey. John T. Kelley followed with his signature song, "If It Wasn't for the Irish and the Jews" ("I really heard Belasco say / You couldn't stage a play today / If it wasn't for the Irish and the Jews"). The song was even more appropriate now than it had been in 1898.

Lillian then made her entrance, in a white chiffon gown studded with diamonds and pearls, to sing "The Island of Roses and Love." It was followed by her signature song, "Come Down, Ma Evening Star," which brought tears to both the company and members of the audience.

Enter William Collier to sing and dance — neither of which he had done for years. When he was out of breath, Lillian, as Mrs. Wallingford Grafter, came on stage to begin their routine. They quickly abandoned the script and traded jokes, to the great amusement of the audience. Then came Bailey and Kelly again, followed by Fay Templeton, who brought the audience to their feet with a rousing rendition of "Ma Blushin' Rosie." Finally, accompanied by sounds of scuffling in the wings and the loud complaint "Don't poosh me, Meyer!", Weber and Fields made their entrance. Leaping to their feet, an appreciative audience cheered and applauded them for ten minutes.

Lillian, with Joe Weber, William Collier and Lew Fields in the "Poker Scene" for *Hokey-Pokey*, their 1912 Jubilee production. Lillian considered her days with the Weberfields to be the most enjoyable she ever had on stage.

Lillian had two other routines to perform: as participant in the familiar poker game with Weber, Fields and Collier; and as the sly purchaser of sculpture in the gladiator statue skit, in which Weber and Fields dressed in short skirts and covered themselves with whitewash. For three glorious hours, the audience was treated to vintage Weber and Fields, and thrilled to every moment. When the show ended, no one wanted to leave the theater. The reunion had succeeded beyond anyone's expectations.

The *Dramatic Mirror* called *Hokey-Pokey* a "classic of its kind," in which the "actors hauled and mauled each other to the supreme delight of a house full of admirers." As for Lillian:

> There was the famous poker game, which included Lillian Russell and William Collier. Miss Russell, much the same as ever, strolled on every little while to sing, and she busied herself off-stage by changing from one gorgeous gown to another.[20]

At the Broadway Theater, 110 performances grossed over $300,000. The company's 36 city tour — all one-night stands — made another $105,000. It was the largest amount of money any touring show had ever made. Weber and Fields, as well as Lillian Russell, had been rediscovered by a new and enthusiastic audience.

For Lillian, as for all the company, it was the most enjoyable and satisfying tour ever experienced. And waiting for Lillian in Pittsburgh was Alex Moore, attending to their wedding arrangements. What a way to end a tour!

When the company stopped in Baltimore, Lillian held a late supper for Jim Brady in her private car. Brady had been confined to the Johns Hopkins hospital for several weeks; it was reported he was close to death.

Near the end of April, Brady seemed to have disappeared from Broadway, and rumors flew that he was dying or already dead. Speculation about Brady caused as much excitement as the sinking of the *Titanic*. In fact, he had been transported from New York to Baltimore because of a kidney stone obstruction. An emergency operation by Dr. Hugh H. Young saved Brady's life. By the time the Jubilee Company reached Baltimore, Brady had recovered enough to be carried to Lillian's dinner party. The party included Alex Moore and members of the Weber and Fields troupe. It lasted until 2:30 A.M., when the train was scheduled to depart for Pittsburgh, for the company's last road performance and the Russell/Moore wedding ceremony. There was no question that Lillian was as happy to see Brady alive as he was to be so honored by longtime friends.

Conducted by Reverend Dr. F. H. Lewis, pastor of the First Methodist Church, the marriage took place on June 12, at 11 A.M., in the parlor of the Hotel Schenley. In attendance were Moore's two brothers and their wives; Harry Davis, the local theater manager; Attorney Clarence Burleigh and Col. Oliver S. Hirschman, political friends of Moore; Dorothy and Susan; and the entire Weber and Fields company. William Collier, Jr., served as page; Dorothy Fields, eight years old, was maid to Lillian.

The company had just arrived in Pittsburgh by train that same morning. Lillian dressed for the ceremony in her private car. She wore a mauve silk gown, a hat of the same color trimmed in white, and a modest selection of diamonds and pearls, highlighted by a pendant. Diamonds embedded in crystal graced her bodice. A waiting convertible automobile carried her to the hotel, where all awaited her arrival.

After the ceremony, breakfast was served. The wedding breakfast had to end at 1 P.M., since the company was due at the theater to perform the matinee. The show itself was dominated by good-natured joking directed at Lillian. "You've changed husbands several times, haven't you?" "Who's the latest?" "What's your name now?" "New monogram on your china?" "An M?" "You don't spell Moore with an M, do you?"

After the matinee, dinner for the entire company was served in Lillian's dressing room. The evening performance, last in their tour, continued to chide Lillian about her marriage. To the delight of the audience, the show ended with a shower of rice and old shoes.

The next day, a rival Pittsburgh newspaper reported that Moore had tried to arrange a church wedding; puritanical deacons had declined to permit it, no reasons given. Displaying rather more divine beneficence than had his deacons, the pastor (a close friend of Moore) agreed to perform the nuptials at the hotel. The wedding certificate showed Lillian's birthplace as Clinton, Iowa, and her birth date as December 4, 1865.

Chapter Ten

Old Specialties, New Platforms

Lillian and Alex Moore separated only three hours after the closing of Weber and Fields' Jubilee tour, Moore attending the Republican convention in Chicago, Lillian returning to New York with the Jubilee Company.

A general malaise pervaded the Jubilee train. While the performers felt satisfaction that their tour had made many new friends, and a good deal of money, the Weberfields also recognized that their artistry was already a matter of public nostalgia. On the ride home, they shared their melancholy about the passing of the good old days.

Though elated by her marriage, Lillian wondered whether this stage "fling" might be her last. Unlike her colleagues, she had no dates to perform, acts to rehearse or contracts to sign. Her summer was to be spent at home in Chelsea, playing the role of homemaker and hostess. Moore would be in attendance frequently, but he had a newspaper to run and a presidential candidate to support.

The trip back to New York also gave Lillian and other company stars a chance to assess the current direction of musical theater. Astute observers of trends in entertainment, they all agreed that major changes were in process, that what was familiar today would be changed drastically in a few years. They also had to admit that their type of performance was "getting old." What were the trends in musical theater? The opportunities? The biggest threats?

All concurred that movies were fast becoming the public's primary form of leisure entertainment. Not as important, but still influential, were changes in the record industry, dance, cabarets and musical tastes. But the Jubilee performers also admitted to constraints within their own field of endeavor.

Musical theater seemed to have lost its creativity. Attractions were still unduly influenced by foreign imports and composers. And the development of new shows was inhibited by increasingly high costs of production.

For Lillian, it meant a considerable shrinking of the number of performance venues suited to her talents and abilities. A few months ago, this realization had influenced her quick acceptance of the offer from Weber and Fields. But it also suggested that her skills no longer satisfied current audiences as they had in the past. Still, she argued, she had a need to perform. Dealing with that dilemma would have to be postponed, however, as Lillian contemplated the immediate issue: her new role as Mrs. Alex Moore.

The Chelsea cottage, a sprawling wooden structure with six bedrooms, had a front porch that stretched the length of the building. On the far side of the frontage road lay the beach, which extended for hundreds of feet before meeting the ocean. Just down the road was a small park, perfect for picnics.

Lillian often said she looked forward to "keeping house" like normal people. Chelsea gave her the opportunity to fulfill the responsibilities of the typical moneyed matron. Now she could prove her talents as an authentic homemaker, albeit with the help of a Chinese cook to prepare most of the meals.

As always, Lillian adhered to a strict daily routine. Up at six A.M., exercise (now with a punching bag and weights), breakfast, making-up and dressing, singing (she continued to practice each day), lunch, an afternoon rest, dealing with business affairs, dinner and evening activities, which ranged from entertaining guests to attending theater. The locals had become familiar enough with Lillian that she was rarely bothered, for which she was grateful. On weekends, Moore was usually home; they would often tour the countryside in their new Hupmobile roadster. One such trip prompted a wager about how fast they could make the trip between Atlantic City and New York. The run was completed in five and a half hours, and Moore won the bet. Lillian had calculated seven.

Dorothy was again living at home. Susan continued to maintain the apartment in New York and visited Chelsea frequently to help Lillian write articles for the *Chicago Tribune*. Susan had signed for a road tour with a Cohan production and was negotiating a possible trip to California to appear in the movies. Jim Brady visited often. Excursions to see Lillian were a welcome respite from his usual round of New York restaurants and theaters, particularly since he wasn't feeling so robust these days. Old stage friends dropped by frequently. When conversation focused on performances and road tours, Lillian requested they talk about other topics. "This is my vacation," she said, "and I don't wish to talk of stage business." Moore often brought along political friends for the weekend, to conduct strategy sessions regarding the upcoming presidential campaign.

Dinners on these occasions fell barely short of staged entertainments. Lillian's Chinese cook created Oriental feasts of select meats and vegetables. Four Japanese girls, costumed to complement the colors of the china, waited on the guests. At one such dinner, one of Moore's friends, attempting to compliment his hostess, proclaimed, "How remarkably well you are looking, Miss Russell." Apparently taking offense at the comment, Lillian responded, "Did you expect me to come out with crutches?"

It was through these meetings that Lillian was persuaded to assist the Republican candidate, Theodore Roosevelt, against Democrat Woodrow Wilson. Lillian agreed to operate a "Progressive" store that would cater to New York society and club women, selling souvenirs to raise funds and distribute campaign literature. She would also tour a number of large Eastern cities to speak on behalf of Roosevelt, such events to be interspersed with talks on suffrage. Lillian particularly disliked Wilson because of his refusal to support women's suffrage.

Her suffrage speeches were most satisfying. Here was a venue unlike anything she had experienced on stage. Her views and opinions seemed to gain her more positive, unquestioning attention than had any stage performance. People came to hear what she had to say, not necessarily to gaze at her beauty and manner of dress, though both these factors helped to draw an audience. Lillian was being taken seriously and fast becoming an important spokesperson for women's rights. In addition, she found herself to be an excellent orator — a superior "salesperson," Moore suggested. Lillian noticed that her comments about suffrage were now featured in the newspapers in the same way that her statements about plays, performances and producers had made headlines in the past.

"How about suffrage?" she would be asked.

"I was brought up on mother's milk and suffrage. Don't you know that my mother was the famous Cynthia Leonard, who ran for President years ago? Ah, yes, I'm for suffrage and hope that it comes soon in my time, so that I can vote, and I'll vote good and stiffly."

"Then you firmly believe in women?"

"I never find a single fault with a woman. I can give the men a jolly calling down at times. Women have such great ideals, even if they are tied in knots by husbands; they have aspirations, even if they have not as yet learned to walk on the other side of the street."

Lillian's opening remarks at her talks on suffrage always drew applause, and set the tone for the messages that followed.

> You know that suffrage has always been a thing in our family. Our mother was very keen on it years ago. If she had been alive today, she would have been right in the movement. I want women to vote, and I believe they will. The idea was first brought home to me by a colored servant I had. He went out to vote, and when he came back he said: "I'm superior to you, Miss Nellie, because I can vote and you can't." Well, that got me, and ever since that day I've been eager for suffrage.[1]

When Lillian spoke on "How To Win Men — to the cause of votes for women," anti-suffrage reporters remarked she would no doubt prove to be an effective speaker on that subject.

"And the stage? Is that still being pursued?" Lillian avoided answering the question, but an article in the *Dramatic Mirror* suggested that she was still interested:

> If rumor be true, Lillian Russell may be back on Broadway again this year. If Lillian does return to the stage after her fourth marriage, it will probably be in a straight comedy, for musical comedy is said to have lost its charm for her. The question now appears to be whether one that is suitable can be found.[2]

Apparently, Roosevelt's loss to Wilson helped Lillian to decide. Just after the election, Lillian wrote a series of articles for the Pittsburgh *Leader*, interviews with various stage performers who were appearing in the city. On her birthday in December, she announced that she planned to embark on a lecture tour, speaking about women's health and beauty. Lillian had been approached in this regard by Tunis F. Dean, manager of the Baltimore Academy of Music and a close friend of Blanche Bates. A film of Lillian demonstrating exercises and makeup application would supplement the lectures. Some filming would be done in New Jersey and some in California, where "I will pose for two weeks in the open air for views that will be added to the film." Lillian boasted she was going to become, as Sarah Bernhardt put it, "a film."

The entire film supplement was to be shot in color by the Kinemacolor Company, using a process that had been developed in England in 1906 and had its first commercial showing in 1909. Interestingly, the American film trust prevented further development of the process because they believed it would add too much expense to filmmaking.

Just before Lillian boarded the train to Los Angeles, Susan gave her sister a farewell dinner. Crowds greeted Lillian when she arrived, and crowds surrounded her when she was filming. The title of her lecture was to be "How To Live a Hundred Years and Die Young." The *Dramatic Mirror* thought the title appropriate because "she is without doubt the best preserved woman on the American stage."[3]

The actual filming took place at Westlake Park in Los Angeles, a popular spot where neighbors took their children to play and feed ducks in the pond. Lillian, to the delight of park habitués, routinely arrived before the day's shooting to feed the ducks. She entertained them by demonstrating how feeding ducks could be turned into an exercise. A New York company supplied a red plush throne-chair, placed next to the stage, from which Lillian expounded to the crowd on the virtues of sleep and facial care. Everyone sleeps about one-third of each day, she noted. Thus, if one were 45 years old and had slept a third of that lifetime, he or she would really be only 30 years old. A Los Angeles reporter, amused by her logic, wrote:

> Several thinkers bethought themselves of this and went away to catch a little surplus life that they had been robbed of.[4]

Participating in the making of a film was a unique experience for Lillian, one she found herself enjoying because of its intimacy with the audience. Yet, as the noise coming from spectators was quite loud, it was fortunate that the shooting captured no sound. Talking among themselves, whistling when Lillian exercised, applauding when she completed each task, her audience made the event seem like a party. When Lillian demonstrated the use of the punching bag, shouts of "Hit it, Lillian!" caused her to laugh, and the scene had to be repeated a number of times. When the filming was completed and the park cleared of motion picture equipment, someone put up a small sign proclaiming, "Lillian Russell stopped here to feed and exercise the ducks."

When she returned to Chicago in January, a brief illness forced Lillian to postpone her opening lecture but gave her an extra week to practice her presentation. The opening lecture took place on February 22 at Chicago's Orchestra Hall, to a sellout crowd. A combination of heavy advertising and her celebrated name had guaranteed a large turnout. Many were curious to discover how Lillian would perform when she moved from amusing people to instructing them. Lillian wondered about it, too.

When the announcer came on stage to introduce the program, he was met with a mixture of cheers and boos — cheers when he said the show was about to begin, boos when he said a film would be shown before Lillian came on stage. The film, he boasted, was 1,000 feet long, featured Lillian, and would show (fanfare) "the blossom was as beautiful as the bud." Loud cheers.

The motion picture began by showing Lillian getting out of bed in her nightgown (whistles and foot stomping). It showed her applying her makeup (murmurs of appreciation) and exercising in a gym with a medicine ball and punching bag (cheers). She then modeled various kinds of dress (whistles from the men) and demonstrated how a woman's wardrobe could be purchased at reasonable prices (nods of approval from the women). Examples of men's styles were also featured, along with "the right things for them to do socially" (cheers from the women). The film concluded with Lillian's preparations for a healthy night's sleep (whistles and foot stomping again).

After a four-minute intermission for "pondering her demonstrations," the second part of the program began with a fanfare. "The Personal Appearance of Miss Russell," proclaimed the announcer. Loud cheers and applause.

With the introduction, Lillian made her entrance, bowed gracefully and declared, "I'm going to beat old Father Time at his own game." Loud cheers. Dressed in a blue velvet gown, trimmed with embroidery and embellished by appropriate jewelry, Lillian discoursed on cold cream, bathing, punching bags, diet and exercise. Wake with a smile, she advised. Drink hot water; exercise before an open window; eat one egg, toast and coffee each morning; rest an hour, reading or writing; punch a bag. Each pronouncement met with a cheer.

The *Chicago Tribune*, for whom Lillian was writing a beauty column, naturally headlined her appearance:

Tribune's Beauty Expert Starts Sane Living Campaign

Lillian Russell, actress, songstress, writer, reached Chicago yesterday prepared to add "lecturer" to her list of accomplishments. She is here to tell Chicago women how to live a hundred years and die young. Her first appearance as the priestess of the art of living sanely, correctly, and preserving health and beauty is in Chicago.[5]

Lillian was quoted as saying, "Years ago I began my career in Chicago as an entertainer. Now I am to begin a new career in Chicago—that of a missionary of happiness."

The lecture appealed to both men and women, and they were equally entertained. When Lillian began demonstrating the use of the punching bag, men in the audience smiled indulgently. Yet, when the bag began flying in all directions under her skillful blows, the smiles soon faded. When she completed her expert demonstration, men applauded enthusiastically. "Let me tell all my friends here tonight," she said, "the sooner you become acquainted with the punching bag, the sooner your husbands will come home to dinner." Her lecture ended with loud cheers.

The following week, Lillian arrived in New York to present her lecture at the Fulton Theater. The success of these lectures prompted Alan Dale to write a feature article about Lillian and "Eternal Youth."

After all, the one name that may be relied upon invariably to draw an audience is contained in the household words—Lillian Russell.[6]

He went on to praise her dedication to the stage, her good humor, self-confidence and beauty lectures. When he met her at the theater, he had found her to be "the concentration of all the pleasant features" of all the roles she had performed. Lillian's most important attributes, Dale concluded, were her ceaseless energy, persistent effort, tireless thought and spectacular femininity. "Miss Russell is the most striking instance of feminine success that any writer can find in his list of popular women."

With such glowing reviews and positive audience response to the lectures, Lillian seemed satisfied with the change in her performance role, even though it came at the expense of admitting to a certain "length of service." Rather than dismissing her as "an old and tired performer," audiences and critics alike embraced her as a symbol of all those things that were considered distinguished about theatrical performance. Temporarily at least, this triumph buoyed her desire to persevere on stage.

Lecture successes continued through stops in Boston, Cleveland, Baltimore and Washington, D.C., with enthusiastic audiences every-

Lillian lectured and gave demonstrations on "How to Live 100 Years," a program that appealed to both men and women. Over the years, her health, exercise and beauty testimonials inspired countless women to emulate her fitness regimen. (Museum of the City of New York, 34.79.600. Gift of Gilbert J. Holden.)

where acknowledging Lillian as an expert beauty and health instructor. Acton Davies, the *New York Sun* theater critic, summarized her current achievement:

> As a lecturer, Miss Russell is a huge success. Beautiful as were many of the kinemacolor pictures, just to watch the living, breathing Lillian was at all times a cure for sore eyes. It can honestly be said that Miss Russell entertained her audience thoroughly and proved a most charming instructor.[7]

To everyone's surprise, Lillian abruptly cancelled the remainder of her tour in early April. Reporters sought to find a reason for this apparent retreat from a success. The fact was that Lillian was responding to a telegram from Alex Moore. Her husband had fallen ill and wanted her at his side. Setting her health and beauty crusade aside, she immediately stopped the tour and returned to Pittsburgh.

The extraordinary success of her lectures, however, had captured the attention of a number of vaudeville managers. When they discovered that her lecture tour was ending, they quickly contacted her to appear at their theaters. The Keith and Proctor people offered an interesting possibility: Why not combine Lillian's singing with a condensed version of her beauty lecture on a vaudeville bill? Lillian concurred, agreeing to a ten-week contract, at $2,500 a week.

Lillian opened her vaudeville run at the Colonial Theater, New York, April 21, singing her usual repertoire of songs and lecturing about how to become and stay beautiful. Any manager having a problem attracting women to his theaters found the problem instantly solved by Lillian's appearance.

Lillian's second week in vaudeville took the company to Pittsburgh and gave her a chance to be with Moore, who was now recovering. The tour ended in Brooklyn in mid-June, Lillian returning to her apartment on the Upper West Side to await Moore and make preparations for their summer trip to Europe. Before leaving, however, she and John Cort — manager and owner of the Cort circuit of vaudeville houses — agreed on conditions for a 15-week tour, to start in September. It was reported that she would receive more than $50,000 for the entire run.

The trip to Europe was supposed to combine two objectives. It would give both Lillian and Moore a chance to rest; some spas were listed on the itinerary. Lillian would also study women's living conditions in the countries they planned to visit. On behalf of the suffrage movement, she planned to observe and interview European women, then share her findings in public speeches upon her return to the U.S. There are no indications, however, that any such material was publicly presented, if indeed it was ever collected.

The newspapers did report on Lillian's shocked reaction to the latest Parisian fashions. The "rooster effect" dresses, she said, made it difficult for women to sit down. Overall, American fashions were much more practical, she observed. Upon her return to New York, reporters informed Lillian that French designers, in response to her comments, had called her "out of date." She just laughed, remarking how very "French" such designers were.

Lillian immediately began rehearsals for her upcoming tour on the Cort circuit. Despite vigorous training with her singing coach, she noticed that each time she prepared for a singing assignment, it took her longer to be ready. Cort had already begun advertising the show as the "costliest theatrical venture on the American stage," very likely the truth, thanks to Lillian's extraordinary salary.

Lillian's portion of the vaudeville program consisted of four songs, the usual encores, an abbreviated speech on health and beauty and a display of the latest in Parisian gowns. Performing a skit on the same bill was William Farnum, fresh from his motion picture triumphs. The remaining acts were rotated each week.

Lillian Russell's Big Feature Festival opened September 29 at the Hermanus Bleeker Theater in Albany, first stop on a tour that would take the company to major cities throughout the U.S. Initial reviews of the show were good and houses were filled. But as the show traveled to the Midwest, reviews became more critical and receipts declined. This was partly attributable to recent shifts in leisure time pursuits, but it was also a function of the changing tastes of a new generation of theatergoers, a younger audience who did not share the same respect for Lillian shown by their elders. A review in a Madison, Wisconsin, newspaper summed up current perceptions of Lillian's performance, and it undoubtedly bothered her:

> The name of Lillian Russell once was the synonym of "standing room only." Players who have tested popularity never know when to quit. And Lillian has gone all the way from light opera to this tragedy. Nothing is sadder than the fall of a theatrical star. Some real good honest friend ought to take Lillian by the hand and gently lead her home that we might be left with a happy memory of the days when she was in her prime.[8]

Cort was distressed by the reviews and the continued decline in receipts. He would have liked to close the tour, but his investment was so large that any returns would help reduce his debt. His contract with Lillian required him to pay her the full amount whether she performed or not. Lillian, too, was disturbed by the situation, but she preferred to perform. A brief interruption in January (Moore had another operation which required Lillian to return home) only prolonged the disappointing tour to the end of the month.

Personal picture of Lillian, 1914. She was about to begin a 15-week vaudeville tour on the Cort Circuit, an experience that persuaded her to consider retirement from the popular stage. (Museum of the City of New York, 34.79.606. Gift of Gilbert J. Holden.)

The train ride back to Pittsburgh provided Lillian time to evaluate the whole affair, and examine her remaining chances for a performing career, if indeed she had any at all. The critics now seemed clearly to be telling her, "It's time to retire!"

Theater business during the early years of the second decade of the century was generally poor, 1913 and '14 being the worst on record until the depression of the 1930s. Musical theater was in the doldrums, relying only on Ziegfeld revues and the Shuberts, who tried hard to emulate Ziegfeld. Little in the way of original American shows was successful. Even Cohan's latest efforts failed to inspire audiences.

The popularity of ragtime music was rapidly diminishing, soon to be replaced by jazz. But the time between marked a period of indifference, as if the public was waiting expectantly for a new and different musical experience.

An experiment by Jesse Lasky and Henry B. Harris introduced a new form of entertainment, a combination of restaurant and music hall borrowed from the

French — the cabaret. By 1912, many of the best-known New York restaurants, such as Martin's, Rector's and Shanley's, had incorporated the cabaret format. It attracted many stage performers and audiences from the theaters, but it, too, seemed to be no more than an entertainment "filler" until new directions were found.

Motion pictures were doing the most damage to popular theater. By 1910, the star system had evolved. In a matter of a few years, performers like Mary Pickford increased their salaries from $200 to $1,500 a week. In Pickford's case, she soon reached six figures annually by bartering herself between the studios. Charlie Chaplin had begun at $150 a week making movies for Mack Sennett. Within two years, he was earning $10,000 a week.

One-reel films became five-reel epics, and prices increased accordingly. When Bernhardt's *Queen Elizabeth* was released, tickets were sold for $1, considered an outrageous price. Griffith's 1913 masterpiece *Birth of a Nation* startled the viewing public. Nothing like it had ever been seen before. Multiple-reel films and higher ticket prices soon became standard.

Stage stars like John Drew, Maude Adams, David Warfield and Ethel Barrymore were quickly signed to appear in movies; the exodus of luminaries from Broadway was considerable. Performers soon realized they could earn more in movies, which further offered the opportunity to reach many thousands more people, more quickly, than any stage production might ever hope to achieve.

Simultaneous with increased motion picture production and the development of a controlled distribution organization, new movie "temples" were being built. The new theaters were designed primarily for films and only incidentally for vaudeville. All this development was laying the foundation for a dramatic resurgence in popular entertainment, now poised to begin.

Lillian was sensitive to these activities and wrestled with their significance throughout early 1914. Yet she remained insistent about performing. She still desired an audience, lights and applause. If she couldn't have a stage, maybe she could have a platform.

The summer began unpleasantly. Lillian came down with a cold that became pneumonia, and she spent a month in bed at the Chelsea cottage. While recovering, she suffered an attack of appendicitis and had to be taken to a Pittsburgh hospital for an operation. Doctors suggested that the pneumonia had somehow caused the appendix inflammation. Throughout this ordeal, Moore was at her side. By contrast, Dorothy was off on another amorous adventure.

Late July newspaper stories revealed that Dorothy was again to be married, for the fourth time. (Headlines flattered neither mother nor daughter: "Dorothy Beats Mama Lillian's Famous Record!"[9]) Prospect number four was Edward O'Reilly, a nephew by marriage. While on vacation during the summer, O'Reilly had met Dorothy at Chelsea. She invited him for a swim, and he became a daily visitor to the house. Begged for her hand, Dorothy consented to O'Reilly's proposal. They eloped to Pleasantville, New Jersey, and were married by a justice of the peace on August 19. Dorothy phoned Lillian to tell her the news.

Lillian was disturbed, and Moore's negative comments about Dorothy's emotional instability did not help. According to Dorothy, however, her mother responded to the news with characteristic grace and wit: "All I have to say is, it's some jump from Einstein to O'Reilly." There is no evidence of how Lillian really felt about the marriage at the time, but later indications suggest she did not care for Dorothy's husband.

The Moores, as they were now being called, moved into a new apartment on the Upper West Side, at 2 West 86th Street. But Moore soon had to return to Pittsburgh to run his newspaper. By October, fully recovered, Lillian was again attending first nights with Jim Brady, an event that always captured the attention of theatrical newspapers. She was reported to be "thinner and as lovely as ever." Audiences were quickly abuzz whenever they discovered Lillian was in attendance. When she entered the auditorium, someone would invariably exclaim, "Here comes the Queen!" People would stand and applaud politely until she reached her front row seat. For many in the audience, seeing Lillian was as exciting as seeing the show.

In November, Lewis Selznick, then head of the World Film Corporation, telephoned Lillian to make an appointment. He wanted to discuss a movie proposal. Selznick's idea was to produce a film version of *Wildfire*, with Lillian playing the same role she had performed on stage. Both he and Lillian believed it could be a profitable enterprise because the play had been so well received seven years ago. Shooting would take place at World's Fort Lee, New Jersey, studios. Co-starring with Lillian would be Lionel Barrymore, 17 years younger than she, but readily aged by appropriate makeup. Lillian agreed to a contract worth $10,000. Recalling her enjoyable experiences in Los Angeles the previous year, she was very excited about the prospect of appearing in movies. Immediately after the contract was signed, World released the announcement:

> Lewis J. Selznick, general manager of the World Film Corp., has arranged to present Lillian Russell in a photo-play based on one of her greatest stage successes, *Wildfire*.[10]

New Jersey in December, she soon learned, was not Los Angeles. The studio was cold and drafty. Lillian was chilled to the point of having to wear a fur coat and gloves between scenes. The shooting schedule was more rigorous than her previous filming experience; 12-hour days were common. Barrymore's antics also delayed completion of the film. Often, when he and Lillian appeared together, his glib off-camera comments made her laugh, forcing them to reshoot the scene. He would sometimes deviate from the script, which disrupted Lillian's timing. Though scheduled for release on January 11, 1915, the film was actually released two weeks later. Selznick was so sure the film would be successful that he ordered distribution of 236 prints, a much larger number than usual.

But reviews of *Wildfire* were mediocre. Similar to Lillian's experiences with her latest vaudeville tour, critics took the opportunity to note that Lillian was "not youthful anymore." The movie, they observed, "points out the difference of beauty from Lillian between yesterday and today." *Photoplay*, the top movie magazine of the day, remarked:

> When one sees her, one realizes how fast our standards of beauty have changed. Together with militant suffrage and the feminist movement has come the ultimatum that a beauty of the twentieth century must be lithe and slim and boyish, and Lillian Russell still adheres to the princess gown which fits without a wrinkle, the lines of a "perfectly molded" figure.[11]

Lillian quickly realized that she would not have a movie career. *Wildfire* was her only venture into motion pictures.

Nor was her fifty-third birthday a gala event. Lillian had just been informed by the *Chicago Tribune* editor that the paper wanted her to refrain from writing on any subjects other than health and beauty. Evidently, some of her recent work had included references to women's suffrage. Lillian was not entirely pleased by the editor's suggestion and decided that it might be time to seek another newspaper as outlet for her views.

Along with Moore, Lillian's sisters and perennials Digby Bell and Jim Brady, Dorothy and her new husband also attended Lillian's birthday party. Lillian's less-than-positive feelings about O'Reilly were apparently communicated directly and succinctly. He soon excused himself from the proceedings. Dorothy later suggested that the event had been the beginning of the end of their marriage.

In addition, Lillian seemed perturbed by the amount of attention Moore was now receiving. Apparently pursuing a new story angle about Lillian and Moore, some reporters had questioned him about how it felt to be the husband of a celebrated star. In jest, Moore talked about the "penalty of marrying a famous woman," but insisted he enjoyed the role. He referred to himself as Miss Russell's "current husband." He also told a story about rearranging the pictures on his desk so that Lillian would be "topping the bill."

Lillian's recent positive stage reviews were never mentioned by reporters. They only asked her about prospects for the film of *Wildfire* and how getting into the movies would affect her career. She admitted to uncertainty about that prospect.

With the apparent failure of the cinematic *Wildfire,* Lillian announced that she was going to embark on a number of activities in support of women's suffrage. Alan Dale was one of the first to interview her on the issue. His article in *The Theater* magazine outlined her views.

Lillian again emphasized her mother's suffragist activities and influence. She discussed the many contributions to the cause made by women in the acting profession and reminded readers of the difficulties encountered by women who wished to pursue theatrical careers in previous years. She ended the interview by declaring she might run for mayor of New York City, "just as soon as the people have voted on equal suffrage." Her platform, she continued, would include school lunches, no children under 15 working, clean streets, and free markets for poor people to buy food. Some reporters suggested that Lillian was sounding just like her mother, who had run for mayor 30 years earlier and voiced the same "progressive" arguments.

Along with her public pronouncements, Lillian actively involved herself in suffrage activities. Early in 1915, the women's suffrage association in New York was lobbying the state legislature to approve a bill giving women the right to vote. Led by Carrie Chapman Catt, former national suffrage president and current leader of the New York chapter, the campaign was vigorously contested. Lillian not only spoke in favor of the vote, but also was active in soliciting funds. At one such speech, with Catt and Ida Husted Harper in attendance, $15,000 was collected.

Lillian again assumed an active role in the Woman's Professional League, lobbying its members to play a larger role in the suffrage movement. Programs now included speakers talking about suffrage. Skits dealt with suffrage issues. Donations were made to suffrage groups.

When the suffrage association staged its giant parade up Fifth Avenue, Lillian participated, carrying a placard along with other marchers. Using her celebrity status to sell women's suffrage, Lillian had now wholeheartedly assumed the role of political campaigner. With Lillian among its members, no man could claim the movement wasn't feminine. Boos and jeers changed to applause and cheers when Lillian was recognized among the marchers.

Due to disagreements over content, Lillian and the *Chicago Tribune* ended their three-year relationship. A fortuitous conversation with the editor of the *Chicago Record-Herald*, a *Tribune* competitor, resulted in another writing assignment. Lillian could now write on anything she pleased, not only health and beauty, but also suffrage and love. Moore remarked to the papers that Lillian was thoroughly enjoying her new role as social crusader.

Lillian's activities on behalf of suffrage extended to encompass her continuing contributions to charity. While Lillian had always participated in benefits, these fund-raising events now became additional outlets for her views on suffrage. She spoke (and sang) at a benefit for homeless children in New York. She sold souvenirs and gave a brief speech on women's rights at the annual Actors' Fund benefit. At the Lambs' Gambol, another benefit for actors, she sold programs and solicited funds for suffrage. In Pittsburgh, Lillian sold baseball tickets at Forbes Field in support of the cause.

Of special significance to Lillian was her benefit appearance at the Metropolitan Opera House. When master of ceremonies Henry E. Dixey informed the audience that Lillian was about to appear, they quieted, in rapt anticipation. When, ever-elegant, she entered from the rear of the house, the audience rose and remained silent until she sat down. When she sang, their loud and sustained applause declared that her reputation among fellow professionals remained strong, if mostly reverential.

Lillian's suffrage activities continued until summer. Her work was briefly interrupted by Moore's illness and, closely following his recovery, Dorothy's hospitalization for pneumonia. All plans for the summer now had to be canceled to care for Dorothy, who was gravely ill. Her illness was complicated by a fall that broke her left foot. Rumors circulated that she had attempted suicide or had been drunk or had fallen from a stage; the real reason for the accident was never revealed. Further diagnosis indicated she had cracked three vertebrae. Dorothy's recovery took many months, and she still had difficulty walking. A year later, further complications forced doctors to amputate her disabled foot.

Fortunately, Lillian's public exposure and positive reviews had prompted Martin Beck, manager of the Orpheum Circuit, to offer her a vaudeville tour during the upcoming season. For Lillian, the call of the stage remained strong. And, most importantly, this opportunity to perform arrived as an emotional antidote to recent professional misfortune. She signed a ten-week contract, to open at the Palace Theater, New York, in November. Immediately, her singing coach was called.

The renowned Palace Theater had opened March 24, 1913, one of those so-called temples, spacious, lavish in crimson and gold decor. Its first show was attended by more theater professionals than public. Yet initial reactions from both professionals and public were negative. All indications were that the theater was a flop. *Variety* reported bets being made that the Palace would die before the end of the theater season. By the end of the sixth week of operation, however, attendance began to increase. Two women — Ethel Barrymore and Sarah Bernhardt — turned incipient failure into heralded success; two more women — Fritzi Scheff and Nora Bayes — made the Palace "the place for the best in vaudeville in New York."

By the end of 1915, the Palace had not only become New York's showplace, but performers who played there received additional public recognition. Just prior to Lillian's opening, stars like Mrs. Leslie Carter, Vernon and Irene Castle and Madame Emma Calvé, played the theater.

Lillian opened on November 3, to a full house. She sang six songs, including "Evening Star." Renold Wolf, critic from the *New York Telegraph*, wrote:

> Lillian Russell was given an enthusiastic reception. "There she is! That's our American Beauty! Is there any wonder that we are proud of her?" Miss Russell in appearance, in grace, in her beautiful gown and her wealth of jewels, and in the effectiveness with which she sang justified the confident approval of her assembled admirers.[12]

The *New York Star* suggested why Lillian was still a paragon:

> Miss Russell has something that is sadly lacking in so many of our young actresses today — technique. She is an artiste to her fingertips, and it is a joy and revelation to see the exquisite manner in which she handles herself on the stage.[13]

Lillian's entire week at the Palace consisted of SRO performances. Two weeks at the Majestic Theater continued the success. After stops in the East, where, according to the newspapers, "all records were broken," the company headed for the Midwest. In deference to her drawing power, Beck asked Lillian to extend the tour to 15 weeks, to which she agreed with no hesitation. A sidelight of the tour was Lillian's attendance at ladies' teas, convened in each city, which afforded her the opportunity to talk about suffrage.

Closing in early March, the tour was seen as a financial and performance triumph. It enlightened Lillian to the sudden reawakening of popular theater but, at the same time, the admitted fact that her voice was foundering.

As unkind as 1913 and 1914 had been to American theater entertainment, 1915 and 1916 seemed to rekindle public consciousness of its potential. Part of this revival was due to the war in Europe. A growing anti-German sentiment carried over to public opinion about operetta and foreign imports in general. Moreover, the war had effectively stopped all theatrical production in Europe.

Old composers had died or retired, and youngsters like Jerome Kern, Cole Porter and George Gershwin were being recognized for their characteristically "Yankee" styles. Ragtime music was being discarded for jazz, an "insistent" music, improvisational in presentation, with Negro origins. The first advertised public use of the word "jazz" occurred in 1915, when a New Orleans band played at Chicago's Lamb's Café.

ASCAP (American Society of Composers, Authors and Publishers) had been founded by Victor Herbert and friends in 1914, to prevent the evasion of royalty payments to songwriters and composers. Record industry sales dramatically increased because original patents expired and new manufacturers hired new performers to feed the public's desire for music in the home. Flat records, which had entirely replaced cylinders by 1912, allowed for easy and cheap availability. This further accelerated expansion of the sheet music business. Dancing became a widely popular new sport, both in action and in observation. Dance halls opened by the hundreds. In 1915, the Cakewalk was added to the national dance repertoire of the Hesitation Waltz, the Turkey Trot and the Tango. The Victor Talking Machine Company produced a series of dance records, featuring the celebrated duo of Vernon and Irene Castle.

A fragmented movie industry was now consolidating into powerful studio empires, with as much intrigue and double-dealing as had existed among theater impresarios three decades earlier. Paramount and Goldwyn Pictures were formed; leading directors like D.W. Griffith, Mack Sennett and Cecil B. De Mille set up their own companies. Successful producers were not only gaining control of distribution outlets, but were also acquiring control of theaters. Hollywood was fast becoming the film capital of the world.

As a keen observer of the entertainment scene, Lillian knew that her performance career had reached its end. Her last tour had been a success; she could leave the stage "on top." One can live on past success only so long; reputations die quickly. Her voice could no longer beguile, nor could her beauty compete with younger, more contemporary styles. Too many performers didn't know when or how to retire. Leaving the stage voluntarily would be much better than leaving by popular demand.

A sudden death seemed to influence Lillian's decision. Ida Kate Schultze, Lillian's oldest sister, died June 5, 1916, in Rutherford, New Jersey. Ida Kate had taken care of Cynthia during her last years. Due to a nervous breakdown, Kate was being cared for by her own daughter when she died. The entire family, including Lillian, attended the simple funeral. Burial was in the local cemetery.

Her parents gone; now her sister. Life is finite. It was time to withdraw from the stage.

Once the decision was made, the Moores determined to find a permanent home in Pittsburgh. Lillian would sell her New York apartment; it was no longer needed. A month later, they purchased a home on Squirrel Hill, an exclusive section of the city. The house already possessed the kind of reputation that befitted its new residents:

> It is one of the handsomest residences in Pittsburgh and has been celebrated for the elaborate entertainments given there.[14]

After making the necessary arrangements for their new home, the Moores left for their Chelsea cottage to enjoy the summer. Dorothy, her two-year marriage fast dissolving, was soon to join them.

Chapter Eleven

God, Mother, Country
and Lillian Russell

$\mathcal{T}$he fall and winter of 1916 found Lillian commuting between Pittsburgh and New York. Weekends were spent at home, where she enjoyed what soon became a tradition—Sunday afternoon get-togethers with Pittsburgh society matrons who represented various local charities. Since many of the participants belonged to more than one charity and their duplication of effort wasted a good deal of time and money, it was Lillian's idea to coordinate the activities of these charities so they could be more efficient. The wisdom of her strategy was quickly appreciated, as the combined effort increased contributions well beyond what had previously been collected. Lillian also used this opportunity to continue her lobbying for the woman's vote.

The trips to New York were for the purpose of establishing a cosmetics business, an idea Lillian had wanted to exploit for some time. With the manufacturers who would supply the products, she formed Lillian Russell's Own Preparations, Inc. The line was to consist of creams, powders and rouges, to be distributed through department stores and small beauty shops. Beyond simply lending her name to a list of products, Lillian planned to participate in company operations and visit outlets to promote her line. It took her only a short time to see that beauty shop distribution would be a financial liability, and they were soon closed. While Lillian and her investors hoped to make substantial profit selling cosmetics using her name, sales proved only average. Nor did it encourage Lillian when her partners abruptly discontinued monthly royalty payments. Rather than getting into a legal squabble at this time (she had an investment to protect), Lillian instead involved herself all the more in company operations. She decided to wait and see how the company performed before determining her future involvement. World events would soon influence her decision.

Jim Brady was ailing again. Since his confinement at Johns Hopkins Hospital in 1912, Brady had been under medical supervision, physicians constantly monitoring the state of his health. His doctors had instructed him to modify his eating habits and social activities, but Brady rejected their advice and continued his exuberant ways. Brady's customary answer to his medical critics: "Hell, I gotta have some fun; I haven't much longer to live." In November 1916, he suffered an attack of what seemed to be his old malady, gastric ulcers. Yet, upon examination by Dr. Hugh Young, his favorite physician, he was found to be suffering from a combination of angina, diabetes and kidney problems, as well as ulcers.

Brady was told he had only a short time to live — *how* short the doctors weren't sure. He acknowledged the news by deciding to live out his days with characteristic flair. He moved to Atlantic City and established himself at the elegant Sherburne Hotel, in a large apartment complex with a glass enclosed balcony overlooking the ocean. Atlantic City was close enough that his friends could visit, and it was usually the place new shows were tried out before going to Broadway.

After months of wasting away, Diamond Jim Brady died in his sleep on April 13, 1917, no one at his bedside. For a man who had devoted his life to cultivating friends and donating a fortune to good causes, it was an ironic and lonely end.

As befit the man, a special train returned his body to New York to lie in state in the living room of his 86th Street home. From newsboys and hotel managers he had befriended, to industrial executives and theatrical stars he had associated with and entertained, hundreds of people came to pay their respects.

Jim Brady's funeral was held at St. Agnes Roman Catholic Church at 43rd Street and Lexington. It was as elaborate as any ever seen by New Yorkers. Police patrols were assigned to control the large crowds. Among the many theatrical performers who attended the services was Lillian. Like many others, she cried openly as priests recited the liturgy honoring the dead. Burial was in Greenwood Cemetery, in a gilded and elaborately decorated mausoleum, Brady's final contribution to a fast-disappearing era of display and opulence.

As Brady's casket was lowered into the ground, Lillian reflected on their long and intimate relationship, particularly those times when his staunch support and counsel had comforted her and helped to alleviate self-doubts and indecision. Had she been wrong not to marry him? Had she taken advantage of his generosity, like all the others upon whom he showered gifts? Had she really been a faithful friend to him? The doubts would remain.

Less than a week prior to Brady's death, the U.S. declared war on Germany. Earlier in the year, Germany had announced that its submarines would sink any ship going to or coming from any Allied port, hoping the offensive thrust would provide a decisive victory over the Allies before the U.S. could enter the war. In March, German U-boats sank several American supply ships without warning. After two years of attempts to maintain a semblance of neutrality, President Wilson and Congress reluctantly declared war. All along, however, Congress had been preparing for eventual entry into the fighting by voting to increase the size of the army and allocating more than $7 billion for national defense. Wilson had also authorized U.S. merchant ships to carry guns as protection against submarines.

With preparations for war now accelerating, the country changed its mood from the pursuit of leisure to the promotion of patriotic fervor. A selective service system was immediately established, requiring men to register for the military draft. Public information programs were launched to explain why the U.S. was involving itself in a European conflict. Sales of Liberty Bonds were the country's most significant civilian war effort. Advertising promoted slogans such as "Food Will Win the War." A tough-looking, finger-pointing Uncle Sam glowered grimly from recruiting posters stating, in bold and colorful letters, "I Want You." George M. Cohan's song "Over There" told the world the Yanks would soon be on their way.

A few weeks after the U.S. entered the war, Lillian was approached by Navy recruiters in Pittsburgh to assist in their activities. Could she join them to sign up recruits? Would she be willing to perform and speak on behalf of the war effort? Would she travel throughout the state with them? Lillian's answer to all these questions was an unqualified "yes," an agreement that would launch her on an extensive two-year crusade (at the time, a unique professional endeavor for a stage performer).

On her first effort, in McKeesport, Pennsylvania, Lillian recruited 259 men. Reports of her successes traveled quickly. She was immediately besieged by various government officials — not unlike the theatrical managers from an earlier day — to donate her time, energy and reputation to other wartime causes. To all these requests, she agreed. For Lillian, the remainder of 1917 became a whirlwind tour of cities, army camps and Liberty Bond gatherings.

At home, she converted the extensive lawn in front of her house into a Victory garden, growing vegetables to be donated to local military camps. She presented the colors to the first Pennsylvania regiment on its way to Europe. She persuaded her Sunday afternoon matrons to make "comfort kits" for the soldiers and delivered thousands of them during an almost two-year period. During the summer of 1917, Lillian visited embarkation depots to teach troops some basic French. To the First Field Artillery, she gave out 2,000 books of French language lessons.

Lillian's Liberty Bond activities were even more extensive, taking her to cities and towns all over the Northeast. Wherever she appeared, crowds were large. After listening to a brief speech on behalf of Liberty Bonds, the audience invariably implored her to sing. After a few songs, she repeated her petition that they purchase Bonds; sales always seemed to increase after she had entertained. Reporters remarked that her appearances turned otherwise dull and predictable appeals into "patriotic pep rallies."

Sponsored by the Theater War League, a major Liberty Bond rally was staged at the Hippodrome Theater in New York. More than 5,000 people attended to hear a number of government officials press the case for Bond purchases. Lillian and a number of other theatrical people were on stage to entertain and sell. The *New York Times* reported that Lillian was "an eloquent pleader for subscriptions, a delightful added attraction, and one of the big hits of the show."[1] The event raised almost $32,000, one of the largest amounts collected to that point in time.

Lillian's tireless activities during this first year of the war effort were favorably noticed by the War Department, at the time headed by Newton Baker, who also happened to be one of the strongest supporters of women's suffrage in Wilson's administration. Through Gen. Barnett of the Marines, Baker proposed that Lillian be "enlisted" in the Marines branch of the service as a recruiting sergeant, to recognize her efforts on behalf of the country. The enlistment also proved to be an excellent promotional device to take advantage of her popular appeal. From the day of her appointment, Lillian appeared in a Marine sergeant's uniform at all events. She would be the only woman in the history of the U.S. Marines ever to be honored with such an appointment.

Lillian herself recalled some of these thrilling events, likening them to the kind of euphoria she had once experienced in early stage appearances:

> As I stepped upon the platform, I saw before me about ten thousand people. It had started to rain and umbrellas were raised. I shouted: "Men and women — our boys are knee deep in mud in the trenches in France, fighting for you and me. It's raining there. Do those boys have umbrellas? In five seconds, every umbrella was down."[2]

Lillian compared her successful first nights to these impassioned appeals for Liberty Bonds, as crowds "came to the call of Uncle Sam." She talked about returning soldiers, some of them wounded, who helped her sell Bonds "by exhibiting themselves on the stage." In uniform, Lillian caused as much audience response as she had when wearing elegant Worth gowns. Her recruiting speeches now inspired young men to enlist, just as her health and beauty lectures had previously persuaded young women to exercise. The honest and sincere tone of her patriotic messages received the same rapt attention as her

Lillian in her Marine Corps sergeant's uniform, 1917. Her patriotic endeavors earned her this military appointment, an honor that no other woman has ever achieved. (Harry Ransom Humanities Research Center, the University of Texas at Austin.)

singing. Lillian was no longer an actress, the press announced; she had now become an exemplar of America's patriotic spirit.

When Lillian traveled from city to city, she regularly stopped at military camps to entertain the troops. Often, she was accompanied by fellow performers such as old friend Fay Templeton, who came out of retirement to offer her services. The songs they sang were the popular ones of the day; their skits were reminiscent of the old Music Hall jokes and patter. When Lillian volunteered to go overseas to entertain, she was dissuaded because of her importance to the war effort on the home front. "A bill headed by Lillian," Alan Dale wrote, "guaranteed SRO as it had consistently done for her many years in comic opera." He added that "her empire was now one of Good Deeds."

In early 1918, Lillian realized her cosmetics business was failing, due mainly to the war. Having already lost considerable money on her investment, Lillian sold her remaining shares for $10,000. She was lucky she did. The company went bankrupt six months later.

While she was giving speeches in Detroit in February 1918, Raymond Hitchcock, playing the same city in his current hit *Hitchy-Koo,* asked Lillian for a special favor. In Chicago, the company's next stop, would she appear in the show as a stand-in for the bedridden female star? Lillian could not refuse an old friend.

After a few days off to learn her lines, playing opposite Hitchcock, Leon Errol and Irene Bordoni, the top musical theater stars of the day, Lillian opened with the company, to rave reviews. There was no question that everyone, fellow performers and audiences alike, enjoyed Lillian's performances. At curtain calls, in recognition of her professional status, she was asked to sing a few songs, which she graciously did. This brief return to the stage reminded Lillian of the excitement such performances had brought her.

Throughout the spring and summer, Lillian continued her patriotic activities: more Bond rallies, more shows for the troops, more recruiting. At the Nixon Theater in New York, donning a Red Cross uniform, Lillian auctioned seats for Bonds and raised more than $10,000. She continued her recruiting for the Navy. She sang farewell concerts to the troops at Camp Merritt before they were shipped out. She and Fay Templeton went on a brief recruiting tour in Pennsylvania for the Marines. In addition, it was reported, Lillian made a personal tour of the barracks to find out what the men needed. The result was the purchase of medical supplies and washing machines, purportedly paid for by Lillian.

Ever ready to leap at an opportunity for profit, the Keith Circuit recognized Lillian's renewed popular appeal, as well as the loss of many performers to military service, by offering her a contract to appear in vaudeville on a 15-week tour. Unable to refuse this possibly last opportunity to perform, Lillian accepted E.F. Albee's offer. Yet, faithful to her current responsibilities, she stipulated that she appear on stage in her Marine uniform and, as part of the show, make recruiting and Bond-selling speeches. In addition, she donated her salary to wounded soldiers awaiting rehabilitation to civilian life. These Keith Circuit appearances became not only a farewell tour for Lillian, but a patriotic triumph as well.

On October 29, 1918, at the Palace Theater, New York, Lillian, dressed in her Marine uniform, gave her audience 29 minutes of song and war effort messages. The *New York Telegraph* reflected the kind of respect now bestowed on Lillian:

> It has become evident that Miss Russell is more than America's Queen of beauty and song. Everyone present realized that Miss Russell of all theatrical stars is easily the most popular in the sense of beloved woman of the American stage."[3]

The Dramatic Mirror honored her likewise, praising both her youthful beauty and patriotic zeal:

> Lillian Russell has the exclusive prescription for perennial youth, unfailing charm and public popularity. Her present tour of the Keith houses is in the nature of a triumph. She is a fiery patriot and her red-hot little speeches in

the uniform of a sergeant of the U.S. Marines is Americanism served with tabasco, gunpowder and TNT. To raise money for bonds, she is working in Keith vaudeville. She never tires and her gracious personality never lets down into anger or temperament or the blues. She's just a wonderful person.[4]

The vaudeville tour played to the middle of February 1919. Even though the war had ended the previous November, every show was SRO. While recruiting was no longer needed, Lillian concentrated on selling Bonds. As she stated to the *Cleveland Plain Dealer*:

> The present tour is strictly patriotic. I am devoting the funds I receive to the Marine Corps and patriotic work. But, more than that, I want to impress upon the people that the war is not over. Far from it. Actual fighting has ended, but the boys are coming back. This is the work of reconstruction; and there is the work that must be done until every one of those youngsters is reestablished at home, and normal conditions at home, and abroad, become a reality.[5]

At the end of each of these shows, Lillian brought wounded Marines on stage, introduced them and had them tell their battle stories to the audience. At her final tour performance, at the Hippodrome in Houston, the audience recognized Lillian's contributions with a five-minute, standing ovation:

> The applause that greeted Lillian Russell was a remarkable little study in psychology. It started before the star appeared, stopped for a moment as the audience gasped in amazement at the vision, and then started up again with greatly renewed enthusiasm. If the feminine expressions all over the house could be epitomized, they would probably crystallize into the inter- rogation "How does she do it?" For Lillian is radiant with a mature beauty that is far from fading.[6]

No sooner had the tour ended and Lillian returned to Pittsburgh than she renewed her efforts on behalf of women's suffrage. By the middle of 1919, Con- gress had finally approved the women's suffrage amendment. The challenge now was getting 36 states to ratify the amendment. Lillian's speeches and lobbying efforts helped to make the Pennsylvania legislature one of the first to pass the amendment. Instead of continuing these speeches outside the state, however, she chose to remain at home, pleading exhaustion from her many months of travel. She indicated that it was now time to rest and tend to local affairs. Lillian took to visiting conva- lescing soldiers at Pittsburgh hospitals, giving mini-concerts and delivering candy, magazines and books. In addition, she renewed her activities in local charities and played hostess at social benefits. Her front lawn soon returned to its previous ver- dant condition.

Little is recorded about Alex Moore during the time Lillian spent on her patri- otic missions. He had his newspaper to run. He remained active in Republican pol- itics, looking toward the next election, devising possible campaigns to defeat the Wilson forces. He was often seen with Lillian on weekends, wherever she happened to be playing or speaking, but remained in the background. Yet his support for her throughout this period demonstrated the new freedoms women had achieved in mar- ital relationships. In unassuming fashion, Lillian continued to be a symbol, as she had in earlier years, of the "new" woman, now mature, confident and comfortable with her independent role.

The summer of 1919 was spent at Chelsea to rest. At 57, after two years of non-stop performance for the government, Lillian admitted she was fatigued and wished to concentrate on domestic activities. Alex was home every weekend. Friends visited often. Having terminated her latest marriage, Dorothy was also home, recovering from a recent automobile accident. The welcome rest was cut short, however, when Lillian was asked to return to New York to assist fellow performers in a new and more volatile confrontation with theatrical producers.

Six years earlier, Actors Equity had been formed by performers in legitimate theater. Their primary purposes were to protect the rights of actors by means of a standard contract that guaranteed a minimum wage, limited unpaid rehearsal time, and ensured that, no matter how briefly a show might run, actors would be paid for at least two weeks' work. For their part, musicians and stagehands had already extracted an agreement from producers by joining an AFL union.

During the last few years, the White Rats had attempted a number of strikes, with little success. In 1917, they confronted producers and, in a bitter battle, were almost totally destroyed. After this struggle, their membership reportedly declined from 11,000 to no more than several hundred.

Now it was time for renewal of the contract between Actors Equity and producers. There seemed to be agreement on most issues, but a few items, considered insignificant by producers, remained unresolved. Actors wanted to be paid for extra matinees on legal holidays and for other extra performances. Producers, however, refused to negotiate on these issues, expressing surprise that such minor items blocked agreement. This impasse led actors to strike on August 6, closing down practically all shows on Broadway and stopping all those in preparation or in rehearsals, estimated to be another 60. The strike quickly spread to other cities, paralyzing both Syndicate and Shubert operations. There were no negotiations for two weeks, as the warring parties refused to meet.

Performers took to the streets of New York to explain their strike to the public. On a rainy day in the middle of August, more than 2,000 actors marched down Broadway from Columbus Circle to advance their claims and demands. A number of fund-raising shows, featuring many of the stars of musical theater, were staged at the Lexington Avenue Opera House. Theatergoers had a unique opportunity to see all their favorites on one stage, and several thousand dollars were collected at each show. Lillian performed at one of these benefits, on September 3. While all such events were serious business for the strikers, the public found the shows supremely entertaining and supported the actors strongly.

Losses to the producers amounted to an estimated half a million dollars every week. When musicians and stagehands joined the strike, producers realized it was time to negotiate. In addition, the White Rats and the Associated Actresses of America had by now joined with Actors Equity to form a united effort.

When negotiations were about to begin, Francis Wilson, one of the leaders of the strike, called Lillian to gain her support. Though Alex Moore noted with disapproval that the organization was union-affiliated, Lillian retorted, "My place is with my people," and traveled to New York, ready to assist in any way she could. Other prominent members of the strike included Eddie Foy, Marie Dressler, Ed Wynn, Eddie Cantor and Ethel and Lionel Barrymore.

The confrontation also pitted two highly esteemed actor/producers against one another. Lew Fields had a profitable show closed by the strike, yet sided with the actors in their dispute. George M. Cohan, who had previously crusaded to protect actors' rights, now sided with the producers. In fact, Cohan didn't merely support management, he vehemently opposed the actors' union.

Three members of Actors Equity were selected to negotiate with the producers: Francis Wilson, Eddie Foy and Lillian Russell. For two weeks, they met to discuss the unresolved issues. When a final agreement was reached, Wilson not only thanked Lillian for her involvement, but called her "one of the toughest negotiators" he had ever seen. He recalled a particular exchange between Lillian and one of the managers as exemplary: At one meeting, a manager suggested that the strike couldn't last much longer since the actors out of work would starve. Lillian laughed in his face. "You managers taught them to starve," she responded. "They are used to it."

The strike lasted one month. In the end, Actors Equity won the right to bargain for all stage people. It also obtained one-half pay for choruses after four weeks of rehearsals, minimums for choruses in New York, and regular pay for all touring actors required to play extra matinees. Lillian knew what this meant for performers; she had endured these same battles 20 years earlier.

The benefits of the strike were more than just financial. Actors were now viewed as full-fledged members of the working world. They were represented by a union that could halt shows when necessary. Their higher salaries, along with greatly increased production costs, changed musical theater performances from extravagant displays to intimate ensembles, setting the foundation for America's new writers and composers.

It also ended the era of the combined actor/producer, as exemplified by Fields and Cohan. One had to be either a producer or an actor, management or labor. Neither Fields nor Cohan could readily accommodate. Times were changing; they did not.

After settlement of the strike, Lillian returned to Pittsburgh to become a homemaker and again participate as a member of the city's social elite. Her most significant activities for the remainder of the year were parties she gave for performers who were playing local theaters. In fact, performers looked forward to stopping in Pittsburgh so they could spend an evening at the Moore home, enjoying lively conversation and delicious food. At a dinner attended by Irene Franklin and her husband, Irene enthused: "It's real soup, with soup in it." From her farm just outside the city, Fay Templeton often visited Lillian. They talked about their days at the Music Hall, and Lillian never forgot to tease Fay about her "avoirdupois."

For Lillian, the spring of 1920 was unusually quiet. She attended the Professional Woman's League Ball in New York and, as had always been the case, was continually followed by reporters eagerly awaiting any comment she might make on any topic. For a Shakespeare Pageant held at the Metropolitan Opera House, Lillian agreed to play the role of Queen Catherine. The Queen could not have been more typecast. Surrounded by liveried retainers, deployed regally on a raised dais, gowned in elegant velvet and fur robes, crowned with an ornate, gem-studded tiara, Lillian appeared almost divine. Although the production was a series of dioramas, at curtain time the audience insisted that Lillian sing some of the songs she had made famous.

While Lillian thought little of performance during this time, performance was about to summon her again. In her memoirs, Lillian noted the occasion:

> I took a respite from public life and never thought I would go on the stage
> again, until the campaign started for the President of the United States in
> June 1920.[7]

The Republican National Convention was held in Chicago. Both Moore and Lillian attended, Moore as a Pennsylvania delegate, intent on promoting old friend Senator Hiram Johnson of California for the presidency. Johnson, however, was quickly eliminated from consideration, his place taken by Leonard Wood. Still, the delegates were unable to reach agreement, and the convention was thrown open to the possibility that a "dark horse" candidate might capture the nomination. After four days of debate and much back room bargaining, Ohio Governor Willis nominated Ohio Senator Warren G. Harding for delegate consideration. Moore was one of Harding's sponsors.

After Harding was nominated the Republican candidate, Moore asked Lillian, "Will you go on the stump for him?" Lillian replied, "I will go for the Republican cause, for it needs every patriot in America." But typical of her concern about men in powerful positions, she stipulated, "I must meet Senator Harding and know him, and I must learn for myself whether I can make speeches for him."

The meeting took place a few weeks later at Harding's home in Marion, Ohio. Seated next to the presidential candidate at both lunch and dinner, Lillian had an opportunity to hear him speak to various groups of supporters and to discuss with him what she might do to help. Although she admitted liking Mrs. Harding better, she found Harding a charming man and both of them gracious hosts. When Harding told Lillian about his mother and missionary sister, Lillian offered her support, convinced that Harding would win the election.

Quickly, Lillian was appointed a member of the "Flying Squadron," a group of Pennsylvania women who were to travel the Eastern states making speeches and getting out the vote. For one full month before the election, Lillian made three or four speeches a day in 15 states. Again, her name and reputation brought out large and enthusiastic crowds, as much to see her as to demonstrate support for Harding. When she spoke, Lillian made fiery denunciations of the League of Nations and accused the Democrats of plotting to entangle the U.S. in European affairs.

With the Democrats in disarray due to Wilson's illness and his League of Nations policies, Harding won the election easily. It was also the first election in which women had the right to vote for president. To the disappointment of suffrage leaders, only one-third of eligible women exercised their new political franchise.

Shortly after the election, Lillian met Mrs. Harding in New York to assist her in choosing gowns for the inaugural festivities. A story in the newspapers suggested that Lillian had specially selected an azure gown, her own favorite hue, for Mrs. Harding. The color later became known as "Harding Blue."

As insiders, Lillian and Moore not only attended the inauguration but were received as special White House guests. Ready to relax again, Lillian returned to Pittsburgh to resume her homemaking activities.

Only two weeks later, an editor from *Cosmopolitan* magazine visited Lillian, asking if she would be interested in writing a serialized history of her life. After a brief negotiation, Lillian agreed to write her autobiography, with the stipulation that she would have full editorial control over its content. This contract allowed Lillian to eliminate two marriages and divorces, one child, confrontations with theater managers and various failed shows. At the same time, it provided the welcome opportunity to embellish previous reports of performances, salaries, admirers, and suitors. Her mother would be portrayed as a saint, her daughter as a talented and dutiful child, herself as a respectful and respectable religious woman. Since little else regarding Lillian's life became available through the years, the information in her autobiography would help to construct an elaborate mythos surrounding her personal life and public career.

In August 1921, Lillian's sister, Leona Ross, died in Rutherford, New Jersey. Leona was buried next to Cynthia and Ida Kate. The remaining family members attended the funeral. Susan returned from Hollywood, as did Leona's daughter, son-in-law and granddaughter. The press reported that granddaughter Leona Brammell was a child actress in a movie, *The Scarlet Letter.*

Returning to their summer cottage in Atlantic City, the Moores prepared a post–Labor Day dinner in honor of President and Mrs. Harding. Their retinue included Secretary of Commerce Herbert Hoover, a dozen Secret Service men and another dozen reporters. After the elegant dinner, reported to have been catered from New York, Harding expressed a desire for a poker game, his favorite evening pastime. Instead of the men going off to play cards by themselves, Lillian suggested they all play together.

The first Actors Equity Ball since the strike was held at the Hotel Astor, New York, in November. Lillian attended and received many kind expressions of gratitude for her support of the organization. It was described that, when she entered the ballroom, De Wolf Hopper leapt to the podium and announced, "Here comes the Queen!" The music stopped; dancers on the floor separated to make way for her and applauded as she walked down the aisle. "The Queen still reigns," trumpeted the *New York Telegraph.*

After but one year in office, Harding had already acquired a notorious reputation for conferring appointments upon his friends and supporters. It was apparently no different in Lillian's case. She had expressed a desire to become ambassador to China, mainly because of her interests in Chinese art and culture. But since the U.S. had only a legation in Pei-ching at the time, she was told that such an appointment would be premature. Instead, Secretary of Labor Davis suggested she become a special commissioner of immigration and study conditions among people eager to migrate from Europe. Lillian agreed to take the job, with the provision that she be allowed to work for a salary of one dollar.

The *New York Times* announced her appointment, stating that she had been "for a long time immensely interested in the problems of immigration." They added, "The American Beauty still retains her charm of speech and manner, and she is still a beautiful woman. Her blond hair, piled high on her head, is as yet without a thread of gray."[8]

The newspapers never missed an opportunity to comment on Lillian's beauty and attire, no matter her other activities. When she appeared at the Ritz-Carlton Hotel to tell of her assignment, the *Times* described her manner of dress in detail:

> She wore a black crepe de chine dress embroidered with red and steel beads made in a tube style. Jewels adorned her fingers and over her heart she wore the little pearl and diamond elephant that Anna Held gave her when she died.[9]

As for her acceptance of the commission, she was quoted as saying:

Lillian with fourth husband Alexander Moore, prior to her trip to Europe to study the immigration problem for Congress. She had just celebrated her sixty-first birthday. (Harry Ransom Humanities Research Center, the University of Texas at Austin.)

Mr. Davis wants me to look into the immigration problem. We have had talks and discussion about immigration. He had known for a long time of my interest in those poor people who come here only to be turned back because of some defect. I want to find out why these reports occur and why such people are ever allowed to make the journey that ends in disappointment.[10]

Her travels in Europe, through England, France, and Italy, took seven weeks. She visited embassies, embarkation points, hospitals and health offices, interviewing government officials at all of these places. She toured various facilities, studied their operations, but talked to few people who were themselves enduring the immigration process. The manner in which she was treated befitted royalty. In a number of cities she visited, Lillian spoke at official gatherings of Americans.

Toward the end of her tour, she began to advocate that immigrants be examined by American doctors in the immigrants' countries of origin, so as to "insure against fraud," before they were allowed to sail to the U.S. In response to her comments, some foreign newspapers questioned her knowledge of their medical practices and suggested her views, if accepted by Congress, could become inflammatory. In rebuttal, Lillian said she had learned that unofficial inspectors were issuing passports to any and all—"defectives" included—and taking all their savings, leaving the unfortunate émigrés with only enough to admit them to the U.S. European newspapers suggested she return home as soon as possible.

Lillian had planned to spend another week in London, but she became ill while in Paris and sailed for the U.S. from Cherbourg. The trip back was evidently uncomfortable for her. A dispatch from the ship indicated she had fallen and injured her leg. Yet when asked about these problems, Lillian refused to admit any difficulties. She and Moore arrived in New York, March 20, on the *Aquitania*, and were immediately questioned by reporters.

"All immigration should be entirely stopped for a period of five years," the papers quoted her as declaring. When she was interviewed, she read from a prepared statement:

> I have a detailed report that will amaze Secretary of Labor Davis. Our representatives in Washington have no real conception of the immigration situation. It has been "overpropagandeered." Stories of suffering humanity in Europe and oppression all have the dollar sign back of them. It is my own personal belief that there are organizations financed for the sole purpose of making money out of what they call humanity.
>
> It seems to me a crime that American boys have to wait until they are 21 before they have a vote when such aliens as I saw abroad can, within a period of five years, have the privileges our forefathers fought for. Our slogan should be America for Americans.[11]

She concluded her statement with a spontaneous remark, which the papers also published:

> It makes my blood boil when I think of what may happen to this country unless our legislative bodies act on this important question at once.

That said, she and Moore returned to Pittsburgh, for Lillian to prepare her formal report to Secretary Davis and recover from her unidentified illness. Lillian's physicians recommended she take a month's rest so that "proper medical treatment could restore her to health." She refused. She was due in Washington in two weeks to meet with Secretary Davis and a Congressional committee. Lillian knew she was ailing, but did not want to delay her report.

On April 6, Lillian met with Secretary of Labor Davis and the House Immigration Committee. She recommended "an immigration holiday of from one to five years." She went on to recommend that compulsory blood tests of immigrants be made before they sailed; that "objectionable" people be refused passports; and that all immigrants be required to read, write and speak the English language. Lillian concluded her report by suggesting that "America should care for Americans first."

Lillian also proposed that the U.S. should place American "teachers" on incoming ships to educate the "more ignorant" about the country and help them decide where they might expect to find "the greatest advantages of life." Her comments elicited sharp debate from members of the House and Senate, both for and against her recommendations. Senate Democrats wanted her to appear before their own immigration committee, but Republicans blocked it. Instead, portions of her report were read into the Senate record, leading one committee member to question her expertise:

> I admit she is a pretty high authority on matters theatrical and perhaps on cosmetics, but I never knew until now that she had entered the field of immigration.[12]

To supplement her report to Congress, and to support the Republican position on immigration, Secretary Davis asked Lillian to make a brief tour of Eastern cities to speak on conditions abroad, and why her recommendations were so important to the country. Although perceptibly ill, she agreed to undertake the tour, which continued to early May. As always, she was greeted by large audiences, some of which were very vocally against her position. Brief trips back to Pittsburgh during this time resulted in arguments with Moore and her physicians, who urged her to stay home and rest.

At the end of April, Lillian made her last public appearance on stage, singing for a charity benefit at New York's Palace Theater. In May, she attended a benefit for Actors Equity held at the Metropolitan Opera House. Unannounced, she walked on stage to thunderous applause. Dorothy, in attendance to assist her mother, adoringly reported the event:

> Lillian Russell was more than a star on that occasion. She had reached heights in the lay world that no other woman of the stage had ever attained.[13]

Yet Lillian was so ill that night that Dorothy had begged her not to attend. "You don't understand," Lillian protested. "I must go. Think what it would mean if I were to disappoint Equity!" The next morning, Lillian returned to Pittsburgh, barely able to walk.

Doctors ordered her to stay in bed, since they were not yet entirely sure how to diagnose her illness. A nurse was assigned. But none of this prevented Lillian from spending the next week shopping, going to the hairdresser and attending the theater. At the end of the week, she complained of tiredness and finally took to bed.

Tests by the doctors indicated her problems were probably due to complications of diabetes. The prognosis was not good. It was obvious she had been suffering from this disease for some time, and little had been done about it. Years of continuous activity and stress, along with excess weight and a habit of overeating, had contributed to the malady. Intermittent dieting and regular exercise had probably delayed the ultimate effect on her health.

For the next few days, Lillian spent time receiving guests and, when alone, reading the Bible. The pastor of her church came by often to visit, inquiring of any needs she might have. Everyone noticed her diminishing strength. On June 4, Lillian complained of pain and the doctor-in-charge called in a number of colleagues for consultation. They agreed that members of the family should be called to her bedside immediately. Through the evening, she slept and awakened frequently, talking to Alex and Dorothy about making arrangements in case of her death. Handing some keys to Dorothy, Lillian counseled, "You may need these. Don't lose them."

At 2:20 A.M., June 6, 1922, Lillian Russell died in her sleep. She was 61 years old. Alex, Dorothy, Mildred Martin, a niece, and Dr. C.B. Schieldecker were at her bedside. Her last words were reported to be, "I have no fear. As we are, so shall we be received." The valediction served as apt summary of all the performances during her lifetime.

The official medical report stated the cause of her death to be uremic poisoning. Nonetheless, the doctor announced to the press that the "primary cause of her illness and death occurred when she was violently thrown on the ship [returning from Europe] during a storm." No one questioned how an accident three months previously, with an interval of two months during which Lillian traveled and spoke extensively, could be responsible for her death. For a person of her legendary status, a fatal injury sustained while performing civic duties was apparently deemed more appropriately romantic, infinitely more fitting than dying from an obscure, hard-to-explain, somewhat less than elegant disease.

LILLIAN RUSSELL HON-
ORED BY NOTABLES

THOUSANDS AT RITES FOR
LILLIAN RUSSELL

ALL THE WORLD
MOURNS

THRONGS PAY TRIBUTE
TO DEAD STAR

NEW YORK CITY SERVICE OF THE
NATIONAL TRIBUTE
In B. F. Keith Theatres Throughout America
IN MEMORY OF
LILLIAN RUSSELL
———
Arranged in Loving Esteem and Devotion by
E. F. ALBEE
To Commemorate the Exalted Position She Held in Public Life and the
High Estate to Which Her Example and Deeds Lifted Her Profession.

In Memoriam

LILLIAN RUSSELL

*A thing of beauty is a joy forever
Its loveliness increases; it will never
pass into nothingness.*—KEATS.

B. F. KEITH'S
Palace Theatre
BROADWAY AND 47TH STREET
NEW YORK CITY

SUNDAY MORNING
JUNE EIGHTEENTH
NINETEEN TWENTY-TWO
AT ELEVEN-FIFTEEN

Program for the memorial service in honor of Lillian at Keith's Palace Theater in New York. E.F. Albee, a former member of the powerful Syndicate and one-time adversary of Lillian, arranged the memorial "in Loving Esteem and Devotion," a final tribute to her distinguished performance career. (Harry Ransom Humanities Research Center, the University of Texas at Austin.)

were a few of the headlines, among hundreds, that filled newspapers announcing Lillian's death. President Harding declared three days of national mourning for her, an honor never previously — nor ever since — bestowed on any theatrical performer.

Lillian's body lay in state for two days. The first day, at home, close friends and relatives were permitted to view the body. Two marines were assigned to keep vigil beside her, and great baskets of flowers filled the room. Thousands of letters and telegrams, all expressing grief and sadness at her passing, were piled high on a table near the casket.

On the morning of the second day, escorted by a detachment of Marines, the body was moved to Trinity Episcopalian Church, where the public paid their last respects. Hundreds of people — including writers, actors, statesmen, soldiers, shop girls, letter carriers and newsboys — comprised the crowd of mourners. The funeral service, conducted by Lillian's pastor, Rev. Travers, began at 2:30 P.M., before an audience that filled the church. Thousands of others stood with bared heads in the churchyard and surrounding streets. No eulogy was given. Lillian's favorite hymns were played and sung by a choir. A wreath sent by President Harding lay atop Lillian's casket.

At the completion of the service, accompanied by the somber strains of Chopin's "Funeral March," the body was taken from the church. Escorted by a flotilla of police and Marines, the cortege made its way to the cemetery. Members of the 107th Field Artillery, to whom Lillian had presented their standard before they left for Europe, met her bier at the cemetery gates and escorted it to the receiving vault. As Lillian was paid final tribute by the Marine contingent, American Legion riflemen fired a last salute.

Among those attending the funeral were Senator Hiram Johnson, the governor of Pennsylvania, Secretary of Labor Davis and many other prominent people from the political, social and theatrical worlds. Honorary pallbearers included Senator Johnson, Secretary Davis, producer E.F. Albee, artist Howard Chandler Christy and a number of local government dignitaries. Although the family had requested no flowers at the graveside, many of the mourners placed single roses on her casket as they slowly filed past.

Two days later, a memorial service for Lillian was held at the Hippodrome Theater in New York. Sponsored by the theatrical community and attended by church and military representatives, the service attracted more than 4,000 people. Flanked by a Marine and a sailor, a life-size picture of Lillian dramatically held center stage. Bouquets of flowers entirely covered the front of the stage. The Navy Band, led by John Philip Souza, played "The Star Spangled Banner" at the beginning of the service. Hymns were sung, prayers offered and brief eulogies spoken by former theatrical colleagues. The firing of a volley by Marines and the sounding of "Taps" ended the ceremony.

At the eulogies, the audience both cheered and cried.

Old friend De Wolf Hopper, speaking on behalf of the theatrical profession, recalled:

> She gave a wonderful example of loyalty to the world. Do what she could for others was her motto. Her evolution from the trying surroundings of her early career to the most beloved woman of the universe — such an evolution should be our inspiration. We called her "Queen" because that word best befitted her regal self. Lillian Russell, by her individual spiritual self, has done more than anyone else to dissipate the prejudice against our profession.[14]

Francis Wilson, who had led the Actors Equity strike three years previously, remarked:

> We actors adored Lillian Russell, not only because she was beautiful; not only because of the charms of her person, but because she was big enough to stand up and defend the rights of her profession.[15]

A few days after this ceremony, another memorial service was conducted at the Palace Theater and, simultaneously, in B.F. Keith theaters throughout the country. Attending the service in New York were representatives of the U.S. government, the City of New York, the Armed Forces, churches and the theatrical profession. The entire memorial was arranged by E.F. Albee, president of the Keith Circuit and, ironically, a former leader of the Syndicate.

In the program commemorating Lillian was printed a poem written by Philander Johnson. His verse gracefully captured both the public's and fellow performers' feelings about her:

> Lillian Russell! Lady Fair
> Gifted with attainments rare
> That we scarce knew how to praise
> As we paused to hear or gaze!

> Lillian Russell, Queen of Song
> Worshipped by the listening throng;
> Lillian Russell, Beauty's Queen
> With a majesty serene!
> Yet your greatest loveliness
> Simple worth must still express,
> As this earthly scene you leave
> While fond, helpless memories grieve,
> E'en when at Fame's highest crest,
> Kindly to the lowliest;
> Take this tribute as your due, —
> Lillian Russell, woman true![16]

Variety, too, recognized Lillian for her commitment to the stage:

> Lillian Russell is in her grave, but her image and her memory can never die in stagedom. Nor does the world outside theatricals want to forget her. Lillian Russell was a national figure, made so first through her beauty, later and while still retaining that glorious and remarkable appearance, becoming even more nationally known and revered through her kindliness and charm. The stage people will never forget her. It's a magnificent tribute to a magnificent product of the footlights, one who was ever ready, long after she had retired professionally, to lend her talents and her presence whenever called upon for a worthy object.[17]

And Alan Dale, the most renowned of theater critics, a long-time follower and judge of Lillian's career, had these final words:

> She has passed on. It is cruel to realize it. She never would have grown old, and now she never will! We can remember her as she was at the last — spendidly effulgent, radiant, radiating, graciously interested in everything, intensely altruistic, diffidently dominant. ... She was always there — the old reporters finest subject, the critic's inevitable target. A talk with Lillian! It was bound to make a feature. She was so vibrantly interesting.... All the "celebrities" of the day knew and adored Lillian Russell. And now she will meet many of them again.... She has left here thousands of friends who are inclined to mourn. But why mourn? With no regrets, no disturbing thoughts, no disillusionment, no rust, no canker and no dismay, she has exchanged one sphere for another. And that is all.[18]

Chapter Twelve

The Queen Is Dead!
Long Live the Queen!

"It was terrible for us to go through Lillian's property," said Susan. "Her wonderful collection was a record of her successes and reminders of her friendships. My sister's treasures should have been placed in a museum instead of being dispensed to the world."

In 1944, Susan Westford rocked slowly in her chair on the porch of the Percy Williams nursing home in Bayshore, Long Island. Eighty years old, the last survivor of the Leonard family, Susan was now a picturesque, fragile woman who was always seen publicly wearing an ostrich-feathered hat, a reminder of her sister's glamour days.

"We were all so sad," she continued. "It was as if a light had gone out of our lives. I don't think any of us realized how important she really was. The rest of the world knew it, though, and showed how much they loved her."

"She was a good businesswoman, but we didn't think she did a good job planning her will. She allowed Moore to have too much control over it."

Two weeks after Lillian's funeral, her will was filed for probate. It contained only three provisions: certain amounts of money, known only to her husband, would go to specific charities; Dorothy would receive a stipend of $50.00 a week for the remainder of her life; and Moore would sell off all of Lillian's remaining property. Lillian's will manifested her confidence in her husband, concluding with the statement, "...knowing that he will carry out my wishes with regard to certain charities and provisions for my relatives."

Believing she should have been given more, Dorothy was not at all happy with her mother's will. Nor was sister Hattie satisfied with the will's provision to sell off Lillian's property. Lamenting the loss, Hattie complained, "Each piece had its own story of love, of misfortune, and the many vicissitudes of personages with whom Lillian had come in contact."

Nevertheless, in December 1922, a series of auctions was held to sell Lillian's art objects and personal property, which included household furniture, embroideries and rugs. Originally, it was estimated that her estate amounted to more than $100,000. In the sale, however, only $62,000 was realized, according to the auctioneers, because "a quarter of the items cataloged for sale had not been shipped from Pittsburgh." At the time, no one seemed to question this omission. Ten years later, however, it would become a key element in a lawsuit between Dorothy and Moore's estate.

A week later, Lillian's Chinese porcelain collection was sold. Valued at more than $50,000, it netted only $6,447. An auction of Lillian's book collection did better, realizing over $12,000. All of the monies accumulated from the auctions were to go to the care of Dorothy, now an invalid, and to the stipulated charities.

A number of Lillian's old theatrical friends purchased some of her possessions. Charlotte Greenwood and Theda Bara obtained various household furnishings. John Golden bought a beaded bag, gold buckles, and a vanity case. Movie producer William Fox paid thousands for some unique pieces of jewelry, said to have been given to Lillian by Jim Brady.

An article in the *New York Times* suggested that the total amount collected "would not be sufficient to give Dorothy $50.00 a week after paying inheritance taxes." Moore promised he would assist Dorothy, if necessary.

Lillian's name disappeared from the newspapers for the next few years, to surface again when it was announced that Alex Moore and Enrico Caruso's widow Dorothy planned to marry. Moore had given her a ring, formerly owned by Lillian, to seal the betrothal. Dorothy Russell objected and claimed the ring belonged to her, as part of her mother's estate. She further claimed that the ring was one of a number of items that had never made it to auction. Her arguments were quickly forgotten when the Moore/Caruso engagement was broken. Nevertheless, Dorothy Caruso retained possession of the ring. Newspaper coverage of the episode produced a number of articles reminiscing about Lillian's career. Most noticeable about these features was the singular emphasis on her legendary beauty and disputes with theater managers, the remainder of her career neatly overlooked or forgotten.

At about the same time, the B.F. Keith organization held a grand opening to dedicate the Lillian Russell Room at their Philadelphia theater. It had been five years since she last appeared there, attired in her Marine Corps uniform, singing and recruiting. A life-size painting of Lillian hung from one wall; photographs from various shows adorned another. Large bouquets of American Beauty roses decorated the room. Miss Julia Arthur, a well-known actress from the legitimate stage, gave the dedication address:

> Miss Russell represented the highest type of the past generation of actresses. She was always noted for her affability and her great kindness and so I dedicate this room to "Happiness." Let this room typify the women of the theatrical profession.[1]

In 1929, Dorothy wrote a serialized biography of her mother for *Liberty* magazine. Much of the information was taken from Lillian's autobiography in *Cosmopolitan*, written just months before she died. Dorothy added her own observations, which presented an interesting, if biased, view of her own life, her marital adventures and her relations with Lillian. It also revealed the dysfunctional emotional life of a young woman who tried somehow to live beyond the colossal shadow cast by her mother, yet seemed to fail at every attempt. The articles provided sad illustrations of a person trying to reinvent her own life. Dorothy did, however, make a number of accusations about Alex Moore that suggested they never had been friendly. Their enduring disagreements, kept quiet for so long, would soon erupt into open warfare.

Alexander Moore died of tuberculosis in Los Angeles, California, February 17, 1930. He was 63 years old. Moore had just been appointed ambassador to Poland by President Herbert Hoover. His activities during the past eight years reflected continuing close ties to international affairs and Republican party politics.

Less than a year after Lillian's death, Moore sold the *Pittsburgh Leader*, giving as his reason the increasing costs of production. A month later, President Harding appointed him ambassador to Spain. He served in this capacity for two years, enjoying a close relationship with King Alfonso and his wife Victoria Eugenia, often consulting with them on various financial and trade matters. Moore returned to the U.S. in 1925 to pursue a number of business opportunities. In March 1928, Moore purchased the *New York Daily Mirror* but had been its owner only a few months when President Coolidge appointed him ambassador to Peru.

Due to an unspecified illness, Moore returned from Lima to Los Angeles in August 1929 for medical attention. Initially, he stayed at Charlie Chaplin's home, under the supervision of a personal nurse, then was moved to a Palm Springs hospital for more intensive care. His illness continued, and he was finally admitted to a private sanitarium. There he was diagnosed as suffering from tuberculosis. After contracting bronchial pneumonia, Moore quickly declined. At his bedside when he died were two cousins, along with Marion Davies and William Randolph Hearst. His body was shipped to Pittsburgh, where Moore was buried in Allegheny Cemetery, next to Lillian, after an elaborate funeral.

Lillian was mentioned only briefly when articles about Moore and his life were written. She was noted as his second wife, who had died in 1921. Newspapers identified her only as "Lillian Russell Moore, actress/wife of the diplomat."

When the contents of Moore's will were published, Dorothy reacted swiftly and resolutely. To Queen Victoria Eugenia of Spain, Moore had bequeathed $100,000, to be used for her charitable works on behalf of clinics and hospitals for the poor. Moore also gave $25,000 to Dorothy Caruso, widow of Enrico Caruso, whom he had planned to marry in 1924. Money was also allocated to former business associates, secretaries and relatives. Susan Westford was to receive $3,000, Dorothy only $1,000. She immediately moved to file an injunction against the execution of Moore's estate. The *Herald Tribune* reported on her retaliation:

> It was understood that Dorothy Russell, the step-daughter, would demand
> of the officers of the Union Trust Company, executors, a copy of the will
> and that she would demand one-third of the estate.[2]

The opening challenge to Moore's will occurred a month later, when Dorothy obtained an order for a reaccounting of her mother's estate and a further injunction to withhold distribution of Moore's estate. Her order declared that Moore "fraudulently acquired assets of his wife's estate while acting as executor and has failed to account therefore by his will." Responding to his meager bequest, Dorothy alleged that, in a prenuptial agreement with Lillian, Moore had promised to leave her daughter half of his estate.

Dorothy obtained the order for reaccounting her mother's estate. The investigation found that Lillian had specified that sufficient principal be invested profitably so that Dorothy might realize $50.00 a week for her lifetime. It also found that there were insufficient funds to accomplish this stipulation and that Moore had not made any investments to finance Dorothy's future needs. The inquiry further discovered that many items in Lillian's estate were unaccounted for — the items had never been sent to auction — and that Moore had defrauded the estate by selling various items for large profit. One example given as evidence of his duplicity was a pearl necklace that Moore purchased from the bank for $1,000, and later sold for $8,500.

In court testimony, a number of witnesses described conversations with Moore, who had evidently stated he would care for Dorothy and that, when he died, she would receive one-half of his estate. Bessie Clayton, Lillian's co-star in the Weber and Fields Jubilee Company, recounted a conversation between Lillian and Moore in which they discussed the disposition of their estates. "I will leave Dorothy half of my estate," Clayton quoted Moore as saying. Bert Cooper, who managed Lillian's health and beauty tour, told the court Moore had received the profits of the tour and indicated to Cooper they would be set aside for Dorothy. The money was never accounted for.

In rebuttal, a number of Moore's friends testified that, in conversations after Lillian died, he had stated that Lillian did not love him, that she had "only one love," the daughter Dorothy, born of a previous marriage. Another witness described a conversation with Moore in which he had claimed, "I was crazy about her and wanted to marry her. So did lots of other men, but they would not agree to provide for Dorothy. I had to agree if I wanted to marry her."

It was further revealed that Moore had destroyed the original agreement with Lillian when Dorothy threatened Moore at the time he gave the ring to Dorothy Caruso. He had been further enraged when Dorothy wrote, in her biography of Lillian, some supposedly derogatory remarks about Moore's mother.

Dorothy sued for $300,000, half of Moore's estate. She won the suit but received only $40,000, which, added to the amount left in her account (approximately $34,000) would be the total she would have to live on.

The press followed the lawsuit closely. Articles were frequently published concerning Dorothy's "irregular" life. She was identified as a "child of Lillian Russell"; her early life was portrayed as that of "an abandoned stage child," hence Dorothy's four marriages and divorces. Though Moore stood accused of fraud and other questionable financial transactions, his own reputation remained unblemished.

Dorothy petitioned the court to continue the search for, it was estimated, more than $1,000,000 worth of jade, jewels and porcelain that Lillian had accumulated and which had subsequently disappeared. Her lawyer claimed that much of the treasure had found its way into the hands of wealthy women in Spain and Peru. Included in her suit was a demand for the ring given Dorothy Caruso. Unfortunately for Dorothy, there was no way to trace the disposition of the jewels.

After two years of litigation, Dorothy regained the ring.

> The famous "flawless emerald" ring for which the late Lillian Russell, famed stage beauty, paid $75,000 thirty years ago was turned over to her invalid daughter Dorothy today. The ring had been in the possession of Mrs.

Dorothy Benjamin Caruso Holder, now of Paris, who obtained it as a
betrothal gift from Mr. Moore.[3]

Dorothy's possession of the ring was short-lived, however. In order to pay off
debts, she turned it over to an auctioneer. At the auction, only two bidders wanted
the ring — Mrs. Kim Moffett, wife of the former Federal Housing Administrator, and
Mrs. E.F. Albee, a friend of Lillian and widow of the famous theatrical producer and
Syndicate leader.

"Sold!" cried the auctioneer, and the ring went to Mrs. Albee for a mere $4,950.
The money Dorothy received for the ring went to satisfying a judgment against her
for arrears in rent. The result of an almost decade-long battle to gain possession of
the jewel left Dorothy little but memories of her famous mother. In 1954, just after
Dorothy died, the remainder of her estate, by then amounting to some $81,000, was
distributed by the court. Ironically, there were only three beneficiaries, all of them
related to Alex Moore.

Lillian's name again surfaced in 1936, thanks to Hollywood's then-current pre-
occupation with musicals and biographies of famous people. Metro-Goldwyn-Mayer,
coming off its successful biography of *The Great Ziegfeld*, announced they were negotiating with Dorothy for the rights to her mother's story. Jeanette MacDonald was the
studio's choice to play Lillian.

Louella Parsons, Hollywood's premier gossip columnist, was unimpressed with
the decision:

> Hope the thousands of Lillian Russell fans won't squawk when they hear that
> Jeanette MacDonald is M-G-M's choice. No imitation Lillian ever will sat-
> isfy the admirers of the former Belle of Broadway. She bears no resemblence
> to the buxom charmer, either in face or figure.[4]

The project never materialized. Instead, 20th Century–Fox, in the person of
Darryl Zanuck, thought that *The Life of Lillian Russell* would prove a profitable enterprise. When movie critics heard the news, they wondered what new lawsuits would
surface when descendants objected to the Zanuck form of "realism."

In 1938, William Anthony McGuire was hired to write the script for the picture
and Irving Cummings to direct. Coincidentally, Cummings had been Lillian's leading man for *In Search of a Sinner*, 27 years earlier. Since no one else involved with
the production had ever met Lillian or seen her perform, Cummings was expected to
lend personal insight to the production. The script went through many revisions,
closely edited by Zanuck. What had begun as a fairly true account of Lillian's life
emerged as a fictitious tale in which only the names were real. The movie script was
notable more for its omissions — two marriages, all divorces, one child, all theater
manager conflicts, Lillian's entire comic opera and dramatic comedy careers, and
everything after 1912 — than its revelations. Lillian's entire life had been telescoped
into what McGuire described as a portrayal of Miss Russell "as she is remembered
rather than as she was." But who remembered her, and what did they remember?

Zanuck was forced to deal with another story element, even more difficult
to resolve. How were women, particularly famous women, to be portrayed in the
movies, in order to make them compatible with existing social mores? To do so, Lillian's personality and life history would have to undergo a Hollywood-mandated
makeover. Thus, she was transformed into an insipid, love sick woman who, by some

remarkable if obscure quirk of luck, gained fame as a beautiful singer. Typical of Zanuck bio-pics, the movie depicted Lillian from age 18 to 51, but the star showed no signs of aging.

Susan and Dorothy were sent contracts by Zanuck to release the studio of all responsibility for his portrayal of Lillian. When she read the script, Susan's reaction was explosive: "It's an abortion, a downright abortion!" She refused to sign the release. Nor did she tear it up, instead putting it aside as a post-mortem memento of her sister's career. Dorothy signed. She needed the money.

The only real elements of the picture were Weber and Fields playing themselves (at age 73, even the best of makeup couldn't make them look 45) and a detailed replica of the Weberfields Music Hall. Alice Faye was chosen to play Lillian, although (even with padded bust) she had neither Lillian's curves, charisma nor voice. Don Ameche played Edward Solomon, a doomed composer who died while writing a great theatrical vehicle for his adored wife. As Diamond Jim Brady, Edward Arnold seemed to laugh his way through the role. Henry Fonda was Alexander Moore, who supposedly waited 30 years for Lillian to return his profound esteem and affection, after having rescued her in a runaway carriage. In the picture, Faye sang two songs 20 years before they were actually written. One of them, John Stromberg's "Come Down, Ma Evening Star," Faye sang for Lillian's audition at Pastor's in 1880.

The movie had its premiere in Clinton, Iowa, May 15, 1940, another of Zanuck's innovative public relations coups. Both of Clinton's movie theaters showed the picture to full houses. Three days of festivities preceded the actual showings, featuring appearances by Don Ameche and Cesar Romero (apparently standing in for Faye, Arnold, and Fonda). Much was made of Lillian's successes and reputation, even though she was never more than a toddler in Clinton before moving to Chicago.

Reviews of the movie were mixed. *Life* magazine gave it "movie of the week" treatment. The *New York Sun* talked about the spectacular stage numbers created by Seymour Felix. *Variety*, however, had a different slant:

> There are a few good scenes in the movie, such as Weber and Fields' funny scene of their card-playing duel.[5]

The *New Yorker* magazine was less complimentary:

> Weber and Fields playing themselves, along with other stars of the period, only contribute to making the movie a confused jumble of social history.[6]

A month after the movie's premiere, Random House published a book by Parker Morell, *The Era of Plush*, a biography of Lillian Russell. It seemed more than coincidental that the book appeared at the same time the movie was in national distribution. Another Zanuck inspiration?

Based on the sources Morell had, he attempted to write her real story. Much, however, was taken from Lillian's autobiography, Dorothy's version of her mother's life, earlier articles, old newspapers and critical reviews. While it seemed adequately researched, reviewers did not favorably consider the book. It seemed to capture little of the excitement of her life and career, and even less of the flavor of the times before and after the turn of the century. Still, Morell's book was seen as "diverting" and "pleasant reading in the dark hour of a tragic world."

Press interest in Lillian died as quickly as the movie. Unlike Zanuck's previous "biographical" successes — all portrayals of men —*Lillian Russell* made little profit. Though videotapes of many other older movies are now available, including the early biographies made by Paramount, Warner Brothers and M-G-M, a video version of *Lillian Russell* has not yet been released.

Pittsburgh remembered Lillian when Perle Mesta was nominated ambassador to Luxembourg in 1949, recalling the city's earlier connections with diplomacy. Alexander Moore was remembered primarily because of his marriage to Lillian and their hosting "some of the most fabulous parties of their day." In that sense, both Mesta and the Moores had much in common:

> Tales still are told of fantastic dinners costing thousands of dollars which the Moores held at their home at Linden and Penn.[7]

Yet there is no evidence that such gala parties ever, in fact, took place.

The articles went on to discuss the relationship between Lillian and Moore, including the legal problems with Lillian's estate and with Dorothy. Moore was described as possessing a "cultivated political bedside manner and social suavity" that made him an excellent diplomat. Lillian was portrayed as "a star of musical comedy, famous for her pretty face and the opulent figure which the taste of a half century ago decreed as the feminine ideal, that made her the nation's first glamour girl." There was not the slightest castigation of Moore's conduct toward Dorothy.

Interest in Lillian was rekindled a few years later in New York when the owner of Luchow's, Jan Mitchell, a retrospective admirer of Lillian, opened the Lillian Russell Museum on the second floor of his 14th Street restaurant. His collection consisted of mementos, costumes, hand props, letters, posters and programs, many of which had been owned by Lillian. How Mitchell gained possession of these items is unknown. Helen Hayes was chosen honorary curator of the museum. At the opening ceremonies, a guest of honor was waiter Hugo Schemke, who claimed to have served Lillian when she worked at Tony Pastor's theater, 74 years previously. In 1961, after Luchow's closed, the entire collection of memorabilia was auctioned by Sotheby Parke Bernet.

Pittsburgh finally established a permanent public memorial to Lillian in 1958 by naming the new Pittsburgh Playhouse dining room in her honor. The room, decorated in turn-of-the-century splendor, with ornately carved tables and velvet-covered chairs, was dominated by a large oil portrait of Lillian. In the dedication, Lillian was identified as "Queen of the Gay Nineties" and "the greatest glamour girl of them all."

Lillian was again recalled in 1962, when Victor and Angel Records released albums of a number of songs associated with her at the height of her comic opera career. In the *Opera News*, an industry periodical, Lillian's life and career were briefly discussed, the author suggesting that "such glorious creatures" as Lillian Russell could only have existed during the Gay Nineties.

Over the last 25 years, little has been written or spoken about Lillian. When she is mentioned at all, only her beauty is recalled. Today, she lacks all context, existing only as a vague, distorted image. At one time so vivid, exciting and awesome, Lillian Russell today remains without a stage upon which to perform.

Shortly after Cynthia retired and went to live in New Jersey, at a time when Lillian was attempting to sort out her personal goals and desires, she described to a friend a vivid dream.

In the dream, a young girl longs to run away from home, and, after many threats to do so, finally carries out her plan. After tramping the streets for several days, tired and hungry, with no one to befriend her, she determines that running away is not much fun. She decides to return to her family and ask their forgiveness. Her family sees her coming home. They decide to punish the girl by ignoring her when she returns. Shamefacedly coming into the house, the girl finds that no one in the family seems to notice her. She speaks to her father, who doesn't reply. When she asks her mother a question, the woman appears neither to see nor hear her. The air seems charged with icy rejection. The girl even begins to imagine that, by some strange phenomenon, she has ceased to exist.

Finally, a friend strolls into the room and, having observed the girl, comes up to greet her sympathetically. This touching welcome so warms the child's heart that she cries and embraces her friend. Seeing that no one else takes notice of them, the two of them depart. As they leave together, the girl looks back over her shoulder and wonders, "Is this the same house I had when I went away?"

The dream succinctly summarizes Lillian's associations with her father and mother. It also suggests her long-term desire to unburden herself of Cynthia's influence and control. The dream seemed to signal a turning point in Lillian's life, when she was finally able to free herself of Cynthia.

Lillian had spent many years of her career alternating successes with self-destructive episodes, constructing self-imposed barriers. It was almost as if Lillian needed to create obstacles before she could enjoy her accomplishments and accept the rewards of her performances.

Besides her mother's retirement, other factors contributed to Lillian's changed perceptions of herself and her career at the time. After much soul-searching, she finally decided to stop performing comic opera, even though it had been primarily responsible for her great success. Audiences seemed to have tired of the genre, and Lillian was tired of performing it.

Lillian now perceived herself to be an experienced and confident performer, an actress who could capably handle any assignment. Moreover, for the first time in her life, she was enjoying a comfortable, undemanding, loving intimacy with a man (Lewisohn), a relationship that supported rather than diverted her career.

The changes in her personality were perceptible to all around her. Traits that surfaced only occasionally among colleagues and friends now became dominant elements of her persona — generosity, kindness, a sense of humor, graciousness and a desire to reach out to others, particularly those who found themselves in unfortunate circumstances. To audiences, she displayed a naturalness, a vulnerability and accessibility that gave them the impression that "what you saw was the real person." She conveyed a sense of calm and confidence, a heartfelt desire to love and be loved. Even though she lived in elegance, her spirit could be embraced by audiences to satisfy their own aspirations and fantasies. So great was her personal appeal, that audiences were able to carry these positive, tender emotions with them, beyond the confines of the theater, establishing Lillian as a household name in America for a quarter of a century.

To this point in time, Lillian had been fiercely concerned with her career. Her voice and beauty had gained her notoriety, money and power. Her use of these attributes to challenge the traditional roles of women had become controversial. Having now internalized these characteristics, Lillian gradually became aware of the social significance of her new performance role. Confidently, she could enter new realms and take on new causes to successful conclusions. She could now transcend her role as a temperamental, authority-challenging actress to become a legitimate spokesperson on a wide variety of issues — from health and beauty to actor's enfranchisement to women's suffrage and politics. This was to be the Lillian Russell known to the world of performance until she died. Ironically, history seems to recall only her beauty and youthful defiance.

While no actual evidence exists, all available information confirms that Lillian possessed an outstanding voice. Dr. Damrosch had been very disappointed when Nellie chose popular stage over grand opera. Critics reported that Lillian "was able to reach high notes with verve and spirit" when she sang comic opera. Both Rudolph Aronson and Henry Abbey believed that Lillian's voice was of grand-opera quality. The fact that friends like Mesdames Nordica and Calvé dissuaded Lillian from entering grand opera says more about their own fear of competition than about any vocal deficiencies she might have had. Madame Nordica was said to have advised Lillian:

> You are queen of comic opera, without any rivals. We all love you, but if
> you become our competitor we shall hate you.

Madame Melba, at the height of her own career, was asked about Lillian's singing comic opera and exclaimed: "What a career that woman would have had in grand opera!"

In 1912, when Lillian was 50, she made her only phonograph recording, "Come Down, Ma Evening Star," for Columbia Records. She was so disappointed with the result, she ordered the recording destroyed. A cylinder copy of the original was discovered years later and reproduced commercially. Those who were familiar with her voice agreed with Lillian's decision. Still, this 1912 recording is the only example we possess of her voice.

Lillian's constant vocal training and stern self-discipline, her determination to maintain the quality of her singing, contributed greatly to the longevity of her career. Nor was she afraid to sing popular hits of the day, from "coon songs" to ballads. Opera singers usually refused to sing popular songs because they believed that to do so was beneath their dignity. Popular singers of the day generally lacked both training and discipline, limiting their vocal capabilities and repertoire. To the delight of her audience, Lillian was never elitist about her singing, ever ready and able to render all styles of songs.

In the late nineteenth century, a boastful and Darwinian America was seeking objective examples of beauty, tangible expressions of the country's new feelings of superiority in an increasingly urban and industrial world. A certain type of American woman was elevated as a symbol of beauty; the ones chosen to embody this symbol were most likely to be stage performers. Lillian didn't specifically seek the title of "American Beauty," but when she recognized its potential, she exploited it. The title became useful because Lillian realized that beauty meant power, and she was able to capitalize on its benefits, whether in stage performance, product endorsements, health and beauty lectures, women's suffrage or patriotic endeavors. Lillian gave beauty itself a legitimacy that other women seemed unable to provide. In time, this legitimacy of beauty became the foundation for female star power, for the acceptability of actresses as sex symbols and as representatives of the "new" class of women in our society.

Lillian was honored as "The American Beauty" because other performers, even if younger, displaying new fashions, or starring in more successful shows, proved unable to usurp her title or equal her longevity. The combination of Lillian's beauty, personal charisma and performance skills made her a larger-than-life icon of the era.

In the succeeding 75 years, three performers have similarly parlayed beauty, talent, sexuality and personal appeal. Mae West, though a talented comedienne, was little more than a cartoon of Lillian. Marilyn Monroe was well on her way to emulating Lillian but died before she was able to test the public prejudice against middle age. Frozen in time, Monroe has achieved icon status. Madonna has already passed through a number of incarnations and, if she lives long enough, may yet come closest to equalling Lillian's legacy. She has matured from sexual provocateur to mature performer. What the twenty-first century version of motherhood and patriotism will be we can only guess. But Madonna may yet fulfill these roles.

Audiences are not fickle; human behavior follows patterns and cycles. Only the tools and manifestations change. Audiences are both sensitive to and critical of the stars they embrace. If a star withdraws from public accessibility, sets up barriers or boasts of superiority, audiences will isolate and punish even previously lauded luminaries. There are social rules for public adoration.

Audiences won't be defrauded. But they are forgiving. When a performer is young, brashness is usually tolerated. As they age, favorites have to build acceptability in order to maintain star power. If stars can last long enough, they stand an excellent chance of becoming icons. Parodying one's self in later years is not a bad bargain, because it displays a sense of humor and suggests humanity, two elements audiences seek in order to justify — indeed sanctify — their choice of icons.

Lillian Russell was *the* sex symbol of her day, the first to achieve national recognition and status in this country. She frightened social arbiters because of her self-sufficiency and drive for equality of the sexes. Her life offered a strong suggestion of sexual license — numerous suitors, four marriages, three divorces and a long-term liaison with Jesse Lewisohn. Indeed, the carefully orchestrated publicity of her deeds helped to establish this exotic and erotic public image.

Romances between theatrical professionals were common, no doubt due to the easy accessibility among performers because their line of work broke down traditional barriers between the sexes. At the time, the theater was probably the only profession in our society where that could occur. Not surprising, then, that the theater became the *avant-garde* for changing social norms, pushing sexual limits and fostering a groundswell of independence for a new, more emancipated middle class of women.

Lillian endured a good deal of disapproval from critics, primarily for her off-stage behavior. Besides reporting on theatrical happenings, critics of the time were moral arbiters and wielded immense power. But they rarely seemed to intimidate Lillian. Each time she was reprimanded for "indecent" behavior, she returned all the more determined to refurbish her public identity. Her ability to share her problems with the audience — and it is the audience that really counts — persuaded them of Lillian's struggle through adversity, that she was bravely returning to regain their confidence.

In later years, her mere presence on stage ignited this intense emotional connection with audiences.

As public suffragist, Lillian followed her mother's example, once her personal conflicts with Cynthia had been resolved. Even before becoming an ardent suffragist, however, she had already won her credentials through years of confrontation with men in important positions. Continuous travel and publicity throughout the country helped. Alex Moore helped. Newspaper articles helped. Political campaigning helped. As an acknowledged beauty, Lillian naturally and obviously counteracted men's arguments about the image of suffragist women. Her activities probably did more to foster the feminist movement, however, than to win women the vote.

As patriot, Lillian was truly an all–American product. She could honestly claim her ancestors had landed at Plymouth Rock. She could rightly praise her father's and mother's contributions to the growth of the country. And Lillian herself was a prime mover in the development of American-rooted popular theater. In an era of fervent nationalism, Lillian's claim to be "American clean through" always met with loud cheers and applause. Apparently, her negative experiences with English and German audiences made her even more partial to American theatergoers; and she wasn't afraid to offer such comparisons in public.

The public saw, in one woman, a transcendent national beauty; and they institutionalized her, one of the reasons contributing to Lillian's success on behalf of the war effort. Her views on immigration were not surprising. They represented her strong sentiment to retain the cultural, if not racial, purity of the country after two decades of record-breaking immigration from Europe and a devastating foreign war. Moreover, aliens could possibly threaten American women's newly earned status and ballot-box power. Lillian was proud of her country and never hesitated to sing its praises. Though seriously ill, only a few weeks before she died, when speaking to Congress, her patriotic zeal remained undiminished: "There was never a time when the flag needed more waving than it does now," she declared, and Congress applauded.

Lillian's longevity attests to her recognition and understanding of changes in theater and her ability to change with them. Through discipline and hard work, she maintained her prominence on stage. In addition, the growing power of the media contributed to her long career. No day was complete without the mention of her name in New York and other major urban newspapers. She not only made news; she *was* news.

Unfortunately, Lillian never got the benefit of the kind of *mass* media attention enjoyed by Cohan, Zeigfeld or Jolson. Their shows, exploits and voices were preserved, aurally and visually, so that we hear and see them frequently in documentaries or on late night TV. If Zanuck's movie on Lillian's life did anything, it probably diminished, rather than increased, her legacy by distorting fact to parody and reforming her persona to meet Hollywood's perceptions of women's morals at the time. Presented honestly today, her story would be fascinating, readily accepted and embraced.

Lillian lived with tremendous gusto. Her beauty was far more than superficial; it radiated true humanity. She helped make American theater intimate and romantic at a time when it was customarily boisterous and brash.

Lillian became the link between foreign-inspired shows and made-in-America productions. She also spanned the eras of individual theatrical impresarios, the omnivorous Syndicate, and the dawn of the age of mass entertainment.

For the past century, every generation has made a place for a Lillian-type personality. Each era has seemed to need such a person — to expand social and sexual parameters, challenge rules, incite controversy, fill newspaper pages, warm the hearts of diligent reporters and satisfy the public's desire for titillating exposé. The ascendance of such an icon can best occur in the world of entertainment. In other aspects of our culture, the gregarious personality remains relatively suppressed.

In America's performance history, there have been others — a few others — like her. There will undoubtedly be more. But Lillian Russell was the first.

Performance Chronology

1877

Time Tries All
December, Christmas program, lead singer, Kimball Music Hall, Chicago

1879

Evangeline
Opened September, chorus, E.E. Rice production, Globe Theater, Boston

Evangeline
Opened October, chorus, E.E. Rice production, Brooklyn Academy of Music, Brooklyn

Patience
Opened December 27, chorus, E.E. Rice production, Park Theater, Brooklyn

1880

Evangeline
Opened January 26, chorus, E.E. Rice production, Haverly's Theater, Brooklyn

Variety
Opened November 22, solo performance, Tony Pastor's Theater, New York, six weeks

1881

Variety
Opened January 3, solo performance, Tony Pastor's Theater, New York, two weeks

Our School Girls, or Fun in a Boarding School
Opened January 17, a singing role, Tony Pastor's Theater, New York, two weeks

Pie Rats of Penn Yan
Opened February 7, Russell as Mabel, Tony Pastor's Theater, New York, five weeks

Olivette
Opened March 12, Russell in lead singing role, Tony Pastor's Theater, New York, two weeks

Willie Edouin's Company leaves on Western tour March 29, Russell loaned to company by Tony Pastor

Sparks
Opened April 2, a singing role, Willie Edouin's Company, Olympia Theater, St. Louis, Missouri, two nights

Sparks
Opened April 18, a singing role, Willie Edouin's Company, Standard Theater, San Francisco, five weeks

Sparks
Opened June 13, a singing role, Willie Edouin's Company, Sixteenth St. Theater, Denver, Colorado, one week (company disbands)

Variety
Opened August 22, solo performance on program, Howard Atheneum, Boston, two weeks

Variety
Opened September 5, solo performance on program, Music Hall, Manchester, New Hampshire, one week (company disbands)

The Grand Mogul
Opened October 29, Russell as D'jemma, Bijou Theater, New York, eight weeks (by arrangement with Tony Pastor)

The Snake Charmer
Opened December 21, revised version of *The Grand Mogul*, new dialogue, new songs, Russell singing lead, Bijou Theater, New York, one week

1882

Patience
Opened January 23, Russell as Patience, Tony Pastor's Theater, New York, eight weeks

Billee Taylor
Opened March 25, Russell as Phoebe, Tony Pastor's Theater, one week

Patience
Opened June 17, Russell as Patience, Niblo's Garden, New York, two weeks

Billee Taylor
Opened September 16, Russell as Phoebe, Bijou Opera House, New York, two weeks

The Sorcerer
Opened October 17, Russell as Aline, Bijou Opera House, New York, three weeks

Patience
Opened November 11, Russell as Patience, Grand Opera House, New York, eight weeks

1883

Virginia
Opened January 9, Russell as Virginia, Bijou Opera House, New York, three weeks

Recitals, Sunday evening concerts
March 4, 11, 18, 25, Cosmopolitan Theater, New York

The Sorcerer
Opened April 24, Russell as Aline, Casino Theater, New York, one week

The Princess of Trebizonde
Opened May 5, Russell as Prince Raphael, Casino Theater, New York, four weeks (Russell left for England during the run, on June 9)

Virginia and Paul
Opened July 16, Russell as Virginia, Gaiety Theater, London, England, four weeks

Pocahontas
Opened August 11, Russell as Pocahontas, Gaiety Theater, London, England, three weeks

1884

Billee Taylor
Opened early January, Russell as Phoebe, tour of Belgium, France and Germany, 14 weeks

Polly
Opened October 4, Russell as Polly Pluckrose, Novelty Theater, London, England, ten weeks

1884-85

Pocahontas
Opened December 26, Russell as Pocahontas, Empire Theater, London, England, five weeks

1885

Recitals, Sunday evening concerts
February 15, 22, March 1, 30 and April 5, Bijou Opera House, New York

Polly
Opened April 27, Russell as Polly Pluckrose, Casino Theater, New York, eight weeks

Billee Taylor
Opened June 20, Russell as Phoebe, Casino Theater, New York, two weeks; on tour two weeks

1885-86

Polly/Billee Taylor
Opened September 17, Peoria, Illinois, on tour 28 weeks

1886

Pepita, or the Girl With the Glass Eye
Opened March 16, Russell as Pepita, Union Square Theater, New York, eight weeks; on tour two weeks

The Maid and the Moonshiner
  (formerly *Virginia and Paul*)
Opened August 16, Russell as Virginia, Standard Theater, New York, two weeks

1886-87

The Mikado; Iolanthe; A Trip to Africa; Gasparone
Duff Opera Co., opened September 6, San Francisco, California, on tour 29 weeks; opened April 11, 1887, Standard Theater, New York, nine weeks

1887-88

Dorothy
Duff Opera Co., opened November 7, Russell as Dorothy, Standard Theater, New York, five weeks; on tour 15 weeks

1888

The Queen's Mate
Duff Opera Co., opened May 2, Russell as Anita, Broadway Theater, New York, eight weeks; reopened August 13, Broadway Theater, New York, five weeks; on tour 14 weeks

1889

Nadjy
Opened January 7, Russell as Etelha, Columbia Theater, Chicago, Illinois, two weeks; opened January 21, Casino Theater, New York, 14 weeks

The Brigands
Opened May 9, Russell as Fiorella, Casino Theater, New York, 18 weeks; on tour 15 weeks

1890

The Brigands
Reopened January 6, Casino Theater, New York, seven weeks

The Grand Duchess
Opened February 25, Russell as the Duchess, Casino Theater, New York, 14 weeks

1890-91

Poor Jonathan
Opened October 14, Russell as Harriet, Casino Theater, New York, 29 weeks

1891

Apollo, or The Oracle of Delphi
Opened May 7, Russell as Phythia, Casino Theater, New York, ten weeks

The Grand Duchess
Opened July 13, Casino Theater, New York, six weeks

1891-92

La Cigale
Lillian Russell Opera Co., opened October 26, Russell as Marton, Garden Theater, New York, 16 weeks; on tour 12 weeks

1892

La Cigale
Lillian Russell Opera Co., reopened September 6, Baldwin Theater, San Francisco, California, three weeks

The Mountebanks
Lillian Russell Opera Co., Russell as Teresa, Baldwin Theater, San Francisco, California, one week

La Cigale/The Mountebanks
Lillian Russell Opera Co., on tour seven weeks, beginning October 3

La Cigale
Lillian Russell Opera Co., on tour five weeks, beginning November 21

1892-93

La Cigale
Lillian Russell Opera Co., opened December 26, Garden Theater, New York, two weeks

1893

The Mountebanks
Lillian Russell Opera Co., opened January 11, Garden Theater, New York, six weeks

Girofle-Girofla
Lillian Russell Opera Co., opened March 3, Russell in dual role as Girofle-Girofla, Garden Theater, New York, four weeks; on tour four weeks

Girofle-Girofla; La Cigale; The Mountebanks
Lillian Russell Opera Co., opened May 6, Columbia Theater, Chicago, Illinois, 16 weeks (Chicago World's Fair)

1893-94

Princess Nicotine
Lillian Russell Opera Co., opened November 20, Russell as Rosa, Casino Theater, New York, 11 weeks; on tour seven weeks

1894

Girofle-Girofla
Lillian Russell Opera Co., opened March 27, Casino Theater, New York, five weeks; on tour four weeks

The Queen of Brilliants
Opened September 8, Russell as Betta, Lyceum Theater, London, England, six weeks

The Queen of Brilliants
Opened November 7, Russell as Betta, Abbey's Theater, New York, four weeks

1894-95

The Grand Duchess
Lillian Russell Opera Co., opened December 4, Abbey's Theater, New York, three weeks; on tour 12 weeks

1895

La Pericole
Lillian Russell Opera Co., opened March 17, Russell as La Pericole, Allan's Grand Opera House, Washington D.C., on tour six weeks; opened April 29, Abbey's Theater, New York, two weeks

The Tzigane
Lillian Russell Opera Co., opened May 14, Russell as Vera, Abbey's Theater, New York, five weeks

The Tzigane
Lillian Russell Opera Co., reopened September 9, Tremont Theater, Boston, Massachusetts, on tour nine weeks

1895-96

The Little Duke
Lillian Russell Opera Co., opened November 11, Russell as the Duke de Parthenay, Columbia Theater, Chicago, Illinois (The Tzigane dropped November 16; The Grand Duchess and La Pericole added), on tour 13 weeks

1896

The Goddess of Truth
Lillian Russell Opera Co., opened February 26, Russell as Princess Alma, Abbey's Theater, New York, four weeks

The Little Duke
Lillian Russell Opera Co., opened April 6, Abbey's Theater, New York, two weeks; on tour five weeks

An American Beauty
Lillian Russell Opera Co., opened September 17, Russell as Gabrielle Dalmont, Lyceum Theater, Rochester, New York, on tour 13 weeks

1896-97

An American Beauty
Lillian Russell Opera Co., opened December 28, Casino Theater, New York, eight weeks; on tour five weeks

1897

The Wedding Day
Opened April 8, Russell as Lucille D'Herblay, costarred with Della Fox and Jefferson de Angelis, Casino Theater, New York, seven weeks

1897-98

The Wedding Day
Reopened September 15, Wieting Opera House, Syracuse, New York, on tour 31 weeks

1898

The Wedding Day
Opened April 18, Broadway Theater, New York, four weeks

Concert Tour
Opened August 29, Winter Garden Theater, Berlin, Germany, six weeks

1899

La Belle Helene
Opened January 12, Russell as Helene, Casino Theater, New York, six weeks; on tour six weeks

1899-1900

Whirl-I-Gig
Weber and Fields Co., opened September 21, Weber and Fields Music Hall, New York, 33 weeks

1900-01

Fiddle-Dee-Dee
Weber and Fields Co., opened September 6, Weber and Fields Music Hall, New York, 32 weeks

1901-02

Hoity-Toity
Weber and Fields Co., opened September 5, Weber and Fields Music Hall, 33 weeks; on tour three weeks

1902-03

Twirly-Whirly
Weber and Fields Co., opened September 11, Weber and Fields Music Hall, New York, 31 weeks; on tour four weeks

1903-04

Whoop-Dee-Doo
Weber and Fields Co., opened September 24, Weber and Fields Music Hall, New York, 19 weeks; on tour 15 weeks

1904-05

Lady Teazle
Opened December 12, Russell as Lady Teazle, Casino Theater, New York, seven weeks; on tour 16 weeks

1905

Vaudeville, Proctor Circuit
Opened October 2, Proctor's 23rd Street Theater, New York, six weeks; on tour four weeks

1906

Vaudeville, Percy Williams
Opened April 4, Orpheum Theater, Brooklyn, New York; on tour six weeks

Barbara's Millions
Opened September 15, Russell as Barbara, Power's Theater, Grand Rapids, Michigan, two days; on tour two weeks; reopened October 8, Savoy Theater, New York, one week

1906-07

The Butterfly
Opened December 21, Russell as Elizabeth Killebrew, Casino Theater, Atlantic City, New Jersey; on tour 33 weeks

1907-08

Wildfire
Opened September 30, Russell as Mrs. Henrietta Barrington, Grand Theater, Cincinnati, Ohio; on tour 34 weeks

1908-09

Wildfire
Reopened September 3, Asbury Park, New Jersey, three days; opened September 7, Liberty Theater, New York, eight weeks; on tour 34 weeks

1909

The Widow's Might
Opened September 10, Russell as Mrs. Laura Curtis, Court Square Theater, Springfield, Massachusetts, two days; opened September 13, Liberty Theater, New York, six weeks; on tour seven weeks

1909-10

The First Night
Opened December 26, Russell as Rose Graham, Broad Theater, Philadelphia, Pennsylvania; on tour 21 weeks

1910-11

In Search of a Sinner
Opened September 16, Russell as Georgiana Chadbourne, South Bend Theater, South Bend, Indiana; on tour 26 weeks

1911

The First Night
Reopened April 10, Blackstone Theater, Chicago, Illinois, two weeks

Vaudeville, UBO Circuit
Opened May 8, Grand Theater, Pittsburgh, Pennsylvania; on tour six weeks

Vaudeville, UBO Circuit
Opened September 18, Keith's Fifth Ave. Theater, New York, one week; on tour nine weeks

1912

Weber and Fields Jubilee Co.
Opened February 15, Broadway Theater, New York, 14 weeks; on tour one month

1913

Vaudeville, UBO Circuit
Opened April 21, Colonial Theater, New York, one week; on tour nine weeks

1913-14

Vaudeville, Lillian Russell's Big Feature Festival
Cort Circuit, opened September 29, Hermanus Bleeker Theater, Albany, New York; on tour 15 weeks

1915-16

Vaudeville, UBO Circuit
Opened November 3, Palace Theater, New York, one week; on tour fourteen weeks

1918

Hitchy Koo
Opened March 17, Colonial Theater, Chicago, Illinois, two weeks (Russell as cast replacement, at the personal request of Raymond Hitchcock, star of production)

1918-19

Vaudeville, Keith Circuit
Opened October 29, Palace Theater, New
York, one week; on tour 14 weeks

1922

Last appearance on Broadway
April 24, Palace Theater, New York, charity
benefit for Actors Equity

MOVIES

How to Live to be a Hundred and Die Young, health and beauty exercises, supplement to lecture
series, Kinemacolor, Los Angeles, California, opened February 22, 1913, Fulton Theater, Chicago,
Illinois; on tour six weeks

Wildfire, World Film Corporation (Lewis Selznick), Peerless Studios, Fort Lee, New Jersey,
released January 25, 1915

PHONOGRAPH RECORDS

(Columbia Records, New York)

19830 "Come Down, Ma Evening Star"

19831 "When You're Away"

19832 "The Island of Roses and Love"

All three songs were recorded on March 22, 1912. All three recordings were rejected as inade-
quate by Russell and Columbia.

In September 1943, Collector's Record Shop, New York City, released a limited edition repress-
ing of "Come Down, Ma Evening Star," taken from the original recording on flat disc rejected
in 1912.

Notes

1—FROM PRAIRIES TO PASTOR'S

1. *The Howland Quarterly,* July, 1956; Mormon Library, Salt Lake City.
2. *History of Clinton County, Iowa,* Clinton Historical Society.
3. Chicago Historical Society: various newspaper articles, *Chicago Tribune.*
4. *Convent of the Sacred Heart,* history annual, 1995.
5. Chicago Historical Society: various newspaper articles, *Chicago Tribune.*
6. A complete biography of Tony Pastor can be found in Parker Zeller's book, *Tony Pastor: Dean of the Vaudeville Stage,* Eastern University Press, 1971.

2—SHE COULDN'T SAY NO

1. Lillian Russell, "Lillian Russell's Reminiscences," *Cosmopolitan,* February 1922, p. 17.
2. *Ibid.,* p. 15.
3. *New York Clipper,* Feb. 9, 1881.
4. *New York Dramatic Mirror,* March 26, 1881.
5. *San Francisco Chronicle,* June 4, 1881.
6. *Clipper,* Nov. 5, 1881.
7. *Clipper,* Jan. 28, 1882.
8. *Dramatic Mirror,* April 15, 1882.
9. *Clipper,* April 29, 1882.
10. *Clipper,* July 8, 1882.
11. *Clipper,* Dec. 30, 1882.
12. *Clipper,* Jan. 6, 1883.
13. Russell, *Cosmopolitan,* March 1922, p. 126.

14. *Ibid.,* p. 126.
15. *Clipper,* June 16, 1883.
16. *Clipper,* June 23, 1883.

3—RETURN OF THE PRODIGAL DAUGHTER

1. *Clipper,* from London correspondent, July 28, 1883.
2. *Ibid.,* Sept. 22, 1883.
3. *Ibid.,* Aug. 4, 1883.
4. *Ibid.,* April 26, 1884.
5. *Ibid.,* Aug. 16, 1884.
6. *London Era,* Aug. 23, 1884.
7. *Clipper,* Nov. 8, 1884.
8. *Ibid.,* Feb. 14, 1885.
9. *Ibid.,* Feb. 21, 1885.
10. *Ibid.,* July 11, 1885.
11. *Ibid.,* April 10, 1886.
12. Russell, *Cosmopolitan,* March 1922, p. 126.
13. *Clipper,* Sept. 18, 1886.
14. *Ibid.,* Oct. 2, 1886.
15. *Ibid.,* Oct. 2, 1886.
16. Russell, *Cosmopolitan,* March 1922, p. 127.
17. *Clipper,* Jan. 12, 1889.
18. *Ibid.,* Jan. 19, 1889.
19. *Ibid.,* Jan. 19, 1889.
20. *Ibid.,* Jan. 19, 1889.

4—THE QUEEN OF COMIC OPERA

1. *Clipper,* May 18, 1889.
2. *Ibid.,* Dec. 14, 1889.

3. *Ibid.*, March 8, 1890.
4. *Ibid.*, March 22, 1890.
5. *Ibid.*, March 25, 1890.
6. *New York World*, Oct. 27, 1890.
7. *Clipper*, Jan. 10, 1891.
8. *Ibid.*, Feb. 21, 1891.
9. *Ibid.*, May 16, 1891.
10. *Dramatic Mirror*, May 16, 1891.
11. *New York Times*, June, 23, 1891.
12. *Dramatic Mirror*, July, 18, 1891.
13. *New York World*, Aug. 17, 1891.
14. *Clipper*, Oct. 31, 1891.
15. *Dramatic Mirror*, Oct. 31, 1891.
16. *Ibid.*, Oct. 31, 1891.
17. *New York Times*, Jan. 30, 1892.
18. *Clipper*, Jan. 23, 1892.
19. *Boston Globe*, March 5, 1892.
20. *Ibid.*, March 7, 1892.
21. *Ibid.*, March 10, 1892.
22. *Dramatic Mirror*, March 19, 1892.
23. *Chicago Tribune*, March 26, 1892.
24. *Dramatic Mirror*, April 16, 1892.
25. *Clipper*, July 30, 1892.
26. *Dramatic Mirror*, Aug. 20, 1892.
27. *Ibid.*, Sept. 3, 1892.
28. *Ibid.*, Sept. 24, 1892.
29. *Chicago Tribune*, Nov. 15, 1892.
30. D. Russell, "My Mother, Lillian Russell," *Liberty*, Oct. 26, 1929, p. 45.
31. *Ibid.*, p. 45.
32. *New York World*, Sept. 9, 1889.
33. *Dramatic Mirror*, Jan. 21, 1893.
34. *Chicago Tribune*, May 13, 1893.

5—THE QUEEN'S CONSORTS

1. *Chicago Tribune*, June 3, 1893.
2. *Clipper*, June 10, 1893.
3. *Dramatic Mirror*, June 26, 1893.
4. *Clipper*, July 22, 1893.
5. Emmett Dedmon, *Fabulous Chicago*. New York: Random House, 1953, p. 269.
6. *Ibid.*, Sept. 9, 1893.
7. *New York World*, Nov. 25, 1893.
8. *Dramatic Mirror*, Nov. 25, 1893.
9. *New York Herald*, Jan. 11, 1894.
10 *Ibid.*, Jan. 11, 1894.
11. *New York World*, Jan. 11, 1894.
12. *New York Press*, Jan. 21, 1894.
13. *Dramatic Mirror*, Jan. 27, 1894.
14. *New York Herald*, Jan. 22, 1894.
15. *Dramatic Mirror*, March 31, 1894.
16. *Ibid.*, June 2, 1894.
17. *New York Herald*, May 26, 1894.
18. *Clipper*, June 16, 1894.

19. *London Referee*, July 21, 1894.
20. *Dramatic Mirror*, Aug. 25, 1894.
21. Cable from London correspondent to the *Dramatic Mirror*, Sept. 13, 1894.
22. *New York Herald*, Nov. 3, 1894.
23. *Dramatic Mirror*, Nov. 3, 1894.
24. *Clipper*, Nov. 17, 1894.
25. *Ibid.*, Dec. 8, 1894.

6—REQUIEM FOR COMIC OPERA

1. *Clipper*, May 11, 1895.
2. *Ibid.*, May 25, 1895.
3. *Boston Globe*, Sept. 14, 1895.
4. *Chicago Tribune*, Oct. 28, 1895.
5. *Ibid.*, Nov. 9, 1895.
6. Russell, *Cosmopolitan*, May 1922, p. 68.
7. *Dramatic Mirror*, Feb. 29, 1896.
8. *Clipper*, Feb. 29, 1896.
9. *Ibid.*, April 18, 1896.
10. *Ibid.*, May 2, 1896.
11. *New York Standard*, June–, 1896.
12. Russell, *Cosmopolitan*, May 1922, p. 92.
13. *Clipper*, Oct. 24, 1896.
14. *Dramatic Mirror*, Jan. 2, 1897.
15. *Clipper*, April 17, 1897.
16. *Ibid.*, May 15, 1897.
17. *Ibid.*, Sept. 18, 1897.
18. *Ibid.*, May 14, 1898.
19. Cable from Berlin correspondent to the *Clipper*, Aug. 27, 1898.
20. Russell, *Cosmopolitan*, June 1922, p. 100.
21. *Dramatic Mirror*, Oct. 22, 1898.
22. *Ibid.*, Jan. 21, 1899.
23. *Clipper*, Feb. 18, 1899.
24. *Ibid.*, March 18, 1899.
25. *Ibid.*, July 8, 1899.
26. *Ibid.*, July 29, 1899.
27. *Ibid.*, Aug. 5, 1899.

7—MUSIC HALL DAYS

1. *Clipper*, Sept. 30, 1899.
2. *Ibid.*, Sept. 16, 1899.
3. Russell, *Cosmopolitan*, July 1922, p. 93.
4. *Dramatic Mirror*, Oct. 21, 1899.
5. Russell, *Cosmopolitan*, July 1922, p. 96.
6. *Dramatic Mirror*, Sept. 15, 1900.
7. *Ibid.*
8. *Clipper*, Sept. 14, 1901.
9. *Ibid.*, Sept. 20, 1902.
10. Russell, *Cosmopolitan*, July 1922 p. 112.
11. D. Russell, "My Mother, Lillian Russell," *Liberty*, Nov. 2, 1929, p. 58.

8—END OF AN ERA

1. *Dramatic Mirror,* Aug. 6, 1904.
2. *Ibid.,* Dec. 17, 1904.
3. *Ibid.,* Jan. 7, 1905.
4. Shubert Archive, March 15, 1905.
5. Shubert Archive, March 16, 1905.
6. *Dramatic Mirror,* July 8, 1905.
7. *Clipper,* Oct. 7, 1905.
8. *New York Herald,* April 14, 1906.
9. *Clipper,* Sept. 22, 1906.
10. *Chicago Tribune,* Sept. 29, 1906.
11. *Dramatic Mirror,* Oct. 13, 1906.
12. *Ibid.*
13. *Ibid.,* Jan. 5, 1907.
14. *Ibid.,* April 20, 1907.
15. *Ibid.,* Oct. 12, 1907.
16. *Clipper,* Oct. 12, 1907.
17. *Ibid.,* Oct. 10, 1908.
18. *New York Times,* April 11, 1908.
19. *Clipper,* May 30, 1908.
20. *Ibid.,* Aug. 8, 1908.
21. *New York Times,* Aug. 27, 1908.
22. *Clipper,* Sept. 5, 1908.
23. *New York Herald,* Oct. 12, 1908.

9—HER IMAGE RENEWED

1. *Clipper,* Sept. 12, 1908.
2. *New York Herald,* Sept. 19, 1908.
3. *Clipper,* Oct. 31, 1908.
4. *Ibid.,* Nov. 14, 1908.
5. D. Russell, "My Mother, Lillian Russell." *Liberty,* Nov. 9, 1929, p. 52.
6. *Dramatic Mirror,* Feb. 27, 1909.
7. *Ibid.,* April 3, 1909.
8. *Ibid.,* June 26, 1909.
9. *Clipper,* Sept. 27, 1909.
10. *Dramatic Mirror,* Jan. 1, 1910.
11. *Chicago Tribune,* Sept. 20, 1910.
12. *Pittsburgh Leader,* Oct. 15, 1910.
13. *Dramatic Mirror,* April 26, 1911.
14. *Chicago Tribune,* April 24, 1911.
15. *Dramatic Mirror,* May 17, 1911.
16. *Pittsburgh Leader,* May 12, 1911.
17. *Dramatic Mirror,* May 31, 1911.
18. *Ibid.,* Aug. 2, 1911.
19. *Ibid.,* Jan. 10, 1912.
20. *Ibid.,* Feb. 21, 1912.

10—OLD SPECIALTIES, NEW PLATFORMS

1. Alan Dale, "Lillian Russell," *Theater,* Jan. 24, 1915.

2. *Dramatic Mirror,* Oct. 9, 1912.
3. *Ibid.,* Dec. 11, 1912.
4. *Los Angeles Times,* Jan. –, 1913.
5. *Chicago Tribune,* Feb. 24, 1913.
6. *New York American,* March 3, 1913.
7. *New York Sun,* March 5, 1913.
8. *Madison (Wisconsin) Democrat,* Nov., 25, 1913.
9. *New York Herald,* Sept. 13, 1914.
10. *Clipper,* Nov. 13, 1914.
11. *Photoplay,* February 1915.
12. *New York Telegram,* Nov. 3, 1915.
13. *New York Star,* Dec. 15, 1915.
14. *Pittsburgh Leader,* July 9, 1916.

11—GOD, MOTHER, COUNTRY, AND LILLIAN RUSSELL

1. *New York Times,* Oct. 19, 1917.
2. Russell, *Cosmopolitan,* Sept. 1922, p. 108.
3. *New York Telegraph,* Oct. 29, 1918.
4. *Dramatic Mirror,* Nov. 23, 1918.
5. *Cleveland Plain Dealer,* Feb. 19, 1919.
6. *Houston Chronicle,* Feb. 4, 1919.
7. Russell, *Cosmopolitan,* Sept. 1922, p. 108.
8. *New York Times,* Jan. 21, 1922.
9. *Ibid.*
10. *Ibid.*
11. *International News Service,* March 20, 1922.
12. *New York American,* April 16, 1922.
13. D. Russell, "My Mother, Lillian Russell," *Liberty,* Nov. 23, 1929, p. 63.
14. *New York Times,* June 17, 1922.
15. *Ibid.*
16. Program, "In Memoriam: Lillian Russell," June 18, 1922.
17. *Variety,* June 16, 1922.
18. *New York American,* June 11, 1922.

12—THE QUEEN IS DEAD! LONG LIVE THE QUEEN!

1. *The Vaudeville News,* Nov. 14, 1924.
2. *New York Herald-Tribune,* March 5, 1930.
3. *New York World-Telegram,* July 26, 1934.
4. *New York American,* July 14, 1936.
5. *Variety,* May 20, 1940.
6. *The New Yorker,* June 3, 1940.
7. *Pittsburgh Post-Gazette,* June 26, 1949.

Bibliography

ARCHIVES, COLLECTIONS, LIBRARIES

Chicago Historical Society
Clinton, Iowa, Historical Society
Convent of the Sacred Heart, Chicago, Illinois
Harvard University, Performing Arts Library
The Howland Quarterly
Institute of the American Musical
Iowa State Historical Society
Library of Congress
Mormon Library, Salt Lake City
Museum of the City of New York
National Portrait Gallery, Smithsonian Institution
New York Public Library at Lincoln Center, Billy Rose Theater Collection
Shubert Archive
University of California, Los Angeles, Microfilm Library
University of Southern California, Special Collections Library
University of Texas, Harry Ransom Humanities Research Center

PERIODICALS, NEWSPAPERS, MISCELLANEOUS PUBLICATIONS

New York Clipper, January 1876 to July 1923
New York Dramatic Mirror, January 1880 to December 1922
Variety, December 1905 to December 1922
Selected issues:
Billboard
Cosmopolitan
Green Book
Ladies' Home Journal
Liberty
Life
McClure's
Scribner's
Stage
Theater
Selected newspaper articles from 1878 to 1968:
Boston Globe
Chicago Tribune
New York Herald
New York Star
New York Sun
New York Times
New York World
Parke-Bernet Galleries, catalog of sales #2029, 1961.
Pittsburgh Leader

BOOKS

Aronson, R. *Theatrical and Musical Memoirs.* New York: McBride, Nast, 1913.
Atkinson, B. *Broadway.* New York: Macmillan, 1970.
Auster, A. *Actresses and Suffragists: Women in American Theater 1890–1920.* New York: Praeger, 1984.
Barnes, D. *I Could Never Be Lonely Without a Husband.* London: Virago, 1985.
Blumenthal, G., as told to A.H. Menkin. *My Sixty Years in Show Business.* New York: Frederick C. Ofberg, 1936.
Boardman, G. *American Musical Theater.* New York: Oxford University Press, 1978.

_____. *American Musical Comedy.* New York: Oxford University Press, 1982.

Bodeen, De Witt. *Ladies of the Footlights.* Pasadena, Ca.: Pasadena Playhouse Assn., 1937.

Brough, J. *Miss Lillian Russell, A Novel Memoir.* New York: McGraw-Hill, 1978.

Brown, H.C. *In the Golden Nineties.* Hastings-on-Hudson, New York: Valentine's Manual, 1928.

Burke, J. *Duet In Diamonds.* New York: Putnam, 1972.

Carter, R. *The World of Flo Zeigfeld.* New York: Praeger, 1974.

Clinton [IA] Historical Society. *History of Clinton County, Iowa.*

Cohan, G.M. *Twenty Years on Broadway and the Years It Took to Get There.* New York: Harper, 1925.

Cook, A., M. Gittell, and H. Mack, eds. *City Life 1865–1900.* New York: Praeger, 1973.

Csida, J. Clinton, and J.B. Csida. *American Entertainment: A Unique History of Popular Show Business.* New York: Billboard, 1978.

Dale, A. *Familiar Chats with the Queens of the Stage.* New York: G.W. Dillingham, 1890.

Dedmon, Emmett. *Fabulous Chicago.* New York: Random House, 1953.

Dressler, M. *Life Story of an Ugly Duckling.* New York: Robert M. McBride, 1924.

_____, as told to Mildred Harrington. *My Own Story.* Boston: Little, Brown, 1934.

Engel, L. *The American Musical Theater.* New York: Macmillan, 1975.

Erenberg, A. *Steppin' Out: New York Nightlife and the Transformation of American Culture 1890–1930.* Westport, Conn.: Greenwood, 1981.

Ewen, D. *The Story of America's Musical Theater.* Philadelphia: Chilton, 1961.

Fields, A., and L.M. Fields. *From the Bowery to Broadway: Lew Fields and the Roots of American Popular Theater.* New York: Oxford University Press, 1993.

Foy, E., and Alvin F. Harlow. *Clowning Through Life.* New York: Dutton, 1928.

Gilbert, D. *American Vaudeville.* New York: McGraw-Hill, 1940.

Golden, G.F. *My Lady Vaudeville and Her White Rats.* New York: The Board of Directors of the White Rats of America, Broadway Publishing Co., 1909.

Goodwin, N. *Nat Goodwin's Book.* Boston: Richard G. Badger, 1914.

Grau, R. *The Business Man in the Amusement World.* New York: Broadway, 1910.

Hamm, M.A. *Eminent Actors in Their Homes.* New York: J. Pott, 1902.

Hapgood, N. *The Stage in America, 1897–1900.* New York: Macmillan, 1901.

Henderson, M.C. *The City and the Theater.* Clifton, N.J.: James T. White, 1973.

Hopper, D.W. *Once a Clown, Always a Clown.* Garden City, N.Y.: Garden City Publishing Co., 1927.

Isman, F. *Weber & Fields,* New York: Boni & Liveright, 1924.

Keaton, B. *My Wonderful World of Slapstick.* New York: Da Capo, 1960.

Kouwenhoven, J.A. *The Columbia Historical Portrait of New York.* New York: Harper & Row, 1972.

Leavitt, M.B. *Fifty Years in Theatrical Management.* New York: Broadway, 1912.

Leslie, A. *Some Players.* New York: Herbert S. Stone, 1890.

Lynes, R. *The Lively Audience.* New York: Harper & Row, 1985.

McCabe, J.D., Jr. *New York by Gaslight.* New York: Arlington House, 1984 (reprint of 1882 edition).

McNamara, B. *The Shuberts of Broadway.* New York: Oxford University Press, 1990.

Marcuse, M.F. *Tin Pan Alley in Gaslight.* Watkins Glen, New York: Century House, 1959.

Mordden, E. *Broadway Babies: The People Who Made the American Musical.* New York: Oxford University Press, 1983.

Morell, P. *Diamond Jim Brady.* New York: American Mercury, 1934.

_____. *Lillian Russell, The Era of Plush.* New York: Random House, 1940.

Morris, L. *Incredible New York.* New York: Random House, 1951.

Odell, G. *Annals of the New York Stage 1883–1889.* New York: Columbia University Press, 1949 (reprint of 1890 edition).

Parker, D., and J. Parker. *The Natural History of the Chorus Girl.* New York: Bobbs-Merrill, 1975.

Rather, L. *Two Lilies in America: Lillian Russell and Lillie Langtry.* Oakland, Ca.: Rather, 1961.

Rovere, R.H. *Howe & Hummel.* London: Arlington, 1947.

Salwen, P. *Upper West Side Story.* New York: Abbeville, 1989.

Smith, C., and G. Litton. *Musical Comedy in America.* New York: Theater Arts, 1981.

Smith, H.B. *First Nights and First Editions.* Boston: Little, Brown, 1931.

Stein, C.W. *American Vaudeville, As Seen by Its Contemporaries.* New York: Alfred A. Knopf, 1984.

Strang, L. *Prima Donnas and Soubrettes of Light Opera and Musical Comedy in America.* Boston: L.C. Page, 1900.

Toll, R.C. *On with the Show: The First Century of Show Business in America.* New York: Oxford University Press, 1976.

Traubner, R. *Operetta, a Theatrical History.* Garden City, New York: Doubleday, 1983.

Zellers, P. *Tony Pastor: Dean of the Vaudeville Stage.* Ypsilanti, Mich.: Eastern Michigan University Press, 1971.

ARTICLES AND ESSAYS

Blum, D. "Lillian Russell, The Toast of the Town." *The Theater,* May 1959.

Dale, A. "Lillian Russell and Eternal Youth." *Green Book Magazine,* August 1916.

Day, C. "Appearing with Lillian Russell." *Saturday Evening Post,* October 26, 1935.

Fields, A. "Lillian Russell, Glamour Queen." *Coronet,* May 1951.

Gibson, I. M. "Breakfast with Lillian Russell." *Green Book Album,* July 1911.

Nathan, G. J. "George W. Lederer's Reminiscences." *McClure's,* May–September, 1920.

Patterson, A. "Lillian Russell — Beauty and Philosophy." *The Theater,* February 1905.

Platt, F. "Lillian Russell." *L'Official/USA,* August 1978.

Russell, D. "My Mother, Lillian Russell." *Liberty,* October 19 through November 23, 1929 (six installments).

Russell, L. "Lillian Russell's Reminiscences." *Cosmopolitan,* February through September, 1922 (eight installments).

"Iowa's Lillian Russell Was the Toast of the 'Yellow Nineties'." *Des Moines Register,* Nov. 24, 1946.

"Lillian Russell." *The Illustrated American,* December 12, 1891.

Index